Jātaka Tales of the Buddha
An Anthology

Volume I

Retold by

Ken and Visakha Kawasaki

Illustrations by

N.A.P.G. Dharmawardena

PARIYATTI PRESS
an imprint of
Pariyatti Publishing
www.pariyatti.org

ISBN: 978-1-68172-310-5 (Print)
ISBN: 978-1-68172-106-4 (PDF)
ISBN: 978-1-68172-104-0 (ePub)
ISBN: 978-1-68172-105-7 (Mobi)
Library of Congress Control Number: 2017956359

First Pariyatti Edition, 2018

Table of Contents

Volume I

Acknowledgments

Just before we left Japan on a world tour in 1978, our late friend Tove Neville took us to the Nara National Museum to view "The Origins of Japanese Buddhist Art." Her brilliant commentary on this seminal exhibition led us to research and photograph Buddhist art as we traveled, which, in turn, introduced us to the Jātakas. For this we owe her a great debt of thanks. We were extremely grateful when, several months later, the kind monks residing at the MahāBodhi Society in Sāñchī opened the library for us. It was there, on those blazingly hot afternoons, that we first read the Jātakas. The inspiration for this book came from our first meditation teacher, Venerable U Khe Min Da Sayādaw of the World Peace Pagoda in Moji, Kita-Kyushu, Japan. Thoroughly versed in Pali and, thanks to his Methodist teachers in Burma, fluent in English, he wove the Jātakas into his teaching and instilled in us a love for the tales.

We must thank Venerable Bhikkhu Bodhi, the President and former Editor of Buddhist Publication Society, who accepted our first efforts at retelling the Jātakas for publication as Bodhi Leaves and encouraged us to continue. For his assistance with difficult Pali terms, we thank the current editor of the BPS, Venerable Nyanatusita.

Special gratitude goes to Venerable Ānandajoti, who read, corrected, and critiqued the entire manuscript with both goodwill and good humor.

We appreciate the many hours Charles Munasinghe spent patiently translating our discussions with Mr. Dharmawardena, the Sinhalese artist who illustrated each story.

Ken and Visakha Kawasaki

Preface

The word jātaka literally means "connected to a former rebirth" and is usually translated as "birth-story." Jātaka is also the name of one of the books in the Pali Tipiṭaka, the canon of sacred scriptures of Theravāda Buddhism. In some ways, the Jātaka collection is the most complex, the most interesting, and the most readable part of all Buddhist literature. It is made up entirely of verses, about 2500 altogether, to which stories have been added in the Jātaka Commentary, the Jātaka-aṭṭhakathā. Each story consists of four parts:

1. The Story of the Present (paccuppanna-vatthu)—This recounts some event in the life of the Buddha which prompted him to tell the Jātaka story. Some of these events are mentioned in the Tipiṭaka itself, but many are not.

2. The Story of the Past (atīta-vatthu)—This is the actual Jātaka story itself, which is in prose.

3. The Verses (gāthā)—It is interesting to note that, while many verses fit well into their story, others can be understood on their own, some make sense only if read with the story, and others don't seem to be related to the story at all. This suggests that the Jātakas were compiled over a long period, by many different hands, and, in some cases, in a rather haphazard manner. Many of the verses are also found in other parts of the Tipiṭaka; e.g., the Dhammapada and the Theragāthā.

4. The Connection (samodhāna)—In this, the Buddha is depicted as identifying who the main characters in the story are in the present, e.g., "Ānanda was the chief minister, the thief was Devadatta, and I was the king."

A point worth emphasizing, because it is often overlooked, despite being crucial to a proper appreciation and understanding of the Jātakas, is that only the verses are canonical and are considered to be the words of the Buddha. The ancients who arranged the Tipiṭaka in its present form were fully aware that the Stories of the Present, the Stories of the Past, and the Connections were apocryphal and later than the verses, a fact verified by modern scholarship. In fact, the Stories of the Present and the Connections may even have been composed much later in Sri Lanka. The Stories of the Past are more complex, as far as age is concerned. As they appear today, they were probably written several centuries after the Buddha, but the stories they tell are very ancient, indeed, and may predate the Buddha by hundreds of years. Interestingly, this fits well with the traditional belief that the events in the Jātaka stories took place during the Buddha's many former lives.

ix

How did these wonderful stories become such an important part of Buddhism? India has a long history of story-telling, going back at least 3000 years. The two most popular types of stories were about the great heroes and kings of the past and animals. The first type can be called proto-historical, i.e., they are a mixture of fact and fiction, history and myth. In the second type, the main characters are animals with human traits, often displaying the best or worst that humans are capable of. Before Prince Siddhattha renounced the world to become an ascetic, he would have learned, as a part of his education, the myths and legends of the Sakyans and, perhaps, of other tribes, as well. In fact, in one discourse,[1] the Buddha briefly recounted one of these legends. He must have also been familiar with popular animal folk tales. It was common in those days for kings to invite traveling story tellers or bards to entertain their courts on special occasions. The evidence shows that the Buddha was acquainted with and sometimes used such "oral literature" in his teaching. In another discourse, he told a Jātaka-like story about a miraculous tree, although this story is not found in the Jātakas.[2] In the Samyutta Nikāya, he used a story of a quail as a simile which is not exactly the same as a story in the Jātakas, but the two are clearly drawn from same source.[3] In the Vinaya, he related one of the Jātakas, although he did not identify any of the characters with himself or with any other people living in the present.[4]

Thus, we can see that these stories and folktales, which had been a heritage common to all, were transformed into something specifically Buddhist. Many stories were known and used by Buddhist teachers, but only certain ones were deemed to be good enough to be preserved. The content of the most popular stories gradually became fixed. At some point, they were collected and arranged. Finally, to give the stories an "official stamp," it was said that the hero of each story was the Buddha in one of his earlier lives, and they became Jātakas.

In the centuries after the Buddha, monks and nuns traveled all over northern India (and later, beyond), teaching the Dhamma "for the good of the many, for the happiness of the many, out of compassion for the world." Of course, they encountered many different types of people. To sophisticated town-dwellers, brahmins, and wandering ascetics, they spoke of dependent origination, non-self (anattā), and the Four Noble Truths. To village folk, farmers, and tradesmen, they would have transmitted the Dhamma, in part, at least, through stories. In doing so, they inevitably drew upon the great store

---

1   Brahmajāla Sutta (Digha Nikāya 1)

2   Dhammika Sutta (Angutarr Nikāya 6,54)

3   Sakunovāda Sutta (Samyutta Nikāya, Mahavāgga, Satipatthāna Samyutta 6) and Tale 71

4   Vinaya Pitaka, Cullavagga, VI and Tale 21

of folklore, tales, and legends already in circulation. Some of these stories had a simple and clear moral and could have been used as they were. Others needed to have a moral added so that they were more than just entertainment. In some cases, two or three stories were woven together to make a single story with a message in accordance with Dhamma. No doubt, some monks and nuns were imaginative enough to create completely new stories.

Be that as it may, the real importance of the Jātakas is the values which they impart. They highlight specifically Buddhist virtues, such as kindness, patience, honesty, courage, civility, simplicity, and detachment. Just as often, they speak of those qualities useful for getting by in the world—thrift, common sense, determination, and perspicacity. All of this is transmitted, not through sermons, but through stories; some of the most delightful stories you will ever read. Expect to be transported to sunny Himalayan meadows, magic islands, and fairy castles. Prepare yourself to meet wise elephants, roguish vagabonds, strong-headed princes, and beautiful maidens. Get ready to laugh and nod in agreement and to gasp and sit on the edge of your seat. Welcome to the wonderful world of the Jātakas.

Shravasti Dhammika

Introduction

It is hard to be born a human;
It is hard to live as a mortal.
It is hard to have the chance to hear the Dhamma;
It is hard to encounter a Buddha.

—Dhammapada 182

Many eons ago, in the presence of Dīpankara Buddha, a young ascetic named Sumedha made an aspiration to become a Buddha like him. At that time, Sumedha had the capacity to achieve arahatship, but he turned his back on Nibbāna in order to attain that more demanding and difficult goal. Dīpankara Buddha confirmed that, indeed, at a time in the distant future, Sumedha's wish would be fulfilled. From that point, during his innumerable existences, until he became Gotama Buddha, he was the Bodhisatta, the Buddha-to-be.

After his Enlightenment under the Bodhi tree, Gotama Buddha was able to remember all his previous lives. During the forty-five years the Buddha taught, he frequently referred to experiences in those earlier lives, and he told stories from them to illustrate various points of Dhamma and to encourage his followers to practice diligently. In these stories, called Jātakas, the Bodhisatta is seen cultivating the Ten Perfections—generosity, morality, renunciation, wisdom, energy, patience, truthfulness, determination, loving-kindness, and equanimity. These are the qualities which must be fulfilled by every Bodhisatta in the course of his spiritual development. Although these Ten Perfections are universal, since all who seek liberation must cultivate them to a certain degree, for a Supreme Buddha, the standard of excellence is so high that the time required is incomparably longer than for other beings. Each perfection must be practiced with full compassion and with the most skillful means. Moreover, the practice must be untainted by any hint of craving, conceit, or wrong view.

In some of the Jātaka tales, the Bodhisatta is the main character, and it is obvious which perfection is being cultivated. In other tales, he is an observer of the action, and, although there is a definite lesson to be drawn from the story, for the Bodhisatta, that particular life was merely one more experience in samsāra, the wearying round of existence. Many of the tales fall between these two extremes, and a case can often be made for his cultivating several perfections in one lifetime.

The Buddha gave no indication of the order of the tales. One took place "five eons ago," and another occurred "at the beginning of the world," but, for most of the stories, there are no clues as to when they happened. In many, "Brahmadatta was reigning in Bārānasi," but, of course, that was another world age, and there were many kings named Brahmadatta.

During this progression, the same as other beings, the Bodhisatta rose and fell in samsāra according to the workings of kamma—from the deva realms, to animal birth, to human birth, to the hell realms, and back. In Tale 208, as Prince Temiya, his memories of his recent suffering in hell were so fresh and powerful that they dictated his response to being reborn a prince. Sometimes, the Bodhisatta was reborn in the animal realm, taking birth as various species, from elephant (the largest) to quail (the smallest), and including many others, such as dog, vulture, rat, deer, buffalo, and lion. Even in these animal births, he was cultivating the perfections. In the human realm, his births ranged from king to thief and from outcaste to brahmin. In the deva realm, he was often reborn as lowly as a tree deva, but sometimes as mighty as Sakka or Mahā-Brahmā. His existence in other realms included rebirths as fabulous creatures, such as kinnara and nāga.

The only Jātaka tale that can be placed with certainty is the last one in the collection. When the Bodhisatta passed away as Vessantara, he was reborn in Tusita Heaven. From there, he was reborn as Siddhattha Gotama and became the Buddha.

The traditional arrangement of the Jātaka tales in Pali is a matter of form. The stories are divided into twenty-two books, according to the number of verses (gāthā) they contain.[1] Most of the tales in Book One (Eka Nipāta) have one verse each. The number of verses increases with each book. The last book (Mahā Nipāta, The Great Book), has ten tales, regarded by many as the most important of all the Jātakas, with very many verses each. The tales in this anthology are arranged in the same order as in the original Pali. In Volume III, the Table of Correspondence gives the number of the Jātaka for each tale and the Book (Nipāta) in which it appears.

Each Jātaka begins with an occasion in the present, which explains what prompted the Buddha to tell a particular story of the past. The main section of each Jātaka is this story of the past, but, in some cases, where the occasion is told in great detail, that is more interesting than the story itself. At the conclusion of each story, the Buddha identified some of the characters in the story, explaining which of his contemporaries had played a part in the story of the past.

---

1   As Venerable Dhammika points out in thge Preface, only the verses are included in the Tipitaka, the Buddhist Canon. The prose narrative, which makes up the tales as they are related herem is given only in the Jātaka Commentary.

Introduction

During his meanderings in samsāra, the Bodhisatta was often accompanied by others who had long before made their own aspirations to become his relatives and followers when he finally became the Buddha. They were like planets to his sun. The Glossary of Personal Names in Volume III will assist the reader in learning more about these contemporaries of the Buddha and in finding the various tales in which they appear.

The Buddha established a dispensation (sāsana) and, for forty-five years, he taught the Dhamma, ordained bhikkhus and bhikkhunīs, and led innumerable beings to Nibbāna. The Jātaka tales offer some instructive contrasts between this world of the Buddha and the many worlds into which the Bodhisatta was born when there was no Supreme Buddha. During those "empty" world ages without a Supreme Buddha, the ancient path to Nibbāna was concealed and forgotten; without a teacher to proclaim the Four Noble Truths, the doors to the deathless were closed to ordinary beings. They could only improve their future circumstances by practicing basic morality, kindness, and generosity or, for those so inclined, by renouncing the world in order to practice asceticism and concentration meditation. During those periods without a Supreme Buddha, perfect insight into reality was possible only for those rare, solitary individuals who, having labored many lifetimes to cultivate the Ten Perfections, were poised on the brink of enlightenment. They required only an example of impermanence, suffering, or non-self (something as slight as the falling of a leaf or the jingling of two bracelets) to achieve insight. When they penetrated the Truth, they were transformed into Pacceka Buddhas, or Silent Buddhas, fully enlightened, but unable to establish a sāsana with an order of monks and nuns. The Jātakas make clear the meaning of the Dhammapada verse cited above: with all the possibilities there are in samsāra, it is rare to be born a human being, rarer to have the opportunity to hear the Buddha's teaching, and even rarer than that to be born at a time when there is a Buddha teaching in the world.

For more than two thousand years, the Jātaka stories have held an important place in Buddhist carving, painting, drama, and literature. The earliest surviving examples of Buddhist art, the and gates of the Bharhut Stupa, carved in India in the second century B.C.E., include many representations of Jātakas. During the same period, the Sri Lankan king, Dutthagāmani had the interior of the relic chamber of the Ruwanveliseya in Anuradhapura painted with murals of Vessantara. In India, the Jātaka stories are prominent in the carving of Amaravati, Nāgājunakonda, Sāñchī, and Ellora, as well as in the painting of Ajanta. In the ancient Buddhist world, from Bamiyan to Borobudur and from Ceylon to China, depictions of Jātaka stories took their place alongside episodes from the life of the Buddha to instruct and to inspire devotees and to inculcate the virtues perfected by the Bodhisatta. Many of these tales, commonly used in teaching, were familiar to Buddhists in all traditions and must have exercised a powerful influence on the people, reassuring them that good will follow from performing virtuous acts of generosity, kindliness, and courage, and that fortitude, nobility of purpose, and self-sacrifice are never in vain.

Though the setting of all the stories is, of course, ancient India, the characters in the Jātakas are not bound to any period or place. The Buddha's message is universal, and the themes of these stories are still relevant today. A popular genre of musical folk theater in Burma, called zatpwe, is based on Jātaka stories. Monks frequently use Jātakas to counsel and encourage lay followers. Dr. Harischandra, a psychiatrist trained in the UK, found in the Jātaka stories remarkably modern diagnoses of mental illnesses and insights into mental health.[2] Some Jātakas seem to be like political cartoons astutely satirizing the foibles of current leaders. The sixteen dreams of King Pasenadi (Tale 33), for example, accurately describe the misrule that afflicts several troubled nations.

The only complete edition of the Jātakas in English is the scholarly translation published by the Pali Text Society at the beginning of the twentieth century. This was a great contribution to Buddhist literature in English. It was our introduction to the Jātakas, and we are extremely grateful. The translators strove hard to render the verses into English verse, and, in some cases, the result was impressive. For the modern reader, however, this version has several drawbacks. One is that the translators, perhaps to express seriousness and respect, adopted elements of Biblical English. Another is that the prose often repeats what is stated in the verses. This becomes even more tedious when the narrator explains a character's intention before the action is carried out.

Recently, quite a few collections of Jātakas have been published. Most of them, however, present the tales as children's stories, omitting both the occasion and the identification. Such a rendering destroys the relationship between the stories of the past and the life of the Buddha and obscures the intertwining relationships between characters in different births and in the Buddha's lifetime. Through seeing these relationships, we gain a clearer understanding of the complex workings of kamma. We see how beings wander through samsāra, how they develop habits and traits of character, both good and bad, and how they often commit the same mistakes or perform the same noble actions again and again.

2   Harischandra, D.V.J., *Psychiatric Aspects of Jātaka Stories*, Upuli Offset, Galle Sri Lanka 1998

Introduction

To make the stories readily accessible to the modern reader, we have incorporated the verses into the prose narration and dialog. We have liberally condensed and abridged the stories, omitting extraneous material, but retaining much of the detail which illustrates the culture of ancient India. In some cases, we have added information from other texts to clarify the situation or to enhance the plot. We have tried to be careful, however, not to change any important points of the stories.

Our anthology is not complete; of the original 547 Jātakas, it contains only 217 tales, though we have tried to make it representative and to include the most important ones. Some readers who are familiar with the original Jātakas may complain that we have omitted certain favorites. We apologize. Our selection is entirely personal. We hope that, with this modern retelling, these Jātaka tales, so rich in morality, compassion, and wisdom, will become better known to readers of English throughout the world.

The English titles of the tales in this anthology are not translations of the Pali. They are entirely our own creations. The original Pali title of each Jātaka has been included in order to facilitate identification by readers who are familiar with the originals. In most cases, we have retained the Pali for the names of characters. The notable exception is King Half-Penny (Tale 163). In many of the stories, a person's name identifies a predominant characteristic of that person, and that meaning is immediately understood by the reader of Pali. When put into English, however, those names may not sound appropriate. For example, Faith and Joy are acceptable English names for women, and Rock can be a man's name, but Princess Beautiful and Prince Goodness, sound very much like characters from fairy tales. In some cases, we have provided the meaning of a name.

In addition to the Glossary of Personal Names and the Table of Correspondence, Volume III contains a Glossary of Terms which will help to explain many of the Buddhist terms and concepts that recur throughout the stories. Generally, however, when a term appears only once, it has been placed in the footnotes rather than in the Glossary. A table of The Thirty-one Planes of Existence illustrates where beings can be reborn in samsāra. Finally, there is a map of ancient Jambudīpa indicating the relative positions of many of the various kingdoms and cities mentioned in the Jātaka tales.

1

Crossing the Wilderness
Apannaka Jātaka¹

While the Buddha was staying at Jetavana Monastery near Sāvatthī, the wealthy merchant, Anāthapindika, went one day to pay his respects. His servants carried masses of flowers and huge quantities of perfume, cloths, robes, and catumadhu. Anāthapindika paid his respects to the Buddha, presented the offerings he had brought, and sat down in a proper place.² At that time, Anāthapindika was accompanied by five hundred friends who were followers of other teachers. His friends paid their respects to the Buddha and sat close to the merchant. The Buddha's face appeared like a full moon, and his body was surrounded by a radiant aura. Seated on the red stone seat, he was like a young lion roaring with a clear, noble voice as he taught the Dhamma full of sweetness and beautiful to the ear.

After hearing the Buddha's teaching, the five hundred gave up their false practices and took refuge in the Triple Gem. After that, they went regularly

---

1   According to the commentaries, this Jātaka will be among the last to be forgotten when the Dhamma disappears from the world.
2   When sitting with a respected person, one should not sit higher than, upwind from, directly in front of, directly behind, too far from, or too near that person.

1

with Anāthapindika to offer flowers and incense and to hear the teaching. They gave liberally, kept the precepts, and faithfully observed the Uposatha days. Soon after the Buddha left Sāvatthī to return to Rājagaha, however, these men abandoned their new faith and reverted to their previous beliefs.

Seven or eight months later, the Buddha returned to Jetavana. Again, Anāthapindika brought these friends to visit the Buddha. They paid their respects, but Anāthapindika explained that they had forsaken their refuge and had resumed their original practices.

The Buddha asked, "Is it true that you have abandoned refuge in the Triple Gem for refuge in other doctrines?" The Buddha's voice was incredibly clear because throughout myriad eons he had always spoken truthfully.[3]

When these men heard it, they were unable to conceal the truth. "Yes, Blessed One," they confessed. "It is true."

"Laymen," the Buddha said, "now here between the lowest of hells below and the highest heaven above, nowhere in all the infinite worlds that stretch right and left, is there the equal, much less the superior, of a Buddha. Incalculable is the excellence which springs from obeying the precepts and from other virtuous conduct."

Then he declared the virtues of the Triple Gem. "By taking refuge in the Triple Gem," he told them, "one escapes from rebirth in states of suffering." He further explained that meditation on the Triple Gem leads through the four stages of Enlightenment. "In forsaking such a refuge as this," he admonished them, "you have certainly erred."

"In the past, too, men who foolishly mistook what was no refuge for a real refuge, met disaster. Actually, they fell prey to yakkhas in the wilderness and were utterly destroyed. In contrast, men who clung to the truth not only survived, but actually prospered in that same wilderness."

Pressing his palms together and raising them to his forehead, Anāthapindika praised the Buddha and asked him to tell that story of the past. "In order to dispel the world's ignorance and to conquer suffering," the Buddha proclaimed, "I practiced the Ten Perfections for countless eons. Listen carefully, and I will speak."

Having their full attention, the Buddha made clear, as though he were releasing the full moon from behind clouds, what rebirth had concealed from them.

Long, long ago, when Brahmadatta was reigning in Bārānasi, the Bodhisatta was born into a merchant's family and grew up to be a wise busi-

---

3   During his innumerable lives in quest of Buddhahood, a Bodhisatta can break all the moral precepts except abstaining from false speech..

nessman. At the same time, in the same city, there was another merchant, a very stupid fellow, with no common sense whatsoever.

One day, it so happened that the two merchants each loaded five hundred carts with costly wares of Bārānasi and prepared to leave in the same direction at exactly the same time. The wise merchant thought, "If this silly young fool travels with me and if our thousand carts stay together, it will be too much for the road. Finding wood and water for the men will be difficult, and there won't be enough grass for the oxen. Either he or I must go first."

"Look," he said to the other merchant, "the two of us can't travel together. Would you rather go first or follow after me?"

The foolish merchant thought, "There will be many advantages if I take the lead. I'll get a road which is not yet cut up. My oxen will have the pick of the grass. My men will get the choicest wild herbs for curry. The water will be undisturbed. Best of all, I'll be able to fix my own price for bartering my goods." Considering all these advantages, he said, "I will go ahead of you, my friend."

The wise merchant was pleased to hear this because he saw many advantages in following after. He reasoned, "Those carts going first will level the road where it is rough, and I'll be able to travel along the road they have already smoothed. Their oxen will graze off the coarse old grass, and mine will pasture on the sweet young growth which will spring up in its place. My men will find fresh sweet herbs for curry where the old ones have been picked. Where there is no water, the first caravan will have to dig to supply themselves, and we'll be able to drink at the wells they have dug. Haggling over prices is tiring work; he'll do the work, and I will be able to barter my wares at prices he has already fixed."

"Very well, my friend," he said, "please go first."

"I will," said the foolish merchant, and he yoked his carts and set out. After a while, he came to the edge of a wilderness. He filled all of his huge water jars with fresh water before starting the sixty-yojana trek across the desert.

The yakkha who haunted that wilderness had been watching the caravan, and, when it reached the middle, he used his magic power to conjure up a lovely carriage drawn by pure white young bulls. With a retinue of a dozen disguised yakkhas carrying swords and shields, he rode along in his carriage like a mighty lord. His hair and clothes were wet, and he had a wreath of blue lotuses and white water lilies around his head. His attendants also were dripping wet and draped in garlands. Even the bulls' hooves and carriage wheels were muddy.

Because the wind was blowing from the front, the merchant was riding at the head of his caravan to escape the dust. The yakkha drew his carriage beside the merchant's and greeted him kindly. The merchant returned the greeting and moved his own carriage to one side to allow the carts to pass while he and the yakkha chatted.

"We are on our way from Bārānasi, sir," explained the merchant. "I see that your men are all wet and muddy and that you have lotuses and water lilies. Did it rain while you were on the road? Did you come across pools with lotuses and water lilies?"

"What do you mean?" the yakkha exclaimed. "Over there is the dark-green streak of a forest. Beyond that there is plenty of water. It is always raining there, and there are many lakes with lotuses and water lilies." Then, pretending to be interested in the merchant's business, he asked, "What do you have in these carts?"

"Expensive merchandise," answered the merchant.

"What is in this cart which seems so heavily laden?" the yakkha asked as the last cart rolled by.

"That's full of water."

"You were wise to carry water with you this far, but there is no need for it now, since water is so abundant ahead. You could travel much faster and lighter without those heavy jars. You'd be better off breaking them and throwing the water away. Well, good day," he said suddenly, as he turned his carriage. "We must be on our way. We have stopped too long already." He rode away quickly with his men. As soon as they were out of sight, they turned and made their way back to their own city.

The merchant was so foolish that he followed the yakkha's advice. He broke all the jars, without saving even a single cupful of water, and ordered the men to drive on quickly. Of course, they did not find any water, and they were soon exhausted from thirst. At sunset, they drew their carts into a circle and tethered the oxen to the wheels, but there was no water for the weary animals. Without water, the men could not cook any rice, either. They sank to the ground and fell asleep. As soon as night came, the yakkhas attacked, killing every single man and beast. The fiends devoured the flesh, leaving only the bones, and departed. Skeletons were strewn in every direction, but the five hundred carts stood with their loads untouched. Thus, the heedless young merchant was the sole cause of the destruction of the entire caravan.

The wise merchant allowed six weeks to pass after the foolish merchant had left before setting out with his five hundred carts. When he reached the edge of the wilderness, he filled his water jars. Then he assembled his men and announced, "Let not so much as a handful of water be used without my permission. Furthermore, there are poisonous plants in this wilderness. Do not eat any leaf, flower, or fruit which you have never eaten before, without showing it to me first." Having thus carefully warned his men, he led the caravan into the desert.

When they had reached the middle of the wilderness, the yakkha appeared on the path, just as before. The merchant noticed his red eyes and fearless manner and suspected something strange. "I know there is no water in this desert,' he said to himself. "Furthermore, this stranger casts no shadow.[4] He must be a yakkha. He probably tricked the foolish merchant, but he doesn't realize how clever I am."

"Get out of here!" he shouted at the yakkha. "We are men of business. We do not throw away our water before we see where more is to come from!"

Without saying any more, the yakkha rode away.

As soon as the yakkhas had left, the merchant's men approached their leader and said, "Sir, those men were wearing lotuses and water lilies on their heads. Their clothes and hair were wringing wet. They told us that up ahead there is a thick forest where it is always raining. Let us throw away our water so that we can proceed more quickly with lightened carts."

The merchant ordered a halt and summoned all his men. "Has any man among you ever heard before today," he asked, "that there was a lake or a pool in this wilderness?"

"No, sir," they answered. "It's known as the 'Waterless Desert.'"

"We have just been told by some strangers that it is raining in the forest just ahead. How far does a rain-wind carry?"

"A yojana, sir."

"Has any man here seen the top of even a single storm cloud?"

"No, sir."

"How far off can you see a flash of lightning?"

"Four or five yojanas, sir."

"Has any man here seen a flash of lightning?"

"No, sir."

"How far off can a man hear a peal of thunder?"

"Two or three yojanas, sir."

"Has any man here heard a peal of thunder?"

"No, sir."

"Those were not men, but yakkhas," the wise merchant told his men. "They are hoping that we will throw away our water. Then, when we are weak and faint, they will return to devour us. Since the young merchant who went before us was not a man of good sense, he was most likely fooled by the yakkhas. We may expect to find his carts standing just as they were first

_____
4 A yakkha has no shadow because his body is only an apparition created to allow people to see him.

loaded. We will probably see them today. Press on with all possible speed," he told his men, "but do not throw away a drop of water!"

Just as the merchant had predicted, his caravan soon came upon the five hundred carts with the skeletons of men and oxen scattered about. He ordered his men to arrange his carts in a fortified circle, to take care of the oxen, and to prepare an early supper for themselves. After the animals and men had all safely bedded down, the merchant and his foremen, swords in hand, stood guard all through the night.

Early the next morning, the merchant replaced his weakened carts with stronger ones and exchanged his common goods for the most costly of the abandoned merchandise. When he arrived at his destination, he was able to barter his stock of wares at two or three times their value. He returned to his own city without losing a single man out of all his company.

Having concluded his story, the Buddha said, "Thus it was, laymen, that in times past, the foolish came to utter destruction, while those who clung to the truth escaped from the yakkhas' hands. They went on to reach their destination safely, and safely they returned to their homes. Clinging to the truth not only endows happiness even up to rebirth in the Brahma heavens but also leads ultimately to arahatship. Following untruth entails rebirth either in the four lower realms or in the lowest conditions of mankind." After he taught the Dhamma, those five hundred disciples attained the first path.

Then the Buddha identified the birth: "At that time, Devadatta's followers were the foolish merchant's men, and Devadatta was the foolish merchant. My followers were the wise merchant's men, and I was the wise merchant."

2
Determination in the Desert
Vannupatha Jātaka

It was while staying in Sāvatthī that the Buddha told this story about a bhikkhu who gave up striving.

A boy from a family in Sāvatthī heard the Buddha speak, understood that craving leads to suffering, and ordained as a sāmanera. After five years, he was eligible for higher ordination. After he became a bhikkhu, he received a subject of meditation from the Buddha, retreated to the forest, and spent the rainy season in solitude. Despite striving for the full three months of the rains retreat, however, he could not develop even a glimmer of insight, and he thought, "The Buddha said there are four types of men, and I must belong to the lowest of them.[5] It seems that, in this birth, there will be neither path nor fruit for me. There is no point in staying here anymore. I'll go back to Jetavana, stay with the Buddha, and listen to his sweet teaching."

When his friends saw him, they wondered. "You got a meditation theme from the Buddha himself and went to the forest. Now you are back, going

---

5   (1) One of quick understanding, (2) one who understands after extensive explanation, (3) one who needs guidance, and (4) one who understands, at most, the words.

here and there, enjoying company. Have you already achieved your goal? Have you gotten beyond rebirth?"

"Friends, I have accomplished nothing. I got discouraged because I could not achieve any insight whatsoever, so I gave up and came back."

"You have done a great wrong, friend. How could you give up after ordaining in this great teaching? Come with us to see the Buddha!"

Although the Buddha immediately realized what had happened, he asked, "Bhikkhus, why are you bringing this bhikkhu to me against his will? What has he done?"

"Venerable Sir, after obtaining a meditation subject from you, this bhikkhu has quit striving. He has given up and returned here."

The Buddha asked him, "Is what they are saying true? Have you given up?"

"Yes, Lord. It is true."

"How can you, after devoting yourself to this liberating doctrine, be dissatisfied? Why aren't you contented with solitude? Why do you lack perseverance now? After all, wasn't it you who were so wonderfully valiant in times past? Didn't you single-handedly, by your own diligence, save an entire caravan in a barren desert? Through your indomitable spirit, water was found so that the lives of men and oxen were spared. How can you give up now?"

Heartened by the Buddha's stirring words, the bhikkhu resolved to resume his solitary meditation.

Hearing what the Buddha had said, the others asked him, "Sir, we're well aware of this bhikkhu's faintheartedness, but we know nothing about his managing to find water in the desert and saving a whole caravan. Please tell us about that."

With that request, the Buddha made clear what rebirth had concealed.

Long, long ago, when Brahmadatta was reigning in Bārānasi, the Bodhisatta was born into a merchant family. After he grew up, he regularly traveled on family business with five hundred carts.

On one occasion, he came to an arid, sandy wilderness sixty yojanas across. The sand of this desert was so fine that it slipped right through the fingers of a closed fist. As soon as the sun rose, the sand became too hot to walk on. Anyone wishing to cross this desert had to carry ample rations of water, oil, ghee, rice, and firewood, for there was nothing on the way. Of course, due to the tremendous heat, travel was possible only at night. At dawn, all the carts had to be drawn up into a circle and an awning stretched overhead. After taking an early meal, the drovers rested in the shade until the sun went down. Then they ate their evening meal. Only after the ground had cooled, could they yoke their oxen and proceed. Traveling on this desert at night was like voyaging over the sea. Each caravan was guided by a "desert-pilot," who used his knowledge of the stars to guide the wagons safely through the barren waste.

One evening, when the caravan was only about one yojana from the end of the desert, the merchant thought, "Tonight, we'll be out of this sandy desert, at last."

After the men had eaten their supper, the merchant ordered that the excess water casks and wood be thrown away. Without the unnecessary provisions, the caravan set out, much lighter than before.

The pilot sat in the front cart, observing the stars. Having been without sleep for a long time, however, he was thoroughly exhausted. He started nodding, dozed off, and was soon fast asleep. All night, the oxen kept up a steady pace, but the slumbering pilot was unaware that they had circled back, retracing their steps. When he awoke at dawn, he observed the position of the stars overhead and shouted, "Turn the carts around!"

Hurriedly, the drovers turned the carts, but, as they were lining them up, the sun came up. "Heaven help us!" they cried. "This is where we camped yesterday, but all our water is gone. We are doomed!" As soon as they had circled the carts and stretched the awning, the men threw themselves down in despair.

The merchant quickly assessed their situation. Realizing the gravity of their plight, he thought, "If I give up, all of us will perish." Determined to save his caravan, he walked all around the campsite while it was still early and somewhat cool. At last, he came upon a clump of kusa grass.

"This grass must mean there is water below!" he reasoned. He ordered his men to bring a spade and to dig a hole there. When they had dug sixty hatthas, their spades struck a rock, and everybody lost heart. The merchant climbed down into the hole, put his ear to the stone, and listened. He was sure that he could hear the sound of water flowing beneath the rock. He climbed back up and said to a young lad standing there, "My boy, if you don't make an effort, we will all perish. We all depend on you, so you must take heart. Go down into the hole with this iron sledge-hammer, and break the rock."

Resolute, while all the others were in despair, the boy obeyed his master's command. With one great blow, the huge stone damming up the spring split in two. Water gushed out of the hole in a fountain as high as a palm-tree. The whole caravan rejoiced as men drank and bathed. They chopped up their spare axles and yokes to cook rice. After the men had eaten, they fed their oxen. As soon as the sun set, they hoisted a bright flag by the side of the well for other travelers and continued on to their destination.

Once there, they bartered their goods for far more than they had expected. All the men of the caravan became wealthier than they had ever dreamed possible. After a life spent in generosity and other good deeds, the merchant passed away to fare according to his deserts.

Having concluded his story, the Buddha taught the Dhamma. As soon as he had finished, the fainthearted bhikkhu attained the highest fruit of all, which is arahatship.

Then the Buddha identified the birth: "At that time, this bhikkhu who was discouraged was the young man who, persevering, broke the rock and gave water to all the people; my followers were the other members of the caravan; and I was the wise merchant."

3
The Traders of Seriva
Seri-Vānija Jātaka

It was while staying in Sāvatthī that the Buddha told this story to encourage a disheartened bhikkhu to persevere so that he would have no regrets in the future. "If you give up your practice in this sublime teaching which leads to Nibbāna," the Buddha told him, "you will suffer long, like the trader of Seriva who lost a golden bowl worth one hundred thousand coins."

When asked to explain, the Buddha told this story of the distant past.

Five eons ago, the Bodhisatta was an honest trader selling fancy goods in the kingdom of Seriva. Sometimes he traveled with another trader from the same kingdom, a greedy fellow, who handled the same wares.

One day, the two of them crossed the Telavaha River to do business in the bustling city of Andhapura. As usual, to avoid competing with each other, they divided the city between them and began selling their goods from door to door.

In that city, there was a ramshackle mansion. Years before, the family had been rich merchants, but, by the time of this story, their fortunes had dwindled to nothing, and all the men of the family had died. The sole survivors were a girl and her grandmother, and these two earned their living by working for hire.

That afternoon, while the greedy peddler was on his rounds, he came to the door of that house, crying, "Beads for sale! Beads for sale!"

When the young girl heard his cry, she begged, "Please buy me a trinket, Grandmother."

"We're very poor, dear. There's not a cent in the house, and I can't think of anything to offer in exchange."

The girl suddenly remembered an old bowl. "Look!" she cried. "Here's an old bowl. It's of no use to us. Let's try to trade it for something nice."

What the little girl showed her grandmother was an old bowl which had been used by the great merchant, the late head of the family. He had always eaten his curries served from this beautiful, expensive bowl. After his death, it had been thrown among the pots and pans and forgotten. Since it hadn't been used for a very long time, it was completely covered with grime. The two women had no idea that it was made of gold.

The old woman asked the trader to come in and sit down. She showed him the bowl and said, "Sir, my granddaughter would like a trinket. Would you be so kind as to take this bowl and to give her something or other in exchange?"

The peddler took the bowl in his hand and turned it over. Suspecting its value, he scratched the back of it with a needle. After just one covert look, he knew for certain that the bowl was really made of gold.

He sat there, frowning and thinking, until his greed got the better of him. At last, he decided to try to get the bowl without giving the woman anything whatever for it. Pretending to be angry, he growled, "Why did you bring me this stupid bowl? It isn't worth even one cent!" He threw the bowl to the floor, got up, and stalked out of the house in apparent disgust.

Since it had been agreed between the two traders that the one might try the streets which the other had already covered, the honest peddler came later into that same street and appeared at the door of the house, crying, "Beads for sale!"

Once again, the young girl made the same request of her grandmother, and the old woman replied, "My dear, the first peddler threw our bowl on the ground and stormed out of the house. What have we got left to offer?"

"Oh, but that trader was nasty, Grandmother. This one looks and sounds very kind. I think he will take it."

"All right, then. Call him in."

When the trader came into the house, the two women gave him a seat and shyly put the bowl into his hands. Immediately recognizing that the bowl was gold, he said, "Mother, this bowl is worth one hundred thousand coins. I'm sorry, but I don't have that much money."

Astonished at his words, the old woman said, "Sir, another peddler who came here a little while ago said that it was not worth anything. He got angry, threw it on the floor, and went away. If it wasn't valuable then, it must be because of your own goodness that the bowl has turned into gold. Please take it, and just give us something or other for it. We will be more than satisfied."

At that time, the peddler had only five hundred coins and goods worth another five hundred. He gave everything to the women, asking only to keep his scales, his bag, and eight coins for his return fare. Of course, they were happy to agree. After profuse thanks on both sides, the trader hurried to the river with the golden bowl. He gave his eight coins to the boatman and got into the boat.

Not long after he had left, the greedy trader returned to the house, giving the impression of having reluctantly reconsidered their offer. He asked them to bring out their bowl, saying that he would give them something or other for it, after all.

The old woman flew at him. "You scoundrel!" she cried. "You told us that our golden bowl was not worth even one cent. Lucky for us, an honest peddler came after you left and told us that it was really worth one hundred thousand coins. He gave us one thousand coins for it and took it away, so you are too late!"

When the trader heard this, an intense pain swept over him. "He robbed me! He robbed me!" he cried. "He got my golden bowl worth one hundred thousand coins!" He became hysterical and lost all control. Throwing down his money and merchandise, he tore off his shirt, grabbed the beam of his scales like a club, and ran to the riverside to catch the other trader.

By the time he got to the river, the boat was already in midstream. He shouted for the boat to return to shore, but the honest trader, who had already paid, calmly told the ferryman to continue on.

The frustrated trader could only stand there on the riverbank and watch his rival escape with the bowl. The sight so infuriated him that a fierce rage welled up inside. His heart grew hot, and blood gushed from his mouth. Finally, his heart cracked like the mud at the bottom of a pond dried up by the sun. So intense was the unreasoning hatred which he developed against the other trader because of the golden bowl that he perished then and there.

The honest trader returned to Seriva, where he lived a full life spent in generosity and other good deeds and passed away to fare according to his deserts.

Having concluded his story, the Buddha identified the birth: "At that time, Devadatta was the greedy trader, and I was the honest trader. This was the beginning of the implacable grudge which Devadatta has held against me through innumerable lives."

4

Carpe Diem
Cullaka-Setthi Jātaka

It was while staying at Jīvaka's mango grove near Rājagaha that the Buddha told this story about Venerable Culla-Panthaka.

His mother was the daughter of a wealthy merchant in Rājagaha. Before her parents could arrange a marriage for her, she became intimate with a slave. Fearing that her misconduct would be discovered, she urged him to run away with her, saying, "We can't stay here; if my parents find out about our affair, they'll kill us!" Taking only what they could carry, they fled the city to make a life for themselves far away.

When she became pregnant, she told her husband that she wanted to go back to her parents' home to have the baby. Although he agreed to take her, he kept postponing their departure. The days slipped by until she thought to herself, "This fool is so ashamed of his misconduct that he doesn't dare go back. Still, when a woman is in trouble, her parents are her best friends. With him or without him, I am going back home."

A little later, after her husband had gone out, she put everything in order and headed off to her parents' house, telling her next-door neighbor where she was going. When her husband returned, he learned that she had left and hurried after her. He caught up with her, but she had already gone into labor beside the road.

She delivered a son then and there. Since the baby's birth was the reason for the journey, the couple took their newborn boy back home. Because he had been born on the road, they called him Panthaka, which means "by the wayside."

The second time she became pregnant, things happened much as they had before. Since their second son had also been born by the road, they also named him Panthaka. To distinguish between the two boys, they called the older child Mahā-Panthaka and the younger boy Culla-Panthaka.

While they were growing up, the older child heard other boys talking about grandparents, aunts, and uncles, so he asked his mother whether he had family as the other boys did.

"Oh yes, my dear," said his mother; "but they don't live here. Your grandfather is a wealthy merchant in the city of Rājagaha, and you have plenty of relatives there."

"Why don't we go and visit them?" he asked.

She gave him excuses, but when both children began asking about their family, she finally said to her husband, "The boys are always pestering me. Let's take them to see their grandparents. My parents are not going to eat us alive."

"I don't mind taking them," he reluctantly agreed, "but I really cannot face your mother and father."

"Never mind. Just as long as the boys get to see their grandparents," she said.

They took the children to Rājagaha and stayed in a public resthouse near the city gate. The woman sent a message to her parents announcing their arrival. In reply, the parents sent a servant with message which said: "We have not renounced the world, so it may seem strange for us to be living without our children, but that is the way it has worked out. Given the circumstances, we have no wish to see the guilty couple. Here is some money for them to use as they like. If they wish, they can send the children to live with us."

Taking the money, the merchant's daughter and her husband handed the children over to the servant and returned home alone. Thus, the children grew up in their grandparents' house.

Culla-Panthaka was just a child, but his brother was old enough to go with his grandfather to hear the Buddha teach. After hearing the Dhamma, the youth was so moved that he said to his grandfather, "With your permission, I would like to join the Sangha."

"What is this I hear?" cried the old man. "Nothing in the world would give me greater joy than to see you in robes! Become a bhikkhu, if you feel able to," he declared and took his grandson to the Buddha.

"Well, sir," said the Buddha, "I see that you have you brought your grandson with you again today."

"Yes, Venerable Sir. This is my older grandson, Mahā-Panthaka, and he wishes to ordain."

The Buddha immediately sent for a bhikkhu and told him to admit the lad to the Order. The bhikkhu taught him the meditation on the thirty-two parts of the body and ordained him as a sāmanera. By the time Venerable Mahā-Panthaka was twenty, old enough to be fully ordained as a bhikkhu, he had already perfectly memorized many of the Buddha's teachings. He devoted himself to meditation and attained arahatship.

One day, Venerable Mahā-Panthaka thought of his younger brother and wanted to share the great happiness of the Dhamma with him. He went to his grandfather and said, "With your consent, I would like to admit Culla-Panthaka to the Order."

"Please do so, Venerable Sir," the old man replied.

Venerable Mahā-Panthaka thus ordained his younger brother. Venerable Culla-Panthaka tried to learn the Dhamma, but he was so dull that he could not master even a single verse. Each time he tried to memorize a new line, he forgot the line he had just learned. (Long before, during the days of Kassapa Buddha, Culla-Panthaka had been a brilliant and learned bhikkhu. At that time, he had mocked another bhikkhu who was struggling to memorize a passage. This had so confused the young bhikkhu that he was unable to remember anything at all. Now, as a result of that occurrence long ago, Culla-Panthaka himself had become a dullard.)

Venerable Culla-Panthaka struggled unsuccessfully with a single stanza for four months. At the end of that time, his elder brother said, "Culla-Panthaka, you are not equal to this doctrine. In four whole months you have not been able to learn this one verse. How can you hope to succeed at your vocation? Leave the monastery."

Although he had been expelled by his brother as a failure, Venerable Culla-Panthaka did not want to return to lay life.

Not long after that, the physician Jīvaka visited the monastery to offer incense and flowers and to listen to a discourse by the Teacher. Afterwards, he asked Venerable Mahā-Panthaka, who was acting as monastery steward, how many bhikkhus were staying there with the Buddha. Venerable Mahā-Panthaka answered that there were five hundred.

"I would like to invite all five hundred of you, with the Buddha at your head, to my house for your meal tomorrow."

Venerable Mahā-Panthaka replied, "Sir, there is one here named Culla-Panthaka. He is a dolt and has made no progress in his studies. I accept the invitation for everyone except him."

Venerable Culla-Panthaka overheard this and thought, "In accepting the invitation, my brother excludes me. His affection for me is dead. What is the point of my continuing my monastic life? I will become a layman and practice generosity and other good deeds."

Early the next morning, he got up, intending to disrobe and to return to lay life.

As always, at daybreak, the Buddha surveyed the world. He immediately was aware of Venerable Culla-Panthaka's intention. Going out early, he paced back and forth on Venerable Culla-Panthaka's path. When the sāmanera came out of his room, he saw the Buddha and greeted him.

"Where are you going at this hour, Culla-Panthaka?" the Buddha asked.

"My brother has banished me from the Order, Venerable Sir, so I am going to leave."

"Culla-Panthaka, you took your vows under me. Why didn't you come to me when your brother expelled you? A layman's life is not for you. You will stay here with me."

With those words, the Buddha led Venerable Culla-Panthaka to the door of his Perfumed Chamber and sat him down facing east. The Buddha gave him a perfectly clean cloth and said, "As you handle this cloth, repeat the words: 'Removal of impurity; removal of impurity.'"

At the proper time, the Buddha, accompanied by the Sangha, went to Jīvaka's house for the meal.

All the while, Venerable Culla-Panthaka continued rubbing the cloth and repeating, "Removal of impurity; removal of impurity." Gradually, the cloth became dirty, and Venerable Culla-Panthaka observed, "A few minutes ago this cloth was perfectly clean, but I have spoiled its original purity and made it dirty. Impermanent, indeed, are all compounded things!"

Instantly aware that Venerable Culla-Panthaka had achieved that insight, the Buddha appeared before him and said, "Never mind this mere piece of cloth which has become dirty. Within you are the impurities of greed, anger, and delusion. Remove them!"

As the vision of the Buddha spoke, Venerable Culla-Panthaka attained arahatship with the four branches of knowledge which included full knowledge of all the sacred texts.[1]

---

1   This would include: (1) the understanding of the sense of the sacred books, (2) the un-

(In ages past, Culla-Panthaka had been a king. While making a solemn procession around his capital, this king had wiped the sweat from his brow with a pure white cloth. Upon seeing the stained cloth, he had thought, "This body of mine has ruined the purity of the cloth and soiled it. Impermanent, indeed, are all compounded things." Both times, it was the removal of impurity which led to his insight into the nature of impermanence.)

In the meantime, at Jīvaka's home, the doctor began pouring the Water of Donation, but the Buddha put his hand over the vessel, and asked, "Jīvaka, are there no other bhikkhus in the monastery?"

Venerable Mahā-Panthaka spoke up and said, "There are no bhikkhus there, Venerable Sir."

"Oh yes, Jīvaka, there are," the Buddha said.

Jīvaka ordered a servant to go to the monastery and to check whether there were any other bhikkhus still there.

Venerable Culla-Panthaka immediately knew that his brother was declaring that there were no bhikkhus left in the monastery, so he decided to prove him wrong. Using his newly-acquired extraordinary powers, Venerable Culla-Panthaka created the illusion of one thousand bhikkhus. He filled the whole mango grove with bhikkhus, some making robes, others dyeing cloth, and still others reciting suttas.

Astonished, the servant hurried back and reported that the mango grove was full of bhikkhus.

The Buddha instructed the servant to return to the grove and to announce, "The Buddha sends for the one named Culla-Panthaka."

The servant did as he was told, but all of the one thousand bhikkhus answered, "I am Culla-Panthaka!"

The bewildered servant returned to the Buddha and said, "Venerable Sir, all of them answered, 'I am Culla-Panthaka.'"

"Well, go back one last time," said the Buddha, "and take the hand of the first one who says that he is Culla-Panthaka."

Again, the servant did as he was told. As soon as he took Venerable Culla-Panthaka's hand, all the phantom bhikkhus disappeared. The servant respectfully led Venerable Culla-Panthaka to Jīvaka's house.

When the meal was finished, the Buddha said, "Jīvaka, take Culla-Panthaka's bowl; he will give anumodana." Venerable Culla-Panthaka's sermon of thanks ranged eloquently through the whole of the Buddha's teachings.

---

derstanding of their ethical truth, (3) the ability to justify an interpretation grammatically, logically, etc., and (4) the power of public exposition.

After Venerable Culla-Panthaka had finished speaking, the Buddha returned to the monastery, accompanied by the five hundred bhikkhus.

That evening, in the Hall of Truth, the bhikkhus were talking about these events. "Mahā-Panthaka failed to recognize his younger brother's real abilities. He even tried to expel him from the monastery as a hopeless dullard, but, during the course of a single meal, the Buddha led Culla-Panthaka to arahatship with both extraordinary knowledge and powers. How great is a Buddha's power!"

The Buddha knew perfectly well what the bhikkhus were discussing, and he decided to join them. As soon as he entered, the bhikkhus broke off their talk and were silent. Looking at the assembled bhikkhus, the Buddha thought, "This company is perfect! Not a man is guilty of moving hand or foot improperly; not a sound, not even a cough or a sneeze, is to be heard! In their reverence for the Buddha's majesty, none dares to speak before I do, even if I sit here in silence for the rest of my life. However, let me open the conversation." Then he asked the bhikkhus what they had been discussing.

"Venerable Sir," the bhikkhus replied, "we were not speaking idly. We were talking about how you led Culla-Panthaka to arahatship."

"Bhikkhus, because of me, Culla-Panthaka has now realized great things in my Sāsana. In the past, he acquired great wealth, also through me." At their request, the Buddha told this story of the past.

Long, long ago, when Brahmadatta was reigning in Bāranasi, the Bodhisatta was born as the son of the city treasurer. When he grew up, he became treasurer himself. An extremely clever man, he had a keen eye for signs and omens.

One day, on his way to the palace, he noticed a dead mouse lying on the road. Considering the position of the stars, he commented to himself, "Any young fellow with his wits about him has only to pick up that mouse and start a business."

An impoverished young man of good family overheard the treasurer's words and thought, "That man always has a good reason for what he says." Accordingly, he picked up the mouse, which he sold for a penny to a tavern keeper for his cat.

With the penny, he bought treacle. He filled a water-pot with drinking water and set out. Soon, he met a band of thirsty flower-gatherers returning from the forest. He offered them the treacle and water and received a handful of flowers from each in exchange.

He easily sold the flowers and bought more treacle. The next day, he met the flower-gatherers again, and again offered them water and treacle.

This time, they gave him flowering plants, which he sold for a profit of eight pennies.

Not long after that, on a stormy day, the wind blew down so many branches in the king's pleasure garden that the royal gardener was unable to clear them away without help. Seeing this, the young man offered to clean the entire garden if he could have the wood and leaves to do with as he pleased. The gardener was delighted with the idea and immediately agreed.

The young man hurried to the playground nearby and offered treacle to the boys and girls there, in exchange for cleaning the garden and piling the branches, sticks, and leaves in a heap at the garden gate.

Just as the children were finishing, the royal potter happened to pass by. "My good man," he said to the merchant's son, "I have been desperately searching for fuel to fire my kiln. This pile of wood and leaves would be ideal. I will buy the lot from you for sixteen pennies. As a bonus, I offer you five of my bowls and a few extra pots as well." The young man accepted the deal without hesitation.

With his capital of twenty-four pennies, the young man devised a plan. He filled a large jar with drinking water and carried it to an area near the city gate, where five hundred men were cutting grass. He offered all of them free water to quench their thirst.

The mowers were very grateful. As they drank and refreshed themselves, they thanked him warmly. "Friend," they said, "you have done us a great favor. How can we repay you?"

"Don't mention it," he replied. "I'll let you know when I can use your help."

About the same time, he became friendly with two merchants, one trading overland and the other, by sea. One day, the land trader gave him a tip, saying, "Tomorrow, a horse trader with five hundred horses to sell is coming to town."

The young merchant quickly went to meet the mowers. "Today I would like each of you to give me a bundle of grass." They all agreed. "Also," he continued, "I would like to ask you not to sell your grass until I've sold mine."

"Certainly," they agreed cheerfully. The five hundred bundles of grass were soon delivered to his house.

When the horse trader found himself unable to get grass for his horses elsewhere, he bought the young man's grass for one thousand coins.

A few days later, his sea-trading friend brought him news of the arrival of a large ship. This gave him another idea.

For eight pennies he hired a grand carriage and rode to the port. His demeanor was so impressive that he was able to purchase the ship's entire cargo on credit, simply by depositing his signet ring as security. The young man then erected a magnificent pavilion nearby and instructed his servants that any merchants who came to see him should be shown in with impressive formality by three successive ushers.

Just as the young man had expected, one hundred merchants from the town soon arrived at the port, expecting to buy some of the cargo. All of them were told that the entire cargo had already been purchased by a great merchant, and they were pointed in the direction of the pavilion.

When each merchant appeared at the pavilion, he was treated with great respect and even greater formality. As arranged, he was passed from usher to usher until, at last, he stood before the young merchant seated at his desk. Each of the merchants gave the young man one thousand coins for a share of the cargo, and, together, they offered him another one hundred thousand to buy him out entirely. Thus, the young man was able to sell the entire cargo, sight unseen, for two hundred thousand coins, having made only a very meager investment. The clever young man dismantled his pavilion and returned to Bārānasi.

Wishing to show his gratitude, he put half of his wealth in a sack and went to call on the treasurer.

"How did you acquire all this wealth?" the treasurer asked him.

"I was able to amass this fortune in only four months, simply by following your advice," the young man replied. Then he told the treasurer the whole story, starting with the dead mouse.

"This is a most remarkable young fellow!" the treasurer thought. "I must see that he does not end up in anybody else's family!" The treasurer offered his own daughter, and, as soon as they were married, he settled all his property on his new son-in-law.

When the treasurer passed away to fare according to his deserts, his clever son-in-law became the new treasurer of the city.

Having concluded his story, the Buddha added, "From such a humble beginning and with trifling capital, a shrewd and able man will rise to wealth, just as a small breath can fan a flame.

"Through me, Culla-Panthaka has risen to great things in my Sāsana, just as, in times past, he achieved great things in the way of wealth through my tutoring, for, of course, Culla-Panthaka was that clever young man, and I was the treasurer."

5

A Measure of Rice
Tandulanāli Jātaka

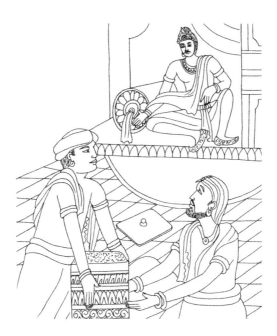

It was while staying at Jetavana that the Buddha told this story about Venerable Lāludāyi.

At Jetavana, Venerable Dabba the Mallan held the post of meals' designator for the Sangha. One of his responsibilities was to allot tickets for the lottery meals at the homes of devotees.

Generally, the senior bhikkhus were offered meals at the houses with the best rice, but where each bhikkhu actually went depended on how many bhikkhus there were in each seniority group on any particular day. It was understood that each bhikkhu would agree silently to go to whichever house he was assigned.

If Venerable Lāludāyi received inferior rice, however, he was not quiet. Instead, he would loudly complain about the allotment. "Is Dabba the only one who knows how to give out tickets?" he would shout. "Some of us could do just as well as he does!"

One day, when he was making a disturbance, the other bhikkhus handed him the ticket basket and said, "Here, Friend! From now on, you may give out the tickets! Show us what you can do!"

Lāludāyi, however, could not distinguish between the houses with higher quality and lower quality meals. Nor did he know how to arrange the bhikkhus according to seniority. After they had been arranged one day, he made marks on the wall and on the floor to indicate the limit of each seniority group. The next day, although the numbers of bhikkhus in the groups were different, Venerable Lāludāyi insisted on using the marks for the previous day for his allotment.

"Friend," the other bhikkhus protested, "the numbers are different today from what they were yesterday. The lottery and the allotment of tickets for the better meals should be according to seniority, but your marks are not correct."

"What do you mean?" Venerable Lāludāyi retorted. "These marks were correct when I made them. No one's seniority has changed! Why aren't you standing according to the marks? Why should I trust you instead of my marks?"

Finally, the boys and sāmaneras dragged him out of the hall. "Friend Lāludāyi," they shouted, "you are not fit to allot the tickets! When you give them out, nobody receives what he deserves! Get out of here!"

Hearing the noise, the Buddha asked Venerable Ānanda what was happening. Venerable Ānanda explained that Venerable Lāludāyi had made a muddle of the food allotments, and the Buddha replied, "This is not the first time that Lāludāyi, through his stupidity, has deprived others of what they deserve. He did the same thing before." At Venerable Ānanda's request, the Buddha told this story of the past.

Long, long ago, when Brahmadatta was reigning in Bārānasi, the Bodhisatta was the king's official appraiser. It was his job to value horses, elephants, jewels, gold, and real estate and to pay the owners the proper price for their goods or property.

King Brahmadatta was a greedy man, and his greed suggested to him that he was losing wealth because of the appraiser's honesty. "This appraiser, with his naive style of valuing will soon deplete my wealth. I ought to get myself another appraiser." He opened his window and looked down into the palace courtyard. There he saw a simple-looking farmhand whom he judged a likely, docile candidate for the post. The king impulsively sent for the fellow and asked him whether he thought he could do the job.

"Oh, yes, Sire! It sounds easy enough." answered the farmhand, and the king immediately appointed him royal appraiser.

Of course, the fool had no idea of the true worth of elephants, horses, gold, and jewels. He set their value according to his own fancy, which was constantly changing. Because of the power of his position, however, whatever value he set for any item had to be accepted as correct.

One day, a trader arrived from the northern part of the kingdom with a herd of five hundred horses, and the king sent this appraiser to fix the value of the animals. The man looked at the horses and declared that the entire herd was worth one measure of rice. He ordered that this amount be paid to the dealer and that the horses be driven into a corral adjacent to the royal stable.

The astonished horse trader hurried to the former appraiser, explained what had just happened, and appealed for help.

"What you need to do," the former appraiser suggested, "is to give him a bribe and to ask him to state, in the presence of the king, the value of one measure of rice. I will be there when he does."

The horse trader went back to the appraiser, slipped him a bribe, and said, "Sir, knowing, as we do now, that our horses are worth a single measure of rice, we are curious to learn from you the precise value of one measure of rice. Would you be so kind as to state its value in the king's presence?"

"Of course, sir," replied the appraiser. "Let us go to the king now."

They went to the throne room, where the king was, surrounded by many ministers and advisors. The former appraiser stood inconspicuously at the side.

After paying his respects to the king, the horse trader said, "Sire, I am not disputing your appraiser's decision that the value of my five hundred horses is a single measure of rice. I would request, however, if I may, that Your Majesty ask your appraiser to declare the value of that one measure of rice."

Since he had not been informed of all that had already taken place, the king did not understand what the horse trader was asking. "Appraiser," the king asked, "what is the value of this man's five hundred horses?"

"One measure of rice, Sire," he replied.

"Well, then, my friend," asked the king, "if five hundred horses are worth one measure of rice, what is the value of that measure of rice?"

Of course, this fool had undervalued the horses to please the king, but, having received the bribe, he now wanted to please the horse trader, so he declared, "Sire, it is worth all Bārānasi and its suburbs!"

At his ridiculous answer, all the ministers and advisors clapped their hands and laughed merrily. "How silly of us!" one of them cried. "We imagined that Bārānasi was beyond price, but now we learn that the entire city, including the king and his palace, is worth just one measure of rice!"

"What a clever appraiser we have!" shouted another.

"How has this talented fellow kept his job so long?" asked a third.

"You forget, my friend," said another under his breath, "that this idiot pleases our king!"

Openly put to shame, the king was compelled to send the foolish bumpkin packing and to restore the former appraiser to the office.

When his life ended, the wise appraiser passed away to fare according to his deserts.

Having concluded his story, the Buddha identified the birth: "At that time, Lāludāyi was the foolish appraiser, and I was the wise appraiser."

6
Seeking Righteousness
Devadhamma Jātaka

It was while staying at Jetavana that the Buddha told this story about a wealthy bhikkhu.

A rich landowner of Sāvatthī decided to join the Sangha after his wife died. Before he ordained, however, he had accommodations built for himself, including a day room, a sleeping room, a room for the fire, and an ample storeroom. Not until his apartments were finished and his storeroom well-stocked with rice, ghee, jaggery, and oil did he finally join the Order. Even after he became a bhikkhu, he ordered his old servants to cook his favorite curries for him. He was richly provided not only with the requisites, but also with robes for the daytime and a change of robes for nighttime. He stayed in his rooms at the edge of the monastery, aloof from the other bhikkhus.

One day, after he had spread out his robes, bedding, and bedclothes to air, some visiting bhikkhus happened to pass by, and they saw all these belongings.

"Whose things are these?" they asked.

"Mine, sirs," he replied.

"What are you saying, Friend?" they cried. "All these upper robes, outer robes, bedclothes, and bedding? All this is yours?"

"Yes, nobody's but mine."

"Friend," they protested, "the Buddha allows each bhikkhu to possess only three robes. Since the Buddha himself is restrained in his wants and since you have ordained in his order, how can you boldly proclaim that this whole pile of requisites belongs to you?

"Please come with us to see the Teacher!" they urged, as they led him to the Buddha.

When the Buddha saw them, he asked, "Why have you brought this bhikkhu here against his will?"

"Venerable Sir, this bhikkhu is well-to-do and has a great stockpile of requisites."

"Is it true, Bhikkhu, that you are wealthy?"

"Yes, Blessed One."

"Why have you amassed so many belongings? Don't I extol the virtues of renunciation, contentment, solitude, and making effort?"

Angered by the Buddha's question, he flung off his outer robe and, standing there in only his waist-cloth, he cried, "In that case, I'll go about like this!"

Rather than chastising the bhikkhu for his rudeness, the Buddha gently asked, "Was it not you, Bhikkhu, in days gone by, who, as a yakkha, sought righteousness for twelve years? How can you now fling off your outer robe and stand here devoid of shame?"

As soon as he heard the Buddha's words, his sense of honor was restored. He immediately put on his robes again, paid his respects to the Buddha, and seated himself respectfully at the side.

The bhikkhus gathered there asked the Buddha to explain this story of the past, so he made clear what had been concealed by rebirth.

Long, long ago, when Brahmadatta was reigning in Bāranasi, the Bo-dhisatta was born to the king and queen and was named Prince Mahimsāsa. By the time Prince Mahimsāsa could run about, a second son was born, and the king named him Prince Canda (Prince Moon). While Canda was just a toddler, their mother died.

Soon afterwards, the king took another queen, who became his joy and delight. In time, the new queen gave birth to yet another prince, whom they named Prince Suriya (Prince Sun). In his happiness at the birth of this third boy, the king promised to grant the queen a boon on the child's behalf. The queen requested that she be allowed to postpone her wish and to claim it in her own good time. The king agreed.

Years later, when her son was grown, she said to the king, "Sire, when my boy was born, you granted me a favor. I would like to claim it now. Let my son be king."

"That's impossible," said the king. "I have two other bright and promising sons. I cannot give the kingdom to your boy."

No matter how firmly the king refused her request, however, the queen continued plaguing him to make her son the heir-apparent. Afraid that his wife might plot against his older sons, he sent for them and said, "My boys, when Prince Suriya was born, I granted his mother a boon. Now the queen is asking me to give the kingdom to him. I do not want to do that, but I am afraid that she will do you some harm. Both of you had better retire to the forest for the time being. Remember, however, this kingdom, by rights, belongs to you. When I am dead, return and claim the throne."

The king wept bitter tears, kissed his two elder sons on the head, and sent them away.

While this was taking place, young Prince Suriya was playing in the courtyard. When he saw his brothers leaving the palace, he asked them where they were going. Hearing that they were leaving to live in the forest, he asked to go with them.

Without telling anyone else, the three brothers set out together for the Himavat. Along the way, they stopped to rest at the foot of a tree. Prince Mahiṃsāsa said to his youngest brother, "Suriya, dear, you must be tired. Run down to the pool over there. Get yourself a drink and bathe. When you have finished, bring us back some water in a lotus leaf."

It so happened that that particular pool had been given by Vessavana to a certain yakkha with permission to eat all wayfarers who entered into the water of the pool except the one who knew what righteousness was. For many years, the yakkha had asked everyone who entered the pool, but no one could tell him what righteousness was, and he had devoured them all.

Of course, Prince Suriya knew nothing of this as he gleefully ran toward the pool. As soon as he stepped into the cool water, he was grabbed by the yakkha, who asked, "Do you know what righteousness is?"

"Oh, yes," he answered readily. "It is the sun and the moon."

"Ha! You don't know!" said the yakkha, as he hauled the prince down into the depths of the pond and imprisoned him there.

Noticing that his brother had been gone a long time, Prince Mahiṃsāsa sent Prince Canda to find him and to fetch some water. The yakkha grabbed him too, and asked, "Do you know what righteousness is?"

"Oh yes," said Prince Canda. "It is the four quarters of heaven."

"Ha! You don't know, either," said the yakkha, and he hauled him off to the same prison.

When his second brother failed to return, Prince Mahimsāsa became worried that something had happened to both of them. He went himself to the pool, following their footprints down to the water's edge. He realized at once that some yakkha inhabited the pool, so he buckled on his sword, took up his bow, and waited.

The yakkha could see that Prince Mahimsāsa had no intention of entering the water, so he took on the appearance of a forester and approached the prince from behind. "Greetings, my dear young man," he said warmly to the prince, "you must be tired from your journey. Why don't you step into this lovely pool, bathe, and have a drink of cool water? Refreshed, you can comfortably resume your journey."

Immediately recognizing the forester as a yakkha, Prince Mahimsāsa said, "You have seized my brothers, haven't you?"

"Yes, I have," the yakkha admitted.

"Why?"

"Because all who go into this pool belong to me."

"All?"

"All except the one who knows what righteousness is."

"Do you want to know what righteousness is?"

"Yes, I do," said the yakkha hopefully.

"Then I will tell you what righteousness is."

"Please tell me, and I will listen with full attention," said the yakkha, now beginning to show respect to the prince.

"Well," the prince said slowly, "I would like to begin, but I am tired and dirty after my long journey."

The yakkha bathed the prince and gave him water to drink. He adorned the prince with flowers and created a lovely pavilion with a soft couch.

Prince Mahimsāsa sat on the couch, the yakkha sat at his feet, and the prince began, "Listen, and you will hear what righteousness is. Only those who shrink from evil are righteous. Those with pure minds who follow the good are righteous."

When he heard this, the yakkha was pleased and offered Prince Mahimsāsa a reward. "Man of wisdom, I am pleased with you. I will give you back one of your brothers. Which one shall I bring?"

"The youngest."

"Man of wisdom, though you know what righteousness is, you don't act on your knowledge."

"How so?"

"You take the younger in preference to the elder, without regard to his seniority."

"Yakkha, I not only know what righteousness is, I also practice it. It was on this boy's account that we had to leave our home and seek refuge in the forest. His mother asked our father to give him the kingdom. Our father refused her demand and sent us away for our own protection. This dear lad came with us, never thinking of turning back. Who would believe me if I said that he had been devoured by a yakkha in the forest? It is fear of that blame that compels me to ask for his return."

"Excellent, man of wisdom! Excellent!" cried the yakkha in approval; "you not only know righteousness but also practice it."

To show his appreciation and approval, he returned both brothers to the prince.

Then Prince Mahimsāsa said to the yakkha, "Friend, because of your own evil deeds in the past you were born as a yakkha living on the flesh and blood of other creatures. In this present birth, you are continuing to do evil. This wicked conduct will ensure that you are born again and again in the lower realms. From now on, renounce evil, and live righteously."

The yakkha followed this advice and offered to protect the princes as long as they wished to remain in that pleasant spot. The three brothers accepted the yakkha's invitation and stayed there. One night, Prince Mahimsāsa saw in the stars the signs that their father had died. Taking the yakkha with him, he returned with his brothers to Bārānasi and took possession of the kingdom. He appointed Prince Canda crown prince and Prince Suriya commander-in-chief.

King Mahimsāsa reserved a beautiful garden as a home for the yakkha and made sure that he received the choicest food and garlands. The king ruled in righteousness until he passed away to fare according to his deserts.

Having concluded his story, the Buddha taught the Dhamma, and that bhikkhu attained the first path. Then the Buddha identified the birth: "At that time, the wealthy bhikkhu was the yakkha, Ānanda was Prince Suriya, Sāriputta was Prince Canda, and I was the eldest, Prince Mahimsāsa."

7

The Wood Gatherer's Son
Katthahāri Jātaka

It was while staying at Jetavana that the Buddha told this story about
Vāsabha-Khattiyā.[2]

Vāsabha-Khattiyā was the daughter of Mahānāma the Sākyan by a slave
named Nāgamunda. After she grew up, she was married to King Pasenadi,
the king of Kosala, and had his son. When the king learned of her servile
origin, however, he demoted her from her queenly rank and degraded her
son, Vidūḍabha. After that, she and her son never went outside the palace.

When he learned of this, the Buddha went to the palace at dawn, attended
by five hundred bhikkhus. Sitting down on the seat prepared for him, he
asked the king, "Sire, where is Vāsabha-Khattiyā?"

Then the king told him the whole story of what he had done.

"Sire, whose daughter is Vāsabha-Khattiyā?"

"Mahānāma's daughter, Venerable Sir."

---

2   The occasion for this story is the same as part of that for Tale 179, where it is related in
detail.

"When she left Kapilavatthu, whose wife did she become?"

"Mine, sir."

"Sire, she is a king's daughter. She is married to a king. To a king she has borne a son. Why, then, is that son not the crown prince of his father's realm? In the distant past, a monarch who had a son by a simple wood-gatherer gave that son sovereignty."

When the king asked him to explain, the Buddha made clear what had been concealed by rebirth.

Long, long ago, when Brahmadatta was reigning in Bārānasi, he went to his pleasure garden to enjoy the fruit, flowers and fresh air there. As he wandered about, he came upon a young woman, merrily singing to herself as she gathered sticks and twigs in a shady grove.

Infatuated at first sight, the king seduced her. Immediately aware that she was pregnant, the woman told the king. He gave her the signet ring from his finger and told her that, if the baby was a girl, she should sell the ring and use the money to support her daughter. If the child was a boy, however, she should bring the ring and the baby to him.

When it was time for her to deliver, she gave birth to a son, who grew into a strong and handsome boy. Sometimes, when they were playing, the other children mocked him, saying, "No-father has hit me!" or "Let's give it to No-father!"

Finally, the boy ran to his mother and demanded to know who his father was.

"My dear, you are the son of the king of Kāsi."

"What proof do you have, Mother?"

"My dear boy, before you were born, the king gave me this signet ring and told me, 'If you have a daughter, spend the price of this ring on her. If the child is a son, bring the ring and the boy to me.'"

"Why don't you take me to my father, Mother?"

Realizing that the proper time had, indeed, come, she took him to the palace. At the gate, they asked that their presence be announced to the king, and they were summoned inside. The woman bowed to the king and said, "Sire, this is your son."

The king was fully aware that this was the truth, but, feeling embarrassed in front of the court, he quickly replied, "He is no son of mine."

"But here is your signet ring, Sire. Surely, you recognize this," she stated, holding up the ring for all to see.

"My dear woman," the king retorted, "that is not my signet ring."

"Sire, I have now no witness to prove my words," the woman declared. "All I can do is to appeal to the truth. If you are the father of my child, I pray that he may hover in mid-air. If you are not, may my son fall to the ground and die."

She grabbed her little boy by the foot and threw him up into the air.

The child remained poised in mid-air and said in a sweet voice, "Your Majesty, I am indeed your son. Raise me! Since the king is father to the kingdom, he must also rear his own son!"

Hearing the truth spoken from mid-air, the king stretched out his hands and cried, "Come to me, my son! I alone will care for you!"

Many hands were stretched out to catch the boy, but he descended into the arms of his father and seated himself in the king's lap.

The king proclaimed the boy crown prince and made his mother queen-consort.

When the king died, the new king was called Katthavahana.[3] After ruling righteously, he passed away to fare according to his deserts.

Having concluded his story, the Buddha identified the birth: "At that time, Queen Mahā-Māyā was the mother; King Suddhodana was the father; and I was King Katthavahana."

---

3   Kattha means "firewood." Katthahāri means "firewood gatherer." Katthavāhana means "One who rides on firewood."

8

What Happiness!
Sukhavihāri Jātaka

It was while staying at Anupiya mango grove[1] near the town of Anupiya that the Buddha told this story about Venerable Bhaddiya.

Bhaddiya was the head of an aristocratic Sākyan family in Kapilavat-thu. He was close to the young Anuruddha, so, when Anuruddha asked his mother for permission to become a bhikkhu, she replied that she would agree only on the condition that Prince Bhaddiya, the Sākyan chieftain, also leave the home life. Of course, she expected that Bhaddiya was so attached to the power, prestige, and worldly pleasures that came with his position that he would refuse.

"Bhaddiya," Anuruddha told his friend, "my ordination depends on yours. Let us go forth together into homelessness."

---

1   Anupiya, in the kingdom of Malla, lay to the east of Kapilavatthu. After the Bodhisatta renounced the home life and cut off his hair, he spent one week there in the mango grove. As the Buddha, he revisited the Anupiya mango grove after leaving Kapilavatthu, where he had gone to see his relatives. It was in this mango grove that he ordained the Sākyan princes.

"Whether it depends on me or not," Bhaddiya replied, "there should be ordination. I shall..." He broke off in the middle of the sentence. He had intended to say, "I shall come with you," but, regretting his initial agreement, he said "Go and be ordained, according to your wish."

Anuruddha pleaded again and again with Bhaddiya, reminding him that he needed his mother's permission. Unable to refuse completely, Bhaddiya asked the young prince to wait for seven years.

"Seven years is too long, Friend," Anuruddha replied. "I cannot wait for seven years." Step by step, he forced Bhaddiya to reduce the delay to seven months, to seven weeks, and, finally, to seven days. Bhaddiya explained that he needed that much time to settle his worldly affairs and to arrange for a successor. True to his word, Bhaddiya prepared to renounce the household life in seven days.

Anuruddha's example encouraged other Sākyan princes to leave the home life and to ordain in the Buddha's Sangha. Pretending that they were going on an outing to the royal pleasure garden, Bhaddiya, Anuruddha, Ānanda, Kimbila, Bhagu, and Devadatta, accompanied by their barber, Upāli, left Kapilavatthu with an armed escort. After a while, however, they dismissed their guards and slipped across the border into Malla. They took off their jewelry, tied it into a bundle, and handed it to Upāli.

Upāli accepted the bundle and started back to Kapilavatthu, but it occurred to him that, if he returned without the princes, the Sākyans would assume that he had murdered them for their jewelry. He hastily hung the bundle on the branch of a tree and hurried to join the others. "If you are going to take up the homeless life, why shouldn't I?" he asked, and the others allowed him to join them.

In fact, when they asked the Buddha for ordination, they requested that he ordain Upāli first. "We Sākyans are proud," they told the Buddha. "This Upāli, the barber, has served us for a long time. If you ordain him before us, he will be our senior, and we will have to respect his seniority. That will humble our Sākyan pride."

Among this group of Sākyans, Venerable Bhaddiya was first to attain arahatship. Venerable Anuruddha acquired the divine eye, and Venerable Ānanda attained the first path. Later, all of them, except Devadatta, attained arahatship, but Devadatta never achieved more than mundane extraordinary powers.

In Kapilavatthu, Bhaddiya had had many duties of state and had been carefully protected at all times. After his ordination, he recalled that he had constantly lived in a state of anxiety and that, even at night on his elegant couch in his private apartments on the upper floor of his palace, he had never been able to relax completely. Comparing those stressful days with the total absence of fear that he experienced as an arahat, he repeatedly uttered, "What happiness! What happiness!"

Hearing this, several bhikkhus told the Buddha, "Bhaddiya is declaring the bliss that he has won!"

The Buddha replied, "This is not the first time that Bhaddiya's life has been happy. He was also happy long ago." At the request of those bhikkhus, the Buddha told this story of the past.

Long, long ago, when Brahmadatta was reigning in Bārānasi, the Bodhisatta was born into a wealthy and proud northern brahmin family. Realizing, however, the evil of lust and the blessings that come from renouncing the world, he became an ascetic. He practiced concentration meditation in the Himavat, perfected the eight jhānas, and became the leader of five hundred ascetics.

Once, as the rainy season was beginning, he left the Himavat with his followers to get salt and vinegar and to find a place to stay. Eventually arriving in Bārānasi, they stayed in the royal park and received alms and hospitality from King Brahmadatta. At the end of the rainy season, the ascetic went to the palace to take leave of the king.

"You are old, Venerable Sir!" exclaimed the king. "At your age, why should you go back to the Himavat? Send your students back by themselves, and stay on here in my royal park."

The master accepted the king's invitation and instructed his eldest student, who had also perfected the jhānas, to become the leader of the others.

After staying in the Himavat for some time, that disciple felt a great longing to see his master again. He told the other students to continue practicing diligently and promised to return after he had visited their master.

He went directly to Bārānasi, paid his respects to his master, and greeted him with affection. Then he lay down beside his master on a mat which he had spread there.

At that time, King Brahmadatta happened to arrive at the park to visit the old ascetic. The king greeted him and sat at one side. Although the visiting ascetic was aware that the king had come, instead of rising, he continued lying beside his master, all the while, exclaiming with great feeling, "What happiness! What happiness!"

Displeased that the younger ascetic had not risen, the king complained to the elder, "Venerable Sir, it seems that this ascetic has had more than enough to eat, in that he continues to lie there so contentedly!"

"Sire," the ascetic replied, "when he was younger, this ascetic was a great king like you. He is remembering that, in those days, though he lived surrounded by regal luxury and stateliness, he was constantly guarded by many soldiers and that he never knew such happiness and freedom as he now experiences. This is the happiness of the ascetic's life and the happiness that the jhānas bring. It is this extraordinary happiness which moves him to make his emotional cry. Consider, Sire, that the man who neither guards nor is guarded lives happily and is freed from craving and lust."

Placated by this explanation, the king paid his respects and returned to his palace. The disciple soon took leave of his master and returned to the Himavat. The old ascetic stayed in the royal park with his concentration unbroken for the rest of his life. When he passed away, he was reborn in the Brahma heavens.

Having concluded his story, the Buddha identified the birth: "At that time, Venerable Bhaddiya was the disciple, and I was the teacher."

9
Leadership
Lakkhana Jātaka

It was while staying at Veluvana, the bamboo grove near Rājagaha, that the Buddha told this story about Devadatta.

At one time, Devadatta insisted that the Buddha impose five rules on the Sangha.[1] When the Buddha refused, Devadatta took five hundred newly-ordained bhikkhus from Vesāli to Gayāsīsa, thereby creating a schism in the Sangha.

After a while, the Buddha said to Venerable Sāriputta, "Your five hundred students, who were lured away by Devadatta, are now wiser. Go to Gayāsīsa, properly teach them the Dhamma, and bring them back with you."

Venerable Moggallāna and Venerable Sāriputta went to Gayāsīsa and found Devadatta imitating the Buddha. They preached to those five hundred bhikkhus and took them back to Veluvana.

---

1 (1) Bhikkhus should spend their whole lives in the forest; (2) bhikkhus should eat only food received on almsrounds; (3) bhikkhus should wear only robes made of discarded rags; (4) bhikkhus should stay under trees and never under a roof; and (5) bhikkhus should abstain completely from eating meat and fish.

Later, a group of bhikkhus was discussing this and said to the Buddha, "Venerable Sir, the glory of the Captain of the Teaching, when he returned with those five hundred bhikkhus, was very great, while Devadatta lost his entire following."

The Buddha replied, "This is not the only time, Bhikkhus, that Sāriputta has achieved glory for protecting his followers. Likewise, this is not the only time that Devadatta has lost all his following. The same thing happened to both long ago." At their request, the Buddha told this story of the past.

Long, long ago, in Magadha, the Bodhisatta was born as a deer. When he was a mature stag, he became the leader of a great herd of one thousand deer and had two sons named Lakkhana and Kāla. The great deer watched his sons grow into fine stags, and, feeling old himself, he decided to give them the responsibility for the herd. He placed five hundred deer under the care of each.

In Magadha, as the harvest season was approaching, villagers set snares, dug pits, hid sharpened stakes, and laid traps to protect their crops from marauding deer. It became dangerous for deer to remain anywhere near the fields of ripening grain, and, every year, many deer died from these devices.

One day, the old stag summoned his sons and said, "The crops are ripening in the fields, and it is dangerous for so many to stay here. Those of us who are old know about the dangers, and we can manage, but you must take the young deer to the hills until the crops have been harvested and it is safe to return."

The two promptly agreed to do as their father wished and prepared to leave right away.

Hunters were well aware of this annual migration, and lay in wait in blinds along the trails leading into the hills. Oblivious to the danger, Kāla moved with his herd during the day, and many of his deer were shot and killed. Every night, he led his herd close to villages, hoping to find food, but more were killed there. He reached the hills with only a few survivors.

Lakkhana, much wiser than his brother, traveled with his herd only after it was dark. He was careful to give wide berth to all signs of human habitation, and he did not lose a single member of his herd.

The deer stayed in the hills for four months until they could be sure that the crops had been gathered and that the fields were empty. On the return journey, Kāla made the same careless misjudgments and lost the rest of his herd. He was the only survivor. Lakkhana, however, exhibited the same caution as before and returned safely with all five hundred of his followers.

When their father saw his two sons returning, he observed, "Behold Lakkhana's glorious triumph as he leads his kin back home! Behold the foolish Kāla, who returns alone!"

After the king of the deer had reached a ripe old age, he passed away to fare according to his deserts.

Having concluded his story, the Buddha identified the birth: "At that time, Devadatta was Kāla, Devadatta's followers were Kāla's herd, Sāriputta was Lakkhana, my followers were Lakkhana's herd, and I was the father deer."

10
The Pregnant Doe
Nigrodha-Miga Jātaka[1]

It was while staying at Jetavana that the Buddha told this story about Venerable Kumāra-Kassapa.

In Rājagaha, a wealthy merchant had a daughter who, even as a child, had been uninterested in frivolous things. Unlike other girls her age, she was disgusted by the usual career of marriage and motherhood and wished to become a bhikkhunī instead. Although she begged to be allowed to take the vows, her parents refused because theirs was a wealthy family and she was the only daughter.

Undeterred, she thought to herself, "After I am married, I will get my husband's consent to become a bhikkhunī."

She did, indeed, marry and become a devoted wife, living a life of goodness and virtue in her new home. After some time, she conceived, although she was unaware of her pregnancy.

Shortly after that, there was a big festival. The city was decorated like heaven itself, and people were enjoying the holiday. Despite the festivities,

---

1 Nigrodha means "banyan tree."

45

she continued the same as usual. Noticing this, her young merchant husband said, "Dear wife, everybody has gotten dressed up and is celebrating the holiday. You are still wearing your ordinary clothes. You have not put on any make-up, and you are not wearing any of your beautiful jewelry."

"Husband," she replied, "the body is made up of thirty-two parts. What is the point of adorning it? It comes from a bloody womb, born to parents themselves liable to decay. The body is born to waste away and to expand the graveyard. It is a source of sorrow, subject to innumerable diseases. It is only the repository of the workings of kamma. Foul inside, it seeps and oozes foulness. Why decorate and perfume such a nasty thing?"

"Wife," retorted her husband, "if you think this body is so disgusting, why don't you become a bhikkhunī?"

"If I could, husband, I would take vows this very day."

"Very well," he agreed. "I will help you enter the Order." He offered hospitality to the Sangha and escorted her to a monastery, where she was ordained under Devadatta. She rejoiced at the fulfillment of her life's desire.

As her pregnancy advanced, the other bhikkhunīs noticed the signs and said, "Lady, you seem about to become a mother; what does it mean?"

"I have led a virtuous life."

The bhikkhunīs took her to Devadatta. "Venerable Sir," they said, "this young gentlewoman, who became a bhikkhunī with the reluctant consent of her husband, is now expecting a baby. Whether this dates from before her admission to the Order or not, we cannot say. What should we do?"

Not being a Buddha, and lacking generosity and compassion, Devadatta figured that rumors that one of his bhikkhunīs was pregnant might cause him damage. "It must not be thought that I condone the offense. My course is clear! I must expel this woman from the Order."

Without any enquiry, he had her thrown out immediately.

The bhikkhunīs paid their respects to Devadatta and started back to the monastery, but the young woman pleaded with them, saying "Ladies, Devadatta is not the Buddha. My ordination was into the Buddha's Order. Don't deprive me of the vocation which I won with great difficulty. Take me to the Buddha at Jetavana." Moved by her supplications, they accompanied her on the journey of forty-five yojanas from Rājagaha to Sāvatthī. After paying their respects to the Buddha, they explained the matter to him.

The Buddha listened and thought, "Even though the baby was conceived while she was still a laywoman, unbelievers will talk if I decide by myself to accept a bhikkhunī expelled by Devadatta. In order to avoid such talk, this case must be examined in the presence of the king and his court."

The next morning, he asked King Pasenadi and the great lay disciples, Anāthapindika and Visākhā, to come to the monastery, along with other influential persons. When all bhikkhus, bhikkhunīs, and lay disciples were present, the Buddha instructed Venerable Upāli, who was foremost in knowledge of the Vinaya, to clear up the matter of the young bhikkhunī.

First, Venerable Upāli called upon Visākhā and asked her to determine when the young woman had conceived and whether it had occurred before or after she had joined the Order. Visākhā compared the days and months and discovered that the conception had, without doubt, taken place before she had become a bhikkhunī. When this was reported, Upāli proclaimed to the assembly that the bhikkhunī was innocent. With her innocence clearly established, she paid her respects to the Buddha and the bhikkhus and returned to her own monastery with her companions.

In due time, she delivered a strong and healthy son, for whom she had prayed at the feet of the Buddha Padumuttara many ages previously.

One day, when the king was passing the monastery, he heard an infant's cry. Asking his courtiers to find out the source, he learned that the crying came from the baby which the young bhikkhunī had recently delivered.

"Caring for a child will be a burden to the bhikkhunīs in their religious life; let us take charge of him." He offered to take the baby and handed him over to his commander, who gave him to the women of his own family. The baby was named Kumāra-Kassapa, Prince Kassapa, and was raised in the king's court as a prince.

At the age of seven, Kumāra-Kassapa became a sāmanera under the Buddha, and, when he was twenty, was fully ordained as a bhikkhu. Venerable Kumāra-Kassapa became famous as a preacher of the Dhamma, and the Buddha declared him foremost among the bhikkhus in eloquence. Both he and his mother attained arahatship.

One day, the bhikkhus were talking about the attainments of Venerable Kumāra-Kassapa and his mother. "Because Devadatta lacked generosity and compassion," one of them said, "he almost ruined Venerable Kumāra-Kassapa and his venerable mother. The Buddha, however, perfect in generosity, love, and pity, became their refuge."

When the Buddha heard what they were discussing, he said, "This is not the first time, Bhikkhus, that I have been the refuge of these two. Long ago, also, I was their refuge." At the request of the bhikkhus, he told this story of the past.

Long, long ago, when Brahmadatta was reigning in Bārānasi, the Bodhisatta was born as a deer. While a fawn, he was a beautiful golden color, with bright eyes, horns like silver, and lacquered hooves. After he matured, he led five hundred deer and was known as King Nigrodha. In the same forest, there was another deer, also with a herd of five hundred. He was called Sākha.

King Brahmadatta demanded meat at every meal and was passionately fond of hunting. He regularly conscripted his subjects, townsfolk and countryfolk alike, to act as beaters for him on his hunting expeditions.

"This king interferes with our work," the people grumbled. While they were discussing the hardship imposed upon them by the king's frequent hunting trips, one of them suggested, "Why don't we sow grass and provide a water supply in the king's own pleasure garden? We can drive deer into the enclosure, and the king can hunt them at his pleasure!"

Everyone agreed that this was a great idea. They chose a suitable corner of the king's pleasure garden, planted it with lush grass, and erected a sturdy fence. With the gate opened wide, they armed themselves with sticks and noise makers and surrounded about a yojana of forest to catch the deer. Their circle included the haunts of the herds of both of the deer kings Nigrodha and Sākha. As soon as the people saw the deer, they beat the trees, bushes, and ground with their sticks. The noise so startled the animals that they all ran, trying to flee. Of course, they ran straight into the enclosure. As soon as all the deer were inside the garden, the men shut the gate.

They chose a spokesman to inform the king, "Sire, your frequent hunting trips have so interrupted our work that we have created a deer park in your pleasure garden. There you may hunt as much you like, and there are plenty of deer for your table."

The king inspected the new park and was very pleased. Among the deer, he saw the two golden stags, Nigrodha and Sākha, and granted them immunity.

Thereafter, the king enjoyed hunting without disturbing his subjects, and, at other times, he sent his cook to kill a deer for the meat. At the sight of the bow, the deer would dash off in fear. Sometimes, several deer were injured as they fled. Sometimes, the deer that was shot was able to escape but would later collapse and die. Thus, on some days, many deer were injured, and several died accidentally.

Some of the deer described this to Nigrodha, who sent for Sākha and said, "Friend, our deer know that they cannot escape death, but they are being destroyed in great numbers, and many are being needlessly injured. Let us establish a system whereby the deer go to the block by turns, one day one from my herd, and next day one from yours. The deer on whom the lot falls must go to the place of execution and lie with its head on the block. In this way, the deer will escape unnecessary suffering." Sākha readily consented. When they understood what their leaders had discussed, the other deer also agreed. Whenever the cook arrived at the park, he found a deer waiting to be slain. He, too, was pleased at how easy his work had become.

One day, the lot fell on a pregnant doe from Sākha's herd. She approached Sākha and said, "Sire, I am with young. After I have delivered my little one, there will be two of us to take our turns. Please allow me to be passed over this time."

"No," he said curtly, "I cannot make your turn another's. You must bear the consequences of your own fate. Go!" Finding no sympathy from him, the doe went to Nigrodha and repeated her story. He immediately told her not to worry and promised that he would get her exempted from the lottery. After reassuring her, Nigrodha himself went to the execution block and placed his head there.

When the cook saw him, he cried out, "Would you look at that! Here's the king of the deer! What can this mean?" He rushed off to tell the king what he had seen. The king immediately mounted his chariot and hurried to his garden, followed by a large retinue. "My friend, king of the deer," he said, "I granted you immunity. Why are you here?"

"Sire, a doe heavy with fawn came to me and begged that she and her unborn young be spared. I promised to spare her, but, not wanting to pass her doom onto another from my herd, I decided to take it upon myself."

"My Lord, golden king of the deer," said the king, "even among men, I have never seen one so abounding in generosity, love, and compassion as you. I am simply delighted! Stand up! Once more, I spare your life, and I spare her life as well."

"Though two be spared, what about the rest, Sire?"

"I spare their lives, too, Your Majesty."

"Sire, only the deer in your pleasure garden will have immunity. What about all the rest?"

"I spare their lives, too!"

"Sire, deer will thus be safe, but what about all the other four-footed creatures?"

"I spare their lives, too, Your Majesty."

"Sire, four-footed creatures will thus be safe, but what about the flocks of birds?"

"They, too, shall be spared."

"Sire, birds will thus be safe, but what about the fish?"

"I spare their lives, also, Your Majesty."

Having thus interceded with the king for the lives of all creatures, Nigrodha arose and established the king in the five precepts. "Walk in righteousness," he advised the king. "Be just toward all so that, when this life ends, you may be reborn in heaven."

The stag Nigrodha remained in the garden for a few more days to instruct the king. Then, with his herd, he returned to the forest.

Often, however, the deer, enjoying full immunity, wandered into the farmers' fields and ate their crops. The farmers did not dare hit the deer or drive them away. Unable to endure the depredations wrought by the voracious deer, the men assembled in the king's courtyard and complained.

"When the deer Nigrodha won my favor," the king answered, "I promised him a boon. I would rather lose my kingdom than break my word. My promise stands! Not a man in my kingdom may harm the deer."

When Nigrodha heard about the problem, he called his herd together and instructed them to stop eating men's crops. Then he sent a message to the farmers explaining that he had forbidden his followers to eat their crops. "From this day forward," his message continued, "farmers need not fence their fields. It will be enough to indicate a field by simply tying leaves around it."

That was the beginning of the custom of tying up leaves to mark a field, and never was a deer known to trespass on a field so marked.

The doe delivered a fair fawn, who sometimes played with Sākha's herd. "My child," his mother warned him, "don't go about with those deer. Stay with Nigrodha's herd. Death in Nigrodha's company is preferable to the longest life with Sākha."

Nigrodha always admonished the members of his herd to be virtuous. At the close of his long life, he passed away to fare according to his deserts. After spending the rest of his life in performing good deeds, according to the teaching of Nigrodha, King Brahmadatta, too, passed away to fare according to his deserts.

Having concluded his story, the Buddha taught the Dhamma. Then he identified the birth: "At that time, Devadatta was the deer Sākha, his followers were that deer's herd, the bhikkhunī was the doe, Kumāra-Kassapa was her offspring, Ānanda was King Brahmadatta, and I was Nigrodha."

11
The Wind Antelope
Vāta-Miga Jātaka

It was while staying at Jetavana that the Buddha told this story about Venerable Culla-Pindapātika Tissa.

Once, when the Buddha was residing at Veluvana, Kumara Tissa, the heir of a wealthy family, heard a discourse and resolved to join the Sangha. Though his parents refused to give their consent, he finally got it, grudgingly on their part, by fasting for seven days.

About a fortnight after his ordination, the young bhikkhu accompanied the Buddha to Jetavana. In Sāvatthī, he undertook the dhutanga practices, and became known as Culla-Pindapātika Tissa, after the third of those practices, which is eating only almsfood. So strict was his practice that he was a shining example of good conduct among the Buddha's disciples.

At that time, a festival was proclaimed in Rājagaha. Venerable Culla-Pindapātika Tissa's parents put all his jewelry and trinkets in a silver casket and bewailed his becoming a bhikkhu. "For previous festivals," they cried, "our darling son used to wear this pendant and these rings. Now our only son has been stolen away from us by the sage Gotama. He is far from us

51

in Sāvatthī, and we are all alone! Where is our son staying? How does he manage, eating the leavings of others!"

A slave-girl noticed the lady of the house weeping and asked her what was wrong. After she had heard everything, she said, "Madam, tell me what your son was most fond of."

The bhikkhu's mother carefully described his favorite foods and beverages.

"Well, if you will give me authority, I'll fetch your son back."

"Very good," the lady agreed. She gave the servant enough money for all her expenses and dispatched her with a large entourage. "Go!" she said to the girl, sending her off. "Please find a way to bring my darling son back!"

The girl rode in a palanquin to Sāvatthī and took up residence in the street where the bhikkhu walked for alms. The next morning, from the window of her mansion, she watched him as he began his almsrounds. As soon as he entered the street, she came out, accompanied only by her own servants so that he would not see anyone from his father's household, and offered him his favorite food and drink, prepared exactly the way his mother had described.

After repeating this for several days, she was confident that he was becoming bound by the craving of taste, and she invited him to sit inside the house. Later, when she was sure that her offerings of delectable food had him firmly in her power, she feigned sickness and lay down in an inner chamber.

When Venerable Culla-Pindapātika Tissa came to the house on his almsrounds, the servants took his bowl and made him sit down inside.

"Where is the lay-sister?" he asked.

"She is ill, sir! She would be glad to see you."

Overcome by the craving of taste, he broke his vows and went to where she was lying.

As the bhikkhu approached her couch, she told him why she had come to Sāvatthī. Unable to resist her power over him, he agreed to leave the Order. She made room for him in the palanquin, and they rode back together to his parents' house in Rājagaha.

That evening, at Jetavana, one of the bhikkhus exclaimed to the others, "Friends, have you heard that a slave-girl trapped Venerable Culla-Pindapātika Tissa with the craving of taste and carried him off!" and they discussed the matter at length.

When the Buddha heard what they were discussing, he said, "Bhikkhus, this is not the first time that, in bondage to the craving of taste, he has fallen into her power. In bygone days, also, he fell into her power in a similar manner." Then he told this story of the past.

Long, long ago, when Brahmadatta was reigning in Bārānasi, he had a gardener named Sañjaya. One day, a shy and elusive wind antelope entered the king's pleasure garden but fled swiftly away at the sight of Sañjaya. The gardener let it go without frightening the timid creature. After several more visits, the antelope began to roam freely around the garden.

Every day, Sañjaya gathered flowers and fruit from the garden and took them to the king. One day, the king asked him whether he had seen anything strange or interesting recently.

"The only thing, Sire, is a wind antelope that sometimes comes into the garden."

"Do you think you could catch it?" asked the king.

"Oh, yes. If I had a little honey, I could bring it right into Your Majesty's palace."

The king immediately commanded a servant to bring some honey. Sañjaya took it to the garden and brushed it on the grass where the wind antelope usually grazed. Then he hid nearby. After a short time, the wind antelope came into the garden. Once it had tasted the honeyed grass, it was so taken by the wonderful taste that it went nowhere else to graze. Seeing the success of his trick, the gardener slowly emerged from his hiding place.

As soon as the wind antelope saw the man, it took flight. This happened for a couple of days, but, eventually, the sight of the gardener grew familiar to the cautious animal. Gradually, the wind antelope gathered enough confidence to eat honeyed grass directly from Sañjaya's hand.

When Sañjaya was sure that the creature's natural fears had been overcome, he strewed broken boughs like a carpet to make a path. He tied a gourd full of honey on his shoulder such that the honey dripped onto a bunch of grass stuck under his belt. As he walked slowly toward the palace, he dropped wisps of honeyed grass in front of the wind antelope and proceeded to lead the creature right inside the palace itself.

As soon as the wind antelope was inside, the guards shut the doors. At the sight of these men, the wind antelope, terrified for its life, dashed to and fro about the hall. When the king came down from his chamber, he saw the trembling creature and said, "So timid is the wind antelope that it won't revisit a place where it has seen or smelled a man. Once it has been frightened in a particular place, it will never go back there again, its whole life long. Yet, ensnared by the lust of taste, this wild creature from the forest has actually been lured into my palace! Truly, my friends, there is nothing more dangerous in the world than this craving of taste. How else could Sañjaya deliver such a wild and elusive animal to this palace in the heart of the city!" Then the king commanded the guards to open the doors and to allow the wind antelope to return safely to the forest.

Having concluded his story, the Buddha identified the birth: "At that time, this slave-girl was Sañjaya, Culla-Pindapātika Tissa was the wind antelope, and I was the king of Kāsi."

12
The Goat That Laughed and Wept
Matakabhatta Jātaka

It was while staying at Jetavana that the Buddha told this story about a
Feast for the Dead.

One day, some bhikkhus asked the Buddha whether there was any
benefit in sacrificing goats, sheep, and other animals as offerings for departed relatives.

"No, Bhikkhus," replied the Buddha. "No good ever comes from taking
life, not even when it is for the purpose of providing a Feast for the Dead."
Then he told this story of the past.

Long, long ago, when Brahmadatta was reigning in Bārānasi, a brahmin
decided to offer a Feast for the Dead and bought a goat to sacrifice. "My boys,"
he said to his students, "take this goat down to the river, bathe it, brush it,
hang a garland around its neck, give it some grain to eat, and bring it back."

"Yes, sir," they replied and led the goat to the river.

While they were grooming it, the goat started to laugh with a sound like
a pot smashing. Then, just as strangely, it started to weep loudly.

The young students were amazed at this behavior. "Why did you suddenly laugh," they asked the goat, "and why do you now cry so loudly?"

"Repeat your question when we get back to your teacher," the goat answered.

The students hurriedly took the goat back to their master and told him what had happened at the river. Hearing the story, the master himself asked the goat why it had laughed and why it had wept.

"In times past, brahmin," the goat began, "I was a brahmin who taught the Vedas like you. I, too, sacrificed a goat as an offering for a Feast for the Dead. Because of killing that single goat, I have had my head cut off four hundred and ninety-nine times. I laughed aloud when I realized that this is my last birth as an animal to be sacrificed. Today, I will be freed from my misery. On the other hand, I cried when I realized that, because of killing me, you, too, may be doomed to lose your head five hundred times. It was out of pity for you that I cried."

"Well, goat," said the brahmin, "in that case, I am not going to kill you."

"Brahmin!" exclaimed the goat. "Whether or not you kill me, I cannot escape death today."

"Don't worry," the brahmin assured the goat. "I will guard you."

"You don't understand," the goat told him. "Your protection is weak. The force of my evil deed is very strong."

The brahmin untied the goat and said to his students, "Don't allow anyone to harm this goat." They obediently followed the animal to protect it.

After the goat was freed, it began to graze. It stretched out its neck to reach the leaves on a bush growing near the top of a large rock. At that very instant, a lightning bolt hit the rock, breaking off a sharp piece of stone, which flew through the air and neatly cut off the goat's head. A crowd of people gathered around the dead goat and began to talk excitedly about the amazing accident.

A tree deva had observed everything from the goat's purchase to its dramatic death, and, drawing a lesson from the incident, admonished the crowd. "If people only knew that the penalty would be rebirth into sorrow, they would cease from taking life. A horrible doom awaits one who slays." With this explanation of the law of kamma, the deva instilled in his listeners the fear of hell. The people were so frightened that they completely gave up the practice of animal sacrifices. The deva further instructed the people in the precepts and urged them to do good.

Eventually, that deva passed away to fare according to his deserts. For several generations after that, people remained faithful to the precepts and spent their lives in generosity and meritorious deeds, and many were re-born in heaven.

Having concluded his story, the Buddha identified the birth: "At that time, I was that tree deva."

13

The Hollow Canes
Nalapāna Jātaka

It was while journeying through Kosala that the Buddha told this story.

When he came to the village of Nalakapāna, he stayed near Nalakapāna Lake. One day, after bathing in the pool, the bhikkhus asked the sāmaneras to fetch them some canes for needle-cases. After getting them, however, the bhikkhus discovered that the canes, rather than having joints like common canes, were completely hollow. Surprised, they went to the Buddha and said, "Venerable Sir, we wanted to make needle-cases out of these canes, but from top to bottom they are quite hollow. How can that be?"

"Bhikkhus," said the Buddha, "this was my doing in days gone by." Then he told this story of the past.

Long, long ago, on this spot, there was a lake, surrounded by a thick forest. In those days, the Bodhisatta was born as the king of the monkeys. As large as the fawn of a red deer, he was the wise leader of a troop of eighty thousand monkeys that lived in that forest.

He carefully counseled his followers: "My friends, in this forest, there are trees that are poisonous and lakes that are haunted by yakkhas. Remember always to ask me first before eating any fruit you have not eaten before or drinking any water from a source you have not drunk from before."

"Certainly," the monkeys agreed.

One day, while roaming the forest, the monkey troop came to an area they had never before visited. Thirsty after their day's wanderings, they searched for water and found this beautiful lake. Remembering their master's warning, the monkeys refrained from drinking. They sat and waited for their leader. When he joined them he asked, "Well, my friends, why don't you drink?"

"We waited for you to come."

"Well done!" said the monkey king. Then he walked a full circuit around the lake. He noticed that all the footprints led down into the water, but none came back.

"My friends," he announced, "you were right not to drink from this lake. It is undoubtedly haunted by a yakkha."

Suddenly, the yakkha, in a hideous guise, rose up out of the lake and appeared before them. He had a blue belly, a white face, and bright-red hands and feet. "Why are you sitting here?" he asked the monkeys. "Go down to the lake, and drink."

The monkey king asked him, "Aren't you the yakkha of this lake?"

"Yes, I am. How did you know I was here?"

"I saw the footprints leading down to the water but none returning. Do you prey on all those who go down to the water?"

"Yes, I do. From small birds to the largest animals, I catch everything which has come into my water. I will eat all of you, too!"

"Oh, no, Yakkha," said the monkey king, "we are not going to let you eat us."

"You must be parched. Just drink the water," taunted the monster.

"All right, Yakkha, we will drink some water, but we are not going to fall into your power."

"How can you drink water without entering the lake?"

"Yakkha!" the monkey king cried. "We need not enter your lake at all. All eighty thousand of us can drink through these canes as easily as through a hollow lotus stalk. We will drink, and you will not be able to harm us."

The monkey king requested that a cane be brought to him. Then, recollecting the Ten Perfections he was developing, he recited them in a solemn asseveration of truth and blew into the cane.

Instantly, the joints disappeared, and the whole length of the cane became hollow. After hollowing several more in the same way, the monkey king toured the lake. "Let all canes growing here become perfectly hollow throughout," he commanded. Because of the great virtues of Bodhisattas, their commands are always fulfilled. Therefore, every single cane that grew around that lake instantly became hollow and has always remained so.[1]

At last, the monkey king seated himself with a cane in his hands. The other eighty thousand monkeys, likewise, arranged themselves around the lake, each with a cane. They all dipped their canes into the water and drank. They satisfied their thirst, but the yakkha could not touch a single one of them. Frustrated and furious, he returned to his home in defeat.

When all had finished, the monkey king led his followers back into the forest.

Having concluded his story, the Buddha identified the birth: "At that time, Devadatta was the yakkha; my disciples were the eighty thousand monkeys; and I was the king of the monkeys, so fertile in resourcefulness."

---

1   There are four miraculous phenomena which will endure throughout this entire eon;
(1) the figure of the rabbit can be seen in the moon [Tale 121]; (2) fire will not touch the
spot of the baby quail's nest [Tale 20]; (3) no rain will fall on the site of Ghatīkāra's house
[Ghatīkāra Sutta, Majjhima Nikāya, 81]; and (4) the canes that grow around this lake will
remain perfectly hollow.

14

The Case of the Gnawed Leather
Kukkura Jātaka

It was while staying at Jetavana that the Buddha told this story about acting for the good of relatives.

Long, long ago, when Brahmadatta was reigning in Bārānasi, the Bodhisatta was born as a dog. He lived in a great charnel ground as the leader of a pack of several hundred dogs.

One day, the king rode out to his pleasure garden in the royal chariot drawn by milk-white horses. After amusing himself all day in the garden, he returned to the city, well after sunset. Hungry and tired, the king's men hurriedly unhitched the horses, but they left the chariot in the courtyard, with harness and reins still attached. During the night, it rained heavily.

The next morning, the grooms discovered that the leather of the chariot and harness had gotten wet and had been gnawed. They immediately went to the king. "Sire," they reported, "Your Majesty's chariot has been ruined. It seems that, during the night, dogs entered the courtyard through the sewers and gnawed the straps and the beautiful leatherwork covering the chariot."

Enraged, the king shouted, "Kill every dog you see."

The king's soldiers immediately began roaming the streets of the city, killing every dog they found. The dogs were terrified by this wanton slaughter and sought safety in the charnel ground.

"Why are you here in such great numbers?" asked the chief. "What is happening?"

"The king is so infuriated by reports that dogs gnawed the leatherwork and straps of his carriage," they answered, "that he has ordered that all dogs be killed. Throughout the city, dogs are being destroyed wholesale. We are in great danger!"

The leader thought about this and reasoned to himself, "The palace is closely guarded. It would be impossible for an animal from outside to get inside. This must have been done by the king's own thoroughbred dogs, but now innocent creatures are being executed, while there is no punishment for the real culprits. I must try to save the lives of these dogs, my followers."

He comforted his relatives, saying, "Have no fear! I will save you, but to do it, I must see the king."

Protecting himself with thoughts of loving-kindness and calling to mind the Ten Perfections, the leader stealthily made his way alone into the city. Because of his kindly thoughts, he was able to reach the palace safely without encountering anyone.

He ran straight to the Hall of Justice, where the king was seated, and dived under the throne. The king's servants tried to catch him, but the king stopped them.

Emboldened by this, the great dog emerged from under the throne, bowed to the king, and asked, "Sire, was it you who ordered that all the dogs be destroyed?"

"Yes, it was I."

"What was their offense, Your Majesty?"

"Dogs gnawed the harness straps and the beautiful leatherwork of my chariot and ruined it."

"Do you know which dogs actually did the mischief?"

"No, I do not."

"But, Your Majesty, if you do not know for certain who the real culprits are, is it right to order that every dog be destroyed?"

"It's very simple. Dogs gnawed the leather of my carriage, so I ordered that all dogs be killed. That way, I am sure to punish the guilty dogs."

"Do your men kill all dogs without exception, or are there some dogs who are spared?"

"Some are spared, of course. I am not going to kill the thoroughbred dogs of my own palace."

"Sire, just now, you said that you had ordered the slaughter of all dogs because dogs had gnawed the leather of your chariot. Now you say that the thoroughbred dogs of your own palace are spared. In this, you are following four evil ways—partiality, dislike, ignorance, and fear. Such behavior is wrong, and not king-like. When a king tries a case, he should be as unbiased as the beam of a balance. In this instance, however, you are allowing the royal dogs to go free, while you are mercilessly massacring poor stray dogs. What you are carrying out is not the impartial destruction of all dogs, but rather the slaughter of the poor. Your Majesty is not acting with justice!"

The king listened carefully and replied, "You speak wisely, and I am impressed. Tell me. In your wisdom, do you know who actually gnawed the leather of my chariot?"

"Yes, Sire, I do."

"Who was it?"

"It was the thoroughbred dogs of your palace."

"Can you prove this?"

"I will demonstrate it to you."

"Do so, wise creature."

"Please provide me with a little buttermilk and kusa grass, and send for your dogs."

When this was done, the great dog instructed the king's men to mash the grass, to stir it into the buttermilk, and to feed it to the thoroughbred dogs.

A few minutes after the dogs had drunk the mixture, they began to vomit. When the king's men examined the vomit which the palace dogs had brought up, they discovered bits of leather.

"There is your evidence, Sire!" the wise dog exclaimed.

"What a perfect judgment!" cried the king. He was so pleased that he offered the royal umbrella to the king of the dogs, who established the king in the five precepts. Then he returned the white umbrella of kingship and encouraged the king to be steadfast and righteous.

The king immediately ordered that the slaughter of dogs be stopped and, further, that all dogs be given food fit for the king himself. The king was so moved by the teaching that he also ordered that the lives of all creatures in the realm be protected. He spent the rest of his life in generosity and other good deeds and, when he died, was reborn in heaven. The wise dog lived to a ripe old age before passing away to fare according to his deserts. His teaching endured for ten thousand years.

Having concluded his story, the Buddha identified the birth: "At that time, Ānanda was the king, my followers were the dogs of the pack, and I was their wise leader."

15

Great Joy
Nandivisāla Jātaka

It was while staying at Jetavana that the Buddha told this story about the Gang of Six.

These bhikkhus often disagreed with respectable bhikkhus, taunting them and heaping ten kinds of abuse[1] on them. When the harassed bhikkhus reported this behavior to the Buddha, he sent for the Gang of Six and asked whether the charges were true. When those six bhikkhus admitted their misbehavior, the Buddha scolded them, saying, "Bhikkhus, even animals are irritated by harsh words. Once, an animal caused the man who spoke harshly to him to lose one thousand coins." Then he told them this story of the past.

Long, long ago, in Takkasilā, the capital of Gandhāra, the Bodhisatta was born as a calf. While he was still quite small, his owner donated him to a

---

1   These are: (1) by referring to race, class, or nationality; (2) by referring to name; (3) by referring to family or lineage; (4) by referring to occupation; (5) by referring to craft; (6) by referring to disease or handicap; (7) by referring to physical characteristics; (8) by referring to defilements; (9) by referring to offenses; (10) by using an abusive form of address. [From Vinaya, Sutta Vibhanga].

brahmin, who named him Nandivisāla (Great Joy). The brahmin treated the calf like his own child, feeding him delicious rice-gruel and expensive rice. By the time the calf became a fully grown bull, he was incredibly strong. One day he thought to himself, "This brahmin has brought me up kindly. In all of Jambudīpa there is no bull to equal me when it comes to pulling. I would like to use my strength and ability to repay my master the cost of raising me."

"Go, Brahmin," he said aloud, "and find a rich merchant. Wager one thousand coins that your bull can pull one hundred loaded carts."

Trusting his faithful bull, the brahmin found a merchant and got into a discussion about whose oxen were the strongest. The merchant boasted that when it came to real strength, there were no oxen which could compare with his.

"But I have a bull who can pull one hundred loaded carts," said the brahmin.

"Where is such a bull to be found?" laughed the merchant.

"I've got him at home," said the brahmin.

"Make it a wager." the merchant challenged.

"Certainly," said the brahmin, "I'll wager one thousand coins that my bull, Nandivisāla, can pull one hundred carts loaded with sand, gravel, and stones."

"Agreed!" cried the merchant.

The brahmin loaded the carts and lashed them together, one behind the other. Then he bathed Nandivisāla, gave him a measure of perfumed rice to eat, and hung a garland around his neck.

He fastened the yoke onto the pole and put the bull on one side. He secured the other side by fastening a smooth piece of wood from the yoke on to the axle, so that the yoke was taut and could not skew in either direction. In this way, a single bull could draw the load, even though the yoke was made to be drawn by two. When all was ready, the brahmin took his seat on the front cart. "Now, you rascal," he shouted as he waved his whip in the air, "pull these carts! Let's go, you rascal!"

"I'm not the rascal he is calling me," Nandivisāla thought. Angry that the brahmin should speak to him in such a way, he planted his four feet in the ground, leaned back, and refused to budge an inch.

Of course, the brahmin had to pay the one thousand coins to the merchant. His money gone and feeling very discouraged, the brahmin unharnessed Nandivisāla from the cart and walked slowly home. As soon as he reached his house, the brahmin lay down on his bed and wept bitter tears over his misfortune. Surprised to see the brahmin lying down in the middle of the day, Nandivisāla asked if he were taking a nap.

"How could I be taking a nap," asked the brahmin, "when I have just lost one thousand coins?"

"Brahmin," Nandivisāla replied in a soft voice, "during the entire time I have lived in your house, have I ever broken a pot, pushed up against anybody, or made a mess?"

"Never, my child."

"Then, why did you call me a rascal? You are to blame, not me. Go and find that merchant again. Bet him again that I can pull one hundred carts, but increase your wager to two thousand coins. Just remember, though, not to abuse me by calling me a rascal."

The brahmin jumped out of bed, hurried to find the merchant, and laid a wager of two thousand coins. Just as before, he tied the one hundred carts together and harnessed Nandivisāla, looking very sleek and fine, to the lead cart.

The brahmin seated himself on the cart, gently stroked Nandivisāla on the flank, and called out to him, "Now, my fine fellow, pull these carts along! Let's go, my fine fellow!"

With a single great tug, Nandivisāla pulled the whole string of one hundred carts until the last cart stood where the front one had started.

The merchant, amazed that any bull could be so strong, paid the two thousand coins to the brahmin. Other people, too, bestowed large sums on the bull. All of this wealth went to the brahmin who prospered mightily because of Nandivisāla.

Having concluded his story, the Buddha added, in rebuking the six misbehaving bhikkhus, "Thus, you see, that harsh words please no one." Then he identified the birth: "At that time, Ānanda was the brahmin, and I was Nandivisāla."

16

The Adventures of Magha
Kulāvaka Jātaka[2]

It was while staying at Jetavana that the Buddha told this story about a bhikkhu who drank water without straining it.[3]

Two young bhikkhus left Sāvatthī to practice in the countryside. They found a very pleasant spot and stayed there. After some time, they decided to return to Jetavana to see the Buddha.

One of them had a water strainer, but the other did not, even though a water strainer is one of the requisites a bhikkhu must possess. Since the two were good friends, they shared the same strainer before drinking. One day, however, they had an argument. After that, the owner of the strainer stopped lending his strainer to the other bhikkhu. The second bhikkhu, unable to endure his thirst, drank water without straining it.

At last they reached Jetavana, where they paid their respects to the Buddha and took their seats. After friendly words of greeting, the Buddha asked where they had come from.

2   1. Kulāvaka means "nest."
3   One of the bhikkhu's requisites is a water strainer, used to prevent the killing of water-borne creatures when using water from a well or a stream.

"Venerable Sir," they answered, "we have been living in a hamlet in Kosala. We have come here in order to see you."

"I trust," the Buddha said, "that your friendship is as strong as when you left."

The bhikkhu without a strainer replied, "Venerable Sir, along the way, he quarreled with me and would not lend me his water strainer."

"Venerable Sir," the other added, "not having a water strainer, he did not strain his water. He intentionally drank water with all the living creatures it contained."

"Is this true, Bhikkhu?" the Buddha asked. "Did you knowingly drink water containing living things?"

"Yes, Venerable Sir. I drank unstrained water."

"Bhikkhu, a wise and good being of long ago, when fleeing in full retreat back to his deva realm, refused to destroy living creatures, even to preserve his own power. Instead, he chose to turn back his chariot, in order to save the lives of some garula nestlings." Then Buddha told this story of the past.

Long, long ago, when King Magadha was reigning in Rājagaha, the Bodhisatta was born into a brahmin family in the village of village of Macala, which contained only thirty families. He was named Magha, and, when he was old enough, his parents chose a wife for him from a family of equal rank with their own. Magha and his family faithfully kept the five precepts and excelled in generosity.

One day, while the men were standing in the middle of the village discussing village affairs, Magha cleared the dust and pebbles away from the spot where he was standing. As soon as someone else moved into that place, Magha quietly stepped aside and cleared another spot, only to have that place taken over as well. Again and again, Magha cleared new spots, until he had made smooth standing places for every man there.

At another time, he erected a pavilion for the village, which he later pulled down and replaced with a hall with benches and a communal water jar. In time, the twenty-nine other men of the village were influenced by Magha's deeds and began following his example. Magha established them in the five precepts, and, together, they performed many good deeds around the town. The thirty men regularly got up early, took their hoes, axes, and shovels, and set to work improving the village. They cleared the stones from the highways and roads and smoothed rough places, they cut down trees that could break chariot axles, they made causeways, they dug water tanks, and they built halls. In this way, the men of the village lived according to Magha's teaching, practiced generosity, and kept the precepts.

Seeing this, the village headman grumbled, "Before, when these men got drunk and committed crimes, I made a lot of money out of them, not only from what they spent on liquor but also from the fines they paid. Now, however, this young Magha has them all keeping the precepts, and he has put a stop to crime. He can't do this to me! I'll teach them to keep the five precepts!"

The headman went straight to the king and said, "Sire, there is a band of robbers going around pillaging villages and committing other outrages." The king ordered the headman to catch them.

The headman immediately arrested Magha and his friends and accused them of all sorts of crimes. Without any enquiry, the king sentenced them to be trampled to death by an elephant. Soldiers laid the condemned men in a row in the courtyard and sent for the executioner elephant. As they lay there, Magha urged his companions, "Bear in mind the precepts. Extend loving-kindness to the slanderer, to the king, and to the elephant. Wish for them to be as happy as you yourself would like to be." His friends listened to his words and extended loving-kindness to all.

When the elephant was brought into the courtyard, it refused to touch the condemned men. No matter how much the soldiers prodded it, the great beast would not trample them. Instead, the elephant raised up its tail, trumpeted loudly, and ran away. The soldiers brought in other elephants, but each animal acted in exactly the same manner.

The king ordered that the prisoners be searched to see whether they were hiding some drug which was warding off the elephants, but none was found.

"They must be uttering some spell," said the king. "Ask them whether they have a spell."

When the soldiers posed this question, Magha replied that he and his companions did, indeed, have a spell. The king summoned the prisoners into his presence and said, "Tell me your spell."

Magha answered, "Sire, the only spell we have is this. Not one of us ever kills, steals, commits adultery, or tells a lie. None of us drinks alcohol or uses drugs. We practice loving-kindness and generosity to all. It is our custom to level roads, to dig tanks, and to build public halls. This morality is our spell, our safeguard, and our strength."

When the king heard this, he was so furious with the headman who had falsely accused them that he stripped him of all his wealth. The king awarded an elephant and the revenue from the village to Magha and his friends. The former headman became their slave, and Magha became the new head of the village.

Magha and his friends continued their meritorious work with even stronger commitment. One of their most ambitious projects was the construction of a large hall at the main crossroads in the village. Since these men had lost all interest in relations with women, they did not want to allow any woman to share in this project.

Magha, however, had four wives named Sudhammā (Goodness), Cittā (Thoughtful), Nandā (Joy), and Sujā (Well-born). One day, Sudhammā secretly sought out the chief carpenter, gave him a present, and said, "Brother, please arrange it so that I become the principal donor of this hall."

"Very good," he said, accepting her gift. Before doing any other work on the building, he laid aside pieces of special wood. After appropriately drying and treating them, he fashioned them into a magnificent pinnacle, which he wrapped in cloth and gave to Sudhammā. Without telling anyone else about the pinnacle, she hid it in her house.

When the hall was almost finished, the carpenter exclaimed, "Alas, my masters, there is one thing we have not yet prepared."

"What's that?" Magha and his friends asked in surprise.

"We need a pinnacle for the roof."

"All right," they instructed. "Go ahead and make one."

"Ah, it is not so easy as that! One cannot make a proper pinnacle out of green wood. I must have special wood which has been suitably dried, treated, and shaped."

"Well, what can we do?"

"Let's look around to see if anyone happens to have a ready-made pinnacle for sale."

Of course, they found one in Sudhammā's house, but she refused to sell it at any price.

"I will give this pinnacle to you for no money at all," she offered, "if you will allow me to be a partner in your good work."

"That is impossible," they replied, "We have declared that no women will share in our merit."

"Masters, what are you saying?" the carpenter asked them. "Except for the Brahma heavens, there is no place in the universe without women. It is foolish for you to bar them from sharing in your meritorious work. If you agree to Sudhammā's condition and accept the pinnacle, we can finish the hall."

Agreeing with the carpenter and seeing the wisdom of his words, they accepted the pinnacle from Sudhammā and placed it on the roof of the hall. It fit perfectly, like the crown on a king's head. Around the hall, they built a wall with a splendid gate. Inside the wall they spread fresh sand, and, outside, they planted a row of fan-palms. In preparation for the dedication ceremony, they set up benches, arranged jars of water, and boiled a great quantity of rice.

Following Sudhammā's example, Cittā laid out a garden with every kind of flowering and fruit-bearing tree.

Nandā provided a water tank in which she planted the five kinds of lotuses, creating a beautiful addition to the garden.

Sujā watched all of this activity, but she did not take part.

Throughout his life, Magha took upon himself seven vows: to maintain his parents; to respect elders; to use gentle language; never to utter slander; being free from greed, to practice generosity and kindness; to speak the truth; and to be free from anger. Because of this praiseworthy way of life, he was reborn in Tāvatimsa, the Heaven of the Thirty-three, as Sakka, king of the devas. His friends were also reborn there as devas.

In those days, the asuras were also dwelling in Tāvatimsa. Sakka, however, was not happy sharing his realm with these lower beings and decided to get rid of them. He got them inebriated by giving them the delicious liquor of the devas. When they were thoroughly drunk, he had them hurled head-first down the steep slopes of Mount Sineru. They tumbled all the way to the bottom of the mountain into a realm which came to be called the asura realm. Their new domain was identical to Tāvatimsa in every way, including size, except for one thing. In Tāvatimsa, there was a red coral tree called Paricchattaka, which bore beautiful red flowers. In the asura realm, there was a similar tree called Cittāpatali, but this tree bore white flowers. When the asuras awoke from their drunken stupor, they saw the white flowers and immediately realized that they were no longer in Tāvatimsa. They also recollected how they had come to be where they were.

"We have to win back our heavenly city from Sakka," they cried, as they began climbing up the side of Mount Sineru, like ants up a pillar.

As soon as Sakka heard the alarm warning that the asuras were coming, he mounted his chariot, Vejayanta, and rode out to battle. He was quickly defeated by the furious asuras, and fled in the chariot along the crests of the ocean on the southern side of Mount Sineru.

When he arrived at the silk-cotton tree forest called Simbalivana, which was the home of the garulas, the chariot's enormous wheels mowed down the mighty trees like weeds and knocked them into the ocean. As the baby garulas were hurled from their nests, they shrieked loudly with terror.

"Mātali," Sakka asked his charioteer, "what is that heartrending sound?"

"Sire, that is the garula nestlings crying out in fear. The rush of your chariot has just uprooted their forest."

"Mātali!" he cried, "those baby birds must not be harmed because of me. Let us not destroy life! Turn the chariot around! Even if I have to sacrifice my own life to the asuras, I will protect those garulas."

Mātali immediately turned the chariot back and headed toward Tāvatimsa by an alternate route.

When the asuras saw the chariot turning, they were alarmed and cried out in fear, "Look! Sakka has turned his chariot around. Reinforcements must be coming!" They retreated as fast as they could, neither stopping nor looking back until they reached the asura realm.

Sakka reentered Tāvatimsa in a victory procession. He stood in the middle of the city, and all the devas sang his praises. At that moment, a magnificent palace, also called Vejayanta,[1] one thousand yojanas high, rose up from the earth. To prevent any further attack, he had five walls built around the city, each protected by guards—nāgas, garulas, kumbhandas, yakkhas, and the Four Great Kings, respectively, Thus protected by faithful and powerful sentinels, Sakka enjoyed great glory as king of the devas.

In the meantime, Sudhammā died and was reborn in Tāvatimsa as one of Sakka's wives. The result of her gift of the pinnacle was a glorious mansion called "Sudhammā Hall." It was five hundred yojanas high and studded with heavenly jewels. In one of the rooms of this hall, under a royal white canopy, was Sakka's marble throne.

Cittā and Nandā were also reborn as Sakka's wives. Cittā's donation of the pleasure garden resulted in an exquisite garden in Tāvatimsa, called Cittālatavana, which contained many kinds of creepers bearing beautifully colored flowers. Nandā's donation of the pond resulted in a beautiful lake called Nandāpokkharani.

One day, Sakka realized that only three of his former wives had arrived in Tāvatimsa. "There's no sign of Sujā," Sakka said to himself. "I wonder where she has been reborn." He discovered that she had been reborn as a paddy bird and went to visit her. Then he brought her back to Tāvatimsa and showed her all the delightful places there. "Observe this magnificent hall, this delightful garden, and this beautiful lake. These three," he said, "named after Sudhammā, Cittā, and Nandā, are the results of the meritorious deeds of these three, who have been reborn here. As Sujā, however, you did nothing of the kind. Therefore, you have been reborn in the animal world. Let me teach you the five precepts, which I urge you to keep from now on." Having established her in the precepts, he returned her to the world.

Not long afterwards, Sakka wondered whether she was following his instructions and keeping the five precepts. He descended once more to the world, transformed himself into a fish, and lay down in front of her, belly up. Supposing the fish to be dead, the paddy bird took it by the head. The fish wagged its tail. "Oh, I think it's alive," she cried and released it.

---

1   Jaya means "victory."

Revealing his true form, Sakka commended her. "Very good, my dear. Continue to keep the precepts." Then he returned to Tāvatimsa.

When the paddy bird died, she was reborn into a potter's family in Bārānasi. Sakka again wanted to know whether she was keeping the precepts. He disguised himself as an old man and filled a cart with cucumbers made of solid gold. In the middle of the village, he cried, "Cucumbers! Cucumbers!" The townsfolk crowded around him, asking for some of his precious vegetables. "I give these cucumbers to those who keep the precepts," he said. "Do you keep them?"

"We don't know what you mean by 'precepts.' Just sell us your cucumbers."

"No, I don't want money. I will give these cucumbers freely, but only to those who keep the precepts."

"Who is this joker?" someone asked.

"He's just a fool," someone else answered. "No one has ever heard of precepts. He's not worth our time." They all left him alone.

When the potter's daughter heard about the peddler, she thought, "That old man must be looking for me." She went to where he had set up his cart and asked for some of his cucumbers.

"Do you keep the precepts, madam?" he asked.

"Yes, I do," she replied.

"Aha!" he cried. "It was for you alone that I brought these." He pushed his cart to her house, left all the golden cucumbers at her door, and returned to Tāvatimsa.

Throughout her life, the potter's daughter faithfully kept the precepts as she had been instructed. After she died, she was reborn as the daughter of Vepacittiya, the asura king. Her name was Sujā, and, because of her goodness, she was rewarded with great beauty.

When she reached the proper age for marriage, Vepacittiya decided to call together all the asuras and to let his daughter pick one of them for a husband. When Sakka learned of this, he declared, "If Sujā chooses a husband after her own heart, I will be her choice." He assumed the guise of an asura and descended to the asura realm.

The princess dressed herself in her finest clothes, entered the assembly hall, and surveyed the row of suitors. As soon as her eyes fell on Sakka, the love she had felt for him in her previous existence welled up and filled her mind. She pointed at Sakka and announced, "I choose him for my husband!" Sakka boldly stepped forward and bowed to the king. Then he quickly embraced the princess, and, before the asuras realized what was happening, he escaped with her from the hall. He carried her off to his heavenly city, where he made her his queen.

When Sakka's life ended, he passed away to fare according to his deserts.

Having concluded his story, the Buddha rebuked that negligent bhikkhu with these words, "Thus, Bhikkhu, the wise and good ruler of the devas forbore, even at the sacrifice of his own life, to be guilty of slaughter. How can you, who have devoted yourself to so liberating a creed, drink unstrained water with all the living creatures it contains?"

Then the Buddha identified the birth: "At that time, Ānanda was Mātali the charioteer, and I was Sakka."

17

The Dance of the Peacock
Nacca Jātaka

It was while staying at Jetavana that the Buddha told this story about a bhikkhu with many belongings.

One day, a group of bhikkhus brought a bhikkhu to the Buddha, saying, "Venerable Sir, this bhikkhu has many belongings."

"Bhikkhu," the Buddha asked, "is it true that you have a lot of property?"

"Yes, sir," the bhikkhu admitted, "it is so."

"Why do you own so many things?" the Buddha asked.

Without answering, the bhikkhu tore off all of his robes and stood stark naked before the Buddha. "All right!" he cried. "I'll go around like this!"

"Oh, for shame!" exclaimed the other bhikkhus.

The bhikkhu ran away and reverted to lay life.

Later, when the bhikkhus were gathered together, they talked about his shocking impropriety. The Buddha came in and asked about their discussion. "Sir, we were talking about that bhikkhu's indecency in your presence. How shameless of him to stand there as naked as a village urchin. On top of that, he has given up the life of a bhikkhu."

"Bhikkhus, this is not the only time that his lack of shame caused him loss." At their request, the Buddha told this story of the past.

Long, long ago, in the first cycle of the world's history, the animals chose the lion to be their king. The fish chose the great fish called Ānanda, and the birds chose a wise golden goose.

The king of the birds had a lovely young daughter, and he granted her a boon. The favor she asked was to be allowed to choose a husband for herself. In fulfillment of his promise, the king made an announcement to all the birds in the Himavat that his daughter would choose a husband. Males of every species came to woo the princess. Her suitors included a quail, a hawk, a peacock, various ducks and swans, and many songbirds. After all of these birds had arranged themselves on a great plateau of bare rock, the king called for his daughter and told her to choose a husband after her own heart. As she reviewed the crowd of birds, her eye lighted on the peacock with his shimmering jeweled neck and magnificent tail. Overwhelmed by his beauty, she looked straight at the peacock and cried out, "Let him be my husband." The other birds gathered around the peacock and congratulated him on being selected by the princess.

"My friends," the peacock exclaimed, carried away by joy, "you have never seen how active I can be!" Forgetting where he was, he spread his wings, displayed his magnificent tail, and began to dance. During his dance, however, he violated all rules of propriety and exposed himself.

This so disgusted the king that he exclaimed, "This fellow has no modesty nor any sense of decency. I certainly will not give my daughter to one so shameless. Master Peacock, you have a pleasing song, a beautiful back, a gorgeous neck, and a magnificent tail, but your dance is disgusting! You will not marry my daughter!"

He immediately dismissed the peacock and chose for his daughter a handsome young goose, one of his nephews.

Overcome with shame at losing the princess, the peacock flew away and was never seen there again.

Having concluded his story, the Buddha added, "Thus, Bhikkhus, you see that shamelessness causes loss. This time, he has lost the jewel of faith. Then, it cost him the jewel of a wife." Then the Buddha identified the birth: "At that time, the bhikkhu with the many belongings was the peacock, and I was the royal goose."

18

The Wages of Strife
Sammodamāna Jātaka[1]

It was while staying at Nigrodhārāma near Kapilavatthu that the Buddha told this story about a squabble over a porter's head-pad.[2]

"Strife among relatives is unseemly," the Buddha said. "In bygone times, a flock of birds was utterly destroyed when they quarreled."

At the request of his royal relatives, the Buddha told this story of the past.

Long, long ago, when Brahmadatta was reigning in Bārānasi, the Bodhisatta was born as a quail. He lived in the forest and became the leader of a huge flock of quails. There was a clever fowler who often hunted in that forest. Hiding behind a tree, he imitated a quail's cry, which lured many birds. When enough had gathered together, he flung his net over them, whipped the sides of the net together, and trapped all the birds inside. Then he crammed the helpless birds into his basket, carried them off, and sold them in the market.

---

1   Sammodamāna means "rejoicing."
2   The cloth which a porter twists into a ring and places on his head so that he can carry a heavy load.

One day, the leader of the quails said to his followers, "This fowler is wreaking havoc among our relatives. I have an idea which will save us. The very moment you feel the net, each one of you must put your head through a hole in the mesh and spread your wings. If we all fly together, we can carry the net to a thorn-brake and escape from the net."

"That is a very good plan," they all agreed.

The next morning, when the fowler arrived, the quails were ready. As soon as the net was cast over them, they put their heads through the holes and spread their wings. Flying together, they lifted the net and carried it to a thorn-brake. Just as their leader had told them, they were able to drop down into the bush and escape unharmed.

It was evening by the time the angry fowler finished disentangling his net, and he had to go home empty-handed.

For several days, the fowler cast his net, but, every time, the quails played the same trick. Every day, the fowler had to disentangle his net from the thorns and to return home with an empty basket.

Naturally, the fowler's wife was upset and scolded him. "Day after day," she complained, "you return empty-handed. I guess you're supporting a second wife somewhere else."

"No, my dear," answered the fowler. "I don't have a second wife. The fact is, those blasted quails have started working together. The moment my net is over them, they fly away with it and land on a thorn-brake. They're all able to escape through the bush, but it takes me all day to free my net. Don't worry, though. Right now, they're all working together, but it won't last. I just have to wait until they start bickering among themselves. Then I'll bag the lot. You'll see, and that'll make you smile!"

A few days later, as one of the quails was landing on the feeding ground, he accidentally bumped another quail's head.

"Who stepped on my head?" cried the disgruntled quail.

"I did," admitted the first quail. "I'm sorry. I didn't mean to. I'll be more careful next time. Please don't be angry!"

The second quail refused to accept the apology and began taunting the other. "I suppose you think that you alone have been lifting up the net? You seem to think that you're the hero, the one who's been rescuing the rest of us!"

This so upset the first quail, that he fired back some sharp insults. Soon, both of them were arguing fiercely and mocking each other. The leader listened to this and thought, "There's no safety with those who are quarrelsome. The time is coming when they will stop cooperating. Then they will no longer lift the net, the fowler will win, and the flock will be destroyed. It's not safe to stay here any longer." He called together his faithful followers and explained what was happening. They decided to leave the main flock and to find a new place to live.

The next day, the fowler returned. The same as always, he made a cry like a quail, many birds came, and he threw his net.

This time, however, the offended quail shouted to the other, "OK. Show us how you can lift the net!"

"Now that you're old enough to fly, it's your turn," rejoined the other.

With those two bickering, each daring the other to lift the net, the others were not able to do it by themselves, and the fowler easily trapped them all. He quickly stuffed them into his basket and carried them home. When his wife saw all the plump little quails, her face broke into a broad smile. "That's my husband!" she cried happily.

Having concluded his story, the Buddha added, "Thus, you can see that a quarrel among relatives is unseemly and can only lead to disaster." Then the Buddha identified the birth: "At that time, Devadatta was the foolish quail who kept up the quarrel, and I was the wise leader of the quail."

19

The Slave of Passion
Maccha Jātaka

It was while staying at Jetavana that the Buddha told this story about passion.

When a bhikkhu admitted that he was being tempted by his former wife and that he was still feeling passion for her, the Buddha said, "Bhikkhu, this woman is a danger to you. Long ago, too, she was the cause of your downfall, but I managed to save you." Then he told this story of the past.

Long, long ago, when Brahmadatta was reigning in Bārānasi, there was a group of fishermen on the Gangā. One day, as they were casting their net, a large fish was swimming along amorously intent on seducing his mate. Suddenly, she sensed the presence of the net ahead and turned sharply to avoid it. He was so distracted by his passion that he didn't even notice that she had turned, and he swam right into the mesh. As soon as the fishermen felt him hit the net, they hauled it in. "Wow! He's a big one!" they cried when they saw him. "Let's roast him for lunch!" They tossed him alive onto the riverbank, and, while one man began whittling a skewer, the others busied themselves with building a fire.

As the fish lay on the wet sand, he lamented, "It isn't the fear of the skewer piercing my body or of the fire burning me to death that distresses me most! I cannot bear the thought that my mate might think that I have been unfaithful to her and that I have gone off with another."

Just as he was saying this, the king's chaplain, who understood the language of animals, happened to be passing by with several attendants, on his way to bathe in the river. He heard the fish's lament and thought, "This poor fish is suffering from blind passion. If he dies in this unhealthy, deluded state of mind, he will be reborn in hell. I will save him."

"Friends," the chaplain called to the fishermen, "don't you supply the palace with fish every day for our curry?"

"That's right, sir," they replied. "If you are looking for fish now, please take whatever you any you fancy."

"Thank you, but I want only this one," he said, pointing to the large fish on the sand.

"He's yours, sir, with our compliments."

The chaplain bent down and picked up the fish. He carried the fish to the water's edge and, looking into the fish's eyes, said, "Friend, if I had not heard you just now, you would have died confused. Cease being the slave of passion." He slipped the fish into the muddy water and returned to the city.

Having concluded his story, the Buddha taught the Dhamma, and the discontented bhikkhu attained the first path. Then the Buddha identified the birth: "At that time, this bhikkhu was the male fish, his former wife was the female fish, and I was the king's chaplain."

20

The Baby Quail
Vattaka Jātaka

It was while on a pilgrimage through Magadha that the Buddha told this story about a jungle fire.

One morning, the Buddha went on his almsrounds through a certain hamlet. After his meal, he went out again, accompanied by a large group of bhikkhus. Just then, a great forest fire broke out, raging fiercely and spreading rapidly, until the jungle was a roaring wall of flames and smoke.

There were many bhikkhus in front of the Buddha and even more behind him. Those bhikkhus who had not yet made attainments were seized with the fear of death. "Let us make a counter fire," they cried; "and then the jungle fire cannot reach us over the ground we have burned." Hastily they started to kindle a fire with their tinder-sticks.

Others said, "What are you doing? You are blind to the sun rising in front of your eyes. Here you are, journeying along with the Buddha who is without equal but you cry out, 'Let us make a counter fire!' You do not know the might of a Buddha! Come with us to the Teacher."

The bhikkhus gathered around the Buddha, who had taken a stand at a certain spot. The blaze rushed toward the bhikkhus, roaring as if it meant to devour them! Suddenly, however, when the fire was sixteen paces[3] from the Buddha, the flames went out like a torch plunged into water. Extinguished and rendered harmless, the fire could not burn any closer to the Buddha.

The bhikkhus burst into praises of the Buddha, saying, "Oh! how great are the virtues of the Teacher! Even fire, though without sense, cannot scorch the spot where the Buddha stands, but goes out like a flame in water!"

Hearing their words, the Buddha said, "It is no present power of mine, Bhikkhus, that makes the fire go out as soon as it reaches this spot of ground. It is the power of a former asseveration of truth of mine. No fire will ever burn in this spot during the whole of this eon."

Then Venerable Ānanda folded a robe into four and spread it for the Buddha to sit on. After he had taken his seat, the bhikkhus paid obeisance and seated themselves respectfully around him. They asked him to explain the matter, saying, "Only the present is known to us, Venerable Sir; the past is hidden. Make it clear to us." At their request, the Buddha told this story of the past.

Long, long ago, the Bodhisatta was born as a quail in Magadha. Until he was able to stand on his own feet and to walk about, he was confined to the nest, and his parents carried food in their beaks and took care of him tenderly.

The area where the nest was located was ravaged annually by jungle fires in the dry season. One day, the flames of a jungle fire swept toward the nest with a mighty roar. Birds panicked with the fear of death and fled their nests shrieking. The parents of the baby quail were as frightened as the others and flew away, abandoning their nestling. Since the baby quail was too young to spread his wings and fly, he lay there alone in his nest. He stretched his neck to see what was happening and thought, "Had I the power to take to my wings, I would fly to safety. If I could use my legs, I would run away. My parents, fearing death, have fled to save themselves, leaving me to fare for myself. I have no protector or guardian in the world. What can I possibly do?"

Then this thought came to him: "In this world there exists the efficacy of goodness and the efficacy of truth. There are those who, through their having developed the Perfections in past ages, have attained Supreme Enlightenment under the Bodhi tree. Those omniscient Buddhas, having achieved liberation by goodness, tranquility and wisdom, possess the knowledge of that liberation. They are filled with truth, compassion, mercy, and patience. Their loving-kindness extends to all creatures alike. There is an efficacy in

---

3   The Pali is sixteen karīsa, which seems not to be an exact or clear unit of measure.

the attributes they have won. Therefore, let me make an asseveration of truth to make the flames retreat and to save myself and the rest of the birds."

Thus, recalling the Buddhas of the past, the little quail loudly proclaimed, "With wings that cannot fly and legs that cannot yet walk, forsaken by my parents, here I lie. With this truth I call on you, dreadful fire, turn back, and harm me not!"

By the power of this asseveration of truth, the fire retreated sixteen paces and went out like a torch plunged into water, leaving a perfect circle around the baby quail unburned. When his life ended, the quail passed away to fare according to his deserts.

Having concluded his story, the Buddha added, "Thus, Bhikkhus, it is not my present power but the efficacy of that asseveration of truth, performed by me when I was a young quail, that has made the flames spare this spot in the jungle." He then taught the Dhamma, at the close of which, some attained the first path; some, the second; some, the third; and some became arahats. Then the Buddha identified the birth: "At that time, my parents were the young quail's parents, and I was that quail."

21
The Morality of the Partridge
Tittira Jātaka

It was while on the way to Sāvatthī that the Buddha told this story about how Venerable Sāriputta was denied a night's lodging.

When the great donor, Anāthapindika, had completed the construction of Jetavana Monastery in Sāvatthī, he sent a messenger to Rājagaha. Thereupon, the Buddha left Rājagaha with a large group of bhikkhus to go to Vesāli, where he planned to stay a while before continuing the journey to Sāvatthī. At that time, the Gang of Six hurried on ahead and secured all available lodgings, which they distributed among their superiors, their friends, and themselves. When the senior bhikkhus arrived, they could find no quarters at all for the night. Even Venerable Sāriputta's disciples, for all their searching, could not find lodging for him. Being without a place to stay, Venerable Sāriputta spent the night near the Buddha's quarters, alternately sitting at the foot of a tree and walking up and down.

Just before dawn, the Buddha came out of his room and coughed. Venerable Sāriputta also coughed.

"Who is that?" the Buddha asked.

"It is I, Sāriputta, Venerable Sir."

"What are you doing here at this hour, Sāriputta?"

After hearing the explanation, the Buddha thought, "Even now, while I am still alive, the bhikkhus lack courtesy and humility. What will they do when I am gone?"

As soon as it was daylight, the Buddha called the bhikkhus together and said, "I have heard that the bhikkhus of the Gang of Six hurried ahead and reserved lodgings, preventing senior bhikkhus from finding lodgings for the night. Is this true?"

"That is so, Blessed One," the bhikkhus replied.

"Tell me, Bhikkhus," the Buddha continued, "who deserves the best lodging, the best robes, and the best rice?"

Some answered that the most deserving was the one who had been a nobleman before becoming a bhikkhu. Others thought that it was the one who was originally a brahmin or a wealthy man. Some answered that the most deserving was the one who was well versed in the rules of the Vinaya, the one who could expound the Dhamma, or the one most skilled in the jhā-nas. Others said that the most deserving was the bhikkhu who had attained arahatship or, at least, the first, second, or third paths.

The Buddha listened to all of these opinions and said, "In my Sāsana, precedence in the matter of lodging and other requisites is not by noble birth or by possession of wealth before ordination. It is not by familiarity with the Vinaya, with the Suttas, or with the Abhidhamma. Precedence is not determined by the ability to achieve jhānas or by having made attainments on the path. Bhikkhus, the sole standard for determining who deserves re-spect in word and deed is seniority.[1] Seniors should enjoy the best lodging, the best robes, and the best alms. This is the true standard. Therefore, these things should be reserved for the senior bhikkhu. Because of his seniority, Bhikkhus, Sāriputta, my chief disciple, who keeps turning the Wheel of the Law that I set in motion, deserves to have a lodging after me. Yet Sāriputta spent last night at the foot of a tree without lodging! If you lack respect and subordination now, what will your behavior be as time goes by?

"In times past, Bhikkhus, even animals realized that it was not proper for them to live without respect, without subordinating one to another, without order in their everyday life."

Then the Buddha told this story of the past.

Long, long ago, near a great banyan-tree on the slopes of the Himavat, there lived three friends—a partridge, a monkey, and an elephant. They

---

1   In the Sangha, seniority is determined by the number of rains retreats that a bhikkhu has observed since his ordination

stayed together happily enough, but they came to realize that their life lacked order and that they had no one to respect. The more they thought about this, the more they wanted to know which of them was the oldest so that they could honor him.

One day, as they were sitting beneath the banyan tree, they had an idea. The partridge and the monkey asked the elephant, "Friend elephant, how big was this banyan when you first remember it?"

"When I was a baby, this banyan was a mere bush, and I used to walk over it. When I stood right over it, its topmost branches just touched my belly. I've known this tree since it was a mere bush."

The elephant and the partridge posed the same question to the monkey.

"My friends," he replied, "when I was just a baby and sat here on the ground, I had only to stretch out my neck to eat the topmost sprouts of this banyan. I've known this banyan tree since it was very tiny."

Finally, the monkey and the elephant looked to the partridge for his answer.

"Friends," he began, "long ago, there was a great banyan tree some distance away. I ate its seeds and voided them here. That was the origin of this tree. Since I have knowledge of this tree from before it was born, I must be older than either of you."

"Indeed, Friend," the other two animals exclaimed, "you are the oldest. From now on, we will pay you honor. We will show you due respect in word and deed, and we will seek your guidance. From now on, please give us advice whenever we are in need of it."

The partridge, accepting their respect as the most senior, counseled them wisely from that day on. He also established them in the precepts, which he himself faithfully observed. In this way, their daily life acquired more order. Established in the precepts, they lived together respectfully and properly, thereby, at life's close, earning rebirth in heaven.

Having concluded his story, the Buddha added, "The aims of these three came to be known as the 'Morality of the Partridge.' Knowing that these three animals, Bhikkhus, lived together in harmony because of age, how can you, who have ordained in this Sangha, live together without proper respect? Henceforth, I declare that respect and all due service be paid to seniority. Seniority shall receive the best lodging, the best robes, and the best alms. Nevermore, let a senior be kept out of a lodging by a junior. Whosoever shows disrespect for his senior in such a way commits an offense. Those who honor age will be praised in this life and will find their reward in the future, as well." Then the Buddha identified the birth: "At that time, Moggallāna was the elephant, Sāriputta was the monkey, and I was the wise partridge."

22

The Pit and the Lotus
Khadirangāra Jātaka

It was while staying at Jetavana that the Buddha told this story about Anāthapindika.

Anāthapindika valued nothing more than the Triple Gem. He had spent over fifty-four crores to build Jetavana Monastery. Whenever the Buddha was staying there, this pious layman visited at least three times every day—at daybreak, after breakfast, and in the evening. Thinking that the sāmaneras and temple boys might need something, he never went empty-handed. When he went in the early morning, he took rice-gruel; in the afternoon, he took ghee, butter, honey, jaggery, and other medicines; in the evening, he offered incense, flowers, and robes. His generosity knew no bounds.

The great layman was like mother and father to the bhikkhus, sāmaneras, and bhikkhunīs. Some times, he invited the Buddha to his house, along with the eighty great disciples. In his house, rice for at least five hundred bhikkhus was prepared daily, but the number of bhikkhus who received alms there was beyond count.

Anāthapindika's house was seven stories high, and each story had its own entrance. Over the doorway of the fourth floor, lived a deva who was not a devotee of the Buddha. Nevertheless, whenever the Buddha or senior bhikkhus arrived, she had to show respect by taking her children and going down to the ground floor. This very much upset the deva, and she grumbled, "As long as this Gotama and his disciples keep coming to this house, I will have no peace. I can't be forever going downstairs. It's intolerable! There must be a way to stop them from visiting here!"

Shortly afterwards, she appeared to Anāthapindika's business manager as he rested after work.

"Who are you?" he asked.

"I am the deva who lives over the fourth doorway."

"What do you want?"

"Surely, you, of all people, can see what Anāthapindika is doing. He's neglecting his business and spending his money and resources to enrich the ascetic Gotama. The merchant is no longer engaged in any commerce or trade. He is ruining himself! You must advise him to attend to his business. Perhaps you could arrange it so that Gotama and his disciples no longer come to the house."

Her speech made the manager very angry. "Foolish deva!" he shouted. "The merchant is spending his money on the Buddha Sāsana which leads to liberation. Even if he were to sell me as a slave, I would never say anything to him about that. Get out of my sight!"

Undeterred, the deva went to Anāthapindika's eldest son with the same advice. He reacted in the same way as the business manager had and ordered her out. Being rebuffed by these two in no way changed the deva's mind, but she didn't dare speak directly to Anāthapindika himself.

What the deva said about Anāthapindika's business, however, was somewhat true. He had lent more than eighteen crores to various traders but never bothered calling in this money. Another eighteen crores of the family property had been lost in a great storm. The treasure had been buried in brass pots which were swept away when the river banks collapsed. These pots lay under water, with the seals still intact.

As a result of Anāthapindika's unbounded generosity, his treasury was greatly diminished. Since he was no longer doing business, his income had shrunk to nothing. The quality of the food served in the house and of the clothing worn by his family gradually deteriorated to the point that they appeared to be living in poverty. In spite of this, Anāthapindika continued to offer meals to bhikkhus, even though the meals were not the feasts they had once been.

One day, after Anāthapindika had paid obeisance, the Buddha asked him, "Householder, are alms being offered at your house?"

"Yes, Venerable Sir, but there is only a little broken rice and sour gruel."

"Don't be distressed, householder. Even if you can only offer something unappetizing, if your intention is good, the gift is fruitful. When the heart is pure, alms given to Buddhas, Pacceka Buddhas, and Buddhas' disciples are always good.[1] The fruit of those alms is great. One who has faith in his heart cannot give an unacceptable gift. No gift he gives to a Buddha or to his disciples is small. There is merit in any gift, even broken rice and sour gruel, given to those who have entered on the Noble Eightfold Path. Long ago, as the brahmin, Velāma, I was renowned throughout all of Jambudīpa for my generosity in giving the seven precious things, but I could find no one worthy of my gifts, not even one who kept the five precepts. Rare, indeed, are those who are worthy of offerings. Therefore, do not let yourself be troubled by the thought that your alms are not so delicious."

The unbelieving deva had not dared to speak to the merchant before, but now that he was poor, she supposed he would listen to her. Emboldened, she entered his bedroom at midnight and made herself visible.

"Who's that?" asked the merchant.

"I am the deva, sir, who dwells over the fourth doorway."

"What brings you here?"

"I wish to give you counsel."

"All right. I'm listening."

"Sir, you are not thinking about your own future or that of your children. You have lavished vast sums on the ascetic Gotama. In fact, since you are not undertaking new business, you have been reduced to poverty by your generosity to him. Yet, even in your poverty, you do not shake off the ascetic Gotama! His followers are in and out of your house every day, just the same as ever! What they have taken from you cannot be recovered. That is for certain. I urge you to stop going to the ascetic Gotama and to forbid his disciples to set foot inside your house. Give up the ascetic Gotama, attend to business, and restore your family fortune."

"Is this the counsel you came to give me?"

"Yes, sir, it is."

"Those are wicked words!" Anāthapindika shouted. "Neither you nor one thousand like you could ever shake my faith in the Buddha. My wealth has been spent on the Sāsana that leads to liberation. I will not continue to

---

1   This is explained in the Velāma Sutta (Anguttara Nikāya, 9, 20), which the Buddha taught at this time

live under the same roof with you! Leave my house at once and seek shelter elsewhere!"

Being ordered out by the merchant himself, the deva had no choice but to leave. Reluctantly, she took her children by the hand and departed, nonetheless determined to find a way to appease the merchant and to return to his house. She first went to the tutelary deity of the city. "My lord," she said to him, "I spoke imprudently to Anāthapindika. He became angry and drove me out of my home. Please come with me and help make peace between us so that he will let me live there again."

"What did you say to the merchant?"

"I told him not to support the ascetic Gotama anymore and not to let him or his disciples set foot in the house again. That is all I said, my lord."

"Those were wicked, wicked words. You struck a blow aimed at the Buddha. I cannot go with you to see him."

Getting no support from him, she went to the Four Great Kings. When they learned of her offense, they repulsed her in the same way. Next she went to Sakka, and repeated her story. "Your Majesty," she pleaded, "please either come with me and speak on my behalf to Anāthapindika or give me some place to live. I have been wandering about homeless, leading my children here and there. I cannot go on like this!"

"You have done an evil thing, maligning the Buddha," Sakka told her. "I will not speak to the merchant on your behalf, but I will suggest a way that you might be able to get him to pardon you."

"Thank you, Your Majesty," cried the deva.

"Traders have borrowed eighteen crores from him. Disguise yourself as his agent, and go to their houses. Show them their promissory notes and intimidate them with your powers. Say to them, 'Here's your IOU. Our merchant did nothing about this while he was affluent, but now he is poor. You must immediately repay what you owe.'

"In this way, you can get back those eighteen crores of gold and replenish the merchant's empty treasury. He had another treasure buried near the Aciravatī River, but when the bank collapsed, the treasure was washed away. Using your extraordinary power again, reclaim that money and place it in his treasury. Lastly, there is another unclaimed treasure of eighteen crores buried nearby. Take that, too, and place it in his vault. When you have atoned by the recovery of these fifty-four crores, ask the merchant to forgive you."

"Thank you, Your Majesty! I'll do as you say," cried the deva, as she hurried away to begin work. In no time, she had recovered all the money and replenished the treasury.

That night, she went to Anāthapindika's chamber and appeared before him.

"Who is there?" the merchant asked.

"It is I, great merchant," the deva replied softly, "the foolish deva who used to live over your fourth doorway. When I spoke to you a few days ago, I was blind to the virtues of the Buddha. I never should have said those wicked words to you. Please forgive me! Sakka told me how I might atone for my sin. I have recovered the eighteen crores owed to you by various debtors, as well as the eighteen crores which had been washed away by a flood. I also found another eighteen crores which lay nearby, buried and unclaimed. These fifty-four crores I have deposited in your empty vaults. You now have enough wealth to offers alms and gifts to the Buddha and his followers as generously as you did before. Please forgive what I did in my ignorance, sir. Please pardon me. With nowhere to live, I am in misery. Please allow me to live in your house again."

"Good deva," Anāthapindika answered, "if you sincerely want me to pardon you, you must ask me again in the presence of the Buddha."

"Very good," she replied, "I will. Take me to the Master."

Early the next morning, Anathapindika took the deva to Jetavana and explained to the Buddha all that she had done.

"You see, householder," the Buddha said after hearing the whole story, "that sinners do not know how evil their deeds are until they have to suffer for them. Then they realize the sins that they have committed. In the same way, the good do not realize the goodness of their acts until they enjoy the fruit. Then they realize the good that they have done."[1]

Upon hearing this, the deva attained the first path. She fell at the Buddha's feet, crying, "I was misled by delusion and blinded by ignorance. I spoke wickedly because I didn't know your virtues. Forgive me!" Both the Buddha and Anāthapindika gladly pardoned her and rejoiced with her.

"Venerable Sir," Anāthapindika added, "this deva tried very hard to stop me from supporting you and your order, but she failed. Though she tried to stop me, I continued giving as many gifts as I could. Wasn't this goodness on my part?"

"Householder," the Buddha answered, "you are a devoted disciple with firm faith and purified vision. It is no wonder that this misguided deva could not stop you. In the distant past, however, when there was no Buddha teaching in the world, it was, indeed, a wonder that even Māra was not able to stop a wise man from giving gifts."

At Anāthapindika's request, the Buddha told this story of the past.

---

1 Dhammapada 119–120.

Long, long ago, when Brahmadatta was reigning in Bārānasi, the Bodhisatta was born into the family of the city's treasurer. He grew up like a prince, surrounded by luxury. By the time he was sixteen years old, he was fully educated and accomplished. At his father's death, he took over the office of treasurer and built six alms-halls—one at each of the four city gates, one in the city center, and one at the gate of his own mansion. He was extremely generous and moral. He was also scrupulous about keeping the precepts and observing the Uposatha days.

One morning, in the Himavat, a Pacceka Buddha rose from seven days of jhānic meditation. Realizing that it was time to go on his almsrounds, he decided to visit the treasurer of Bārānasi. After cleaning his teeth with a toothstick from a neem tree, he rinsed his mouth with water from Lake Anotatta, put on his outer-robe, and took up his bowl. Passing through the air, he arrived at the gate of the treasurer's mansion just as breakfast was being served.

Seeing the Pacceka Buddha, the treasurer got up from the table, called a servant, and asked him to bring the almsbowl.

Māra, the Evil One, realizing that seven days had passed since the Pacceka Buddha had last taken food, became excited. "I will stop the treasurer from giving and destroy the Pacceka Buddha at the same time!" he exalted. In front of the gate of the treasurer's mansion, Māra created a pit, eighty hatthas deep, with a charcoal fire blazing up like the great Avīci hell.

When the servant opened the front door, he was struck with terror by the flaming pit and leaped back from the entrance.

"What is it?" asked the treasurer.

"My lord, there is a great flaming pit in front of the house."

Other servants hurried to the door to see, but they, too, retreated in panic when they saw the pit.

The treasurer asked the servants to step aside and boldly walked toward the door.

He opened the door, stood on the brink of the fiery pit, looked up, and saw Māra poised in mid-air. In order to force the deva to expose himself, he shouted, "Who are you?"

"Māra," was the answer.

"Did you make this pit?"

"Yes, I did."

"Why?"

"To prevent you from giving alms and to end the life of this Pacceka Buddha."

"You cannot stop me from giving alms. Nor can you destroy the life of this Pacceka Buddha. Today, we will see whose strength is greater, yours or mine.

"Venerable Sir," he called to the Pacceka Buddha across the pit, "even if I fall headlong into these flames, I will not turn back. Please accept the food I bring."

Holding the alms he intended to offer, he stepped off the edge of the pit directly into the fire. At that instant, a beautiful lotus rose from the depths of the pit to support him and to protect him from the flames. As he stepped onto the lotus, he was showered with pollen, which covered him from head to foot like gold dust. Standing in the middle of the lotus, he filled the bowl of the Pacceka Buddha with delicious almsfood.

After the Pacceka Buddha had partaken of the food and given anumodana, he flung the bowl upwards, rose into the air, and, appearing to tread the clouds, returned to the Himavat.

Dejected and defeated, Māra vanished.

Still standing on the lotus, the treasurer extolled the merits of giving alms and administered the precepts to the people who had gathered there.

Throughout his life, the treasurer practiced generosity and performed many good deeds, finally passing away to fare according to his deserts.

Having concluded his story, the Buddha added, "With your discernment of the truth, householder, it is no great surprise that you were not overcome by this deva. The real marvel is what that good treasurer did in those days." Then the Buddha identified the birth: "At that time, the Pacceka Buddha passed away, never to be born again, and I was the treasurer of Bārānasi who defeated Māra by giving alms."

23
Always Hungry
Losaka Jātaka

It was while staying at Jetavana that the Buddha told this story about Venerable Losaka Tissa.

In Kosala, there was a prosperous fishing-village with one thousand families. One day, all the fishermen went out with their nets to the rivers and ponds, as they did every morning, but, when evening came, not one of them had caught a single fish. They were astonished for this had never happened before in the entire history of the village. From that day on, bad fortune dogged the village. The catch was never good. Moreover, disaster struck the village with uncanny frequency. Within the space of only eight months, fire destroyed all the houses seven times. Another seven times, the king punished the village by demanding extra taxes. Reeling from these calamities, the villagers wondered why their fortune had suddenly changed so drastically. They concluded that someone among them must have been causing the misfortune. To find out who it was, they decided to divide the village into two groups of five hundred families each.

Sure enough, the next day, one group caught more fish than they could carry, but the other team returned empty-handed. The unlucky group again divided into two, and again only one group caught no fish. The unlucky fishermen continued dividing themselves into groups until they discovered that the cause of the bad fortune was one family. Not only was the wife pregnant, but it seemed certain that the bad fortune had begun on the day she conceived. The villagers all joined together and drove that family away, and the village soon regained its former prosperity.

That family, on the other hand, led a miserable existence. The wife had great difficulty finding enough food to sustain herself during pregnancy, but, when the time came, she gave birth to a son. No matter how much she neglected him and deprived him of food, he survived as though his life was charmed. His parents stayed with him until he could run about, but then, one day, his mother put a broken shard in his hands and sent him off to beg. She and her husband went to another village, leaving him to fend for himself.

Abandoned, the boy scrounged for food the best he could. He never took a bath, and he had no decent clothes, so he looked like a mud-goblin.[1] At the age of seven, he found himself in Sāvatthī, living like a crow, picking up and eating, lump by lump, any food he could find in the back alleys, where people threw away the scrapings of the rice-pots and other garbage.

One morning, as Venerable Sāriputta was entering Sāvatthī for alms, he noticed the child and was immediately filled with loving-kindness towards him. "Come here," he called.

The child obediently approached, bowed to the bhikkhu, and stood before him.

"What village do you belong to?" Venerable Sāriputta asked him gently. "Where are your parents?"

"I live by myself on the street, sir," the child answered. "My parents said they were tired of misfortune, abandoned me, and went away." As the boy stood there, Venerable Sāriputta could see how scrawny he was.

"Would you like to become a bhikkhu?" he asked the boy.

The boy's eyes became very wide, and he answered in a soft voice, "Indeed I would, sir, but who would sponsor a poor wretch like me?"

"I would."

"Then I want to become a bhikkhu."

Venerable Sāriputta took the boy to the monastery, bathed him, and gave him a meal. That same day, the boy was ordained as a sāmanera, and, when he was old enough, he received full ordination as a bhikkhu, with the name Losaka Tissa.

Even as a bhikkhu, Venerable Losaka Tissa continued to be plagued by bad luck. Whenever alms were given, no matter how lavish the generosity,

---

1 Pamsupisācako, a kind of peta.

Venerable Losaka Tissa never got enough to eat. After a single ladle of rice had been placed in his bowl, the bowl appeared full to the brim so that donors skipped him and offered the rest of the rice to the others. When it came time for curry, just as the food was to be put in his bowl, the dishes seemed to vanish, and he never got any.

In time, Venerable Losaka Tissa developed perfect insight and attained arahatship, but he still got very little to eat, and he was always hungry. One morning, Venerable Sāriputta realized that Venerable Losaka Tissa would pass away that day. "Today," he declared, "I will see that Losaka Tissa has enough to eat."

He summoned Venerable Losaka Tissa, and together they walked to Sāvatthī for alms. Because Venerable Losaka was with him, however, Venerable Sāriputta received absolutely nothing. Realizing what was the matter, he asked Venerable Lusaka to go back to the monastery and wait for him. Proceeding on his almsrounds alone, he quickly managed to collect plenty of food as he always before had in that wealthy and generous city. Venerable Sāriputta instructed several other bhikkhus to carry the food back to Jetavana and to offer it to Venerable Losaka Tissa.

Those bhikkhus unaccountably forgot about Venerable Losaka Tissa and ate all of the food themselves. After finishing his own meal, Venerable Sāriputta returned to Jetavana and went to Venerable Losaka Tissa's chamber. "Well, Brother," he asked cheerfully, "did you get the food and enjoy your lunch?"

"I shall, no doubt, get it in good time," Venerable Losaka Tissa answered. Venerable Sāriputta understood what had happened, but, since it was past noon, it was too late for a bhikkhu to eat a meal.

"Please stay here, Friend," said Venerable Sāriputta; "and wait for my return." He went with his bowl to the palace of the king. As soon as King Pasenadi saw Venerable Sāriputta, he ordered that his bowl be taken and filled with catumadhu. Venerable Sāriputta carried the bowl back to Venerable Losaka Tissa, stood before him, holding the bowl, and told him to eat.

Because of his reverence for Venerable Sāriputta, Venerable Losaka Tissa would not touch the catumadhu.

"Please, Friend," Venerable Sāriputta gently urged him, "sit down and eat. I must stand here with the bowl. If the bowl were to leave my hand, everything in it would vanish!"

With respect and admiration for Venerable Sāriputta's kindness and compassion, Venerable Losaka Tissa ate the sweet mixture. Because of Venerable Sāriputta's merit and power, the food did not disappear. Venerable Losaka Tissa was able to eat as much as he wanted and was satisfied. That day, as Venerable Sāriputta had foreseen, Venerable Losaka Tissa passed away, never to be reborn again. His kamma was extinguished.

The Buddha attended his cremation and ordered that a cetiya be built for the collected ashes.

Shortly after this, a group of bhikkhus was sitting in the hall and talking about Venerable Losaka Tissa. "Losaka Tissa," one of them said, "was always unlucky, and little was given to him. I wonder how, with all his bad luck, he was able to win the glory of arahatship."

When the Buddha heard what they were discussing, he said, "Bhikkhus, Lusaka Tissa's actions were the cause of both his receiving so little and his becoming an arahat. Long ago, he had prevented others from receiving, and that was why he received so little himself. He won arahatship for himself, however, by meditating on suffering, impermanence, and the absence of self in all things." Then he told this story of the past.

Long, long ago, in the days of Kassapa Buddha, there was a young bhikkhu living in a small village monastery. He was supported by a well-to-do landowner. The bhikkhu was proper in conduct, and the landowner was pious.

One day, a senior bhikkhu came to that village and stopped in front of the landowner's house, seeking alms. Being impressed with this bhikkhu's demeanor, the landowner took his bowl, led him into the house, paid him every respect, and offered him food.

After eating, the bhikkhu gave him a short discourse. Thoroughly delighted, the man invited him to stay. "Venerable Sir," he said, "There is a monastery close by. Please stay there for the night. I would like to call on you there this evening."

Silently agreeing, the bhikkhu went to the monastery and formally greeted the resident bhikkhu, who received him with all friendliness and asked whether he had received alms that morning.

"Oh yes," he replied.

"Where was that?"

"In the village, at the landowner's house."

Then the senior bhikkhu asked to be shown his room. Putting down his bowl and outer robe, he seated himself in meditation and, being an arahat, began enjoying the bliss of arahatship.

That evening, the landowner went to the monastery, accompanied by servants carrying flowers, incense, lamps, and oil. He paid his respects to the resident bhikkhu and asked whether a guest, a senior bhikkhu, had appeared. The resident bhikkhu replied that he had and indicated which room he had been given. The man went to that room, bowed respectfully to the arahat, seated himself at one side, and listened to a discourse. After the discourse was completed, in the cool of the evening, the landowner lit lamps and incense at the cetiya and Bodhi tree. Before returning to the village, he announced to the resident bhikkhu that he would like to offer a meal the next day to the two bhikkhus and asked him to bring the senior bhikkhu to the house at the proper time.

The resident bhikkhu began to feel threatened by the new arrival. He sat in his room thinking, "This landowner is very pious, and he is obviously impressed by this learned bhikkhu. If this bhikkhu decides to stay here, I could easily lose my place and might soon count for nothing." The more he speculated, the more upset he became. Indeed, he spent most of the night scheming how to make sure that the other bhikkhu did not decide to stay in the monastery.

Early the next morning, the senior bhikkhu went to greet the resident bhikkhu. He tapped on the door, but the resident bhikkhu neither opened the door nor spoke in response. Being an arahat, the senior bhikkhu understood what the other was thinking. "This bhikkhu," he said to himself, "does not realize that I would never trouble him nor threaten his relationship with the landowner who supports him." He returned to his own room and became absorbed in the bliss of his meditation.

When it was time to go, the resident bhikkhu tapped softly on the gong and knocked almost silently on the other's door. Getting no response, he hurried off alone to the landowner's house. His host offered him a seat and immediately asked about the other bhikkhu.

"I have no idea where he is," replied the young bhikkhu. "I struck the gong and knocked on his door, but he did not come out. He must still be sleeping. I suppose that the food yesterday disagreed with him and that he is still in bed not feeling well."

The landowner served the bhikkhu a delicious meal of succulent curries with rice cooked in milk and mixed with ghee, sugar, and honey. After he had finished, servants scoured the bowl and refilled it. "Venerable Sir," the landowner said to the bhikkhu, returning the bowl full of food, "that visiting bhikkhu must be very tired from his journey. Please take this food to him so that he may take his lunch before noon."

The resident bhikkhu accepted the food and went back toward the monastery. As he was walking, he thought, "If our friend gets a taste of this delicious rice, I will never get rid of him, even if I grab him by the throat and throw him out. I can't let him have it, but how can I get rid of it? If I give it away, everyone will talk about it. If I throw it into the river, the ghee will float on the water, and people will see it. If I just throw it away, it will attract crows, and, again, everyone will know what I have done."

Just then, he came to a field that had recently been burned. Very stealthily, he stepped into the field, scraped a shallow hole in the ground, dumped the contents of his bowl into the hole, and covered it with soil and ashes. Then he returned to the monastery with the empty bowl.

In the meantime, the other bhikkhu had washed, dressed, taken his bowl, and gone elsewhere to seek alms, intending never to return.

When the resident bhikkhu found the empty chamber, he realized that the visitor had perceived his jealousy and had left because of it. "Woe is me!" he cried, "My greed has made me commit a dreadful sin! I have prevented the landowner's alms from being offered; I have deprived a senior bhikkhu of his portion; I have abused the requisites; and I have violated my livelihood as a bhikkhu! All for greed! All for greed!"

From that day on, he was tormented by guilt and began to look and to act like a ghost. Not long after that, he passed away and was reborn in hell, where he suffered horribly for hundreds of thousands of years. For five hundred successive births, he was a yakkha and never had enough to eat, except on one occasion when he enjoyed a surfeit of filth. For the next five hundred births, he was a pariah dog. As a dog, too, there was only one occasion when he had enough to eat, and that was when he happened to find a mess of vomit.

Finally, he was reborn as a human being, but it was into a lowly beggar family in a village in Kāsi. As soon as he was born, the family's fortune, that is, their misery, turned from bad to worse. They named him Mittavindaka. As a baby, he never got enough milk from his mother's emaciated breasts, and, as a child, he never got even half as much watery gruel as he wanted.

When his parents finally realized that he was the cause of their misfortune and hunger, they beat him, shouting, "Begone, you curse!" and drove him away.

In the course of his wanderings, the little outcast arrived in Bārānasi, which, at that time, was a remarkably progressive and wealthy city. Even poor boys had their daily rations provided along with their studies. Thus young Mittavindaka became a charity scholar under a renowned teacher who had five hundred other young students.

Despite his improved fortune, Mittavindaka was always fighting with his fellow students. Furthermore, he was extremely disrespectful toward his teacher. Because of Mittavindaka's unruly behavior, the teacher's fees declined. The master tried to reason with him and to correct some of his most obvious faults, but Mittavindaka was intractable. He decided to run away and found himself in a border village, where he was able to eke out an existence by teaching the rudiments of reading, writing, and arithmetic.

The villagers paid him a small salary and gave him a hut at the edge of the village. He married a miserably poor woman and had two children.

Shortly after Mittavindaka arrived, the fortune of that village changed for the worse. Seven times the king's vengeance fell on the villagers; seven times their homes were burned to the ground; and seven times their water tank dried up.

Finally, the villagers realized that Mittavindaka was, indeed, the cause of their misfortunes. Armed with staves, they surrounded his hut and drove him and his family away. Scrounging for food, the little family walked on until they came to a wild jungle, where they were attacked by yakkhas. Mittavindaka was able to escape, but the yakkhas killed his wife and children and ate them.

Once again, Mittavindaka wandered alone, surviving as best he could. Eventually, he came to Gambhīra, a village on the coast. On that very day, there was a ship putting out to sea, and Mittavindaka was able to secure a position on board. For a week the ship sailed steadily on course, but, on the seventh day, it came to a complete standstill in mid-ocean, as though it had run upon a rock. Baffled by this strange occurrence, the crew cast lots, hoping to find the cause of their trouble. Seven times, the lot fell on Mittavindaka, so the other sailors gave him a bamboo raft and bade him farewell, not caring whether he survived or drowned. The instant Mittavindaka left the ship, it began sailing normally once more.

Mittavindaka clambered onto the bamboo raft and floated on the waves. Because he had earned a little merit as a bhikkhu in the time of Kassapa Buddha, he experienced some good fortune. His raft drifted to an isolated island, where he found a beautiful crystal palace. He approached the palace and was greeted by four lovely princesses. For seven days, he was lavishly entertained like a king in the palace. Mittavindaka was sure that his luck had finally turned and that he had, at last, found happiness in this paradise. Unfortunately, the princesses were actually vimāna-petas, who were condemned to alternate between seven days of joy in a divine palace and seven days of suffering in the peta realm. On the seventh day, they told Mittavindaka that they had to leave for a week, but they promised that they would return, and they begged him to wait.

Of course, Mittavindaka did not listen to them. Being impatient, he set off on his raft as soon as they were gone. Before long, he reached another island, where he was even more lavishly entertained by eight ghostly princesses in a silver palace. On the seventh day, they, too, announced that they were leaving for a week and asked him to wait. The same as before, Mittavindaka set out on his raft. Then he successively stayed for one week with sixteen princesses in a palace of jewels and thirty-two princesses in a golden palace.

After leaving the golden palace, Mittavindaka drifted for several days. As he was approaching another island, he expected to find another palace, but all he saw was a herd of goats on a stony beach. Since he was, of course, starving, he decided to make a meal of a goat. Not realizing that these goats were actually yakkhas, he impulsively grabbed the leg of one of the nanny-goats. With all her demonic strength, this yakkhinī gave him such a kick that he was hurled up and away over the ocean. He came down on a clump of thorns on the slopes of the dry moat of Bārānasi, the same city he had fled some years earlier.

That moat happened to be the hiding place of robbers, who regularly killed and roasted goats from the king's herd. At that particular time, however, the king's goatherds were hiding nearby, hoping to catch the thieves red-handed.

No sooner had Mittavindaka picked himself up and dusted himself off, than he spotted the king's goats, seemingly unattended. "Well," he thought, "I was kicked here by a goat on an island in the middle of the ocean. I wonder if one of these goats might just kick me back to one of those lovely islands where the princesses live in magnificent palaces. I should have stayed there in the first place. Let me take hold of the leg of that nanny-goat and see if it works."

Leaping forward, he grabbed the leg of the strong goat, closed his eyes, and waited to be hurled back to an island. Instead of kicking, however, the goat began bleating and tried to run away. Instantly, the goatherds emerged from their hiding places, seized Mittavindaka, and shouted, "This is the thief who has been stealing the king's goats!" They beat him severely, tied him up, and dragged him toward the city.

At that time, Mittavindaka's former teacher was on his way to bathe at the river with some of his students and noticed the goatherds. Recognizing Mittavindaka, he asked why he had been arrested.

"Master," the goatherds said, "we caught this thief in the act of stealing a goat. We are taking him to prison. The king will surely execute him."

"Oh dear!" exclaimed the teacher. "Formerly, he was one of my students. I would hate to see him executed. Would you hand him over to me? He can be our servant, and I will guarantee that he causes no more trouble."

The teacher commanded so much respect that the goatherds gladly agreed. They untied their prisoner and released him into the care of the teacher.

The teacher asked Mittavindaka where he had been and Mittavindaka told him all that had happened.

"By not listening to those who wish you well," the teacher told him, "you have suffered all those misfortunes."

This time, Mittavindaka stayed with the teacher. After several years, both of them passed away, each faring according to his deserts.

Having concluded his story, the Buddha identified the birth: "At that time, Losaka Tissa was Mittavindaka, and I was the wise teacher in Bārānasi."

24

The Bamboo Viper
Veluka Jātaka

It was while staying at Jetavana that the Buddha told this story about a stubborn bhikkhu.

Once, the Buddha asked a certain bhikkhu whether or not the report that he was stubborn was true, and he admitted that it was.

"Bhikkhu," said the Buddha, "this is not the first time you have been self-willed. You were stubborn in former days also, and, as the result of your contrary refusal to follow the advice of the wise and good, you died from a snakebite." At the bhikkhu's request, the Buddha told this story of the past.

Long, long ago, when Brahmadatta was reigning in Bārānasi, the Bodhisatta was born into a wealthy family in the kingdom of Kāsi. Having reached adulthood, he saw how passion caused pain and how bliss came from abandoning passion. With that understanding, he went to the Himavat and became an ascetic. After practicing meditation, he achieved mastery over the higher jhānas. Because of his proficiency, he became the teacher of five hundred other ascetics.

One day, a young venomous viper crawled into one of the huts and stayed there. The ascetic who lived in that hut grew fond of the snake and began taking care of it. He kept it in a joint of bamboo, so he named the creature Veluka. Since the ascetic doted on the viper as if it were his child, the others called the ascetic Velukapitā (Bamboo's father).

When the teacher heard that one of the ascetics was keeping a snake, he sent for him and asked if it was true. When told that it was, he said, "A viper can never be trusted. Let it go immediately."

"But," pleaded the ascetic, "my viper is so dear to me, I cannot not live without him."

"Well," answered the teacher, "I tell you that that snake will cost you your life."

Disregarding his master's warning, the ascetic kept the snake.

A few days later, all five hundred ascetics went to the forest to gather fruit. Finding a spot where fruit was abundant, they stayed two or three days. Of course, the snake was left behind in its bamboo tube.

When Velukapitā returned, he remembered that he hadn't fed the snake. Opening the snake's tube, he stretched out his hand, and said, "Come, my son; you must be hungry."

Angry from being imprisoned so long, the viper bit the ascetic's hand and slithered off into the forest.

Hearing a noise, the other ascetics rushed to the hut, but Velukapitā was already dead. They immediately told the master, who ordered the body cremated. "The stubborn man," he told his students, "who ignores friends who give him kindly counsel will come to grief, the same as Velukapitā."

Living a contemplative life and instructing his students, the teacher, at his own death, was reborn into the Brahma heavens.

Having concluded his story, the Buddha identified the birth: "At that time, you were Velukapitā, my disciples were the other ascetics, and I was the teacher."

25

Long Root or Short?
Ārāmadūsaka Jātaka1

It was while staying in a Kosalan village that the Buddha told this story about despoiling a garden.

One day, a householder invited the Buddha and the Sangha to take a meal at his home. He seated them all in the garden and served them generously. After the meal, as the bhikkhus were strolling through the garden with the gardener, they noticed that one area was completely empty, without any shrubs or trees.

"Everywhere else there is abundant shade, sir, except in this particular spot. Why is this spot bare?"

"Venerable Sirs," the gardener replied, "when this garden was laid out, the village lad responsible for the watering in this area foolishly pulled up the young trees and bushes and watered them according to the length of their roots. Because of that, all the plants in this area withered and died."

When the bhikkhus reported this to the Buddha, he replied, "This is not the first time that that village lad has spoiled a pleasure garden. He did the same thing long ago." Then he told this story of the past.

Long, long ago when Brahmadatta was reigning in Bārānasi, a festival was proclaimed in the city. At the first beat of the drum, people poured out of their homes to celebrate.

The royal gardener also wanted to join the festivities, but he had not yet watered the pleasure garden. He was sure that, if he did the watering, he would miss all the fun, so he was rather disgruntled. Suddenly, he had a good idea and called the chief of the monkey troop that lived in the garden. First, he pointed out the benefits the monkeys enjoyed in the garden, emphasizing all the succulent fruits and flowers they had to eat. "Today," he continued, "there is a festival in Bārānasi. I really want to go out and enjoy myself, but there is something that must be done. Would you and your subjects do me a special favor by watering the trees and shrubs in the garden? It's only for today, and I would really appreciate it."

"Of course! We'd be glad to," the monkey king agreed.

"Thank you very much!" the gardener exclaimed happily. "Here is every-thing you need," he said, giving them the watering skins and wooden buckets filled with water. "Make sure to give everything enough water," he advised as he went off to the festival with a light heart.

The monkey king called his followers and explained what the gardener had told him. The monkeys picked up the watering skins and began enthusiasti-cally sprinkling water around the garden. As they went about their work, the monkey king began worrying. "When this water is gone," he reflected, "it will be difficult for us to get more." He called the monkeys back and told them, "We must be careful not to waste water, and we must make sure that each plant gets just the right amount. Therefore, before you pour any water on a tree or a shrub, you should pull it up and check the length of its roots. Give plenty of water to those with long roots but only a little to those with short roots. In that way, we'll be sure to have enough water!"

"Yes, Sire!" the monkeys answered, as they returned to their work, doing exactly as he had instructed.

A man happened to be passing by the garden at that time and stopped to watch what the monkeys were doing. "Why are you pulling up each tree and shrub before you water it?" he asked one of the monkeys.

"Our king is worried that we will not have enough water," the monkey explained. "He has instructed us to check the length of the roots of each plant before watering it so that we can give the trees with long roots a lot of water and the trees with short roots only a little."

Shaking his head, the man reflected, "It's unfortunate but true that, even when they want to do the right thing, the ignorant only succeed in wreaking harm and causing trouble! If this is the wisdom of their king, how foolish the rest of these monkeys must be!"

Having concluded his story, the Buddha identified the birth: "The village lad who spoiled this garden was the king of the monkeys, and I was the wise passer-by."

26

The Sky Charm
Vedabbha Jātaka

It was while staying at Jetavana that the Buddha told this story about a stubborn bhikkhu.

"This is not the first time, Bhikkhu, that you have been stubborn. Once, because of your obstinate refusal to listen to good advice from the wise, you were cut in two, and one thousand other men also died." Then he told this story of the past.

Long, long ago, when Brahmadatta was reigning in Bārānasi, there was a brahmin who knew a precious charm called Vedabbha. Whenever this incantation was recited during a particular conjunction of the planets, the heavens would rain down the seven precious things.

One day, the brahmin and his very clever student left their village to travel on business to the kingdom of Ceti.

On their way, they had to pass through a forest inhabited by a ruthless gang of five hundred thieves. This gang was known as the Dispatchers be-cause they always made sure that they caught two victims. One they held prisoner, and the other they dispatched to fetch the ransom. If they captured a father and a son, they held the son and sent the father. If they caught a mother and daughter, they dispatched the mother. In case of two brothers, they dispatched the elder.

When the Vedabbha-brahmin and his student reached the middle of the forest, they found themselves surrounded by these ferocious highwaymen. The pair protested that they had no money, but their pleas fell on deaf ears. The brahmin was quickly bound, and the student was instructed to return to the village and hurry back with enough money to rescue his teacher. The thieves gave the student permission to pay his respects to the brahmin before setting out. As he was bowing before his teacher, the clever young man said loudly, "Don't worry! In a day or two, I will return with the ransom." Then, drawing very near the brahmin, he whispered, "Master, please listen! Tonight there will be a conjunction of the planets. Do not give in to temptation. If you repeat the charm and call down the shower of treasures, a terrible calamity will befall you and this entire band of robbers. Don't do it!"

"Thank you for your advice," the brahmin replied. "Now hurry, and bring back the ransom so that we can both continue on our journey."

As it began to grow dark, the brahmin expectantly watched the sky. As soon as the full moon rose over the eastern horizon, he knew that the great conjunction was indeed taking place.

"Why should I suffer this misery?" he thought. "All I have to do is repeat the charm and call down the precious rain. I can pay the robbers the ransom they demand and go free."

"Friends," he shouted to the robbers, "why are you keeping me a prisoner?"

"To get a ransom, of course," they replied.

"Well, if that is all," the brahmin said, "I can give you as much money as you want. Hurry up and untie me. Let me wash my hair and put on some clean clothes. Just leave me alone for a few minutes, and I will get you your reward."

The bemused robbers untied the brahmin and withdrew to let him do what he wanted, but they kept an eye on him from the distance to make sure he did not try to escape. The brahmin quickly bathed and washed his hair. Then he sat down in the middle of the clearing and began gazing at the heavens. When he saw the precise conjunction of the planets, he began repeating the Vedabbha charm. Suddenly a torrent of jewels, silver, gold, and other precious metals fell all around him. The thieves were amazed. This was more wealth than they had ever seen in their lives. They rushed forward and gathered up the treasure, wrapping as much as they could in their cloaks. They heartily thanked the brahmin for his generosity and invited him to join them. Forgetting all about his student, the brahmin marched away with his new friends.

They had not gone far before they were captured by a second gang of five hundred thieves, even more villainous than the first.

The leader of the Dispatchers asked to speak to the leader of the second gang. When the two leaders were together, the first said to the second, "My friend. I know you have captured us for our money."

"That's right," the other assured him.

"Well," the first continued, "listen to this. You can get all you want and more from that brahmin. All you have to do is let him sit by himself for a few minutes. He can gaze at the sky and create a shower of priceless treasure. It's like a monsoon of jewels!"

"All right," the leader of the second gang agreed. "You and your men can go, but if you are not telling the truth, you'll suffer for it."

"My friend," the leader of the Dispatchers replied, as they were setting out to leave, "every word I have said is true. That brahmin is a goldmine."

Untying the prisoner, the leader of the second gang ordered, "Now, Brahmin, give us riches too!"

"Nothing would give me greater pleasure," said the brahmin softly, "but it will be a full year before the necessary conjunction of the planets takes place again. If you will be so good as to wait until then, I will invoke the precious shower for you, too."

"What?" cried the angry robbers. "You infernal scoundrel! You made the other gang rich, but you expect us to wait a whole year! We'll teach you to play the fool with us!" With a slash of his sharp sword, the leader of the gang cut the brahmin in two. The gang threw his body beside the road and hurried after the Dispatchers. Catching them completely by surprise, they killed every one of them in hand-to-hand fighting.

As they were gathering up the treasure, the men began fighting among themselves and killing each other. Finally, only two thieves were left alive. These two agreed to stop fighting and to divide the loot fairly. They managed to carry off the treasure and to hide it in a safe place. One of them stayed there, guarding it, while the other went into the village to get rice for supper.

As the thief was returning with the rice, he mused, "Why should I share the treasure with that no-good thief?" He ate his own portion of the rice, mixed a strong poison into the rest, and continued on his way back to the forest. When he arrived at the hiding place, he called out, "Here's your rice, my friend. It's still hot and very delicious!"

While he was waiting there alone, the first thief had been thinking exactly the same thing. Instantly, he leapt from the shadow and killed the rice bearer with his sword. He covered the body, retrieved the pot of rice, and, gloating over his cleverness, began eating. He had eaten barely a mouthful when he choked and died a very painful death. There was no one left to cover his body where it fell.

The next day, as he had promised, the student returned with the ransom money and approached the clearing where he had left his master. He wondered why he did not hear the thieves. Then he saw a few bits of treasure scattered on the ground, and he immediately realized what his teacher had done. He followed the road into the forest, fearing the worst. Very soon, he came upon his master's body, cut in two and thrown beside the path.

"Oh, no!" he cried, "my teacher is dead because he didn't listen to my warning." He gathered sticks to make a funeral pyre, cremated his master's body, and marked the spot with wild flowers.

Further down the road, he found the corpses of the five hundred dispatchers. Further still, he found the bodies of the other gang scattered as if on a battlefield. Counting almost one thousand, he felt sure that there must have been two survivors. A little further, he found a corpse with a rice bowl overturned beside it. Nearby, he saw the stash of treasure poorly hidden in the leaves. Quickly piecing together the whole story, he looked around and found the bloody remains of the other thief.

"In his stubborn refusal to follow my counsel," he lamented, "my master destroyed not only himself but also one thousand other men. Those who seek gain by misguided means will surely reap ruin, in the same way my master did. Just as my teacher stubbornly insisted on summoning the rain of treasure from heaven and wrought a catastrophe, so, too, will another, seeking his advantage by wrong means, perish himself and bring destruction to others." These wise words brought forth shouts of applause from the deities in the forest. The wise student carried off all the treasure to his own house. He lived out his life, generously giving alms and performing other good deeds, and, when his life ended, he was reborn in heaven.

Having concluded his story, the Buddha added, "Thus, Bhikkhu, this is not the first time that you were stubborn. In bygone days, as well, your obstinacy led you to destruction." Then the Buddha identified the birth: "At that time, you were the Vedabbha-brahmin, and I was the student."

27
The Sacrifice to End All Sacrifices
Dummedha Jātaka

It was while staying at Jetavana that the Buddha told this story about actions done for the welfare of the world.

One day, the bhikkhus were talking about how much the Buddha had done for the world's benefit. When the Buddha heard what they were discussing, he explained that this was not the first time that he had acted for the good of the world. Then he told this story of the past.

Long, long ago, when Brahmadatta was reigning in Bārānasi, the Bo-dhisatta was born to the queen-consort, who named him Prince Brahmadatta. By the time the prince was sixteen, he had been well educated at Takkasilā, and his father conferred upon him the title of crown prince.

At that time, the people of Bārānasi were extremely superstitious. There were many popular festivals in the city. At these festivals, people offered sheep, goats, pigs, chickens, and other beasts, which the brahmins sacri-ficed to the devas.

Once, when the prince observed these bloody ceremonies, he said to him-self, "Misled by superstition, my citizens wantonly sacrifice animals. When

I become king, I must find a way to end this useless destruction of life. I wonder how I can stop this evil without myself harming anyone."

One day, on a ride in his chariot outside the city, the prince saw a majestic banyan tree. Many people were praying to the deva of that tree to grant them children, wealth, and honor. The prince ordered his driver to stop the chariot, approached the tree, laid a garland of flowers, and lit incense. Feigning reverence, he sprinkled the tree with water and circumambulated its massive trunk. Then he mounted his chariot again and returned to the capital. After this, the prince often visited the tree and repeated his ritual.

When the prince became king, he resolved to rule in righteousness, avoiding the four evil courses[1] and observing the ten duties of a king. One day, he called together his ministers, the brahmins, the nobles, the leading farmers, and other influential subjects and asked whether anyone knew to whom he was most grateful for his good fortune. No one could answer him.

"Have you ever seen me reverently worshiping with incense and flowers at a banyan-tree just outside the city gate?"

"Yes, Sire, we have," said the ministers.

"Well, I was making a vow. My vow was that, if I became king, I would offer a sacrifice to the deva of that tree. Now that I am king, I must fulfill my vow and prepare the promised sacrifice. I command you to prepare it immediately!"

"But what are we to sacrifice?" asked the brahmins.

"My vow," said the king, "was to offer in sacrifice one thousand people who persist in breaking the five precepts and pursuing the ten courses of unwholesome action. I have always lived by those precepts and avoided those courses, and I would like to see all of my subjects follow my example. I command you to proclaim, to the beat of a drum, that your king wishes to fulfill the vow he made while still crown prince to sacrifice one thousand subjects who continue to break the precepts. You are to gather these one thousand victims and to prepare them for sacrifice. With their flesh, their blood, their entrails, and their bones, I will make my offering to the deva of the sacred banyan. Go now! Proclaim this throughout the city so that all may understand the five precepts and that all may know my intention. Find me one thousand victims who break the precepts so that I can make my sacrifice and fulfill my vow."

The ministers obediently followed the king's command, proclaiming the message throughout the capital. The brahmins, likewise, prepared for the sacrifice. The proclamation had such a powerful effect on the townsfolk, however, that not a single person could be found breaking the five precepts.

---

1 Catasso agati: lust, hatred, ignorance, and fear.

The populace immediately forsook the practice of sacrificing living animals. For the entire reign of the king, no one was ever convicted of transgressing any of the five precepts, and all lived together in peace and harmony.

At the close of a life of alms-giving and other good deeds, King Brahmadatta passed away to fare according to his deserts. Because of his reforms, his subjects, as they died, filled the ranks of heaven.

Having concluded his story, the Buddha added "So, you see, Bhikkhus, this is not the first time that I have acted for the good of the world." Then the Buddha identified the birth: "At that time, my disciples were the ministers, and I was the King Brahmadatta."

28

Not One Drop of Blood
Mahā-Sīlava Jātaka

The Buddha told this story while he was staying at Jetavana. When a bhik-khu admitted that he had given up, the Buddha asked him, "How can you quit striving when there is so much to be gained? Long ago, when a wise man had lost his kingdom, through resolution alone, he was able to win it back." Then he told this story of the past.

Long, long ago, when Brahmadatta was reigning in Bārānasi, the Bo-dhisatta was born as a prince, and his name was Mahā-Sīlava (Virtuous). When he became king, he built six alms-halls—one at each of the city gates, one in the center of the city, and one at his own palace gate. Every day, he distributed alms at each of these halls. He faithfully kept the five precepts and observed the Uposatha days. King Mahā-Sīlava ruled righteously with patience, loving-kindness, and mercy, caring for his subjects like a father.

One day, it was reported to the king that one of his ministers had com-mitted adultery in the palace. The king summoned the minister, examined the evidence, and decided that the man was, indeed, guilty. "You have com-mitted a serious crime," the king said to the minister. "In any other kingdom, you would probably be executed for what you have done. I will not execute you, but you can no longer stay in my kingdom. You are free to go, but you must take your belongings and leave immediately."

Rather than expressing remorse and gratitude that his life had been spared, the minister resented being sent into exile and developed an implacable grudge against the king. He left Kāsi and entered the service of the king of Kosala. He rose in favor and, in time, became that monarch's most trusted counselor.

"Sire," he said to King Kosala, as they sat in counsel, "the kingdom of Kāsi is extremely rich. It is like a succulent honeycomb, but King Mahā-Sīlava is weak. If you were to attack Bārānasi, I am confident that he would not even fight. With only a trifling force, you would be able to conquer the entire kingdom."

King Kosala knew that Kāsi was both large and wealthy. He did not believe that it could be defeated by a small army, so he accused the advisor of trying to lure him into a trap.

"Your Majesty," the advisor protested, "I am not deceiving you. I would never betray you. I am only telling you the truth. If you doubt me, send some of your men to burn a border village in Kāsi. Let the men be caught, and see how King Mahā-Sīlava treats them. He will not punish them. He will probably load them with gifts and set them free."

"This man is very bold," thought the king. "He must know that, if he is lying to me, I will have him killed. Let me test what he says." The king sent a few soldiers, disguised as outlaws, to harass a village. When the ruffians were captured and taken to Bārānasi, King Mahā-Sīlava asked them, "My sons, why did you bother the peasants in that village and cause so much trouble?"

"We needed money, Sire," they replied. "We have not been able to make a living."

"Why didn't you come to me first?" asked the king. "Don't do this again." Presenting each of them with a sack of coins, he said, "You must use this money to begin a business. Now go and prosper." The soldiers hurried back to report to King Kosala. The king was surprised, but still he was cautious.

He sent a second band to attack a village in the very heart of Kāsi. King Mahā-Sīlava treated these men in the same way as he had the first. King Kosala was even more amazed, but he was still not fully convinced. He sent a third party to commit robbery on the streets of Bārānasi itself. When these men were also pardoned with gifts, King Kosala was at last satisfied that King Mahā-Sīlava was indeed weak and foolish and that it would be easy to capture the kingdom. He immediately set out with troops and elephants.

Actually, the army of Kāsi was very strong. King Mahā-Sīlava had one thousand gallant warriors who would have done anything for their monarch. This matchless band of heroes was prepared to face any charge, even of an elephant in rut, and could have conquered all of Jambudīpa, had the king given the command. When these soldiers heard of King Kosala's approach, they immediately prepared for war and hurried to inform the king. "Sire," they announced, "we will defeat Kosala. We will capture their king before he can even set foot on our soil."

"No, my sons," answered the king. "Not one drop of blood shall be shed because of me. Let those who covet my kingdom take it. You must not fight."

The army of Kosala crossed the border, and the soldiers of Kāsi hurried again to King Mahā-Sīlava. Again the king refused to give them the order to fight. Facing no resistance, King Kosala led his army all the way to the walls of Bārānasi. A third time the soldiers of Kāsi begged King Mahā-Sīlava to allow them to defend him and to stop King Kosala. They assured the king that they would destroy the Kosalan forces and prevent them from entering the city. Again the king refused.

King Kosala sent a message to King Mahā-Sīlava, demanding that he either surrender or suffer defeat in battle. "I will not fight," King Mahā-Sīlava replied, "nor will I surrender. Take my kingdom if you wish."

King Kosala and his men entered the city and marched directly to the royal palace, where they found King Mahā-Sīlava seated on his throne, surrounded by his officers.

"Seize them all!" cried King Kosala. "Tie their hands tightly behind their backs, and take them to the charnel ground! Dig a hole for each one and bury them up to their necks. The jackals can have a feast and dispose of them for me."

The Kosalan soldiers rushed forward with ropes. King Mahā-Sīlava stood up, placed his hands behind his back, and, with a benign smile, signaled for his men to submit. As one, all of them put down their weapons and put their hands behind their backs. When they had all been bound tightly, the Kosalan soldiers hauled them off to the charnel ground. King Mahā-Sīlava did not allow even a trace of anger towards his captors to cross his mind. So great was the discipline among his men, that not even one dared to protest as they were cruelly dragged away.

Following their king's orders, the Kosalan soldiers buried each of the prisoners up to his neck in a hole, with King Mahā-Sīlava in the middle. Before they left, they firmly tamped the ground around the men's protruding heads, so that the bound victims were unable to move at all. King Mahā-

Sīlava comforted his men and instructed them in radiating loving-kindness to their captors and to all beings.

At midnight, a large pack of jackals entered the charnel ground. At the sight of the beasts, the king and his men shouted in chorus, creating a deafening cry, which frightened the jackals away. After the jackals had run a short distance, however, they realized that no humans were pursuing them, and they crept back to the burying ground. A second shout drove them away again, but again they returned. After running away a third time, the emboldened jackals had lost their fear. Even though the men continued shouting louder than before, the jackals did not turn away. They crouched and crept forward, each singling out his own prey, with the leader of the pack making for King Mahā-Sīlava. Remaining calm, the king carefully watched the fierce beast approach and raised his throat as if to receive the animal's bite. At the same instant that the jackal attacked, the king opened his mouth and fastened his teeth on the jackal's throat. Unable to free himself from the king's mighty jaws, the jackal howled in panic. When the other jackals heard this cry of distress, they immediately abandoned their own prey and ran for their lives.

The trapped jackal continued howling as he dug his claws into the ground and jerked madly back and forth, attempting to free himself from the viselike grip of the king's jaws. This loosened the earth around the king. As soon as he was able to move a little, the king released the jackal, who fled in terror. Using his enormous strength to push from side to side, the king was able to free his hands. He clutched the edges of the hole, pulled himself up, and jumped out like a cloud before the wind. Encouraging his companions to be of good cheer, he began digging to free the commander of the army. Then they both dug up and untied other officers. As each man was released, he began digging around another, and, very soon, all of them stood free once more.

It so happened that a corpse had been left in another part of the charnel ground. Two yakkhas who occupied that territory were arguing about how to divide their prize. Unable to decide for themselves, they agreed to appeal to the good King Mahā-Sīlava for judgment. Realizing that the king was nearby, they dragged the corpse to where he stood with his men and said, "Sire, please divide this body, and give us each our share."

"Certainly, my friends," answered the king, "I would be happy to do that, but I am very dirty. First, I must bathe."

Using their magic power, the yakkhas instantly brought the scented water which had been prepared for the bath of King Kosala and gave it to King Mahā-Sīlava. Then they brought him the robes which had been laid out for the usurper to wear. They also brought him precious perfumes, flowers, and a jeweled fan in a casket of gold. When he had adorned himself, the yakkhas asked whether they could be of any further service, and the king mentioned that he was hungry. The yakkhas disappeared again, returning immediately with rice and the choicest meat which had also been prepared for the usurper's table. King Mahā-Sīlava ate some of this delicious food and drank fresh water from the usurper's golden bowl. After the king had rinsed out his mouth, the yakkhas brought him fragrant betel nut to chew and asked whether he had any further commands.

"Fetch me the Sword of State which lies by the usurper's pillow," the king replied. No sooner had he said this than they laid the sword before him. The king set the corpse upright and cut it deftly in two down the breastbone, giving exactly one half to each yakkha. While the yakkhas were contentedly eating their meal, the king washed the blade and strapped the sword to his side.

When they had finished, the yakkhas asked the king what more they could do for him.

"Please use your magic power to carry me to the usurper's chamber and to return each of my men to his own home."

"Certainly, Sire," replied the yakkhas.

In the twinkling of an eye, King Mahā-Sīlava found himself in his chamber of state, where King Kosala was lying sound asleep on King Mahā-Sīlava's royal bed. King Mahā-Sīlava struck the usurper on the belly with the flat of his sword. King Kosala opened his eyes and shrank back in terror. "Sire," he gasped, "aren't you dead? I had you executed. It is midnight. The doors are locked, and there is a guard outside. How did you get in, sword in hand and dressed in those splendid robes?"

King Mahā-Sīlava calmly explained in detail all that had happened. "Your Majesty!" King Kosala cried out in shame, "Even those fierce yakkhas, who feast on the flesh of corpses, knew your worth, but I, a human being, could not appreciate your goodness. Now, at last, I understand, and I vow never again to plot against anyone who possesses such singular virtues as you do. Please forgive me," he begged, as he prostrated himself at King Mahā-Sīlava's feet. "Forgive my wickedness, and let us be friends as long as we live." As a token of his sincerity, he insisted that King Mahā-Sīlava lie down on the royal bed while he himself stretched out on a couch nearby.

At dawn, King Kosala ordered a drum to assemble his army in front of the palace. Standing before his men, the king praised King Mahā-Sīlava, formally returned his kingdom to him, and, in the presence of his entire force, again asked the king's forgiveness. "From now on," he promised King Mahā-Sīlava, "while you rule your kingdom, I will keep watch to protect you. It will be my duty to deal with rebels."

Before returning to his own kingdom with all his troops and all his elephants, King Kosala made sure that the advisor who had encouraged him to invade the kingdom of Kāsi and had so maliciously misrepresented King Mahā-Sīlava was duly punished.

Seated in splendor on his golden throne beneath the white canopy of royalty, King Mahā-Sīlava declared, "Had I not persevered, I would not again enjoy this magnificence, nor would my one thousand warriors still be numbered among the living. It was by perseverance that I recovered the royal state I had lost and that I saved the lives of my one thousand loyal men. Seeing that the fruit of perseverance is so excellent, we should all strive on with dauntless hearts, despite all odds."

King Mahā-Sīlava continued to rule righteously and passed away to fare according to his deserts.

Having concluded his story, the Buddha taught the Dhamma, and the backsliding bhikkhu attained arahatship. Then the Buddha identified the birth: "At that time, Devadatta was the treacherous minister, my followers were the one thousand warriors, and I was the great King Mahā-Sīlava."

29

Hero Without Equal
Pañcāvudha Jātaka

It was while staying at Jetavana that the Buddha told this story about a bhikkhu who had stopped making effort.

Asked whether it was true that he was a backslider, the bhikkhu immediately admitted that it was. "In bygone days, Bhikkhu," the Buddha told him, "the wise and good won a throne by sheer perseverance in the hour of need." Then he told this story of the past.

Long, long ago, when Brahmadatta was reigning in Bārānasi, the Bodhisatta was born to his queen. On the day he was to be named, his royal parents gave a feast for eight hundred brahmins. After the meal, they asked the brahmins what their son's destiny would be. Noting that the child showed promise of a glorious destiny, the soothsayers predicted that he would become a mighty king endowed with every virtue. Winning fame through exploits with his five weapons, he would be without equal in all Jambudīpa. Because of the brahmins' prophecy, the king and queen named their son Pañcāvudha-Kumāra, or Prince Five-Weapons.

When the prince was sixteen years old, the king gave him one thousand coins and sent him to study with a famous teacher in Takkasilā. The prince studied there for several years. When he had mastered all his subjects, the teacher presented him with a set of five weapons. Prince Pañcāvudha paid his respects to his master and left Takkasilā to return to Bārāṇasi.

On his way, Prince Pañcāvudha came to a forest. Some men who were camped at the edge of the forest tried to stop him from going on. "Young man," they warned, "do not try to go through that forest. It is the haunt of a formidable yakkha named Silesaloma (Sticky Hairs) who kills everyone who enters his territory."

Confident of his own strength, Prince Pañcāvudha was undaunted, but, sure enough, in the middle of the forest, the hairy yakkha confronted him. The monster made himself as tall as a palm-tree, with a head as big as a gazebo, eyes like mixing bowls, two sharp tusks, and a hawk-like beak. His distended belly was purple, and the palms of his hands were blue-black.

"Where do you think you're going?" Silesaloma cried. "Stop! You are mine!"

"Yakkha," answered Prince Pañcāvudha calmly, "you do not scare me. Do not come near me, or I will kill you with a poisoned arrow!"

Bravely, the prince fitted an arrow dipped in deadly poison to his bow. He shot it at the monster, but it only stuck to the creature's scruffy coat. The youth shot all fifty of his arrows, one after another, but they all stuck to the yakkha's unkempt fur.

Shaking himself, so that the arrows fell harmlessly at his feet, Silesaloma gave a roar and charged the prince. Prince Pañcāvudha shouted defiance, drew his sword, and struck at the yakkha, but, like the arrows, the sword merely got caught in the yakkha's shaggy hair. Next the prince hurled his spear, but that, too, lodged in Silesaloma's thick pelt. He struck the yakkha with his club, but the club joined the other weapons in sticking to the creature's fur.

The prince maintained his stance, "Yakkha, you have never before heard of me. I am Prince Pañcāvudha. When I entered this forest, however, I put my trust not in these weapons—bow, arrows, sword, spear, and club—but in myself! Now will I give you a blow which will crush you to smithereens." The prince hit Silesaloma with his right fist, but his hand stuck fast to the hair. Next he aimed a blow with his left hand. He kicked the yakkha with his right foot, and with his left. All he accomplished, however, was to get himself stuck to Silesaloma with both hands and both feet.

"I will crush you to atoms!" the prince shouted, as he butted the yakkha with his head, but that too stuck fast.

Though completely ensnared by all four limbs and his head, hanging helplessly like a doll from Silesaloma's coat, Prince Pañcāvudha remained fearless and undaunted.

Silesaloma reflected, "This is a hero without equal, a lion among men. He cannot be an ordinary human being! Although he has been captured by a yakkha like me, he shows no sign of fear. In all the time I've been killing travelers in this forest, I have never seen anyone like him. Why isn't he afraid of me?"

Reluctant to devour Prince Pañcāvudha, the yakkha asked, "How can it be, young prince, that you have no fear of death?"

"Why should I be afraid? Each life must surely end in death. I know that inside my body there is a diamond sword which not even you can digest. If you eat me, this sword will chop your innards into mincemeat. My death will bring about yours." Of course, the prince was referring to the adamantine sword of knowledge.

Silesaloma pondered on this. "This young prince speaks only the truth. Surely I would not be able to digest a morsel of such a hero. I had better release him." Fearful for his own life, the yakkha let Prince Pañcāvudha go free, saying, "Brave youth, I will not eat you. Go free to gladden the hearts of your relatives, your friends, and your country."

"I am free to go, and I will go, yakkha," answered the prince, "but the sins you committed in a past life have caused you to be reborn as a murderous fiend. If you continue your evil ways, you will go from darkness to darkness. Having met me, however, you have the chance to stop killing. To destroy life is to ensure rebirth in hell, as a brute, or as a peta. Even if a killer's rebirth is as a human, it will be miserable and short."

Prince Pañcāvudha taught Silesaloma the evil consequences of violating the moral precepts and explained the blessings that follow from observing them. Having converted him, the prince imbued him with self-discipline and established him in the five precepts.

Before continuing on his way, Prince Pañcāvudha made the yakkha the guardian of that forest, with a right to levy dues, and charged him to remain steadfast. As he passed through the villages at the forest's edge, he announced to everyone that Silesaloma was completely reformed.

Finally, armed with his five weapons, Prince Pañcāvudha returned to the city of Bārānasi and was reunited with his parents.

When he at last became king, he was a righteous ruler. After a life spent in generosity and other good deeds, he passed away to fare according to his deserts.

Having concluded his story, the Buddha added, "Without attachments to hamper one's heart, victory will be achieved by walking righteously." Then the Buddha taught the Dhamma, and that bhikkhu won arahatship. Finally, the Buddha identified the birth: "At that time, Angulimāla was the yakkha, and I was Prince Pañcāvudha."

30

The Buttermilk Sage
Takka Jātaka

It was while staying at Jetavana that the Buddha told this story about a lascivious bhikkhu. On being questioned, the bhikkhu confessed that he was full of lust and passion.

The Buddha said, "Women are often treacherous and ungrateful. Why are you titillated by them?" Then he told this story of the past.

Long, long ago, when Brahmadatta was reigning in Bārānasi, the Bodhisatta renounced the world and went to live as an ascetic on a bank of the Gangā, where he practiced meditation and, in time, achieved considerable extraordinary powers.

In those days, the king's treasurer had a fierce, cruel daughter named Duttha-Kumārī (Princess Wicked), an obnoxious brat, who beat her servants mercilessly.

One day, Duttha-Kumārī went with a large retinue to amuse herself in the Gangā. While she and her friends were playing in the water, the sun began to set, and a sudden storm burst upon them. Everyone else rushed for cover, but the girl's servants stood apart and said to each other, "This is just the chance we've been waiting for! Let's get rid of that nasty creature!"

They quickly grabbed Duttha-Kumārī, threw her into the river, and hurried away. The rain poured down in torrents, and it grew pitch dark. When the servants returned without their young mistress, they said that she had gotten out of the water but that they did not know where she had gone. Her parents searched everywhere, but not a trace of her could be found.

Screaming loudly, the spoiled girl was swept away by the swollen stream. At midnight, she floated past the sage's hermitage. Hearing her cries, he thought, "That is a woman crying. I must rescue her from the river." Holding a torch of grass over the water, he caught sight of her and shouted encouragingly, "Don't be afraid! Don't be afraid!" He waded into the water and, because of his great strength, brought her safely to the bank. Then he made a fire to warm her and offered her some delicious fruit.

After she had eaten, the ascetic asked, "Where is your home, and how did you happen to fall into the river?"

Duttha-Kumārī told him what had occurred.

"You're welcome to stay here for the present," he said.

He let her occupy his hermitage, and he slept in the open air. After several days, he asked her to leave, but, determined to make the ascetic fall in love with her, she asked to stay a little longer.

As time went by, she so beguiled him with her feminine wiles that he gave up his ascetic's life and lost his extraordinary powers. They continued living in the forest, but she did not like the solitude and wanted to live in a settlement. Yielding to her persistent demands, he took her to a border village, where he supported her, as best he could, by selling buttermilk. Because he also had wide practical knowledge, the local people called him Takka-Pandita (Buttermilk Sage). He kept track of the calendar and told them when to plant, and, in return, they gave him a hut to live in at the village entrance.

The area where Takka-Pandita had settled was frequently raided by bandits from the mountains. One day, while the sage was away, a band of thieves descended on the village. After seizing as many valuables as they could find, the bandits took all the villagers to their mountain hideout and held them hostage. Eventually, they released everyone except Duttha-Kumārī. The bandit chief liked her pretty face and decided to keep her as his wife.

When Takka-Pandita learned what had happened, he thought, "She cannot stand to be parted from me. She will soon escape and come back." Comforted by that thought, he stayed on in the village, waiting for her return.

Duttha-Kumārī, however, was quite contented to stay with the bandits. Her only fear was that Takka-Pandita might come to take her back. "I would feel more secure," she thought, "if he were dead. Why don't I send him a message, professing my undying love, and trick him into coming here to his death?" With that vicious intention, she sent the sage a message, saying that she was miserable and begging him to rescue her and to take her back home.

Trusting her implicitly, Takka-Pandita hurried to the robbers' hideout. As soon as he had found her, he called to her in a hushed voice to flee with him.

"Dear husband," she replied tenderly, "if we tried to escape now, we would only fall into the chief's hands, and he would kill us both. Let us postpone our flight until after dark." She hid Takka-Pandita in a room.

A little later, the robber returned, intoxicated with potent local liquor. Duttha-Kumārī sat beside him and tenderly asked, "Tell me, my love. What would you do if my former husband were in your power?"

"Beat him to a pulp!" he replied fiercely.

"Perhaps he is not as far away as you think. In fact, he is in the next room."

The robber jumped up and threw open the door. He grabbed the sage and thrashed him to his heart's content. Despite the blows, Takka-Pandita made no cry. He only murmured, "Cruel ingrate! Slanderous traitor!"

After thoroughly beating the sage, the robber tied him up, finished his supper, and went to sleep. By morning, he had slept off his drunkenness, and he resumed beating the sage, who merely kept repeating the same four words. At last, the robber noticed that Takka-Pandita wasn't crying out for mercy. Curious, he asked the sage why he kept saying those two phrases over and over.

"Listen, and I will tell you," replied the sage. "Once, I was an ascetic staying happily in the solitude of the forest and practicing meditation. I rescued this woman from the Gangā and saved her life. She seduced me, and I lost my concentration and my powers. Because of her, I left the forest and started working to support her in the village from which you carried her away. She sent me a message, saying that she was miserable and begging me to come and to take her back. Now she has delivered me into your hands. That is why I say, 'Cruel ingrate! Slanderous traitor!'"

This got the robber chief thinking. "If she can feel so little for one who is so good and has done so much for her, what harm would she not hesitate to do to me? Wretched woman! She must die."

After reassuring the sage, he woke Duttha-Kumārī up and told her that he was going to kill her former husband. He took up his sword and asked her to accompany them. Outside the camp, he told the woman to hold the prisoner securely. He quickly drew his sword, and, pretending that he was going to kill the sage, he cut her in half instead. That task finished, he showed Takka-Pandita great respect, bathing him, dressing him in clean clothing, and for the next few days, feasting him royally.

"Now that you are free, where do you plan to go?" the robber asked the sage.

"The world has no pleasure for me. I will become an ascetic once more and return to my previous home in the forest."

"I, too, wish to become an ascetic," exclaimed the robber. "Let me come with you!" Thus, the two of them became ascetics and stayed together in the hermitage in the jungle, where they won higher knowledge and attained extraordinary powers. By their intensive practice of meditation on the Four Brahma Vihāras, they won themselves rebirth in the Brahma heavens.

Having concluded his story, the Buddha added, "Thus, Bhikkhu, you see that, sowing dissension and creating strife, women can be slanderers and ingrates. Walk the path of righteousness, and you will surely attain peace and bliss." Then the Buddha taught the Dhamma, and the discontented bhikkhu attained the first path. Finally, the Buddha identified the birth: "At that time, Ānanda was the robber chief, and I was Takka-Pandita."

31

Husband, Brother, Son
Ucchanga Jātaka

It was while staying at Jetavana that the Buddha told this story about a country woman.

One day, the bhikkhus were talking about a woman from a village in Kosala, who had saved three men from unjust punishment by the king. When the Buddha heard what they were discussing, he replied, "This is not the first time, bhikkhus, that this woman has saved these three from peril; she did the same in days gone by." Then he told this story of the past.

Long, long ago, when Brahmadatta was reigning in Bārānasi, a band of thieves raided a village near the capital. The villagers immediately set out to search for the gang, but they could find no trace of them. As they were returning, they saw three men plowing a field near the edge of the forest. "Here are the robbers disguised as farmers!" the villagers shouted. They seized the three men, bound them tightly with ropes, and dragged them to the king.

Not long afterwards, a woman came to the king's palace crying loudly, begging for something to be covered with. The king ordered that she be given a robe, but she refused it, telling the servants that was not what she meant.

She told them that she was referring to a husband. When the king heard this, he had the woman brought before him and asked her to explain her meaning.

"Sire," she answered; "a woman's real covering is her husband. She who loses her husband, even though she is dressed in beautiful silk, is still naked. She is like a kingdom without a king or a stream without water."

Intrigued, the king asked whether one of the three prisoners was, indeed, her husband.

"Yes, Sire. One is my husband, one is my brother, and one is my son."

"Well, Madam, I am impressed with your speech. To show my favor, I will give you one of the three. Which will you take?"

"Sire, why must I choose? Please give me all three."

"No," the king replied. "I have agreed to give you only one. You must choose. Shall I give you your husband?"

"No, Sire. In that case, please give me my brother."

"Your brother?" the king retorted, greatly surprised. "Surely, a brother is not so important to you as your husband or your son. Shouldn't you choose one of them?"

"Your Majesty," the woman replied calmly, "while I am alive, there are plenty of men who will have me, so I can get another husband. I am young enough to get another son easily, too. Since my parents are dead, however, I can never get another brother. Please give me my brother."

Thoroughly delighted with the woman's astute reasoning, the king ordered that all three men be set free.

Having concluded his story, the Buddha added, "Thus, you see, Bhikkhus, that this woman saved these same three men from danger in exactly the same way once before." Then he identified the birth: "At that time, the woman and the three men were the same, and I was the king of Kāsi."

32

A Log Pays a Better Return
Saccankira Jātaka

It was while staying at Veluvana that the Buddha told this story about Devadatta.

One day, the Buddha heard some bhikkhus talking about how Devadatta was ignorant of the Buddha's excellence and had even tried to kill him. "Bhikkhus," the Buddha said, "this is not the first time that Devadatta has tried to kill me. He did the same thing before." Then he told them this story of the past.

Long, long ago, when Brahmadatta was reigning in Bārānasi, he had a son named Duttha-Kumāra (Prince Duttha or Prince Wicked). This prince was as fierce and vicious as a beaten snake. He never spoke to anyone without abuse or blows. As welcome as grit in the eye, he was detested by everyone in the kingdom.

One day, Prince Duttha went with a large entourage to bathe in the river. Shortly after they reached the bank of the river, the sky turned dark with the approach of a great thunder storm. Expecting the prince to order them to return to the capital, the servants began repacking all the royal paraphernalia.

"Hurry up, you lazy scoundrels!" the prince shouted at them. "Why are you so slow! Take me to the middle of the river and bathe me."

After first whispering together, the servants carefully lifted the prince and carried him to the middle of the river. Instead of bathing him, however, they flung him headfirst into the deepest water, shouting, "Good riddance, brute! This is what you deserve!" Knowing that the prince was unable to swim, they watched as he was carried away by the swift current. "After all, what can the king do?" they chortled.

When the servants returned to the palace, the king asked where his son was. "Isn't he here, Your Majesty?" they asked. "We took him to the river to bathe, but a severe storm came up, and we were very busy protecting all the royal trappings we had taken with us. When we didn't see him, we assumed that he returned on his own, so we, also, came back."

The king immediately summoned soldiers and rushed to the riverbank in the driving rain. He ordered the men to search everywhere for his missing son, but they could find no trace of Prince Duttha. Heartbroken, the king returned to the palace.

The prince had, indeed, been carried away by the swift current, but he had not drowned. In the darkness, he happened to strike against a log. Clinging to it, he was able to stay afloat, but the current still bore him rapidly downstream.

Sometime earlier, a wealthy merchant in Bārānasi had died, leaving millions in gold buried on the bank of that river. Because of his attachment to his riches, he had been reborn as a snake at the very spot where his beloved treasure was hidden. Near that same place, another rich man had buried a fortune in gold coins. Because of his craving for his wealth, he was reborn as a rat near his gold. During the great storm, water rushed into the holes in the bank where these two animals lived, and they barely managed to escape with their lives. As they struggled to stay afloat in the flooded river, they came to the same tree trunk to which the prince was clinging. The snake crawled up on one end, and the rat clambered up on the other.

A little further downstream, the storm had uprooted a silk cotton tree which stood on the river bank. When the tree fell, a young parrot who lived in its branches was thrown into the swollen river. Although the bird tried to fly away, the heavy rain beat his wings, and he ended up on the log with the others. The four creatures, more afraid of drowning than of each other, floated downstream together on the log. As the water swirled around him, the prince yelled for help at the top of his lungs.

Further downstream, near a bend in the river, there lived a brahmin, who had renounced the world and become an ascetic. At midnight, as he was walking back and forth, he heard the prince's piteous cries. "Oh, dear," he said to himself, "it sounds like someone is in danger. Having sworn to be compassionate to all, I cannot allow this fellow creature to perish. I must rescue him."

As soon as the ascetic saw the log and the prince, he shouted reassuringly, "Don't be afraid! I'm coming!" He plunged into the water and grabbed the log by one end. Being as strong as an elephant, he pulled the trunk to the riverbank, lifted the prince out of the water, and set him on the ground.

Then the ascetic noticed the three animals who were also clinging to the log. He rescued the poor creatures and carried them to his hermitage, asking the prince to follow. He lit a fire and warmed the animals first, reasoning that they were weaker. When he was sure that the animals were out of danger, he looked after the prince. When all the new arrivals were warm and dry, the ascetic brought out various kinds of fruit, feeding the animals first, before taking care of the prince.

This infuriated Prince Duttha. "This cur of an ascetic pays no respect to my royal birth," he grumbled to himself. "He gives dumb beasts precedence over me!"

A few days later, when all four had recovered their strength and the water had receded, the animals bade farewell to the ascetic. The snake took his leave first. "Father," he said, "you have done me a great service. I am not poor. I have millions in gold hidden away. Should you ever need money, all my hoard will be yours. You have only to come to my place and call, 'Snake!'"

"Father," the rat said next as he took his leave, "you are welcome to my treasure should you ever have need of it. Come to my hole and simply call, 'Rat!'"

Then the parrot bade farewell, saying, "Father, I have no silver or gold, but should you ever want choice rice, come to where I dwell, and call out, 'Parrot!' My relatives and I will give you wagonloads of rice."

The three animals left the hermitage, each going his own way.

The prince observed all of this, but his heart was filled with rancor and ingratitude. He secretly resolved to put his benefactor to death if the ascetic should ever visit him. Disguising his evil intention, however, he said, "Father, come and see me when I am king, and I will give you the four requisites." Having said that, he returned to the palace and, not long afterwards, succeeded to the throne.

One day, the ascetic decided to put the declarations of the four to the test. First, he went to the snake's home and called, "Snake!" The snake immediately emerged from his hole, greeted the ascetic warmly, and said, "Father, buried right here, next to my hole, there are millions in gold. Please dig it up, and take it all."

"Thank you," said the ascetic. "That is fine for now. When I need it, I will not forget."

Next, he went to the rat's hole and called, "Rat!" The rat did exactly as the snake had done, and the ascetic answered in the same way.

When the ascetic called the parrot, the bird immediately flew down from the top of his tree and greeted the ascetic. "Father," he said, "shall my relatives gather paddy from all the regions around the Himavat?"

"Not yet," the ascetic answered, "but when the time comes, I will not forget your offer."

Thoroughly satisfied with these three responses, the ascetic proceeded to Bārānasi and stayed in the royal gardens. The next morning, he carefully arranged his garments and entered the city for alms. The king, who happened to be riding around the city on his royal elephant with a vast entourage, spotted the ascetic and immediately recognized him. "There's that churlish ascetic coming to sponge off me," he grumbled to himself. "I must get rid of him before he tells everyone how he saved my life!"

"Hey, you!" he called to his guards, "that ascetic who is coming to beg from me is a wicked scoundrel. Make sure he does not come near. Seize him, and tie him up. March him to the southern gate, beating him at every crossroads. At the execution ground, chop off his head, and impale his body on a stake."

The guards grabbed the ascetic, bound his arms securely behind his back, and led him through the streets, lashing him with whips at every corner. Despite the harsh flogging, the ascetic remained calm. Though he knew that the guards intended to execute him, he neither cursed them nor begged for mercy. As they led him along, he loudly repeated a single verse, over and over: "They know the world, who spoke this proverb true—'A log pays a better return than some men do.'"

The ascetic repeated his verse each time he was beaten, and, finally, some wise bystanders asked him what good turn he had done for their king. In reply, he related the whole story. "Thus, by rescuing him from drowning," he concluded, "I brought all this trouble upon myself. When I thought how I had ignored those wise words from the past, I couldn't help repeating them as you just heard."

Hearing the ascetic's explanation, not only the citizens but also the soldiers guarding him were outraged. Furious at the injustice, the crowd shouted, "Our king is an ungrateful wretch. The ascetic saved his life, and this is how he rewards him! Down with such a king! Seize the tyrant!" The angry mob rushed toward the procession and dragged the king from his royal elephant. Attacked from all sides, King Duttha died on the spot, and his battered corpse was thrown into a ditch.

Rejoicing to be rid of their ignoble king, the people offered the crown to the wise ascetic, who accepted graciously and ruled in righteousness.

One day, the new king decided once more to test the snake, the rat, and the parrot. Accompanied by a large retinue, he went to the riverbank and called the snake, who immediately came out of his hole, bowed deeply, and said, "Your Majesty, here is your treasure. Please take it."

The king ordered that all the gold be loaded onto carts and invited the snake to accompany him to the rat's hole. Hearing his name, the rat came out, saluted the king, and presented his fortune.

The king ordered that this gold, also, be loaded onto carts, and invited both animals to accompany him to the forest, where he called the parrot. The bird immediately appeared before the king, bowed down at his feet, and asked whether he and his relatives should collect rice for the king.

"Not yet," said the king, "We will not trouble you until rice is needed. Now," he said to the three animals, "let us return to the city."

Back in the palace, the king ordered a golden tube for the snake to live in, a crystal house for the rat, and a golden cage for the parrot. Every day, servants prepared special food, which they served in golden dishes to the three creatures—parched corn for the parrot and the snake and scented rice for the rat.

The king excelled in generosity and good deeds, and the four friends lived in harmony and good will. When their ends came, they passed away, each to fare according to his deserts.

Having concluded his story, the Buddha added, "Thus, you see, Bhikkhus, this is not the first time that Devadatta has tried to kill me." Then the Buddha identified the birth: "At that time, Devadatta was King Duttha; Sāriputta was the snake; Moggallāna was the rat; Ānanda was the parrot; and I was the righteous ascetic who won the kingdom."

33

The Sixteen Dreams
Mahā-Supina Jātaka

It was while staying at Jetavana that the Buddha told this story about sixteen great dreams.

One morning, when the ministers and brahmins went to the palace to pay their respects to King Pasenadi and to inquire whether His Majesty had slept well, they found him lying in terror, unable to move from his bed.

"How could I sleep well?" exclaimed the king. "Just before daybreak I dreamed sixteen dreadful dreams, and I have been lying here terrified ever since! Since you are my advisors, tell me what these dreams mean."

"What were your dreams, Sire?" the brahmins asked. "Surely we will be able to judge their importance."

As the king was telling them his dreams, the brahmins looked very worried, and began wringing their hands.

"Why are you wringing your hands, brahmins?" asked the king. "Is it because of my dreams?"

"Yes, Sire. These are evil dreams. They are full of peril."

"What will come of them?" asked the king.

"They portend one of three calamities, Sire—great harm to your kingdom, to your wealth, or to your life."

"Is there any remedy?"

"These dreams are powerful and extremely threatening. Still, we will find a remedy, otherwise, what is the use of our vast study and learning?"

"How do you propose to avert the evil?" asked the king.

"Wherever four roads meet, we will offer appropriate sacrifices, Sire."

"My advisors," cried the king, "my life is in your hands! Hurry, and do your best to save me!"

Each of the exultant brahmins had the same thought: "We are going to make a fortune from these dreams. Soon we will feast on the choicest viands."

As soon as they had left the king's presence, they began scurrying about, happily giving orders in every direction. They ordered laborers to dig huge sacrificial pits. They demanded herds of various four-footed creatures, all without blemish. They called for baskets of pure white birds of many kinds. Again and again, they discovered something or other lacking. Messengers raced back and forth to inform the king of each new request.

Noticing all the commotion, Queen Mallikā went to the king and asked why the brahmins and their servants kept coming to him.

"I envy you," said the king sarcastically. "A snake in your ear, and you don't even know it!"

"What does Your Majesty mean?" asked the queen.

"I have dreamed such unlucky dreams! The brahmins tell me they point to disaster. They keep coming here because they are anxious to protect me from the evil by offering sacrifices."

"Has Your Majesty consulted the Chief Brahmin of all the worlds about this?" asked the queen.

"Who do you mean, my dear?" asked the king.

"Of course, I mean Lord Buddha. He will surely understand your dreams. Go to Jetavana, and ask him."

"A good idea, my dear," answered the king. "I will go at once."

When the king reached the monastery, he paid his respects to the Buddha and sat down.

"What brings you here so early in the morning?" asked the Buddha.

"Just before daybreak, Venerable Sir, I dreamed sixteen terrifying dreams. My brahmins have warned me that my dreams foretell calamity. To avert the evil, they are preparing to sacrifice many animals wherever four roads meet. Queen Mallikā suggested that I ask you to tell me what these dreams really mean and what will come of them."

"It is true, Sire, that I alone can explain the significance of your dreams and tell you what will come of them. Tell me your dreams as they appeared to you."

"I will, Blessed One," answered the king, and he began relating his dreams.

"In the first dream, I saw four jet-black bulls," the king began. "They came together from the four cardinal directions to the royal courtyard with every intention to fight. A great crowd of people gathered to see the bullfight. The bulls, however, only made a show of fighting, pawing and bellowing. Finally, they went off, without fighting at all. This was my first dream. What will come of it?"

"Sire, that dream will have no result in your lifetime or mine. But, in the distant future, when kings are stingy, when citizens are unrighteous, when the world is perverted, and when good is waning and evil waxing, in those days of the world's decline, no rain will fall from the heavens, the monsoons will forget their season, the crops will wither, and famine will stalk the land. At that time, immense clouds will gather from the four quarters of the heavens as if for rain. Farmers will rush to bring in the rice they had spread to dry in the sun. Men will take their spades and hurry to repair the dikes. The thunder will roar, and the lightning will flash from the clouds. However, just as the bulls in your dream didn't fight, these clouds will retreat without giving any rain. This is what shall come of this dream. But no harm shall come to you from this dream because it applies only to the remote future. The brahmins only said what they said to get some profit for themselves. Now tell me your second dream, Sire."

"My second dream was about tiny trees and shrubs which burst through the soil. When they were scarcely more than a few inches high, they flowered and bore fruit. This was my second dream. What will come of it?"

"Sire," said the Buddha, "this dream will be realized in future days when the world has fallen into decay and when human lives are short. Passions then will be so strong that even very young girls will cohabitate with men. Despite their immaturity, they will get pregnant and have children. The flowers and fruit symbolize their babies. However, you have nothing to fear from this. Tell me your third dream."

"I saw cows sucking milk from their very own new-born calves. This was my third dream. What can it possibly mean?"

"This dream will come about only when age is no longer respected. In that future time, young people will have no regard for their parents or parents-in-law. Children will handle the family estate themselves. If it pleases them, they will give food and clothing to the old folks, but, if it doesn't suit them, they will withhold their gifts. Thus, the old people, destitute and dependent, will survive only by the favor and whim of their own children, like big cows suckled by day-old calves. However, you have nothing to fear from this. Tell me your fourth dream."

"Men unyoked a team of strong, sturdy oxen, and replaced them with young steers, too weak to draw the load. Those young steers refused to pull. They stood stock-still, so that the wagons didn't move at all. This was my fourth dream. What shall come of it?"

"Here again, the dream will not come to pass until the future, in the days of wicked kings. In days to come, unjust and parsimonious kings will show no honor to wise leaders, skilled in diplomacy. They will not appoint experienced, learned judges to the courts. On the contrary, they will honor the very young and foolish and will appoint the most inexperienced and unprincipled to the courts. Naturally, these appointees, because of their ignorance of statecraft and the law, will not be able to bear the burden of their responsibilities. Because of their incompetence, they will have to throw off the yoke of public office. When that happens, the aged and wise lords will remember being passed over, and, even though they are able to cope with all difficulties, they will refuse to help, saying: 'It is no business of ours since we have become outsiders.' They will remain aloof, and the government will fall to ruins, the same as if young steers, not strong enough for the burden, were yoked instead of the team of sturdy oxen. However, you have nothing to fear from this. Tell me your fifth dream."

"I saw an incredible horse with a mouth on each side of its head being fed fodder on both sides. That dreadful horse ate voraciously with both its mouths. This was my fifth dream. What shall come of it?"

"This dream will also come true only in the future, in the days of unrighteous and irresponsible kings, who will appoint covetous men to be judges. These despicable magistrates, blind to virtue and honesty, will take bribes from both sides as they sit in the seat of judgment. They will be doubly corrupt, just like the horse that ate fodder with two mouths at once. However, you have nothing to fear from this. Tell me your sixth dream."

"I saw people holding out a brightly burnished golden bowl which must have been worth a fortune. They were actually begging a mangy old jackal to urinate in it. Then I saw the repulsive beast do just that. This was my sixth dream. What can it mean?"

"This dream, too, will come true only in the remote future, when immoral kings, although from a royal line themselves, will mistrust the sons of their old nobility, preferring instead the lowest-born of the country. Because of the kings' blindness, nobles will decline, and the low-born will rise in rank. Naturally, the great families will be humbled and forced to live dependent upon the parvenu. They will be reduced to offering their well-bred daughters to them in marriage. The union of the noble maidens with the ignoble, nouveau-riche will be like the urinating of the old jackal into the golden bowl. However, you have nothing to fear from this. Tell me your seventh dream."

"I saw a man braiding rope. As he worked, he dropped the finished rope at his feet. Under his bench, unbeknownst to him, lay a hungry jackal bitch, which kept eating the rope as fast as he braided it. This was my seventh dream. What shall come of it?"

"This dream, also, will come true only in far off days. At that time women will crave men, strong drink, extravagant clothes, jewelry, and entertainment. In their profligacy, they will get drunk with their lovers and carry on shamelessly. They will neglect their homes and families. They will pawn household valuables, selling everything for drink and amusements, even the seed needed for the next crop. Just as the hungry jackal under the bench ate the rope of the rope-maker, so these women will squander the savings earned by their husbands' labor. However, you have nothing to fear from this. Tell me your eighth dream.

"At a palace gate, there stood a big pitcher full to the brim. Around it, stood many empty pitchers. From all directions, there came a steady stream of people, carrying pots of water, which they poured into the already full pitcher. The water from that full pitcher kept overflowing and soaking wastefully into the sand. Still the people came and poured more and more water into the overflowing vessel. Not a single person even glanced at the empty pitchers. This was my eighth dream. What shall come of it?"

"This dream, too, will not come to pass until the future when the world is in decline. The kingdom will grow weak, and its kings will be poorer and more demanding. These kings, in their poverty and selfishness, will make the whole country work exclusively for them. They will force citizens to neglect their own work and to labor only for the throne. For the kings' sake, they will plant sugar cane, make sugar mills, and boil down molasses. For the kings' sake, they will plant flower gardens and orchards and gather fruit. They will harvest all the crops and fill the royal storerooms and warehouses to overflowing, but they will be unable even to glance at their own empty barns at home. It will be like filling and overfilling the full pitcher, heedless of the needy, empty ones. However, you have nothing to fear from this. Tell me your ninth dream."

"I saw a deep pool with sloping banks, overgrown with lotuses. From all directions, a wide variety of animals came to drink water from that pool. Strangely, the deep water in the middle was terribly muddy, but the water at the edges, where all those thirsty creatures had descended into the pool, was unaccountably clear and sparkling. This was my ninth dream. What does it mean?"

"This dream, too, will not come to pass until the future, when kings grow increasingly corrupt. Ruling according to their own whim and pleasure, they will never make judgments according to what is right. Being greedy, they will grow fat on lucrative bribes. Never showing mercy or compassion to their subjects, they will be fierce and cruel. These kings will amass wealth by crushing their subjects like stalks of sugar cane in a mill and by taxing them to the last cent. Unable to pay the oppressive taxes, the citizens will abandon their villages, towns, and cities, and will flee like refugees to the borders. The heart of the country will be a wilderness, while the remote areas along the borders will teem with people. The country will be just like the pool, muddy in the middle and clear at the edges. However, you have nothing to fear from this. Tell me your tenth dream."

"I saw a pot of rice on a fire, but the rice was not cooking normally. The rice seemed to be separated into three sections, which were sharply delineated. One part of the rice was sodden, another part was hard and raw, but the third part was perfectly cooked. This was my tenth dream. What will come of it?"

"This dream, too, will not be fulfilled until the future. In days to come, kings will become unrighteous; the nobles will follow the king's example, and so will the brahmins. The townsmen, the merchants, and, at last, even the farmers will be corrupted. Eventually, everyone in the country, the sages and even the devas of the land, will become immoral. Even the winds that blow over the realm of such an unrighteous king will grow cruel and lawless. Because even the skies and the devas of the skies over that land will be disturbed, they will cause a drought. Rain will never fall on the whole kingdom at once. It may rain in the upper districts, but in the lower it will not. In one place a heavy downpour will damage the crops, while, in another area, the crops will wither from drought. The crops sown within a single kingdom, like the rice in the one pot, shall have no uniform character. However, you have nothing to fear from this. Tell me your eleventh dream."

"I saw rancid buttermilk being bartered for precious sandalwood, worth a fortune in gold. This was my eleventh dream. What shall come of it?"

"This will happen only in the distant future, when my teaching is waning. In those days, there will be many greedy, shameless bhikkhus, who for the sake of their bellies dare to preach the very words in which I have warned against greed! Because they desert the Dhamma to gratify their stomachs, and because they side with sectarians, their preaching will not lead to Nibbāna. Their only thought as they preach will be to use fine words and sweet voices to induce lay believers to give them costly robes, delicate food, and every comfort. Others will seat themselves beside the highways, at busy street corners, or at the doors of kings' palaces, where they will stoop to preach for money, even for a pittance! Thus, these bhikkhus will barter away for food, for robes, or for coins, my teaching which leads to liberation from suffering! They will be like those who exchanged precious sandalwood worth a fortune in pure gold for rancid buttermilk. However, you have nothing to fear from this. Tell me your twelfth dream.

"I saw empty gourds sinking in the water. What shall come of it?"

"This dream, also, will not have its fulfillment until the future, in the days of unjust kings, when the world is perverted. In those days, kings will favor the low-born, not the sons of nobility. The low-born will become great lords, while the nobles will sink into poverty. In the king's court and in the courts of justice, the words of only the low-born, who are the empty gourds, will be recognized, as though they have sunk to the bottom and become firmly established. In the assemblies of bhikkhus, it will be the same. Whenever there are enquiries about proper behavior, rules of conduct, or discipline, only the counsel of wicked, corrupt bhikkhus will be considered. The advice of modest bhikkhus will be ignored. It will be as though empty gourds sink. However, you have nothing to fear from this. Tell me your thirteenth dream."

Then the king said, "I saw huge blocks of solid rock, as big as houses, floating like empty gourds upon the waters. What shall come of it?"

"This dream, also, will not come to pass until those times of which I have spoken. At that time, unrighteous kings will show honor to the low-born, who will be come great lords, while the true nobles will fade into obscurity. The nobles will receive no respect, while the ignorant upstarts will be granted all honors. In the king's court and in the law courts, the words of the nobles, learned in the law, will drift idly by like those solid rocks. They will not penetrate deep into the hearts of men. When the wise speak, the ignorant will merely laugh them to scorn, saying, 'What is it these fellows are saying?' In the assemblies of bhikkhus, as well, people will not respect the excellent bhikkhus. Their words will not sink deep, but will drift idly by. However, you have nothing to fear from this. Tell me your fourteenth dream."

"I saw tiny frogs, no bigger than miniature flowerets, swiftly pursuing huge black snakes and devouring them. What can this mean?"

"This dream, too, will not have its fulfillment until those future days of which I have already spoken, when the world is declining. At that time, men's passions will be so strong that husbands will be thoroughly infatuated with their childish wives. Men will lose all judgment and self-respect. Being completely smitten, they will place their infantile wives in charge of everything in the house—servants, livestock, granaries, gold, and silver.

Should the overfond husband presume to ask for money or a favorite robe, he will be told to mind his own business and not to be so inquisitive about property in her house. These abusive young wives will exercise their power over their husbands as if the men were slaves. It will be as though tiny frogs gobble up big black snakes. However, you have nothing to fear from this. Tell me your fifteenth dream."

"I saw a village crow, a vile creature with all the ten vices[1] attended by an entourage of mandarin ducks, beautiful birds with feathers of golden sheen. What shall come of it?"

"This dream, too, will not come to pass until the far distant future, in the reign of weak kings. These kings will know nothing about ruling. They will be cowards and fools. Fearing revolt and revolution, they will elevate their footmen, bath-attendants, and barbers to nobility. These kings will ignore the real nobility. Cut off from royal favor and unable to support themselves, the true nobles will be reduced to dancing attendance on the upstarts, as when the crow had regal mandarin ducks for his retinue. However, you have nothing to fear from this. Tell me your sixteenth dream."

"I saw goats chasing wolves and eating them. At the sight of goats in the distance, the terror-stricken wolves fled and hid in thickets. Such was my dream. What will come of it?"

"This dream, too, will not have its fulfillment until the reign of immoral kings. The low-born will be raised to important posts and will become royal favorites. True nobles will sink into obscurity and distress. Gaining power in the law courts because of the king's favors, the parvenu will claim the ancestral estates of the impoverished old nobility, demanding their titles and all their property. When the real nobles plead their rights in court, the king's minions will have them beaten and tortured, then taken by the throat and thrown out with words of scorn. 'That will teach you to know your place, fools!' they will shout. 'How dare you dispute with us? The king shall hear of your insolence, and we will have your hands and feet chopped off!' At this, the terrified nobles will agree that black is white and that their own estates belong to the lowly upstarts. They will then hurry home and cower in an agony of fear. Likewise, at that time, evil bhikkhus will harass worthy bhikkhus so much that the worthy ones will flee from the monasteries to the jungle. This oppression of true nobles by the low-born and of good bhikkhus by evil bhikkhus will be like the intimidation of wolves by goats. However, you have nothing to fear from this. This dream refers to the future only.

---

1   The crow is (1) destructive, (2) reckless, (3) greedy, (4) gluttonous, (5) rough, (6) merciless, (7) weak, (8) noisy, (9) forgetful, and (10) wasteful.

"It was neither truth nor love for you that prompted the brahmins to prophesy as they did. It was pure greed and selfishness which led them to prescribe sacrifices."

Having completely explained the meaning of the sixteen dreams, the Buddha added, "Nor are you the first to have had these dreams. Long ago, also, they were dreamed by a king. Then, as now, brahmins found in them a pretext for sacrifices." At the king's request, the Buddha told this story of the past.

Long, long ago, when Brahmadatta was reigning in Bārānasi, the Bodhisatta was born into a brahmin family in the northern part of the kingdom. When he grew up, he renounced the world. As an ascetic, he attained a high level of meditation and acquired extraordinary powers.

One day, King Brahmadatta dreamed sixteen mysterious dreams and asked his advisors about them. The brahmins explained that the dreams foretold evil and began preparing great sacrifices.

Seeing this, one of the students of the chief brahmin, a young man of considerable learning and wisdom, approached his teacher and said, "Master, you have taught me the three Vedas. Don't the texts say that it is never a good thing to take life?"

"My dear boy," answered the teacher, "this means money to us—a great deal of money. Why are you anxious to spare the king's treasury?"

"Do as you will, Master," replied the young man. "I will no longer stay here with you." With those words, he left the palace and went to the royal gardens.

That same morning, the ascetic thought, "If I visit the king's garden today, I will save a great number of creatures from death."

The young brahmin found the ascetic, as radiant as a golden image, sitting on the king's ceremonial stone seat in the garden. He sat down in an appropriate place, paid his respects to the ascetic, and entered into pleasant conversation with him. The ascetic asked the young man whether the king ruled righteously.

"Venerable Sir," he answered, "the king himself is righteous, but the brahmins are leading him astray. The king consulted with them about sixteen dreams he had, and the brahmins jumped at the opportunity for sacrifices. How good it would be, Venerable Sir, for you to explain to the king the real meaning of his dreams! Your explanation will save many animals from cruel death!"

"I do not know the king, nor does he know me. If he comes here and asks me, however, I will tell him."

"Please wait here, Venerable Sir. I will bring the king." The young brahmin hurried to the king and told him there was a wondrous ascetic who would interpret the dreams. He asked the king to visit the ascetic and to talk with him.

The king immediately agreed and went to the garden with his retinue. Paying his respects to the ascetic, he sat down and asked whether the ascetic could tell him what would come of his dreams.

"Certainly, Sire," he answered. "Let me hear the dreams as you dreamed them."

The king proceeded to tell the dreams exactly as King Pasenadi told them to the Buddha, and the ascetic interpreted them in the same way.

"Enough!" concluded the ascetic. "You have nothing to fear from any of these dreams."

Having reassured the king and having freed a great number of creatures from death, the ascetic, poised in mid-air, established the king in the five precepts. "From this time on, Sire," he admonished the king, "do not join the brahmins in slaughtering animals for sacrifice!"

Remaining firm in the teaching he had heard and spending the rest of his days in alms-giving and other good deeds, the king passed away to fare according to his deserts.

Having concluded his story, the Buddha added, "Sire, you, too, have nothing to fear from these dreams. Stop the sacrifice!" Then the Buddha identified the birth: "At that time, Ānanda was the king, Sāriputta was the young brahmin, and I was the ascetic."

34
The Miserly Treasurer
Illīsa Jātaka

It was while staying at Jetavana that the Buddha told this story about Kosiya, a tremendously rich royal treasurer, who lived in a town called Sakkara near the city of Rājagaha. Because he was so tightfisted that he couldn't bear to give away even the tiniest drop of oil which you could pick up with a blade of grass, he was called Maccharikosiya, Kosiya the Miser. Perhaps as bad as his stinginess was the fact that he wouldn't even use that minuscule amount for his own satisfaction. His vast wealth was actually of no use to him or to his family, let alone to deserving or needy people.

One day, as Maccharikosiya was returning home, he saw a half-starved farmhand eating a small round cake filled with rice gruel, and the mere sight aroused a fierce craving. Maccharikosiya wanted very much to have a cake like that, but he was so afraid of what to his mind was the ruinous expense of having to share the cakes with someone else that he dared not mention his craving to anyone. He endured his suffering as long as he could, but, finally, after closing all the doors and windows of the house, he told his wife about it in a very soft whisper. He instructed her to collect all the ingredients and utensils and to take them to the top floor of the house. There she was to cook cakes for him to eat, alone and undisturbed.

The next morning, when the Buddha surveyed the world from his Perfumed Chamber in Jetavana, he became aware that Maccharikosiya and his wife were ripe for conversion.

The Buddha summoned Venerable Moggallāna and said, "In Sakkara, forty-five yojanas from here, Maccharikosiya and his wife are on the seventh floor of their house. She is cooking cakes for him, and he is, at this moment, getting ready to eat them all alone. Go there, teach him, and use your power to transport both him and his wife, along with the cakes, here to Jetavana. I will be waiting here with five hundred bhikkhus, and those cakes will suffice for our meal."

Because of his extraordinary power, a moment later, Venerable Moggallāna was standing in mid-air outside Maccharikosiya's seventh-floor window. The unexpected sight of the bhikkhu with his almsbowl infuriated the miser. "I climbed all the way up here to escape such unwelcome visitors," he thought, "and now there's one at the window!"

He shouted, "What do you think you're going to get, standing there in mid-air? You can walk up and down until you've worn a path in the air, but you will still get nothing at all!"

Venerable Moggallāna began to walk back and forth.

That provoked Maccharikosiya to greater anger. "You can sit cross-legged in meditation in the air," he shouted, "but you will still get nothing at all!"

Venerable Moggallāna crossed his legs and began meditating.

Maccharikosiya's face became red. "You can stand on the window sill," he fumed, "but you will still get nothing at all!"

Venerable Moggallāna stepped onto the window sill.

Maccharikosiya's blood began to boil. "You can belch smoke, for all I care," he shrieked, "but you will still get nothing at all!"

Venerable Moggallāna belched smoke which filled the entire room, and the miser's eyes began to burn. The miser was about to dare the visitor to burst into flames, but he caught himself, realizing that that might burn down his house.

"This bhikkhu is certainly persistent!" he thought. "He won't go away empty-handed! I'll have to give him one little cake to make him leave me alone."

He cupped his hand in front of his mouth and whispered, "Wife, cook one tiny cake and give it to that bhikkhu to get rid of him."

His wife obediently measured a small amount of the ingredients and began stirring. For no apparent reason, the dough began to swell and soon formed a large ball which filled the crock.

"You've made too much dough!" the miser complained. "Let me do it!" He grabbed the spoon from her hand and scooped up a tiny bit of the dough, which immediately swelled into an enormous cake.

Completely frustrated, he told his wife to give the bhikkhu one of the cakes that was already cooked. She reached into the basket and took one of the cakes, but all the other cakes stuck to it. She tried to put the other cakes back in the basket, but, try as they might, neither she nor her husband could separate them.

While Maccharikosiya was struggling, all his craving for the cakes died. "I don't want these cakes anymore," he declared to his wife. "Give the whole basket of them to this bhikkhu."

As soon as Venerable Moggallāna saw that the miser's mind had softened, he began to speak. He proclaimed the excellence of the Triple Gem, encouraged the couple in generosity, and taught the Dhamma.

Convinced, Maccharikosiya invited Venerable Moggallāna to enter and to receive the cakes properly.

"Kosiya," Venerable Moggallāna replied, "the Omniscient Buddha is waiting in a monastery with five hundred bhikkhus for a meal of cakes. Please gather all of these delicacies, bring your wife, and come with me. We will go together to the Master."

"Where is the Buddha waiting?" Kosiya asked.

"In Jetavana, which is in Sāvatthī."

"But, Venerable Sir," Kosiya objected, "that is forty-five yojanas from here! How can we go there?"

"If you wish, I will transport you there by my power. It will take no longer than going downstairs," Venerable Moggallāna replied.

Venerable Moggallāna moved the bottom of the staircase to the gate of Jetavana, and they arrived at exactly the proper time for the meal.

The treasurer poured the Water of Donation, and his wife began serving cakes. By the power of the Buddha, the cakes multiplied, and she was able to offer one to the Blessed One and to each of the five hundred bhikkhus. From a never-ending supply, Kosiya was able to serve them milk, ghee, honey, and jaggery, as well.

After the bhikkhus had finished, there were still ample cakes and condiments for Kosiya, his wife, and all the temple boys to eat their fill. Astonished that there were still as many cakes as they had brought, they asked the Buddha what they should do with the leftovers. He instructed them to throw them away. Accordingly, they cast them into a cave near Jetavana, and that cave is still called The Cave of the Crock, after the pot which held the cake dough.

The Buddha offered anumodana, and, as he finished, both Kosiya and his wife attained the first path.

The couple paid their respects to the Buddha and stepped onto the staircase at the gate of Jetavana. Immediately, they found themselves back in their own home.

That evening, while the bhikkhus were sitting together in the Hall of Truth, one said, "How great is the power of Moggallāna! In a moment, he converted the miser to generosity, brought him and his wife to Jetavana, and made it possible for them to attain the first path."

"How remarkable, indeed, is Moggallāna!" the others agreed.

The Buddha entered and asked what they were discussing.

They told him, and the Buddha replied, "A bhikkhu who visits a household should approach without causing disturbance, in the same way that a bee takes nectar from the flower without harming its scent or its hue. Bhikkhus, this is not the first time that Moggallāna has converted this miserly treasurer. Long ago, too, he taught the miser how deeds and their effects are linked together." Then the Buddha told this story of the past.

Long, long ago, when Brahmadatta was reigning in Bārānasi, there was a treasurer named Illīsa, who was worth eighty crores. This man had all the defects possible in a person. He was lame and hunch-backed, and he had a squint. He was a confirmed miser, never giving away any of his fortune to others, yet never enjoying it himself.

Interestingly enough, however, for seven generations back, his ancestors had been bountiful, giving freely of their best. When this treasurer inherited the family riches, he broke that tradition and began hoarding his wealth.

One day, as he was returning from an audience with the king, he saw a weary peasant sitting on a bench and drinking a mug of cheap liquor with great gusto. The sight made the treasurer thirsty for a drink of liquor himself, but he thought, "If I drink, others will want to drink with me. That would mean a ruinous expense!" The more he tried to suppress his thirst, the stronger the craving grew.

The effort to overcome his thirst made him as yellow as old cotton. He became thinner and thinner, and the veins stood out on his emaciated frame. After a few days, still unable to forget about the liquor, he went into his room and lay down, hugging his bed. His wife came in, rubbed his back, and asked, "Husband, what is wrong?"

"Nothing," he said.

"Perhaps the king is angry with you," she suggested.

"No, he is not."

"Have your children or servants done anything to annoy you?" she queried.

"Not at all."

"Well, then, do you have a craving for something?"

Because of his preposterous fear that he might waste his fortune, he still would not say a word.

"Speak, husband," she pleaded. "Tell me what you have a craving for."

"Well," he said slowly, "I do have a craving for one thing."

"What is that, my husband?"

"I want a drink of liquor," he whispered.

"Why didn't you say so before?" she exclaimed with relief. "I'll brew enough liquor to serve the whole town."

"No!" he cried. "Don't bother about other people. Let them earn their own drink!"

"Well then, I'll make just enough for our street."

"How rich you are!"

"Then, just for our household."

"How extravagant!"

"All right, only us and our children."

"Why fuss about them?"

"Very well, let it be just enough for the two of us."

"Do you need any?"

"Of course not. I'll brew a little liquor only for you."

"Wait! If you brew any liquor in the house, many people will see you. In fact, it's out of the question to drink any here at all." Producing one single penny, he sent a slave to buy a jar of liquor from the tavern.

When the slave returned, Illīsa ordered him to carry the liquor out of town to a remote thicket near the river. "Now leave me alone!" Illīsa commanded. After the slave had walked some distance away, the treasurer crawled into the thicket, filled his cup, and began drinking.

At that moment, the treasurer's own father, who had been reborn as Sakka, happened to be wondering whether the tradition of generosity was still kept up in his house and became aware of his son's outrageous behavior. He realized that his son had not only broken with the customary magnanimity of his family but that he had also burned down the alms-halls and beaten the poor to drive them away from his gate. Sakka saw that his son, unwilling to share even a drop of cheap liquor with anyone else, was sitting in a thicket drinking by himself.

"I must make my son see that deeds always have their consequences!" Sakka exclaimed. "I will make him charitable and worthy of rebirth in Tāvatimsa."

Instantly, Sakka disguised himself as his son, complete with his limp, hunch-back, and squint, and entered the city of Bārānasi. He went directly to the palace gate and asked to be announced to the king.

"Let him approach," said the king.

Sakka entered the king's chamber and paid his respects.

"What brings you here at this unusual hour, my Lord High Treasurer?" asked the king.

"I have come, Sire, because I would like to add my eighty crores of wealth to your royal treasury."

"No!" answered the king. "I have ample treasure. I have no need of yours."

"Sire, if you will not take it, I will give it all away to others."

"By all means, treasurer, do as you wish."

"So be it, Sire," Sakka said. Bowing again to the king, he went to Illīsa's house. None of the servants could tell that he was not their real master. He sent for the porter and ordered, "If anybody resembling me should appear and claim to be master of this house, that person should be severely beaten and thrown out." He went upstairs, sat down on a brocaded couch, and sent for Illīsa's wife. When she arrived, he smiled and said, "My dear, let us be bountiful."

When his wife heard this, she thought, "I've never seen him in this frame of mind. He must have drunk a lot to have become so good-natured and generous!" Aloud she said, "Be as charitable as you please, my husband."

"Send for the town crier," Sakka ordered. "I want him to announce to all the citizens of the city that anybody who wants gold, silver, diamonds, pearls, or other gems should come to the house of Illīsa the Treasurer."

His wife obeyed him, and a large crowd of people carrying baskets and sacks soon gathered. Sakka instructed the servants to open the doors to the store rooms and announced to the people, "These are my gifts to you! Take what you like! Good luck to you!"

Townspeople filled their bags and carried away all the treasure they could manage. One farmer yoked two of Illīsa's oxen to a beautiful cart, filled it with valuable things, and drove out of the city. As he rode along, humming a tune in praise of the treasurer, he happened to pass near the thicket where Illīsa was hiding. "May you live to be one hundred, my good lord Illīsa!" sang the farmer. "What you have done for me this day will enable me to live without ever toiling again. Who owned these oxen? You did! Who gave me this cart? You did! Who gave me the wealth in the cart? Again it was you! Neither my father nor my mother gave me any of this. No, it came solely from you, my lord."

These words chilled the treasurer to the bone. "Why is this fellow mentioning my name?" he wondered. "Has the king been giving away my wealth?" He peeped out of the thicket and immediately recognized his own cart and oxen.

Scrambling out of the bushes as fast as he could, he grabbed the oxen by their nose rings and cried, "Stop! These oxen belong to me!"

The farmer leaped from the cart and began beating the interloper. "You rascal!" he shouted. "This is none of your business. Illīsa the Treasurer is giving his wealth away to all the city." He knocked the treasurer down, climbed back on the cart, and started to drive away.

Shaking with anger, Illīsa picked himself up, hurried after the cart, and seized hold of the oxen again. Once more, the farmer jumped down, grabbed Illīsa by the hair, and beat him severely. Then he got back on the cart and rumbled off.

Thoroughly sobered up by this rough handling, Illīsa hurried home. When he arrived, he saw the people carrying away his treasure. "What are you doing?" he shouted. "How dare you do this?" He seized first one man and then another, but every man he grabbed knocked him down.

Bruised and bleeding, he tried to go into his own house, claiming that he was Illīsa, but the porters stopped him. "You villain!" they cried. "Where do you think you are going?" Following orders, they beat him with bamboo staves, took him by the neck, and threw him down the steps.

"Only the king can help me now," groaned Illīsa, and he dragged himself to the palace.

"Sire!" he cried. "Why, oh why, have you plundered me like this?"

"I haven't plundered you, sir," said the king. "You yourself first offered me your wealth. Then you yourself offered your property to the citizens of the town."

"Sire, I never did such a thing! Your Majesty knows how careful I am about money. You know I would never give away so much as the tiniest drop of oil. May it please Your Majesty to send for the person who has squandered my riches. Please interrogate him about this matter."

The king ordered his guards to bring Illīsa, and they returned with Sakka. The two treasurers were so much alike that neither the king nor anyone else in the court could tell which was the real treasurer. "Sire!" pleaded Illīsa. "I am the treasurer! This is an imposter!"

"My dear sir," replied the king. "I really can't say which of you is the real Illīsa. Is there anybody who can distinguish for certain between the two of you?"

"Yes, Sire," answered Illīsa, "my wife can."

The king sent for Illīsa's wife and asked her which of the two was her husband. She smiled at Sakka and went to stand beside him. When Illīsa's children and servants were brought and asked the same question, they all answered that Sakka was the real treasurer.

Suddenly, Illīsa remembered that he had a wart on the top of his head, hidden under his hair, known only to his barber. As a last resort, he asked that his barber be called. The barber came and was asked if he could distinguish the real Illīsa from the false.

"Of course, I can tell, Sire," he said, "if I may examine their heads."

"By all means, look at both their heads," ordered the king.

The barber examined Illīsa's head and found the wart. As he started to examine Sakka's head, the king of the devas quickly caused a wart to appear on his own head, and the barber exclaimed, "Your Majesty, both squint, both limp, and both are hunchbacks, too! Both have warts in exactly the same place on their heads! Even I cannot tell which is the real Illīsa!"

When Illīsa heard this, he realized that his last hope was gone, and he began to quake at the loss of his beloved riches. Overpowered by his emotions, he collapsed senseless on the floor.

At this, Sakka resumed his divine form and rose into the air. "Your Majesty, I am not Illīsa," he announced. "I am Sakka!"

The king's courtiers quickly splashed water on Illīsa's face to revive him. As soon as he had recovered his wits, the treasurer staggered to his feet and bowed before Sakka.

"Illīsa!" Sakka shouted. "That wealth was mine, not yours. I was your father. In my lifetime, I was bountiful towards the poor and rejoiced in doing good. Because of my generosity, I was reborn in this great grandeur. But you, foolish man, are not walking in my footsteps. You have become a terrible miser. In order to hoard my riches, you burned my alms-halls to the ground and drove away the poor. You are getting no enjoyment from your wealth; nor is it benefiting any other human being. Your treasury is like a pool haunted by yakkhas, from which no one may satisfy his thirst.

"If you rebuild my alms-halls, however, and show generosity to the poor, you will gain great merit. If you do not, I will take away everything you have, and I will split your head with my thunderbolt."

When Illīsa heard this threat, he shook with fear and cried out, "From now on I will be bountiful! I swear it!"

Accepting this promise, Sakka established his son in the precepts, preached the Law to him, and returned to Tāvatimsa.

True to his word, Illīsa became diligent in generosity and performed many good deeds. He even attained rebirth in heaven.

Having concluded his story, the Buddha added, "Thus, you see, Bhikkhus, that this is not the first time that Moggallāna has converted this miserly treasurer. Then the Buddha identified the birth: "At that time, the treasurer was Illīsa; Moggallāna was Sakka; Ānanda was the king; and I was the barber."

35

The Would-Be Soldier
Bhīmasena Jātaka

It was while staying at Jetavana that the Buddha told this story about a boastful bhikkhu.[1]

This bhikkhu was constantly bragging about his aristocratic family. "Friends," he said almost every day, "there is no family nobler than mine. I am descended from a long line of princes. My family has vast estates, and our treasuries are full of gold and silver. Even our manual laborers and servants eat fragrant rice with the most delicious meat curries and wear garments made of Bārānasi silk. Of course, now that I have left the home life, I have to be satisfied with coarse food and rough robes, but what splendor I used to enjoy!"

The other bhikkhus got tired of hearing this, and one of them took it upon himself to find out whether or not there was any truth to these claims. He checked on the family background of the boastful bhikkhu and discovered that none of it was true. He exposed the fraud to the whole community, which put an end to the bragging.

---

1   The occasion for this story is the same as that for Tale 49.

Later, the bhikkhus were sitting in the Hall of Truth and talking about how that bhikkhu, despite having left home and entered the Order, had gone about trying to deceive everyone with lies and boasts. When the Buddha heard what they were discussing, he said, "This is not the first time, Bhikkhus, that that man has acted in that way. Long ago, also, he pretended to have great prowess, and it almost cost him his life." Then the Buddha told this story of the past.

Long, long ago, when Brahmadatta was reigning in Bārānasi, the Bodhisatta was born as a dwarf in a town in the northern part of the kingdom. When he was old enough, he studied under an excellent teacher at Takkasilā and mastered all his subjects. He was particularly skillful in archery and became famous as Culla-Dhanuggaha (Little Archer). Leaving Takkasilā, he went to the south in search of a position.

Because of his small stature, Culla-Dhanuggaha knew that it would be difficult to make anyone take him seriously. "Surely, if I present myself before a king," he thought, "he will look at me and laugh, supposing that a dwarf like me would not be of use as an archer. I should find some tall, broad-shouldered fellow to be my front. I could easily earn a living in the shadow of such a man."

One day, as he was scouting in the weavers' quarter, he saw a very large man sitting at a loom. He approached the shop and called out, "Hello, my friend. May I ask your name?"

"It is Bhīmasena," the weaver answered. "Who are you?"

"People call me Culla-Dhanuggaha. May I also ask why a fine fellow like you is working at such a miserable trade as this?"

"My friend, I have no other skills. This is the only way I can make a living."

"Weave no more, my friend. In all of Jambudīpa, there is no finer archer than I, but kings would scorn me because I am a dwarf. I am in need of someone with an imposing figure. I propose, my friend, that you come with me. If you show yourself to the king and proclaim your prowess with the bow, he will hire you immediately. Of course, I will be right there behind you to carry out your duties. In your shadow, I will be able to earn enough for both of us to prosper. All you have to do is follow my orders."

"Excellent!" cried Bhīmasena. "That is the best offer I have ever heard. Let us be off to see the king!"

The two of them set out at once for Bārānasi. Bhīmasena dressed to look like an archer, and the dwarf masqueraded as his page. When they reached the palace gate, Culla-Dhanuggaha instructed his companion how to announce his arrival to the king. When they were summoned into the royal presence, they entered together and bowed before the king.

"What brings you here?" asked the king.

"I am a mighty archer," said Bhīmasena. "There is no one on this entire continent who can use a bow as well as I can."

"I can see that you are very strong," replied the king. "What pay would you want to serve as my chief archer?"

"One thousand coins a fortnight, Sire."

"And who, may I ask, is that short man beside you?"

"He's my little page, Sire. I will take care of him."

"Very well, enter my service."

The two of them were given living quarters near the palace. Bhīmasena took care of Culla-Dhanuggaha, followed his instructions carefully, and gained respect as a skillful archer.

One day, the king was informed that a fierce tiger in the jungle near Bārānasi was harassing travelers on the highway and had already devoured a considerable number of victims. The king immediately sent for Bhīmasena and asked whether he could catch the tiger.

"How could I call myself an archer, Sire, if I could not catch a tiger?"

"Good!" the king replied, "There will be a reward if you can indeed catch the tiger and put an end to the killing of my subjects."

Bhīmasena hurried back and told Culla-Dhanuggaha about his assignment.

"All right, my friend," the dwarf said, "off you go."

"What do you mean?" Bhīmasena asked, terrified at the thought of facing a tiger by himself. "You have to come with me!"

"No, I won't go, but I'll tell you what to do. Here is the plan, and you must follow it carefully." Whispering softly so that no one could overhear, Culla-Dhanuggaha explained exactly what Bhīmasena should do. Bhīmasena listened intently, repeating each step to make sure he understood perfectly. Then he headed off to carry out his instructions.

First, he went to a village near the jungle and gathered a large band of strong farmers armed with clubs, hoes, swords, and various other weapons. "All right," he said to the men, "let's catch that tiger. We can do it if we all work together. Just remember: I will have my great bow ready to protect you." They walked silently toward the jungle keeping an eye out for the beast. Bhīmasena allowed the others to go ahead. He stayed a little to the side with his bow ready. Suddenly, they all spotted the tiger, and all the farmers rushed forward with their weapons raised. Exactly as he had been instructed, Bhīmasena jumped into a thicket and lay down flat on his face. Unaware of this, the farmers charged the tiger and beat the animal to death.

As soon as he was sure that the tiger was dead, Bhīmasena used his teeth to bite off a creeper, and went running toward them, trailing the creeper in his hand. "Who has killed the tiger?" he shouted. "You foolish peasants! I was supposed to take this tiger alive to the king. I never told you to kill it. I was going to bind it with this creeper and lead it back to Bārānasi. I had just stepped into a thicket to get a creeper. The king must know who killed the tiger! Tell me at once who it was!"

Bhīmasena shouted so loudly and was so intimidating that the farmers were more terrified of being punished by the king than they had been of the tiger. They pleaded with him not to let the king punish them. They offered him all their wealth if he wouldn't tell the king that they had killed the tiger. Bhīmasena objected only enough to make sure that they were totally cowed. Finally, he accepted their bribes and sent them back to their village. He carried the tiger's carcass to Bārānasi and received full credit for slaying the beast and protecting the kingdom. As promised, the king gave him a handsome reward.

A few days later, the king sent for Bhīmasena again. In another part of the kingdom, there was a fierce wild buffalo creating havoc along a certain stretch of the road. The king ordered his royal archer to kill it. Bhīmasena informed Culla-Dhanuggaha, and the dwarf devised a plan, very similar to the previous one. Bhīmasena followed his instructions exactly and returned to the capital with the carcass of the buffalo and some generous bribes from the farmers. He was again handsomely rewarded by the king. In addition, this time he was given a title.

Bhīmasena quickly became intoxicated by the honor he was being shown. He spent most of his time with the king's other soldiers and guards. He boasted continually of his daring exploits, regaling the others with the made-up details of how he had killed the animals. He scorned the advice of Culla-Dhanuggaha and began treating the dwarf with contempt. One night, after he returned from drinking with his new friends, Bhīmasena became angry and shouted at the dwarf, "You pipsqueak! You may have helped me a little in the beginning, but I'm the one who did the work. I can get along without you now. Do you think you're the only man around here? The king knows what I can do!" Then, without even saying, "Good night," he went to bed and fell asleep.

Soon afterwards, the king of a neighboring kingdom attacked Kāsi and marched toward Bārānasi. Laying siege to the city, he sent a message to King Brahmadatta, demanding either battle or surrender. King Brahmadatta accepted the challenge to a battle and called Bhīmasena. He ordered the archer to lead the troops into battle to defend the capital and the kingdom.

Pleased that the king trusted him to lead the army and blinded by the admiration he was being shown by the other soldiers, Bhīmasena strode to the stable to mount the war elephant. Culla-Dhanuggaha was listening outside and heard the king's orders. Afraid that Bhīmasena might get himself killed, the dwarf hurried to the stable with his bow and quietly seated himself behind his huge companion.

Surrounded by a great army, their elephant marched out through the city gate toward the battlefield. As soon as the drums signaled the beginning of the battle, Bhīmasena realized with a sinking heart that he had no idea how to fight and that he was in great danger. He started quaking with fear.

"Bhīmasena!" Culla-Dhanuggaha cautioned him. "Get control of yourself. If you slide off now, you will be crushed by our own forces." The dwarf tied a rope around Bhīmasena's waist and fastened it to the howdah to keep him from falling off the elephant. This did nothing, however, to calm the royal archer's fear. The sight of the battlefield, the beat of the drums, and the thought of facing the enemy army so terrified the giant that he lost control of his bowels.

"Aha!" cried Culla-Dhanuggaha. "What has happened? Just the other day you claimed to be a great warrior. You said that you knew what to do. Now your prowess is limited to dirtying your own elephant. You swore that you would vanquish the foe single-handedly, but you can't even control yourself. You just messed your pants!"

Not wishing to humiliate his friend any further, Culla-Dhanuggaha patted the coward on the back and said, "All right, my friend, don't be afraid. I am here to protect you! In fact, why don't you jump down, run home, and wash up. You really are a mess." Bhīmasena meekly agreed. The dwarf untied the rope, helped him get off the elephant, and told him the best way to return safely to the city.

"Now to win the glory I have long deserved," thought Culla-Dhanuggaha. As loudly as he could, he shouted the battle cry and dashed forward into battle. Fighting fiercely, he was able to break through the enemy's lines, to enter their camp, and to capture the king. The invading army quickly retreated. Culla-Dhanuggaha escorted the enemy king to Bārānasi and handed him over to King Brahmadatta. Delighted by the bravery and skill of his new commander, King Brahmadatta bestowed great honor on the dwarf. From that day on, all of Jambudīpa sang the praises of Culla-Dhanuggaha, and no one seemed to notice that he was a misshapen dwarf.

Bhīmasena never again appeared in court. Culla-Dhanuggaha gave him a settlement and sent him back to the weavers' village. The little archer continued to receive great honor. He lived the rest of his life in Bārānasi, excelling in generosity and performing many good deeds, finally passing away to fare according to his deserts.

Having concluded his story, the Buddha said, "Thus, Bhikkhus, this in not the first time that this bhikkhu has been a braggart. He was the same in bygone days." Then the Buddha identified the birth: "At that time, this braggart was Bhīmasena, and I was Culla-Dhanuggaha."

36

A Man Named Trouble
Kālakannī Jātaka

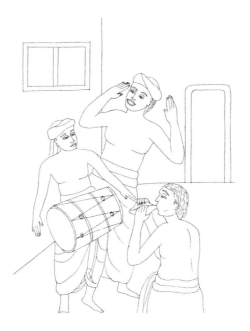

It was while staying at Jetavana that the Buddha told this story about one of Anāthapindika's friends, a man with the unhappy name of Kālakannī, meaning trouble. The two had played together as children and had gone to the same school. As the years passed, however, Kālakannī became extremely poor and could not make a living for himself, no matter what he did. In desperation, he approached Anāthapindika, who welcomed him kindly and employed him to look after his property and to manage all of his business for him. From that time on, it was a common thing to hear someone shouting, "Trouble!" each time a member of the household called him.

One day, some of Anāthapindika's friends and acquaintances came and said, "Sir, don't let this sort of thing go on in your house! It's enough to scare a yakkha to hear such inauspicious speech as 'Come here, Trouble,' 'Sit down, Trouble,' or 'Have your dinner, Trouble.' The man is a miserable wretch, dogged by misfortune. He's not your social equal. Why do you have anything to do with him?"

"Nonsense," replied Anāthapindika, firmly rejecting their advice. "A name only denotes a man. The wise do not measure a man by his name. It is useless to be superstitious about mere sounds. I will never abandon the friend with whom I made mudpies as a child, simply because of his name."

Not long after that, Anāthapindika went with many of his servants to visit a village of which he was headman. He left his old friend in charge. Hearing of the rich man's departure, a band of robbers decided to break into the house. That night, they armed themselves to the teeth and surrounded it.

Kālakannī had suspected that burglars might try something, so he stayed awake. As soon as he knew that the robbers were outside, he ran about noisily as though he were rousing the entire household. He shouted for one person to sound the conch and for another to beat the drum. Soon it seemed that the house contained a whole army of servants.

When the robbers heard the din, they said to one another, "The house is not as empty as we thought it would be. The master must still be at home, after all." They threw down their clubs and other weapons and fled.

In the morning, the discarded weapons were found lying scattered outside the house. When the townspeople realized what had happened, they lauded Kālakannī to the skies. "If such a wise man hadn't been guarding the house," they said, "those robbers would have walked in and plundered as they pleased. Anāthapindika owes this good luck to his staunch friend, Kālakannī." As soon as Anāthapindika returned from his trip, they told him the whole story.

"My friends," Anāthapindika answered, "this is the trusty guardian I was urged to get rid of. If I had taken your advice and sent him away, I would be a poorer man today. It's not the name but the heart within that makes the man!" In appreciation of his friend's services, he raised his wages. Thinking that this was a good story to tell the Buddha, Anāthapindika went to the Master and gave him a complete account.

"This is not the first time, sir," the Buddha said, "that a man named Kālakannī has saved his friend's wealth from robbers. The same thing happened in bygone days as well." Then, at Anāthapindika's request, the Buddha told this story of the past.

Long, long ago, when Brahmadatta was reigning in Bārānasi, the Bodhisatta was the treasurer. He was famous and had a friend named Kālakannī. At that time, everything was the same as it was in the story of Anāthapindika. When the treasurer returned from the village and heard the news, he said to his friends, "If I had taken your advice and had gotten rid of my trusty friend, I would have been a beggar today. A friend is one who goes seven steps to help. He who goes twelve can be called a comrade. Loyalty for a fortnight or a month makes one a relative; long and steady dependability, a second self. How could I forsake my friend Kālakannī who has always been so true?"

Having concluded his story, the Buddha identified the birth: "At that time, Ānanda was Kālakaṇṇī, and I was the treasurer of Bārāṇasi."

37

Omens in Cloth
Mangala Jātaka

It was while staying at Veluvana that the Buddha told this story about a superstitious brahmin.

In Rājagaha, a brahmin became upset when the Buddha retrieved a piece of cloth that he was sure was unlucky and cursed, and the Buddha pointed out the uselessness of his superstition. "Long ago, you were also extremely unreasonable, and you acted in exactly the same way." At his request, the Buddha told this story of the past.

Long, long ago, a righteous king reigned in Rājagaha, the capital of Magadha. In those days, the Bodhisatta was born as a brahmin in the northwestern part of the kingdom. After he grew up, he renounced the world for the life of an ascetic. Living in the Himavat, through concentration meditation, he perfected the five extraordinary powers and the eight jhānas.

On one occasion, the ascetic left the Himavat and happened to stay in the king's park. The king saw him walking for alms in the capital and summoned him to the palace to offer him almsfood. Afterwards, he urged the ascetic to remain in his pleasure garden. The ascetic agreed and began receiving his food from the palace.

In Rājagaha, there also lived a rich brahmin known as Dussalakkhana, who, as his name implied, was famous for reading omens in cloth. One day, after bathing, he called for a clean suit of clothes and the servant brought them, but Dussalakkhana was aghast to discover that they had been gnawed by a mouse, which had found its way into the chest where they were stored.

"If these clothes stay in the house," he thought, "they will bring bad luck. Such ill-omened things are sure to bring a curse. I can no longer wear them, and it is out of the question to give them to any of my children or even to a servant, for whoever owns them will bring misfortune to those around him. They must be thrown away in a charnel ground, but I don't dare ask a servant to do it. A servant might covet the clothes and secretly keep them. That would certainly bring ruin! I can't trust anyone except my son to dispose of these wicked things!"

He called his son and explained the great danger of the situation. He directed his son to carry the garments on a stick, without touching them with his hand, and to fling them away in the charnel ground. After he had done that, he was to purify himself with a ritual bath before returning home.

Following his father's instructions, the young brahmin proceeded to the charnel ground, with the clothes draped on the end of a stick as though they were a dangerous snake. He was surprised to see the ascetic sitting in the charnel ground.

"What are you doing, young man?" the ascetic asked.

"Sir, these clothes, which have been gnawed by mice, are full of evil omens, as deadly as a venomous snake! My father was worried that a servant might be tempted to keep them, so he sent me to dispose of them. I promised him that I would throw them away here. Then I must take a bath and return home. That is my errand."

"Then, by all means, throw the clothes away," the ascetic said.

As soon as the young brahmin had tossed the clothes on the ground, the ascetic picked them up and said, "They will suit me just fine." The young brahmin was horrified and earnestly begged the ascetic not to use the unlucky cloth, repeating how dangerous it was. Impervious to his pleas, the ascetic held the clothes firmly and carried them back to the royal pleasure garden.

The youth hurried home to tell his father what had happened.

"Those clothes," thought the brahmin "are cursed. Even that ascetic cannot wear them without calamity befalling him. If he suffers a disaster, that would bring me into disrepute. I must get him to throw away all of that unlucky cloth."

He and his son hurried to the pleasure garden with a wide selection of robes. When the brahmin came upon the ascetic, he stood respectfully on one side and asked, "Is it, indeed, true, sir, as I hear, that you picked up a suit of clothes that my son threw away in the charnel-ground?"

"Quite true, brahmin."

"Sir, that cloth is cursed! If you use it, it will destroy you. If you are in need of robes, please take these, and throw away those evil clothes."

"Brahmin," the ascetic replied, "I have renounced the world, and I am contented with any rags I find by the roadside, at the garbage dump, or in the charnel ground. I have no belief in superstitions regarding good luck or bad luck. No wise man believes in such omens!"

So powerful were the ascetic's words that, hearing them, the brahmin gave up his superstition.

The wise ascetic continued his practice of meditation and earned rebirth in the Brahma heavens.

Having concluded his story, the Buddha added, "The one who renounces omens, dreams, and signs and frees himself from superstition will triumph at last!" The Buddha taught the Dhamma, and both father and son attained the first path. Then the Buddha identified the birth: "At that time, the father and son were the same, and I was the ascetic."

38

The Straw Worth More Than Gold
Kuhaka Jātaka

It was while staying at Jetavana that the Buddha told this story about a conniving bhikkhu, who was the source of much trouble to others.

Long, long ago, when Brahmadatta was reigning in Bārānasi, a shifty ascetic with long, matted hair lived near a certain little village. The landowner had built a modest hermitage in the forest for him and provided him with excellent food in his own house everyday.

The landowner had a great fear of robbers and decided that the safest course to protect his money was to hide it in an unlikely place. Believing the matted-haired ascetic to be a model of sainthood, he brought one hundred gold coins to the hermitage, buried them there, and asked the ascetic to keep watch over the treasure.

"There's no need to say more, sir, to a man like me who has renounced the world. We ascetics never covet what belongs to others."

"That's wonderful," said the landowner, who went off with complete confidence in the ascetic's protestations.

As soon as the landowner was out of sight, the ascetic chuckled to himself, "Why, there's enough here to last a man his whole life!"

Allowing a few days to elapse, the ascetic dug up the gold and reburied it conveniently by the road. The following morning, after a meal of rice and succulent curries at the landowner's house, the ascetic said, "My good sir, I've been staying here, supported by you, for a long time. Frankly, living so long in one place is like living in the world, which is forbidden to ascetics like me. I really cannot remain here any longer; the time has come for me to leave."

The landowner urged him to stay, but nothing could overcome the ascetic's determination.

"Well, then," said the landowner, "if you must go, good luck to you." Reluctantly, he escorted the ascetic to the outskirts of the village and returned home.

After walking a short way by himself, the ascetic thought it would be a good thing to cajole the landowner. Sticking a straw in his matted hair, he hurried back to the village.

"What brings you back again?" asked the surprised landowner.

"I just noticed that a straw from your roof got stuck in my hair. We ascetics must not take anything which has not been given to us, so I have brought it back to you."

"Throw it down, sir, and go your way!" said the landowner. "Imagine!" he said to himself. "This ascetic is so honest that he won't even take a straw which does not belong to him. What a rare person!" Thus, greatly impressed by the ascetic's honesty, the landowner bade him farewell again.

A traveling merchant happened to witness the ascetic's return with the piece of straw and grew suspicious. He asked the landowner whether he had deposited anything in the ascetic's care.

"Yes," the landowner answered rather hesitantly, "one hundred gold coins."

"Well, why don't you just go and see if your property is still safe?" the merchant suggested.

The landowner went to the deserted hermitage, dug where he'd left his money, and found it gone. Rushing back to the merchant, he cried, "It's not there!"

"The thief is certainly that long-haired rascal of an ascetic," said the merchant. "Let's catch him."

The two men ran after the rogue and quickly caught him. They kicked him and beat him until he showed them where he had hidden the gold. After they had gotten back the money, the merchant looked at the coins and scornfully asked the ascetic, "Why didn't this one hundred gold coins trouble your conscience as much as that straw? Take care, you hypocrite, never to play such a trick again!"

When his life ended, the merchant passed away to fare according to his deserts.

Having concluded his story, the Buddha added, "Thus, you see, Bhikkhus, that this bhikkhu was as conniving in the past as he is today." Then he identified the birth: "At that time, this bhikkhu was the scheming ascetic, and I was the wise and good merchant."

39

Smeared with Poison
Litta Jātaka

It was while staying at Jetavana that the Buddha told this story about using requisites thoughtlessly.

Although the Buddha had exhorted the bhikkhus to be careful in the use of the requisites and had pointed out that their careless use made the bhikkhu liable to rebirth in hell, as petas, or as animals, many bhikkhus failed to heed the warning.

It became necessary, therefore, for the Buddha to lay down the rule: "The thoughtful bhikkhu has a definite object in view when he wears a robe, namely, to preserve modesty and to keep off the cold." He laid down similar rules for the other requisites, as well.[1]

---

1   Bhikkhus are to reflect daily in this way:
"Wisely reflecting, I use the robe only to ward off cold, to ward off heat, to ward off the touch of flies, mosquitoes, wind, and creeping things, and only for the sake of modesty.
"Wisely reflecting, I use almsfood not for fun, nor for pleasure, nor for fattening, nor for beautification, but only for the maintenance and nourishment of this body, for keeping it healthy, and for helping with the Holy Life, thinking, 'I will allay hunger without overeating, so that I may continue to live blamelessly and at ease.
(CONTINUED) "Wisely reflecting, I use the lodging only to ward off cold, to ward off heat,

After establishing these rules, he continued, "Using the requisites heedlessly is like taking deadly poison. Consider those who in bygone days acted thoughtlessly and were, indeed, poisoned. Then he told this story of the past.

Long, long ago, when Brahmadatta was reigning in Bārānasi, the Bodhisatta was born into a well-to-do family in the capital. Even as a boy, he was fond of gambling, so, when he grew up, he made his living by shooting dice. He was very skillful and usually won a lot of money—always honestly. His friends enjoyed playing with him because he never cheated. One day, a professional gambler arrived in Bārānasi and began shooting dice at various venues around the city. It was said that this hustler never left the table without winning a great deal. The young man from Bārānasi wondered how the hustler could be so successful, so he joined some of the games and watched the man carefully. It was not long before he realized what was happening. The hustler had a peculiar habit. As long as he was winning, he kept on playing and urging others to play, but, as soon as his luck turned, he would hide one of the dice in his mouth and claim that it was lost. This would, of course, break up the game, and he would leave with his winnings.

The young man decided to teach this cheater a lesson. He bought some new dice, dipped them in poison, and, after they were quite dry, put them in a silk bag. He found the gambler and challenged him to a game, stipulating only that they use his own new dice. The man examined the dice, found that they were not in any way weighted or loaded, and cheerfully agreed. The dice-board was prepared, and play began. At first, the cunning hustler was winning, and he was very jovial. His hands were moving so quickly that no one could see exactly what he was doing. They only saw that he was winning. Suddenly, he made a couple of bad throws, and it looked like he was going to lose. He quickly popped a die into his mouth and pretended to search for it. His opponent sat calmly and whispered, so that only the hustler could hear, "Swallow now, but you will soon find out how unpalatable it is!"

Even as he speaking, the poison began its work, and the poor hustler grew pale and faint. He bent double with pain, his eyes rolled back in his head, and he fell to the ground.

"Allow me," the young man said, gently pushing the onlookers back. "I must save this rascal's life." He reached into the trickster's mouth and removed the die. Then he mixed a potion and made him drink it so that he

to ward off the touch of flies, mosquitoes, wind, and creeping things, and only for protection from the danger from weather and for living in seclusion.
"Wisely reflecting, I use medicine only to ward off painful feelings that have arisen and for the maximum freedom from disease." (Majjhima Nikāya, 2)

vomited all the poison. After drinking a large glass of ghee with honey and sugar, the hustler was quite restored.

The young man helped the cheater stand up and exhorted him never to do such a thing again. "Not only should one treat one's opponents fairly," he admonished the hustler, "but even a gambler should be careful in how he handles the tools of his trade."

After a life spent in generosity and other good deeds, the honest young man passed away to fare according to his deserts.

Having concluded his story, the Buddha added, "Bhikkhus, the careless use of requisites is like taking a deadly poison." Then he identified the birth: "At that time, I was the wise and good gambler."

40
The Queen's Necklace
Mahāsāra Jātaka

It was while staying at Jetavana that the Buddha told this story about Venerable Ānanda.

One day, the wives of King Pasenadi were talking together. "It is very rare for a Buddha to appear in the world," they said. "It is also rare to be born a human being. We have been born humans during a Buddha's lifetime, but we are not free to go to the monastery to pay our respects, to hear his teaching, and to make offerings to him. We might as well be living in a cage as in this palace. Let's ask the king to allow someone to come here to teach us the Dhamma. We should learn what we can, be charitable, and do good deeds. In that way, we will truly benefit from living at this happy time!" They went to the king and made their request. The king listened and gave his consent.

That same morning, the king decided to enjoy himself in the royal garden and ordered that it be prepared. As the gardener was finishing, he saw the Buddha seated at the foot of a tree. He immediately went to the king and reported that everything was ready but that the Buddha was there sitting under a tree.

"Very good," said the king, "we will go and hear the Master." He mounted his chariot and went to the garden.

When he got there, he found a lay disciple, Chattapāni, sitting at the Buddha's feet, listening to his words. When the king saw this lay disciple, he hesitated. Realizing, however, that this must be a virtuous man, the king approached, bowed, and seated himself on one side.

Out of his profound respect for the Buddha, Chattapāni neither rose to honor the king nor greeted him. This made the king very angry.

Aware of the king's displeasure, the Buddha praised the merits of Chattapāni, who had, in fact, attained the third path. "Sire," the Buddha said, "this lay disciple knows by heart the scriptures that have been handed down, and he has set himself free from the bondage of passion."

"Surely," the king thought, "this can be no ordinary person who is being so highly praised by the Buddha." He turned to Chattapāni and said, "Let me know if you are in need of anything."

"Thank you," Chattapāni replied.

The king listened to the Master's teaching. When it was time, he rose and left ceremoniously.

A few days later, the king met Chattapāni again as he was on his way to Jetavana and had him summoned. "I hear, sir, that you are a man of great learning. My wives are eager to hear the truth. I would be very glad to have you teach them."

"It would not be proper, Sire, for a layman to expound the truth in the king's harem. That is the prerogative of the bhikkhus."

The king immediately realized that this was correct, so he called his wives together and announced that he would ask the Buddha for one of the senior bhikkhus to become their instructor in the Dhamma. He asked them which of the eighty great disciples they would prefer. The women unanimously chose Venerable Ānanda.

The king went to the Buddha, greeted him courteously, sat down, and stated his wives' wish that Venerable Ānanda be their teacher. The Buddha assented, and Venerable Ānanda began teaching the king's wives regularly.

One day, when Venerable Ānanda arrived at the palace as usual, he found that the women, who had always before been so attentive, were distracted and agitated. "What's wrong?" he asked. "Why do you seem anxious today?"

"Oh, Venerable Sir," they replied, "the jewel from the king's turban is missing. He has called his ministers and ordered them to apprehend the thief and to find the jewel without fail. They are interrogating and searching everybody, even all of us women. The entire court is in an uproar, and we have no idea what might happen next to any of us. That is why we are so unhappy."

"Don't worry," said Venerable Ānanda cheerfully as he went to find the king.

Taking the seat which the king prepared for him, Venerable Ānanda asked whether it was true that the king had lost his jewel.

"Quite true, Venerable Sir," said the king. "I have had everyone in the palace searched and questioned, but I can find no trace of the gem."

"There is a way to find it, Sire," Venerable Ānanda said, "without upsetting people unnecessarily."

"What way is that, Venerable Sir?"

"By wisp-giving, Sire."

"Wisp-giving?" asked the king. "What do you mean?"

"Call everyone under suspicion," Venerable Ānanda instructed, "and give him or her a wisp of straw. Say to each of them, 'Take this and put it in a certain place before daybreak tomorrow.' The person who took the jewel will be afraid of getting caught and will give the gem back with the straw. If it is not returned on the first day, the same thing must be done for one or two more days. You will undoubtedly get your jewel back." Without saying anything more, Venerable Ānanda departed.

Following Venerable Ānanda's advice, the king distributed wisps of straw and designated the place where they were to be returned. Even though he did this for three days, the jewel was not recovered. On the third day, Venerable Ānanda came again and asked whether the jewel had been returned.

"No, Venerable Sir," replied the king, "it has not."

"In that case, Sire," Venerable Ānanda said, "have a large water pot filled with water and placed in a secluded corner of your courtyard. Put a screen around it, and give orders that all who frequent the palace, both men and women, are to take off their outer garments and, one by one, to step behind the screen and to wash their hands." Again the king did exactly as Venerable Ānanda had suggested.

"Venerable Ānanda has seriously taken charge of the matter," thought the thief. "He is not going to stop until the jewel is found. The time has come to give it up." He concealed the jewel in his underclothes, went behind the screen, and dropped it in the water. After everyone had finished, the pot was emptied, and the jewel was found.

"Because of Venerable Ānanda," exclaimed the king joyfully, "I have gotten my jewel back!"

"Because of Venerable Ānanda," exclaimed all the residents of the palace, "we have been saved from a lot of trouble."

The story of how his wisdom had returned the jewel spread throughout the city and reached Jetavana.

A few days later, while the bhikkhus were talking together in the Hall of Truth, one of them said, "The great wisdom of Ānanda led to recovering the lost jewel and restoring calm to the palace."

When the Buddha heard what they were discussing, he said, "Bhikkhus, this is not the first time that stolen gems have been found, nor is Ānanda the only one who has brought about such a discovery. Long ago, too, the wise and good discovered stolen valuables and saved a lot of people from trouble." Then he told them this story of the past.

Long, long ago, when Brahmadatta was reigning in Bārānasi, the Bodhisatta completed his education and became one of the king's ministers. One day, the king went with a large retinue to his pleasure garden. After walking about the woods for a while, he decided to enjoy himself in the water and sent for his harem. The women removed their jewels and outer garments, laid them in boxes for their attendants to look after, and joined the king in the royal tank.

As the queen was taking off her jewels and ornaments, a female monkey, hiding in the branches of a nearby tree, watched her intently. The monkey conceived a longing to wear the queen's pearl necklace and waited for a chance to snatch it. At first, the queen's attendant stayed alert, looking all around to protect the jewels, but, after a while, she began to nod. As soon as the monkey saw this, she jumped down, as swift as the wind. Then, just as swiftly, she leaped up into the tree with the pearls around her neck. Fearing that other monkeys would see her treasure, she hid the string of pearls in a hole in the tree and sat, demurely keeping guard as though nothing had happened.

By and by, the girl awoke and saw that the jewels were gone. Terrified at her own negligence, she shouted, "A man has run off with the queen's pearl necklace!"

Sentries ran up from every side and questioned her. The king ordered his guards to catch the thief, and they rushed around the pleasure garden, searching high and low. A poor timid peasant who happened to be nearby became frightened when he heard the uproar and started to run away.

"There he goes!" cried the guards. They chased the poor man, caught him, began beating him, and asked why he stole the precious jewels.

The peasant thought, "If I deny the charge, these brutes will beat me to death. I'd better say I took them." He immediately confessed to the theft and was hauled off in chains to the king. "Did you take those precious jewels?" asked the king.

"Yes, Your Majesty."

"Where are they now?"

"Your Majesty, I'm a poor man," he explained. "I've never owned any-thing of any value, not even a bed or a chair, much less a jewel. It was the treasurer who made me take that expensive necklace. I took it and gave it to him. He knows all about it."

The king summoned the treasurer and asked whether the peasant had given the necklace to him.

Also afraid to deny the charge, the treasurer answered, "Yes, Sire."

"Where is it then?"

"I gave it to the chaplain."

The chaplain was summoned and interrogated in the same way. He said he had given it to the chief musician, who in his turn said he had given it as a present to a courtesan. The courtesan, however, utterly denied having received it, and the questioning continued until sunset.

"It's too late now," said the king. "We will look into this tomorrow." He handed the suspects over to his officers and went back into the city.

The king's wise minister began thinking, "These jewels were lost inside the grounds, but the peasant was outside. There was a strong guard at the gate. It would have been impossible for anyone inside to have gotten away with the necklace. I don't see how a person, inside or out, could have stolen it. I don't believe that any of these five had anything to do with it, but I understand why they falsely confessed and implicated the others. As for the necklace, these grounds are swarming with monkeys. It must have been one of the female monkeys that took it." The minister went to the king and requested that the suspects be handed over to him so that he could look into the matter personally.

"By all means, my wise friend," said the king, "go ahead."

The minister ordered his servants to take charge of the five prisoners. "Keep strict watch over them," he said. "I want you to listen to everything they say and to report it all to me."

As the prisoners sat together, the treasurer said to the peasant, "Tell me, you wretch, where you and I have ever met before today. How could you have given me that necklace?"

"Honorable sir," said the peasant, "I have never owned anything valu-able. Even the stool and the cot I have are rickety. I said what I did because I thought that, with your help, I would get out of this trouble. Please don't be angry with me, sir."

"Well then," the chaplain indignantly asked the treasurer, "how did you pass on to me what this fellow never gave to you?"

"I said that," explained the treasurer, "because I thought that you and I, both being high-ranking officials, would be able to get out of trouble together."

"Brahmin," the chief musician asked the chaplain, "when do you think you gave the jewel to me?"

"I only said I did," answered the chaplain, "because I thought you would help to make the time in prison pass more agreeably."

Finally, the courtesan complained, "You wretch of a musician, you have never visited me, and I have never visited you. When could you have given me the necklace?"

"Don't be angry, my dear," said the musician. "I just wanted you to be here to keep us company. Cheer up! Let's all be lighthearted together for a while."

As soon as the servants had reported this conversation, the minister knew that all his suspicions were correct. He was convinced that a female monkey had taken the necklace.

"Now I must find a way to make her drop it," he said to himself. He ordered his servants to catch some monkeys, to deck them out with strings of beads, and to release them again in the pleasure garden. The servants were to watch every monkey in the grounds. When they saw one wearing the missing pearl necklace, they were to frighten her into dropping it.

The monkeys strutted about with their beads strung around their necks, their wrists, and their ankles. They flaunted their splendor in front of the guilty monkey, who sat quietly guarding her treasure. At last, jealousy overcame her prudence. "Those are only beads!" she screeched and foolishly put on her own necklace of real pearls. As soon as the servants saw this, they began making loud noises and throwing things at her. The monkey became so frightened that she dropped the necklace and scampered away. The servants quickly retrieved the necklace and took it to their master.

The minister immediately took it to the king. "Here, Sire," he said, "is the queen's necklace. The five prisoners are innocent. It was a female monkey in the pleasure garden that took it."

"Wonderful!" exclaimed the king. "But, tell me. How did you find that out, and how did you manage to get it back?"

When he had heard the whole story, the king praised his minister and exclaimed, "You certainly are the right man in the right place!" In appreciation, he showered the minister with immeasurable treasure.

The king continued to follow the wise minister's advice and counsel. After a long life of generosity and meritorious acts, he passed away to fare according to his deserts.

Having concluded his story, the Buddha again praised Venerable Ānanda's merits. Then the Buddha identified the birth: "At that time, Ānanda was the king, and I was his wise minister."

41

A Bowl Full of Oil
Telapatta Jātaka

It was while staying in a forest near the town of Sedaka in the Sumbha region that the Buddha told this story.[1]

"Bhikkhus! Imagine this scene. There is a great crowd of people who are very excited because the most beautiful woman in the land has begun singing and dancing in front of them.

"Now suppose that a young man, full of life, is ordered to carry a bowl of oil, full to the brim, through the crowd, right past the dancing woman. Directly behind him is a fierce man with a razor-sharp sword who will cut off his head if he spills a single drop of oil.

"What do you think, Bhikkhus? Will that man be careless of how he is carrying the bowl of oil? Will he fail to pay attention?"

"Absolutely not, Venerable Sir."

---

1   This incident is also related in the Janapadakalyāni Sutta (Samyutta Nikāya, Mahāvagga, Satipatthāna Samyutta, 20).

"Bhikkhus," the Buddha continued, "one who wants to practice right mindfulness concerning the body must be as careful in not letting his mindfulness drop as that man is in not spilling a drop of oil."

"Venerable Sir," some of the bhikkhus said, "it must be difficult for that man to walk through the crowd with the bowl of oil without being distracted by the charms of the most beautiful woman in the land."

"That is not hard, Bhikkhus. It is an easy task, easy for the very good reason that he is followed by a man threatening him with a drawn sword. The truly difficult task was for the wise and good man of long ago to maintain his right mindfulness, to control his passions, and to avoid being seduced by a woman of incomparable beauty." Then, at their request, the Buddha told them this story of the past.

Long, long ago, when Brahmadatta was reigning in Bārānasi, the Bodhisatta was born as the youngest of the king's one hundred sons. In those days, there were Pacceka Buddhas who took their meals at the palace, where, every day, the young prince served them with great care.

One day, the prince wondered whether, considering all the brothers he had, there was any possibility of his ever inheriting his father's throne. He decided to ask about it.

The next morning, when the Pacceka Buddhas came for their meal, the prince washed and dried their feet and served them as usual, but then he sat down respectfully and posed his question.

"Prince," they replied, "you will never become king in this country, but, in Gandhāra, two thousand yojanas away, there is a city called Takkasilā. If you can reach it in seven days, you will become king there. We must warn you, however, that the road there is very dangerous. Between here and Takkasilā is a great forest, which is infested with yakkhas. Going around the forest would double the distance, and you would never make it in time.

"In the forest, yakkhinīs conjure up all sorts of things to lure travelers. They create fantastic rest-houses and invite travelers in with sweet words. Anyone who is seduced by their wiles is finished. Once he is in their clutches, the yakkhinīs kill him and devour his body while the blood is still warm. Those yakkhinīs are very skillful at appealing to a man's senses. Their charms are incredibly alluring, and the temptation to stop is almost uncontrollably strong. If you can keep traveling for seven days, remaining firm in your resolve and completely controlling your senses, you will become king of Gandhāra."

"Venerable Sirs, after hearing from you of the dangers from those wicked yakkhinīs, how could I even dare to look at them!"

The prince asked the Pacceka Buddhas to give him something to guard him on his journey, and they gave him a sacred thread and some charmed sand. He thanked them and paid his respects.

After bidding farewell to his parents, the prince gathered his men in his own apartments and announced, "I am setting out alone for Takkasilā at once to become king there."

Five of the men immediately stepped forward. "Your Highness, please allow us to accompany you."

"No," the prince replied, "you cannot come with me. The road is very dangerous. The forest is infested with tempting yakkhinīs who destroy anyone captivated by their charms. I have prepared myself, and I will rely on my own strength. I do not wish to subject you to such great danger."

"Your Highness," they begged, "please allow us to go. We, too, will be firm. We will pay no attention to their charms. We will accompany you to Takkasilā."

"If you insist on going, be steadfast," said the prince, and he took those five with him.

In the forest, the yakkhinīs, transformed into gorgeous women, were eagerly waiting for them. With long black hair and complexions as delicate as pale lotuses, they were dressed in the finest silk. They stood in front of elegant pavilions beside the road and beckoned to the travelers. One of the men, an aesthete who prided himself on his fine taste, lagged behind the rest.

"Why are you dropping back?" asked the prince.

"Your Highness, my feet are bothering me. I'll just sit down for a moment in one of those pavilions. Go ahead. After I've rested, I'll catch up with you."

"My good man, those are yakkhinīs," the prince warned him. "Don't be deceived!"

"Don't worry, Your Highness. I really can go no further."

"Well, consider yourself warned," sighed the prince, as he went on with the other four.

As soon as the young man entered the pavilion, he was surrounded by stunning beauties, who quickly seduced him. In the midst of what he thought was the greatest pleasure he had ever experienced, they killed him and ate him.

A little later, another of the men cried, "Listen, do you hear that music? Where is it coming from?" Looking around, he saw a magnificent marquee where lovely and accomplished women sat singing and playing delicate harmonies on various instruments. "There it is. I must go and hear what they are playing."

"Stop!" shouted the prince. "Those are yakkhinīs! Don't be tempted!"

"I just want to listen for a few moments," protested the man. "Go ahead. I'll catch up with you later."

"Consider yourself warned," repeated the prince, as he went on with the other three.

No sooner had the young man stepped into the marquee than he was killed and eaten just as his companion had been.

A little further down the road, another of the men stopped and lifted his nose into the air.

"What is it?" asked the prince.

"That smell," answered the man. "What an incredible fragrance! Where can it be coming from?"

"I'm sure it's from the yakkhinīs," warned the prince.

"No, look! It's coming from that pavilion over there," he cried. As he wandered off, he muttered "Sandalwood! Jasmine! Frangipani! Musk!"

"Consider yourself warned," repeated the prince, as he went on with the other two.

This young man, too, was quickly overcome, killed, and eaten by the yakkhinīs.

Before long, the prince and his remaining companions came upon a restaurant beside the road. His mouth watering from the savory smells, one of the men stopped in his tracks.

"Don't!" said the prince.

"I'm starving," replied the man. "I just need to get a bite to eat."

"Those are yakkhinīs!" warned the prince. "Don't be tempted!"

"Don't worry," the soldier protested. "I have my sword to protect myself."

"Consider yourself warned," repeated the prince, as he went on with his remaining companion.

Before he could swallow a single mouthful of food, the hungry officer was himself eaten by the wicked yakkhinīs.

A little later, the last man also slowed his gait. "Your Highness," he said, "we have been walking all day. Surely, you must be tired, too. Look at these soft, beautiful couches lining the path. Let's just rest for a few minutes. Then, refreshed, we can proceed even faster."

"My friend," replied the prince, "those couches are indeed the most comfortable in the world, but they were created by the yakkhinīs. Don't be tempted by them. Let's keep going!"

"What could be the harm in just sitting down for a moment? I don't even see any yakkhinīs around here."

"Consider yourself warned," repeated the prince, as he went on alone.

No sooner had the indolent fellow sat himself down than he was pounced upon by yakkhinīs, who killed him and ate him as swiftly as they had his four comrades.

Only the young prince was left now, and one of the yakkhinīs followed him, vowing that, in spite of all his stern resolution, she would devour him before she turned back.

"Hey, lady!" some woodsmen called out as they passed. "Who are you following?"

"That is my husband, sirs," she answered.

"Hey, there!" they called to the prince. "Your wife is beautiful and as fair as a flower. Why don't you walk beside her, instead of making her trudge wearily behind you, all alone?"

"She is not my wife," he replied. "She's a yakkhinī. She and her friends have eaten my five companions."

"Alas, gentlemen!" she retorted. "See how anger will drive men to disown their own wives and to say that they are yakkhinīs and ghouls."

"The poor sweet thing!" the woodsmen muttered as they went back to work.

The yakkhinī elicited even more sympathy by simulating pregnancy, but the prince ignored her. When she created a baby and carried the child on her hip, people reviled the prince for treating his wife so ignominiously, but he answered in the same way and continued walking.

As they approached Takkasilā, the yakkhinī made the baby disappear and followed the prince alone. At the gates of the city, the prince entered a rest-house and sat down. Because of his virtue and the talismans from the Pacceka Buddhas, the yakkhinī could not follow him inside. Undaunted, she made herself incomparably alluring and stood on the threshold.

Just then, the procession of the king of Gandhāra happened to be passing by. The king saw her and was overwhelmed by her radiant beauty.

"Go!" he ordered an attendant. "Find out whether or not that woman standing by the rest-house has a husband."

When the attendant asked her, she replied, "Yes, sir. My husband is sitting inside this rest-house."

"She is no wife of mine," the prince announced loudly without moving. "She is a yakkhinī. She and her friends have eaten my five companions."

"Alas, sir!" the yakkhinī said with a sigh. "See how anger will drive men to deny their wives and to say anything that comes into their heads."

When the king heard all of this, he observed, "A treasure trove is a royal privilege," and ordered, "Bring her to me!"

With the yakkhinī seated beside him in the howdah on the back of the royal elephant, the king continued on his procession around the city. When they arrived back at the palace, the king had her dressed in the finest silks. After bathing and perfuming himself, the king ate his evening meal and retired to take his delight in his new consort.

As she lay beside the king, the new queen suddenly burst into tears.

"My dear," the king asked in alarm, "what is the matter?"

"Sire," she replied between sobs, "there are so many women here in the harem that I feel very small. I know that they are going to ask me about my father and mother and about my family connections. They will scorn me and say, 'You were picked up by the wayside.' Sire, I couldn't bear to hear such taunts. Will you give me power and authority over the whole kingdom so that nobody dares to annoy me like that?"

"Sweetheart, even I don't have complete power over everyone in my kingdom. I am king, but I have to obey the rules of the land. I have to rule with justice, and I can punish only those who revolt or break the law. I cannot give you power and authority over the whole kingdom."

"Well," she continued, "if you cannot give me authority over the kingdom, at least, give me authority within the palace. I want to rule over those who dwell in the palace."

Too infatuated by her charms to refuse, the king granted her authority over all within the palace. Satisfied, the yakkhinī allowed the king to amuse himself until he fell asleep. Then she hurried back to the forest and returned with the entire pack of yakkhinīs. After they were all inside the palace, she ordered that the doors be locked and told her companions to begin feasting. She herself killed the king and devoured him. The others gorged themselves on whatever came their way, not sparing a child, a dog, or even a chicken.

The next morning, the townspeople were surprised to find that all the palace gates were still closed and locked. When they finally got inside, they found every room, hallway, and courtyard strewn with bones. As they were pondering the gristly scene and discussing what might have happened, one man exclaimed, "I understand! That man in the rest-house was right! He told everyone that that woman was not his wife and that she was a yakkhinī. Our king, fool that he was, did not believe it and brought her to the palace, made her his queen, and probably even granted her special powers. She must have brought in other yakkhinīs, who devoured the whole court. I'm sure that, by now, they have all gone back to the forest."

Everyone worked quickly to sweep away all the bones and to scrub the floors. They sprinkled perfumes, scattered flowers, decorated the walls with garlands, and burned incense. Soon all evidence of the massacre was gone, but they did not have a king.

"We need a wise man," one nobleman suggested.

Another exclaimed, "What about the man who was able to control his senses to the point of not even looking at the yakkhinī, despite her incomparable beauty. That man is surely steadfast, noble, and wise. With such a man as king, the whole kingdom would benefit. Let us make him our ruler."

There was unanimous agreement. The ministers sent a delegation to the rest-house, where the prince, having sprinkled the charmed sand in his hair and tied the charmed thread around his head, had spent the night, sword in hand, waiting for the dawn.

They escorted him to the palace, adorned him with jewels, and anointed him king of Gandhāra.

For the rest of his life, the king avoided the four evil courses, faithfully observed the ten duties of a king, and ruled his realm in righteousness.

After a life spent in generosity and other good deeds, he passed away to fare according to his deserts.

Having concluded his story, the Buddha added, "Just as one should carry a bowl of oil, full to the brim, with great care, so, too, one who travels to foreign lands should carefully control his own heart!" Then the Buddha identified the birth: "At that time, my disciples were the king's courtiers, and I was the prince who won a kingdom."

42

The Stone Slinger
Sālittaka Jātaka

It was while staying at Jetavana that the Buddha told this story about a bhikkhu who had great skill in slinging stones.[2]

This bhikkhu was from a good family in Sāvatthī, but after higher ordination, he excelled neither in study nor in practice.

One day, as he was standing with another bhikkhu on the bank of the Aciravatī River, two wild geese happened to fly over head. Picking up some stones, he bragged, "I'm going to hit that goose in the eye!"

"You can't do it," said the other bhikkhu.

"I certainly can," replied the first bhikkhu. "Not only that—I can make the stone hit one eye and come out the other!

"That's impossible!"

"Just watch me!" Selecting a triangular stone, he threw it so that it passed by the bird. The goose heard the whizzing sound of the stone, and, sensing danger, it paused in mid-air and turned its head. The bhikkhu quickly threw a small round stone which struck the bird's left eye and exited through the right.

---

2   The occasion for this story is the same as that for Tale 102.

The goose gave a sharp cry, tumbled over and over in the air, and fell dead at their feet.

"You should be ashamed! That was completely improper!" the second bhikkhu cried. He immediately took him to the Buddha and explained what had happened.

"Is this true?" the Buddha asked.

"Yes, Venerable Sir," answered the bhikkhu.

After sternly rebuking the bhikkhu, the Buddha said, "This bhikkhu had the same skill in the past, but then he used it wisely and to advantage." At the bhikkhus' request, the Buddha told this story of the past.

Long, long ago, when Brahmadatta was reigning in Bārānasi, the Bodhisatta was one of the king's courtiers.

The king's spiritual advisor was so talkative and long-winded that, when he got started, no one else could get a word in edgewise. The king was always looking for some way to cure this brahmin of his loquaciousness.

At that time, there was a young crippled boy in Bārānasi who was very skilled in slinging stones. Sometimes, his friends put him in a little cart and pulled him to a huge banyan tree near one of the city gates. If one of the boys said, "Make an elephant for me," the crippled boy threw stone after stone until the shape of an elephant appeared in the foliage, and the ground was covered with fallen leaves. If another boy cried, "Cut out a horse," the lad created a horse in the same way. The boys were so pleased with this entertainment that they gave him coins from their allowance.

One day, as the king was passing by in his chariot on his way to the royal park, he noticed the ingenious designs in the tree, and told his charioteer to stop. The other boys scampered off in fear, leaving their helpless playmate stranded. The king ordered one of his men to find out who had cut all the leaves. When he learned that the crippled boy had done it by throwing stones, the king had a brilliant idea. He had the boy's wagon brought next to the chariot and sent his courtiers out of earshot. "Young man," he said to the boy, "I have an irritating advisor. He is very talkative and can't keep his mouth shut. Do you think you could stop his talking?"

The lad was quick-witted and readily answered, "Sire, I'm sure I could. All I would need is a pea shooter and a good supply of dried goat's dung."

The king had the boy taken to the palace and placed directly in front of the advisor's seat, but behind a curtain with a slit cut into it. The boy was given a pea shooter and a basket of dried goat's dung. The brahmin entered the hall and sat on his appointed seat. From behind the curtain, the boy quietly watched the proceedings. The king had no sooner begun to speak, than the brahmin interrupted and began pontificating. The boy took aim and shot a pellet directly into the advisor's open mouth. The startled advisor swallowed the dung and continued talking. Without so much as a pause, the boy shot one after another. As fast as they landed in his mouth, the advisor swallowed them, pretending that nothing was happening. The pellets of dung were dry when they went down the advisor's gullet, but, in his stomach, they became moist and began to swell. The advisor began to squirm in discomfort, but he continued talking.

Realizing that the boy's ammunition was exhausted, the king abruptly silenced the brahmin. "My dear sir," he said, "while you have been talking, you have swallowed a basketful of goat's dung. I think that you have had enough for one sitting. I advise you to go home and to take a dose of panic seed and water as an emetic. You will feel much better!" Mortified, the brahmin hurriedly left.

From that day on, whenever the advisor was in the presence of the king, he kept his mouth tightly shut, unless he had something extremely important to say.

"Young man," the king said, as he summoned the boy from behind the curtain, "My ears will be in debt to you for this relief." The king rewarded the skillful boy with four villages, which produced an annual income of at least one lakh.

"In this world, Sire," the courtier observed, "skill should be cultivated by the wise. That boy's skill brought him great prosperity."

Having concluded his story, the Buddha identified the birth: "At that time, this bhikkhu was the crippled boy, Ānanda was the king, and I was the wise courtier."

43

The Bran Cake
Kundakapūva Jātaka

It was while staying at Jetavana that the Buddha told this story about a bran cake.

In Sāvatthī, the Buddha and the Sangha were often invited to breakfast. It might have been by a single family, by three or four families, or by all the families on a street. Occasionally, the entire city joined together to entertain them.

One day, all the residents of a particular street were preparing a breakfast of rice gruel and cakes. One of the residents was an extremely poor laborer. In spite of his poverty, this man was determined to offer one cake. He carefully scraped empty rice husks and kneaded the red powder with water into a round cake which he wrapped in a leaf. Since he was too poor to own an oven, he baked his cake in the embers of a fire. When it was done, he resolved that no one but the Buddha should have it.

He lined up with the other donors, but chose a place near the Buddha. As soon as the offering of cakes began, he stepped forward and placed his bran cake in the Buddha's bowl. After having received the poor man's offering, the Buddha held his hand over his bowl, refusing all other cakes. He ate only that one bran cake.

Everyone in Sāvatthī immediately learned that the Enlightened One had not disdained to eat the poor man's cake. Farmers, porters, nobles, and even the king himself rushed there. After paying their respects to the Buddha, they crowded around the poor man. Many people offered him food and money if he would give them the merit of his offering.

Not sure how to respond to these requests, the poor man approached the Buddha, explained the situation, and asked what he should do.

"Take what they offer," said the Buddha, "and let your merit be shared by all living beings."

Having heard that, the man accepted all offerings and shared his merit. In all, he received nine crores of gold. That evening, the king sent for the poor man and appointed him treasurer.

Later, in the Hall of Truth, bhikkhus were talking about this incident. When the Buddha heard what they were discussing, he said, "Bhikkhus, this is not the first time that I have honored that poor man and that, because of me, he became treasurer." Then he told this story of the past.

Long, long ago, when Brahmadatta was reigning in Bārānasi, the people were superstitious and frequently worshiped various devas. During festivals, a family would make offerings at their own particular tree, giving garlands, incense, perfume, and rich oil cakes to their tree deva. One poor man, however, whose deva lived in a castor-oil tree, could not afford any of these gifts. The best he could do was to make a simple bran cake which he baked in an empty coconut shell. When he finished baking his cake, he carried it to the tree.

Standing before the castor-oil tree, the man became embarrassed. "Tree-devas are accustomed to heavenly food," he thought. "Surely the deva of my tree will not want this wretched bran cake. I know it is not good enough for the deva, but I hate to waste it completely. Why don't I just quietly eat it myself?"

As he turned to leave, the deva called out from a fork in the tree. "My good man," he said, "if you were a great lord, I would receive delicate white rolls made from the finest flour. Just because you are poor, don't deprive me of my offering. If you do not offer me your bran cake, I will get nothing! Let me partake of the same fare as you."

Hearing this filled the poor man with great joy, and he gently laid the cake at the foot of the tree. After savoring the cake, the deva asked him, "Why do you worship me?"

"I am a poor man, my lord," he replied, "and I worship you in hope that my burden of poverty will be eased."

"Sir, be of good cheer!" the deva exclaimed. "You have made an offering to one who is grateful for every kind deed. Buried around this tree are many pots of gold. Go to the king, and ask for several wagons. Come back, and dig up the gold. Load all of the pots onto the wagons, take them to the palace, pile them in the courtyard, and you will be rewarded." As soon as he had finished speaking, the deva vanished from sight.

The poor man did exactly as the deva had instructed, and the king was so pleased that he appointed the man treasurer. After many years at his post, the treasurer passed away to fare according to his deserts.

Having concluded his story, the Buddha identified the birth: "At that time, the poor man was the same, and I was the deva of the castor-oil tree."

44

The Jackal's Gold
Sigāla Jātaka

It was while staying at Veluvana that the Buddha told this story about Devadatta.

One day, the bhikkhus in the Hall of Truth were talking about how Devadatta had gone to Gayāsīsa with five hundred followers, whom he was leading into error. Devadatta, they explained to each other, was referring to his teacher as "the ascetic Gotama" and was declaring himself to be the Buddha. By holding a separate Pātimokkha recitation on Uposatha days, he was creating a schism in the Sangha.

When the Buddha heard that they were discussing Devadatta's deceitfulness, he said, "Bhikkhus, this is not the first time that Devadatta has been a great liar." Then he told this story of the past.

Long, long ago, when Brahmadatta was reigning in Bārānasi, a festival was proclaimed in the capital, and many people were making offerings to various devas. To mollify malicious devas, people placed offerings of fish and meat, along with great pots of liquor, in courtyards and at crossroads. The smell of the food attracted a lot of animals.

At midnight, a jackal crept through the sewer and feasted. He ate as much meat and fish as he could and quenched his thirst with the liquor. Stuffed and thoroughly intoxicated, he crawled into a clump of bushes and fell asleep. When he awoke, he saw that the sun had come up, and he realized that he had better be careful not to be seen on the city streets. As he was wondering how he would safely make his way out of the city, he spotted a solitary brahmin on his way to the tank for a morning bath. Suddenly, he had a great idea.

Still hiding in the bushes, he crawled nearer the road. When the man was closer, the jackal called softly, "Brahmin! Brahmin!"

"Who is calling me?" asked the brahmin, looking all around.

"Here I am!" called the jackal. "In the bushes!"

The brahmin saw the jackal and asked, "What do you want?"

"I have a business proposition for you," replied the jackal smoothly. "I know where two hundred gold coins are buried. If you hide me under your outer robe and get me out of the city without my being seen, I'll tell you where that gold is!"

The greedy brahmin could not resist such a lucrative offer. He quickly picked up the jackal and tucked him under his outer robe. Nonchalantly, he walked through the gate and away from the city.

"Where are we now?" asked the jackal.

"I've just passed through the city gate," replied the brahmin.

"Take me to the charnel ground," instructed the jackal.

The brahmin walked to the charnel ground and put the jackal down.

The jackal took the brahmin to the foot of a tree and said. "Spread out your robe here on the ground, use that sharp stick, and dig close to the roots of the tree. You will soon find your reward!" The greedy brahmin quickly spread out his robe, turned toward the tree, and began digging energetically.

While the brahmin was busy excavating for the jackal's gold, the jackal stepped on the man's robe and defecated and urinated on it five times—once in each corner and once more in the middle. Then he scurried off into the woods.

The deva of that tree looked down at the foolish man digging under his tree and shouted, "Brahmin, that drunken jackal has cheated you. No matter how deep you dig, you will not find even find a string of cowry-shells, let alone two hundred gold coins! Better you should wash your filthy robe and bathe yourself as well!"

The embarrassed brahmin snatched up the robe and hurried away. He was rightly chagrined at having been fooled by the crafty beast.

Having concluded his story, the Buddha identified the birth: "At that time, Devadatta was the jackal, and I was the deva of the tree."

45

The Warning
Anusāsikā Jātaka

It was while staying at Jetavana that the Buddha told this story about a greedy bhikkhunī.

This bhikkhunī had come from a good family in Sāvatthī, and was accustomed to gourmet fare. Even after her ordination, she was unable to overcome her desire for special delicacies. In fact, she was so preoccupied with thoughts of food that she often neglected her duties. Every morning, when she went for alms, she visited an area of the city where she was sure to find the best food. No other bhikkhunī knew about this quarter, and she regarded it as her own. Nevertheless, she was constantly plagued by the fear that some of the other bhikkhunīs would find out that delicious almsfood was available there and that she would have to share it. In an attempt to discourage other bhikkhunīs from visiting that street, she warned them that it was very dangerous. Relating tales about the perils of a fierce elephant, a fierce horse, and a fierce dog, she admonished them never to go there for alms. The other bhikkhunīs believed everything she told them, and not a single one dared to venture in that direction.

One day, while that bhikkhunī was walking along that street with her almsbowl, a ram charged her, knocking her down and breaking her leg. Fortunately, she was rescued by passers-by, who set her leg and carried her on a litter to the monastery. The other bhikkhunīs teased her that her broken leg was the result of going where she had warned them not to go.

A few days later, the bhikkhus were talking about the bhikkhunī's accident. When the Buddha heard what they were discussing, he said, "Long ago, too, that bhikkhunī did not follow the warnings she gave others, and she brought harm upon herself." At the bhikkhus' request, he told this story of the past.

Long, long ago, when Brahmadatta was reigning in Bārānasi, the Bodhisatta was born as a bird, who became king of a flock of thousands of birds in the Himavat. In that flock, there was a fierce female bird who had discovered a highway which was always strewn with beans, rice, and other grain that had fallen from loaded wagons. She went there alone every day to feast on these delicious treats. Being extremely greedy, this bird regarded this feeding ground as her own private preserve and guarded the secret from all the other birds. To make sure that none of the other birds went there, she warned them that the highway was a perilous place, with elephants, horses, heavy wagons pulled by huge oxen, and many other dangerous things. She explained that these things were so big and moved so fast that it would be impossible for a bird to take flight quickly enough to escape. She always concluded her emotional descriptions with a dire warning that no bird should ever go there. All the other birds heeded her warning, but she repeated it so often that they began calling her Anusāsikā, or the Warner.

One day, while Anusāsikā was feeding on spilt grain in the middle of the highway, she heard the sound of a carriage. She turned her head and saw that the carriage was approaching, but, thinking that it was still quite a long way off, she continued eating the delicious wheat and millet. The carriage, however, was as swift as the wind and was soon bearing down upon her. The frightened bird tried to fly away, but she found herself trapped by the hooves of the horses and could not escape. Her body was crushed by a wheel of the carriage, which sped on its way.

That evening, the king of the birds noted that Anusāsikā had not returned and ordered a search for her. The scouts found her flattened body on the highway and reported back to the king.

"She warned us of the danger of that highway," the king explained, "but, because she did not follow her own advice, Anusāsikā herself has been crushed. She denounced greed, but she herself fell prey to greed and paid a heavy price."

Having concluded his story, the Buddha identified the birth: "At that time, the bhikkhunī with the broken leg was Anusāsikā, and I was the king of the birds."

46
The Quail's Strategy
Vattaka Jātaka

It was while staying at Jetavana that the Buddha told this story about the son of a rich man.

Uttarasetthi was an extremely rich merchant of Sāvatthī, who had a son, called Uttarasetthiputta or the young Uttara. Having just come from the Brahma heavens, the boy was pure and righteous and grew up to be as handsome as a deva.

When his friends came of age, they all got married, but the young Uttara had no interest in women and was still a virgin. One year, during the Kattikā festival, his companions urged him, "Dear boy, all of Sāvatthī is celebrating this great festival. We want you to come and enjoy the fun with us. How about if we find a charming girl for you?" The young Uttara insisted that he did not want a girlfriend and that he could not have cared less about the festival.

Refusing to take his protestations seriously, his friends found a beautiful young woman and dressed her in the finest silks. They explained to her how to find his room and dropped her off at his house.

She went directly to his room and entered quietly. As soon as she saw him, she began dancing seductively around the room, brushing the fall of her soft silk sari across his back. The young man sat stoically and ignored her. Provoked at this slight to her beauty, she tried even harder. She stood demurely to one side and gave him her most seductive smile. He glanced up and saw her brilliant white teeth, but to him they were just bones. In fact, as he gazed at her curvaceous body, he imagined her as a skeleton and was repulsed. To get rid of her, he gave her some money and sent her away. As she was leaving the house, a nobleman happened to see her and was charmed by her appearance. He offered her a present and invited her to accompany him to his house.

At the end of a week, the festival was over, but the girl didn't return to her own home. Her frightened mother went to see the young man's friends. She asked them where her daughter was, and they, in turn, asked the young Uttara.

He said that he had no idea where she might be. He explained that he had given her money and asked her to leave shortly after she had arrived. He had not seen her since she left his room.

The girl's mother did not believe his story. She demanded that he return her daughter and, despite the young man's protests, took him to the king. The king listened to the mother's complaint, questioned the friends who had taken the girl to the house, and repeatedly demanded that the young Uttara reveal where the girl was. The young man insisted that he did not know. He admitted that the girl had been sent to him but reiterated that he had paid her and that she had left.

The king could not believe that any young man would have acted in such a way and demanded that the young man stop lying and produce the girl.

"Your Majesty," the young Uttara said once more, "I cannot produce the girl because I have no idea where she is."

Suspecting foul play, the king declared, "Either you tell us where the girl is, or you will face immediate execution."

"Sire," the innocent youth insisted, "I have done nothing wrong. The girl tried to seduce me. I gave her some money, and she left. That was a week ago. How can I tell you where she is now?"

"Take him away!" the king commanded.

Guards seized the young man and bound his hands behind his back. Tying a rope around his waist, they led him from the palace and through the streets toward the southern gate. The solemn procession attracted many people, who asked what crime the young man had committed. Hearing the story from the young man's friends, and realizing that he was the son of Uttarasetthi, the crowd became indignant. Many people followed him, shouting, "Unfair! Unfair! How can such a thing be happening? Where is the justice?"

As the young Uttara was marched helplessly toward his doom, he thought, "All this trouble has come to me because I stayed at home. I should have left the household life. If, by some chance, I survive this ordeal, I will renounce the world and become a bhikkhu under the great Gotama, the Perfectly Enlightened Buddha."

Near the southern gate, the missing girl happened to hear the commotion and asked what was going on. As soon as she heard who was being led to execution, she began running and pushing her way through the crowd. "Out of my way! Let me pass!" she screamed. "Let the king's men see me." When she reached the head of the procession, she breathlessly explained who she was and that the youth was innocent. The guards called the girl's mother, who was overjoyed to see her daughter well and healthy. She apologized to the guards and asked them to release the young man.

His friends immediately surrounded him and rejoiced that he was free and safe. They accompanied him to the river, where he bathed to wash off the dust from the streets. Much refreshed, and relieved to be alive, he returned home and had breakfast. Then he informed his parents of his vow to give up the world. Carrying cloth for his robes and followed by a large crowd of people, he went to Jetavana to visit the Buddha. After paying his respects, he asked to be admitted to the Sangha. He was ordained first as a sāmanera and, when he was old enough, as a bhikkhu. From his first day in robes, he meditated intently on the idea of bondage, and he achieved insight. Not long after that, he gained full enlightenment and became an arahat.

One day, in the Hall of Truth, bhikkhus were talking about that bhikkhu's virtues. They remarked that, in the hour of danger, he had recognized the excellence of the Dhamma and had wisely resolved to give up the world for its sake. They praised him for striving and attaining arahatship. When the Buddha heard what they were discussing, he said, "Like the young Uttara, the wise of former times, by thinking carefully in the face of great peril, also escaped death." At their request, he told this story of the past.

Long, long ago, when Brahmadatta was reigning in Bārānasi, there was a clever and successful fowler. Whenever he went to the forest, he caught many birds in his trap. He carried them home carefully and put them in comfortable cages. He fed them so that they became fat, and he was able to sell them in the market for a very good price.

In a flock of quails that the fowler had caught one day, there was a clever young bird who watched his friends greedily gobbling up the food they were given and realized what was happening. "If I eat like the others," he thought,

"I will be sold, and that will be the end of me." At once, he resolved to fast so that he would not get fat.

Every day, he watched the other quails eat and be sold, but he continued his fast and became thinner and thinner. The fowler was so busy selling the birds that he paid no attention to this little quail. The bird's feathers lost their sheen, and his body became no more than skin and bones. Nobody wanted him at any price. At last, all the other birds had been sold, and only he remained lying in the bottom of the cage. The fowler reached in and picked him up. Very gently, he laid the little bird in the palm of his hand and examined him to see what was wrong. As soon as he felt the man relax his guard, the emaciated quail spread his wings and flew off to the forest. Other quails asked where he had been and what he had been doing for such a long time. He explained to them how he had been caught, what had happened to all his companions, and his strategy of taking neither food nor drink, so that he could escape. "The thoughtless are lost," he taught them, "but thoughtfulness saved me from bondage and death. Because I thought things out carefully, I am still alive and free."

Having concluded his story, the Buddha identified the birth: "At that time, I was the quail that escaped death."

47

The Shaft of a Plow
Nangalīsa Jātaka

It was while staying at Jetavana that the Buddha told this story about Venerable Lāludāyi.

This bhikkhu was always saying the wrong thing at the wrong time. At a festival, he would start chanting a gloomy text, such as, "Without the walls they lurk, and where four cross-roads meet." At a funeral, he would chant a gay text, such as, "Joy filled the hearts of devas and men."

One day, the bhikkhus were talking about Venerable Lāludāyi's eccentric behavior. When the Buddha heard what they were discussing, he said, "Bhikkhus, this is not the first time that Lāludāyi's foolishness has led him to say the wrong thing. Long ago, he was just as inept." Then he told this story of the past.

Long, long ago, when Brahmadatta was reigning in Bārānasi, the Bodhisatta was born into a rich brahmin family. After mastering all the arts and sciences, he became a world-renowned teacher with five hundred students.

One of his students was unable to memorize any of the required texts. Furthermore, whenever he opened his mouth, he invariably said the wrong thing. In spite of this, he had been appointed the teacher's personal attendant, and he fulfilled this role faithfully and well.

One evening, as this student turned to go, after rinsing his teacher's hands and feet, the teacher asked him to prop up the foot of his bed. The student put a block under one of the legs of the bed, but, unable to find another block, he sat under the bed and held it up with his hands.

The next morning, the teacher saw the student under the bed and asked why he was still there. "Master," he replied, "I could only find one bed support, so I held up the other leg of the bed myself."

"What devotion!" thought the teacher. "It is hard for me to believe that this is the dullest of all my students. How can I instruct this lad?" The teacher thought about this for a few minutes and decided that, by asking the student about things he saw or did, he could lead him to make comparisons, to see connections, and to understand cause and effect. He hoped that in this way he could develop the boy's mental faculties.

He sent the boy to gather firewood and told him that, after returning, he was to report on what he had seen or heard. The young man understood the assignment and went out.

When he returned from the forest with the firewood, he said, "Master, I saw a snake."

"Excellent!" exclaimed the teacher. "What did the snake make you think of?"

"Well," replied the student hesitantly, "the shaft of a plow."

"Very good! A snake does indeed resemble the shaft of a plow," the teacher said, encouraging the boy. "The next time you gather firewood, please tell me what you see."

When the student returned from the forest the second time, he said, "Master, I saw an elephant."

"Excellent!" exclaimed the teacher. "What did the elephant make you think of?"

"Well," replied the student hesitantly, "the shaft of a plow."

The teacher said nothing, but he thought, "It's not unreasonable to see a resemblance between an elephant's trunk or one of its tusks and the shaft of a plow. Perhaps he is not yet able to express himself with much detail and can only think in generalities, but this may develop." Aloud he said, "The next time you gather firewood, please tell me again what you see."

When the student returned from the forest the third time, he said, "Master, a man gave me some sugar-cane to eat."

"Excellent!" exclaimed the teacher. "What did the sugar cane make you think of?"

"Well," replied the student hesitantly, "the shaft of a plow."

The teacher said nothing, but he thought, "A long piece of sugar cane might possibly make one think of the shaft of a plow, but not a short piece that one eats. That is hardly a good comparison." Aloud he said, "The next time you gather firewood, please tell me again what you see."

When the student next returned from the forest, he said, "Master, today I ate some curd with molasses."

"What did the curd with molasses make you think of?"

"Well," replied the student hesitantly, "the shaft of a plow."

"No!" the teacher cried in despair, as he sat down and put his head in his hands. "This boy is hopeless!" he thought. "He has missed the point entirely. There is only one idea in his head, and he tries to apply it to everything. He is a dullard and will never learn!"

Having concluded his story, the Buddha identified the birth: "At that time, Lāludāyi was the student, and I was the teacher."

48
Steadfastness
Amba Jātaka

It was while staying at Jetavana that the Buddha told this story about a bhikkhu who was scrupulous in fulfilling all his duties. He carefully served his teachers and observed all the rules for bhikkhus. Every day, he swept the monastery, the rooms, the grounds, and the path leading to the monastery. Every day, he prepared fresh drinking water. Because of this one bhikkhu's virtue, lay people regularly offered meals and other requisites to all the bhikkhus in the monastery.

One day, some bhikkhus were talking about how this bhikkhu's goodness ensured their well-being and filled many lives with joy. When the Buddha heard what they were discussing, he said, "This is not the first time, Bhikkhus, that this bhikkhu has been remarkable in fulfilling his duties. Long ago, five hundred ascetics were supported as a direct result of his goodness." Then he told this story of the past.

Long, long ago, when Brahmadatta was reigning in Bārāṇasi, the Bodhisatta was born into a brahmin family in the northern part of the kingdom.

After he grew up, he left the world and became the leader of a group of five hundred ascetics living at the foot of the Himavat.

In those days, there was a severe drought in that region. The rivers and ponds dried up, and the creatures of the forest were desperate. One of the ascetics felt great pity for the thirsty, suffering beasts. He cut down a tree, hollowed out the trunk to make a trough, and worked to fill it with as much water as he could find. So many animals came to drink that the ascetic soon had no time left to gather fruit for himself. Disregarding his own hunger, he continued working to care for the thirsty animals.

The grateful animals realized that the ascetic was sacrificing himself for their sake and said to each other, "This ascetic is so preoccupied with our needs that he has no time to find fruit for himself. He must be very hungry. Everyone who comes here to drink should bring some fruit for him." After that, each animal that came to the trough for water brought fruit, including mangoes, jakfruits, rose apples, and bananas. Their offerings were more than enough to provide not only for the compassionate ascetic but also for all his companions.

Observing this, the leader of the ascetics exclaimed, "See how one man's goodness has been the means of providing all of us with food. Even though he fasted as he toiled for others' welfare, he reaped abundant fruit, beyond his own desire. We should always be so steadfast in doing right!"

Having concluded his story, the Buddha identified the birth: "At that time, this bhikkhu was the good ascetic, and I was the leader of those ascetics."

49

The Imposter
Katāhaka Jātaka

It was while staying at Jetavana that the Buddha told this story about a boastful bhikkhu.[1]

This bhikkhu was constantly bragging about his aristocratic family. "Friends," he said almost every day, "there is no family nobler than mine. I am descended from a long line of princes. My family has vast estates, and our treasuries are full of gold and silver. Even our field-hands and servants eat fragrant rice with the most delicious meat curries and wear garments made of Bārānasi silk. Of course, now that I have left the home life, I have to be satisfied with coarse food and rough robes, but what splendor I used to enjoy!"

The other bhikkhus got tired of hearing this, and one of them took it upon himself to find out whether or not there was any truth to these claims. He checked on the family background of the boastful bhikkhu and discovered that none of it was true. He exposed the fraud to the whole community, which put an end to the bragging.

---

1 The occasion for this story is the same as that for Tale 35.

Later, in the Hall of Truth, the bhikkhus were talking about how that bhikkhu, despite having left home and undertaken the discipline of a bhikkhu, had gone about trying to deceive his fellow bhikkhus with lies and boasts. When the Buddha heard what they were discussing, he said, "This is not the first time, Bhikkhus, that this man has acted in that way. Long ago, also, he pretended high birth." Then he told this story of the past.

Long, long ago, when Brahmadatta was reigning in Bārānasi, the Bodhisatta was one of his treasurers. On the very same day that the treasurer's wife gave birth to a son, a handmaiden in his house also had a baby boy, and the two children grew up together. The treasurer's son was taught to read and write, and the young servant, whose name was Katāhaka, carried his master's tablets to school. Being a clever boy, Katāhaka taught himself to read and write. As he was growing up, he also learned some useful crafts, and became a fair-spoken, handsome young man. One day, Katāhaka thought, "I am only a retainer. Now I am quite at ease being only a personal secretary to my master's son, but the slightest fault on my part could result in my being beaten, imprisoned, or returned to the servant's quarters. It would be an easy matter for me to forge a letter from my master to his friend on the border and to set myself up in a very comfortable position."

He wrote the following letter: "The bearer of this is my son. I would very much like to have our houses united. I would like to suggest that you give your daughter to my son in marriage. If you agree, I further ask that you keep the young couple near you for the present. As soon as I can conveniently do so, I will come to you."

He secretly sealed the letter with the treasurer's private seal and traveled to the border with a well-filled purse, handsome clothing, and rich jewelry. When he arrived at the house, he bowed politely to the merchant.

"Where do you come from?" asked the merchant.

"From Bārānasi, sir."

"Who is your father?"

"The treasurer of Bārānasi."

"What brings you here?"

"My father has sent you this message," said Katāhaka, handing him the sealed letter.

After he had read the letter, the merchant exclaimed, "This is splendid!"

The merchant gladly arranged the marriage between his daughter and Katāhaka and set the young couple up in grand style.

Enjoying his new affluence and privileged position, Katāhaka began to give himself airs. When he sat down to a meal, he would invariably say, "This food is so provincial." Whenever he received new clothes, he complained, "These provincials have no taste and no sense of fashion."

In Bārānasi, the treasurer realized that he hadn't seen Katāhaka for a long time and wondered what could have happened to him. He sent some men to search for him. They scoured the kingdom and finally located him masquerading as the rich man's heir. Without letting Katāhaka know that he had been discovered, they reported everything to the treasurer.

"This will never do," said the treasurer. "I will go and bring him back." He asked the king's permission and departed with a large entourage. The news spread quickly, so it was not long before Katāhaka heard that the treasurer was on his way to the border. Sure that he was the reason for the treasurer's visit, Katāhaka didn't know what to do. He couldn't face losing everything he had gained by running away. At last, he decided that the best way to placate the treasurer would be to meet him on the way and to act like the servant of the old days. To make his plan work and to maintain the deception, he had to prepare his wife's family.

When they all sat down to eat together, he said, "When my parents take their meals, I hand them the plates and dishes, bring the spittoon, and fetch their fans. In my family, I never sit down to eat with my parents. That would show a lack of respect. I prefer to wait on my parents." Couching his behavior in terms of filial piety, he described a servant's duty to a master.

Just before the treasurer arrived, Katāhaka said to his father-in-law, "I hear that my father is coming to see you. Please get ready to entertain him, while I go with a present and meet him on the road."

"Do so, my dear boy," said his father-in-law.

Katāhaka took an expensive gift and set out with a large retinue. As soon as they encountered the treasurer, Katāhaka bowed very respectfully and presented the gift. The treasurer accepted it and reacted in a friendly manner. After breakfast, when he withdrew to answer the call of nature, Katāhaka hurriedly took water to him and fell at his feet. "Oh, Master," he begged the treasurer, "I will do any thing you require, but please do not expose me!"

"Fear no exposure at my hands," the treasurer said reassuringly, quite pleased at the youth's dutiful conduct. In the city, the treasurer was feted with great magnificence and Katāhaka continued to act as his servant.

That afternoon, as the treasurer and the merchant were relaxing, the latter said, "My lord, your letter pleased me very much, and it was an honor for me to give my daughter to your son as a bride. He is a fine young man." The treasurer made a suitable reply about his son, and the merchant was delighted beyond measure. The treasurer, however, realizing the extent of Katāhaka's deceit, came to despise the boy and could barely tolerate the sight of him.

One day, the treasurer sent for the merchant's daughter and said "My dear, please tell me frankly whether my son is a good husband and whether you get on well with him."

"Father-in-law, my husband has only one flaw," she replied. "He often complains about things, such as food and clothes."

"He has always had this weakness," said the treasurer, "but I will tell you how to stop that. Here is a text for you to memorize. Just repeat it to your husband the next time he finds fault with his food. It is in the local language, so you may not understand its meaning." After the treasurer had repeated the verse and she had learned it perfectly, he set out for Bāranasi. Katāhaka accompanied him part of the way and, after giving the treasurer still more precious gifts, took his leave.

The success of passing himself off as the treasurer's son in the presence of the treasurer himself made Katāhaka even prouder, even more boastful and disdainful. One day, not long after that, his wife arranged a sumptuous dinner. At the first mouthful, Katāhaka started to grumble. His wife immediately began reciting the verse her father-in-law had taught her: "If he who lives among strangers far from home talks grandly, his visitor will come back and spoil it all. Come, eat your dinner, Katāhaka."

"Oh no!" thought Katāhaka. "The treasurer has told her my name. Does she know the whole story?" From that day on, he never complained again, and he stopped putting on airs. He humbly ate what was set before him and admired the clothes he was given. At the end of his life, he passed away to fare according to his deserts.

Having concluded his story, the Buddha identified the birth: "At that time, this impudent bhikkhu was Katāhaka, and I was the treasurer of Bāranasi."

50

His Holiness
Bilāra Jātaka

It was while staying at Jetavana that the Buddha told this story about a hypocrite.

When some bhikkhus told the Buddha that another bhikkhu was a hypocrite, the Buddha replied, "This is not the first time he has practiced such duplicity. He was just the same in times gone by." Then he told this story of the past.

Long, long ago, when Brahmadatta was reigning in Bārānasi, the Bodhisatta was born a rat in the jungle. Because of his great size and his wisdom, hundreds of other rats acknowledged him as their leader.

One day, a wandering jackal noticed the large pack of rats and wondered how he could manage to catch them. He watched them for several days and came up with a good scheme. Choosing a suitable spot near the entrance to their hole, he positioned himself. He stood on one leg, facing the sun, and pretended to sniff the wind. When the rats came to search for food, the leader saw the jackal and, taking him for a holy ascetic, approached and politely asked his name.

"Dhammiko (Virtuous) is my name," replied the jackal.

"Why do you stand only on one leg?" asked the rat.

"If I stood on all four legs at once, the earth could not bear my weight."

"Why do you keep your mouth open?"

"To take in air. I live on air. That is my only food."

"Why do you face the sun?"

"I worship the sun."

"What righteousness!" thought the rat. Thereafter, every day, when the rats came out and when they returned, the leader and the other rats paid their respects to the saintly jackal. Each time, however, as the rats were leaving, the jackal swiftly snatched the last one in the line and devoured him without any of the other rats suspecting anything wrong.

As the days passed, the rat pack grew smaller. Some rats noticed that a number of their fellows were missing, and they wondered why. They mentioned this to the leader, but he had no immediate answer, though he suspected the jackal. He decided to test the ascetic.

The next day, he instructed the other rats to go first and to pay their respects to the ascetic, and he positioned himself at the end of the line. As soon as he had paid his respects and turned to go, the jackal sprang at him. He was ready, however, and turned to face the surprised ascetic. "So this is your saintliness, you scoundrel!" the rat leader cried. "Your piety is merely a cloak to hide your villainy! Now we see the true nature of the jackal."

The jackal continued his attack, but the mighty rat leaped at the jackal's throat and severed his windpipe with his sharp teeth. The jackal gasped and fell dead. The other rats hurried back and devoured the jackal's body. They worked so quickly that the entire skeleton had been stripped bare before the last rats arrived. After that, the troop of rats lived happily in peace and quiet.

Having concluded his story, the Buddha identified the birth: "At that time, this hypocritical bhikkhu was the jackal, and I was the leader of the rats."

51
Ingratitude
Asampadāna Jātaka

It was while staying at Veluvana that the Buddha told this story about Devadatta.

One day, the bhikkhus were talking about Devadatta's ingratitude and his inability to recognize the Buddha's goodness. When the Buddha heard what they were discussing, he said, "Bhikkhus, this is not the first time that Devadatta has been ungrateful; he was just as ungrateful in bygone days." Then he told this story of the past.

Long, long ago, in Rājagaha, the capital of Magadha, the Bodhisatta was the king's treasurer. His name was Sankha, and his treasury was worth eighty crores. In Bārānasi, the capital of Kāsi, the king's treasurer was named Piliya, and he was just as wealthy. The two treasurers were great friends.

At one time, Piliya suffered misfortune after misfortune. He lost all his property and was left without a penny or a roof over his head. In his distress, he and his wife left Bārānasi and traveled on foot to Rājagaha to see his friend. Sankha embraced him and treated him as an honored guest, asking, in due course, the reason for the visit.

237

"I am a ruined man," answered Piliya. "I have lost everything and have come to ask your help. You are my only hope."

"My dear friend," Sankha cried, "have no fear! With all my heart I am more than willing to help you! Half of everything I own shall be yours!" From his treasury, he took forty crores of gold and gave it to Piliya. He divided everything, including livestock, grain, and servants into two equal parts and gave half to Piliya. Heartened by this generosity, Piliya went back to Bārānasi and prospered once again.

Some time later, a series of calamities befell Sankha, and he lost every penny he had. Wondering where to turn in his desperation, he decided to visit his friend Piliya. He and his wife set out on foot for Bārānasi.

At the entrance to the city, he said to his wife, "My dear, it is not suitable for you to trudge the streets with me. Wait here until I can send a servant with a carriage to bring you into the city in proper style." He left her in a shelter and went alone to Piliya's house, where he asked to be announced.

"Show him in," said Piliya to the servant. At the sight of the Sankha's shabby clothes, however, Piliya neither rose nor welcomed his friend. In an icy voice, he asked what brought him to Bārānasi.

"To see you," Sankha replied.

"Where are you staying?"

"Nowhere, as yet. I left my wife at the city gate and came straight here."

"I have no room for you," Piliya announced coldly. "Take a measure of rice, find somewhere to cook it, and begone. Never visit me again!"

Piliya ordered a servant to give his unfortunate friend a portion of rough, semi-polished rice, even though, on that very day, one thousand wagon-loads of the best rice had been threshed and stored in his overflowing granaries. The rascal, who had coolly taken four hundred million when he was in need, now doled out this tiny bit of coarse rice to his benefactor!

The servant did as he was told and took the measure of rice to Sankha, who debated in his mind whether or not he should take it. "This thankless wretch breaks off our friendship because I am a ruined man, but, if I refused his paltry gift, I would be as bad as he. It's an ignoble man who scorns a modest gift. I will be true to the principles of friendship." He took the scanty provisions and returned to his wife.

"What did you get, dear?" she asked as soon as he had returned.

"Our friend Piliya has given us this unpolished rice and washed his hands of us."

"Why did you take it?" she cried, bursting into tears. "Is this a fit return for the forty crores you gave him?"

"Don't cry, my dear," Sankha said. "I took it because I did not want to violate the principle of friendship. Our former friend has become a miser, but don't take it to heart. I would rather accept his charity than be the one to break our friendship."

His wife could not stop crying.

At that moment, a servant whom Sankha had given to Piliya happened to be passing by. Hearing the weeping and recognizing his former master and mistress, the servant fell at their feet. He asked what had brought them to Bārānasi, and Sankha told him their story.

Urging them to be of good cheer, their old retainer took them to his own home and prepared a meal for them. He announced to the other servants that their old master and mistress had come, and all of them greeted the couple warmly. A few days later, the man led his fellow servants in a group to the king's palace, where they made quite a commotion.

When the king asked what the matter was, the servants told him the whole story. The king immediately sent for the two treasurers. He asked Sankha whether it was true that he given four hundred million to Piliya.

"Sire," Sankha replied calmly, "when my friend confided in me and sought my aid, I gave him half of my possessions, not only of my money but of my servants, livestock, and grain, as well."

"Is this true?" the king asked Piliya.

"Yes, Sire," he admitted reluctantly.

"When, in turn, your benefactor confided in you and asked for help, did you show him honor and hospitality?"

Here Piliya was silent.

"Did you order that a measure of coarse, unpolished rice be doled out to him?" asked the king.

Piliya remained silent.

After taking counsel with his ministers, the king ordered that all of Piliya's wealth be given to Sankha.

"No, Sire," Sankha protested, "I do not want what belongs to another. Let me be given only what I formerly gave him."

Pleased with this response, the king revised his order. He commanded Piliya to return to Sankha all that he had been given: the forty crores plus the livestock, the grain, and the servants. Sankha and his wife, accompanied by a large retinue, returned to Rājagaha with their recovered wealth, where they prospered once more. After a life spent in generosity and other good deeds, Sankha passed away to fare according to his deserts.

Having concluded his story, the Buddha identified the birth: "At that time, Devadatta was Piliya, and I was Sankha."

52

Feathers of a Golden Goose
Suvanna-Hamsa Jātaka

It was while staying at Jetavana that the Buddha told this story about the bhikkhunī, Venerable Thulla-Nandā (Fat Nandā).

In Sāvatthī, a lay devotee had made a standing offer of garlic as medicine to the Bhikkhunī Sangha. He had stipulated that, whenever a bhikkhunī requested garlic, she was to be given some or allowed to gather it for herself from his field.

During a festival, Venerable Thulla-Nandā asked the family for garlic and was told that there was none in the house. She went to the field and carried off an armload of garlic. When the overseer saw how much she took, he was furious and vociferously complained that the bhikkhunīs were greedy.

The overseer's criticism was widely repeated, which irritated other bhikkhunīs and bhikkhus, who, conscientiously practicing moderation, felt that they were being unfairly accused. Both bhikkhus and bhikkhunīs went to the Buddha and reported what had happened. The Master summoned Venerable Thulla-Nandā and said, "A greedy bhikkhu or bhikkhunī neither instills confidence in those who do not yet believe nor increases confidence in those who already believe. A greedy bhikkhu or bhikkhunī neither invites alms nor helps to maintain regular alms. A bhikkhu or bhikkhunī who practices moderation, of course, does all these things and enhances the Sāsana."

Addressing the assembly of bhikkhus and bhikkhunīs, the Buddha said, "This is not the first time that Thulla-Nandā was greedy." Then he told this story of the past.

Long, long ago, when Brahmadatta was reigning in Bārānasi, the Bodhisatta was born into a brahmin family. When he came of age, he married a woman from a similar family, and they had three daughters, Nandā, Nandavatī, and Sundarīnandā (Joy, Joyful, and Lovely Joy). When he died, he was reborn as a magnificent golden goose, and he had a clear memory of his past.

One day, as he was recollecting his previous life, he realized that his former wife and daughters, who had gone to live with relatives, were scraping by on the charity of others. Still feeling strong affection for them, the golden goose decided to help.

He flew into the house where they were living and landed on a beam. When the woman and her daughters saw the golden goose, they wondered why he had come and where he had come from. He explained their past relationship, and he told them that he would provide for them.

"Take this feather," he said, letting one of his feathers of pure gold fall. "It should make your life easier."

From time to time, the golden goose returned and gave them more feathers, one at a time. Each feather was worth more than they needed for daily life, and, in time, they became quite well-off.

One day, the woman said to her daughters, "We can't depend on that goose! If your father ever decides not to come back, what will we do? We must take no chances. The next time he comes, we should pluck out every feather! That way we're sure to get them all!"

"Mother!" the girls cried in horror. "That would cause him dreadful pain! We could not do such a cruel thing! We could never hurt our father like that!"

The next time the golden goose visited the house, the woman spoke to him very sweetly and invited him to come closer. As soon as he was within reach, she grabbed him with both hands, tucked him under her arm, and pulled out every single feather, not leaving so much as a pin feather or a bit of down.

The goose's golden feathers, however, had a unique property, such that, if they were plucked against his will, they instantly became ordinary white feathers. His greedy wife found herself surrounded by a great pile of white feathers, more than enough for a pillow or a coverlet but of no special value.

Plucked bare, the poor goose was unable to fly away, and the woman, bitterly disappointed, threw him into a barrel with a few scraps of food. In time, his new feathers grew out, but they were all white. As soon as he could, the goose flew away, never to return.

Having concluded his story, the Buddha added, "Thulla-Nandā was as greedy in the past as she is now. Because of greed, she lost gold then, and she has lost garlic now. Learn from this example to be moderate in your desires and to be contented with what you are given. Henceforth, any bhikkhunī who eats garlic must do penance." Then the Buddha identified the birth: "At that time, Thulla-Nandā was the wife, her sisters were the three daughters, and I was the golden goose."

53

The Stonecutter and the Mouse
Babbu Jātaka

It was while staying at Jetavana that the Buddha told this story about Kānā's mother and established a rule of Vinaya.[1]

In Sāvatthī, there was a woman who had attained the first path. Her daughter Kānā lived with her husband in another village. Kānā had gone to Sāvatthī on an errand and was staying with her mother. After a few days, her husband sent a message for her to return home.

Kānā asked her mother about going home, and her mother answered that she should not return empty-handed. She offered to make a cake for Kānā to take. Just as the cake was finished, a bhikkhu passed by on his almsrounds, and Kānā's mother offered him the cake. As the bhikkhu went on his way, he happened to tell another bhikkhu, who passed the house just in time to get the second cake as it came out of the oven. That bhikkhu told a third, and the third told a fourth. In this way, four fresh cakes were successively given to bhikkhus. The result was that Kānā did not start on her way home.

---

1 If a bhikkhu is offered cakes or cooked grain-meal, he may accept no more than two or three bowlfuls, and these are to be shared among the bhikkhus (Vinaya, Suttavibhanga, Pacittiya, 34).

The husband sent other messengers after his wife. The final message was that, if she did not come back immediately, he would get himself another wife. Each message had exactly the same result, with cakes being offered as alms just as soon as they were baked and Kānā postponing her return. In the end, the husband carried out his threat and took another wife. When Kānā heard this news, she wept inconsolably. Kānā was so angry that she began reviling and abusing every bhikkhu she saw, and, eventually, no bhikkhu dared even to enter the street.

Knowing all of this, the Buddha put on his robes early in the morning, went with his almsbowl to the house of Kānā's mother, and sat down on the seat prepared for him. He asked why the daughter was upset and crying and, being told, spoke words of consolation to the mother. The Buddha asked to see Kānā and questioned her about the situation. Finally, she admitted that the bhikkhus were not at fault, since they had only taken what had been given to them. At the end of his discourse, Kānā attained the first path.[2]

Later, in the Hall of Truth, some bhikkhus were talking about how Kānā had been prevented from returning home and had lost her husband by the actions of those four bhikkhus on their almsrounds. When the Buddha heard what they were discussing, he said, "This is not the first time those four bhikkhus have brought sorrow to Kānā's mother by eating her food. Long ago, they did the same thing." Then he told this story of the past.

Long, long ago, when Brahmadatta was reigning in Bārānasi, the Bodhisatta was born into a stone-cutter's family, and, when he was grown, he was an expert in working stone. He found an excellent quarry near a deserted village in the countryside of Kāsi and began working there.

Years before, the village had been the home of an extremely rich merchant who had amassed a fortune of forty crores in gold. One by one, all the members of this family, including the merchant himself, died. In time, the entire village became deserted and the merchant's great wealth and treasure was abandoned and forgotten. The merchant's wife, however, had been so attached to the treasure that, when she died, she was reborn as a mouse and lived in the space above the old storeroom.

As she ran about seeking food, the mouse often saw the skillful stonecutter quarrying and shaping stones near the site of her old mansion. She soon fell in love with him. Realizing that the secret of her vast wealth would die with her, she wanted to enjoy her gold with him.

---

2   Another account of this incident adds that the king saw the Buddha leaving Kānā's home. When the king learned what had happened, he adopted Kānā as his own daughter and arranged for her marriage to a rich nobleman. Afterwards, Kānā's generosity to the Sangha became well-known.

One day, she approached the stonecutter with a coin in her mouth. When he saw her, he very kindly asked, "Mother, why have you brought this coin?"

"It is for you, my son," the mouse answered. "I'd like you to have it to buy some meat for yourself and a little for me, as well."

The stonecutter willingly accepted the money and bought a halfpenny's worth of meat for the mouse. She took the meat and was very happy.

After this, the mouse gave the stonecutter a coin every day, and every day, he supplied her with meat.

One day, however, the mouse was caught by a cat.

"Don't kill me," cried the mouse.

"Why not?" said the cat. "I'm starving, and you are all I have to eat!"

"First, tell me one thing," protested the mouse. "Are you always hungry, or hungry only today?"

"Of course, I'm hungry every day. There is very little to eat around here."

"Well, I can provide you with meat. If you let me go, I will give you meat every day."

"All right," said the cat, releasing the mouse, "but you had better not fail, or you will be in trouble."

This meant that the mouse had to divide her daily ration of meat from the stonecutter in half and to give half to the cat.

Unfortunately, a few days later, the mouse was caught by a second cat and had to purchase her release on the same terms. Thereafter, she had to divide her food into three portions every day.

The hapless mouse was caught by a third and a fourth cat so, with her daily food being divided into five portions, she was not getting enough to eat. She grew so thin that she seemed to be nothing but skin and bone.

The stonecutter noticed how emaciated his friend had become and asked the reason.

The mouse told him all that had befallen her.

"Why didn't you tell me all this sooner?" he asked. "Don't worry! I'll help you out of your troubles."

He took a block of the purest crystal and hollowed out a cavity inside it. When he had finished, he told the mouse to get inside the cavity.

"Just wait there," he instructed her. "When the time comes, you must threaten and revile every cat that comes near you. Provoke them as much as you can!"

The mouse crept inside the transparent crystal cell and waited.

Very soon, one of the cats approached and demanded his meat.

"Away, stupid tabby!" cried the mouse, as loud as she could. "Why should I give you food? Go home, and eat your own kittens if you're so hungry!"

Infuriated at these words and never suspecting that the mouse was inside an invisible crystal, the cat sprang at the mouse to gobble her up. So fierce was his spring that he killed himself striking the hard stone.

The same fate befell all four cats.

From that day on, the grateful mouse brought the stonecutter two or three coins every day, instead of only one. In time, she gave him the whole of her hoarded wealth.

The two lived together in unbroken friendship until their lives ended, and they passed away to fare according to their deserts.

Having concluded his story, the Buddha identified the birth: "At that time, these four bhikkhus were the four cats, Kānā's mother was the mouse, and I was the stonecutter."

54

A Calamitous Day
Ubhatobhattha Jātaka

It was while staying at Veluvana that the Buddha told this story about Devadatta.

One day, the bhikkhus were talking together about Devadatta. Some of them said that he was like a torch from a funeral pyre, charred at both ends and smeared with dung in the middle, unusable as kindling wood, either in the forest or in the village. Having given up the world to follow the Buddha, Devadatta both missed the comforts of lay life and failed in his vocation as a bhikkhu. When the Buddha joined them, he asked what they were talking about. They told him, and he replied, "Yes, Bhikkhus, and in the past Devadatta had a similar twofold failure." Then he told this story of the past.

Long, long ago, when Brahmadatta was reigning in Bārānasi, the Bodhisatta was born a tree deva, near a fishing village.

One day, a fisherman from that village went with his little boy to the river. As soon as he cast his line, the hook caught on a snag, and the fisherman could not pull it up. He was very pleased, imagining a good catch, but then he began to worry. "Son," he called, "I have just hooked a fine fish, but

249

I don't want to have to share it with the other fishermen. Run home, and let your mother know about it. Tell her to start a quarrel in the village so that none of the other men comes down here." Obediently, the boy ran off and told his mother exactly what his father had said.

The fisherman's wife put a palm leaf behind one ear and blackened one eye with soot. Holding a dog as if to nurse it, she went to a neighbor's house.

"Bless me," cried the neighbor woman, "you've gone mad!"

"I'm not crazy!" retorted the fisherman's wife. "How dare you abuse me with such talk! Come with me to the headman, and I'll have you fined for slander."

Bickering angrily, they went to the headman. He listened to the arguments and decided that the one who deserved to be fined was the fisherman's wife. When she heard this, she became so angry that she shouted at him, and he ordered that she be given a beating as further punishment.

Meanwhile, the fisherman, afraid that the line might break, tore off his clothes and jumped into the water to secure his prize. As he groped about for the fish, he struck the submerged tree branch that had snagged his hook, and it poked out both his eyes. While he was thrashing about in pain, another man noticed his clothes lying on the bank and stole them. At last, the unfortunate fisherman gave up trying to find the fish and scrambled out of the water, trembling with cold and pressing his poor eyes to stop the pain. As he felt around, trying to find his clothes, the tree deva saw him and said, "Oh, miserable fisherman! Your work has been in vain both in the water and on land. Your going blind and your wife's beating are a double failure and a double woe!"

Having concluded his story, the Buddha identified the birth: "At that time, Devadatta was the fisherman, and I was the tree deva."

55

Crows' Fat
Kāka Jātaka

It was while staying at Jetavana that the Buddha told this story about a wise teacher.[3]

Long, long ago, when Brahmadatta was reigning in Bārānasi, the Bodhisatta was born a crow. He resided in a huge charnel ground in Bārānasi, where he was the leader of a flock of eighty thousand crows.

One day, the king's spiritual advisor left the city to go to the river to bathe. When he finished, he dressed in brand new clothes, garlanded himself, and returned to the city. On the city gate, sat a pair of crows. The male said to his mate, "I am going to foul this brahmin's head."

"Don't you dare do such a thing!" said his wife. "This brahmin is an important man. It is dangerous to incur the hatred of the great. If you anger him, he may do serious harm to us."

"I don't care. I'm going to do it anyway!" insisted her mate.

"Well, you'll be sorry," said the wife, and she flew quickly away.

---

3   The occasion for this story is the same as that for Tales 136 and 179 where it is told in more detail.

Just as the brahmin passed through the archway, the crow released a considerable dropping, which landed on the man's freshly washed and shaven head.

The indignity he suffered infuriated the brahmin so much that he developed an intense hatred for all crows.

A short time later, a young servant in charge of a granary spread new rice in front of the granary door to dry in the sun. She sat in the door to guard the rice, but the sun made her sleepy, and she dozed off.

While she was sleeping, a shaggy goat went up and started to eat the rice. When the girl woke up, she drove it away. The goat stayed close by, and, as soon as it saw the servant nodding, it returned to eat more rice. Again she awoke and chased the goat away.

After the servant had driven the goat away for the third time, she decided to give the animal such a scare that it would go away and leave the rice alone.

She got a lighted torch, propped it beside her, and pretended to fall asleep again. As soon as the goat resumed eating the grain, she jumped up and struck its back with the torch, which set the goat's shaggy hair on fire. Frightened and in pain, the frantic goat dashed into the hay-shed next to the elephants' stable and rolled in the hay, trying to extinguish the fire. Instead of putting out the fire on its back, the goat set the shed on fire. The flames quickly spread to the elephant stables, where many of the elephants suffered serious burns, beyond the skill of the elephant-doctors to cure.

When the king heard about this, he asked his advisor whether he knew of a remedy to relieve the elephants' pain and to heal their burns.

"I certainly do, Sire," replied the advisor. "The best salve for this type of injury is crows' fat."

The king immediately ordered all crows killed and their fat rendered into an ointment.

Throughout the city, there was a great slaughter of crows, but not a single drop of fat was found on any bird. Undaunted, the king's men went on killing as many crows as they could. Dead crows lay in heaps everywhere. The surviving crows were terrified as they watched their relatives and friends being slain.

After escaping from the king's men, one crow informed the leader of the crows of the danger they were all in. The leader immediately realized that he was the only one who could save the crows from complete annihilation. He reviewed the Ten Perfections and, taking loving-kindness as his protection, flew straight to the king's palace. He entered through an open window and landed under the king's throne. A servant tried to catch him, but, at that moment, the king entered and forbade it.

Again recollecting loving-kindness, the leader of the crows stepped out from under the throne. "Sire," he said calmly to the king, "in ruling his kingdom, a king should remember never to act from passion. Before taking action, a ruler should thoroughly examine a situation. Only then should he do what needs to be done. If, on the other hand, a king acts rashly and without justice, he may cause great fear, even the fear of death, among his subjects. When your advisor prescribed crows' fat, he was merely seeking revenge. He knows that crows have no fat. His intention was to have many crows die simply because he hates them."

These words touched the king's heart. In gratitude, he ordered that the leader of the crows be placed on a golden throne, anointed with the choicest oils, and provided with curries from the royal kitchen, served in vessels of gold. After the wise bird had finished eating, the king said, "Sage bird, you say that crows have no fat. Can you tell me why?

"Your Majesty," the leader of the crows answered in a clear voice, "crows live in perpetual fear of all humans, who are their enemies. Because of this extreme anxiety and apprehension, crows never develop any fat."

King Brahmadatta was so pleased with the crow's teaching that he gave him the white umbrella. After establishing the king in the five precepts, the wise crow urged him to protect all living creatures from harm and returned the kingdom to him.

The king immediately proclaimed a ban on killing any living creature. To crows, he declared special privileges. He ordered that, every day, six bushels of rice be cooked for them and that the leader of the crows be given the same food that he himself ate.

Having concluded his story, the Buddha identified the birth: "At that time, Ānanda was king of Kāsi, and I was the leader of the crows."

56

Bad Friends
Godha Jātaka

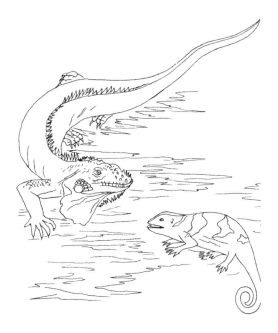

It was while staying at Veluvana that the Buddha told this story about a wayward bhikkhu. This bhikkhu had a friend who had taken ordination under Devadatta. The two friends continued to see one another, sometimes casually, sometimes by visiting each other's monasteries.

One day, the bhikkhu who followed Devadatta asked his friend why he tired himself every day walking for alms. He suggested his friend come to Gayāsīsa, where he could partake of the delicious food provided daily by Prince Ajātasattu. At first, his friend resisted, but Devadatta's follower repeated the offer so many times that, at last, he gave in. After that, the disciple of the Buddha began to frequent Gayāsīsa but was careful to return to Veluvana at the proper hour. It was not long, however, before some of his companions learned what he was doing. When they asked him whether what they had heard was true, he hesitatingly answered, "It is true that I go to Gayāsīsa and eat there, but it is not Devadatta who gives me food; others do that."

His friends reminded him that Devadatta was the enemy of the Buddha and took the bhikkhu to the Hall of Truth to face the Teacher.

After the Buddha had learned the truth from the bhikkhu himself, he said, "Devadatta is a man of bad conduct and bad principle. Having taken ordination here, you should follow my discipline and not eat Devadatta's food. Actually, however, you have always been prone to being led astray by bad friends." Then he told this story of the past.

Long, long ago, when Brahmadatta was reigning in Bārāṇasi, the Bodhisatta was born as a monitor lizard. When he grew up, he lived in a big burrow in the river bank and became the king of a large group of monitor lizards. This monitor lizard king had a son, young and headstrong, who was great friends with a chameleon, with whom he often roughhoused and tussled. When the king heard about this friendship, he sent for his young son and told him that, chameleons being low creatures, the relationship was inappropriate. If the familiarity continued, the king told his son, calamity might befall their whole monitor lizard tribe. He urged his son to have no more to do with the chameleon, but the son stubbornly ignored his father's advice. He spoke with his son again and again about the matter, but his words were of no avail. Foreseeing danger to the monitor lizards from the chameleon, the king had an emergency outlet cut on one side of their burrow, to ensure a secret means of escape, should the need arise.

The young monitor lizard grew to a great size, but the chameleon never got any bigger. What had at first been playful tussling became quite painful for the chameleon, and he began to fear injury or death if it continued. Soon, he came to detest monitor lizards, and he resolved to get rid of them.

One day that summer, after a thunderstorm, winged ants came out, and a few monitor lizards darted here and there catching them. A hunter, who had come into the forest with a sharp spade and a couple of dogs, was catching as many monitor lizards as he could. When the chameleon saw this, he realized that he could deliver a terrific haul to the hunter and thereby settle the score!

He approached the hunter, lay down respectfully in front of him, and asked after his business. "I'm here to catch monitor lizards," the man replied.

"I know the location of a burrow with hundreds of them," offered the chameleon.

"Where is that?" asked the hunter excitedly.

"Follow me," said the chameleon, and he led the hunter toward the monitor lizards' home.

When they arrived, the chameleon said to him, "Here is the monitor lizards' burrow. Gather some brush and build a fire right here. That will smoke them all out." While the hunter did this, the treacherous chameleon withdrew to a nearby spot, where he lay down with his head up to watch the proceedings. "Today I will see the end of my enemy!" he gloated.

When the fire was ready, the hunter set his dogs around the hole, while he stood there keeping his eyes on the exit, holding a heavy stick. Very quickly, smoke filled the burrow, and panic stricken monitor lizards began dashing out. As rapidly as he could, the hunter beat them on the head and piled up the carcasses. The dogs snapped up those he happened to miss. There was a great slaughter among the monitor lizards.

The monitor lizard king knew that this was the chameleon's doing and cried, "A single wicked chameleon has proved the bane of all these monitor lizards. One should never make friends with the wicked, who bring sorrow in their wake! Bad companionship can never have a good end. Because of one treacherous chameleon, our whole tribe has met its end."

With that, he sadly fled by the escape route he had prepared.

Having concluded his story, the Buddha identified the birth: "At that time, Devadatta was the chameleon; this traitorous bhikkhu was the disobedient young monitor lizard; and I was the king of the monitor lizards."

57
Shine Forth in Your Might
Virocana Jātaka

It was while staying at Veluvana that the Buddha told this story about Devadatta's imitating him at Gayāsīsa.

After his extraordinary powers left him and he lost both honor and advantage, Devadatta, in frustration, demanded that the Buddha impose five strict rules on the Sangha.[1] When the Buddha refused, Devadatta and several bhikkhus who sided with him took five hundred young bhikkhus to his monastery at Gayāsīsa. These young bhikkhus were students of the Buddha's two chief disciples, but they had not yet mastered the Dhamma and the Discipline. At Gayāsīsa, Devadatta established a separate order and carried out Sangha business independently from the Buddha, thereby creating a schism in the Sangha.

After some time, knowing that the young bhikkhus had matured sufficiently, the Buddha sent the two chief disciples for them.

When Devadatta saw Venerable Sāriputta and Venerable Moggallāna coming, he began joyfully expounding to his students in imitation of the

---

1 See footnote, Tale 9.

Buddha. After concluding his incoherent lesson late in the evening, Devadatta said to Venerable Sāriputta, "The assembly is still alert and sleepless. Will you be so good as to teach them something or other? My back is aching, and I must lie down."

After Devadatta had gone, Venerable Sāriputta and Venerable Moggallāna delivered an extremely cogent sermon to the young bhikkhus, won them all back, and returned with them to Veluvana.

Early the next morning, Kokālika, one of the bhikkhus who had supported Devadatta most strongly from the beginning, awoke and found the monastery empty. He went to Devadatta's kuti and found him still sleeping. "Master" he cried, "Sāriputta and Moggallāna have taken away the five hundred young bhikkhus, but you still lie here asleep!" He stripped off Devadatta's outer robe and kicked him on the chest with as little compunction as if he were knocking a roof-peg into a mud-wall. The blood gushed out of Devadatta's mouth, and he suffered from the effects of the blow for the rest of his life.[2]

When the chief disciples returned, the Buddha asked, "What was Devadatta doing when you got there?"

Venerable Sāriputta answered that he was imitating the Teacher. He also described the evil that had befallen Devadatta.

"In the same way as now" the Buddha replied, "Devadatta imitated me to his own harm long ago." Then, at Venerable Sāriputta's request, the Buddha told this story of the past.

Long, long ago, when Brahmadatta was reigning in Bārānasi, the Bodhisatta was a maned lion and lived in a golden den in the Himavat. Bounding forth from his lair one day, he looked in all four directions, and roared loudly as he went in pursuit of prey. After slaying a large buffalo and devouring the prime parts of the carcass, he went down to a pool and drank his fill of cool water. As he turned to go to his den, he came face to face with a hungry jackal, who, unable to make his escape, threw himself at the lion's feet.

"What do you want?" the lion asked.

"Lord, let me be your servant," the jackal replied.

"Very well," said the lion, "serve me, and you shall feed on the best meat."

The lion proceeded to his golden den, and the jackal followed.

The lion lay down in his den and instructed the jackal, "Scan the valley for elephants, antelope, buffalos, or other animals that you are fond of. If you see any, come back and report to me. You must say, 'Shine forth in your might, Lord!' Then I will go out and kill the animal. After I have eaten, I will leave a portion for you."

---

2   This incident is related slightly differently in Tale 183.

Following these instructions, the jackal climbed up the mountain every day. Whenever he spotted a beast to his taste, he reported to the lion, fell at his feet, and said, "Shine forth in your might, Lord." Then the lion nimbly bounded away and slew the beast, even a bull elephant. True to his promise, he always shared some of the choice bits with the jackal, who, glutted with his meal, retired to his own den and slept soundly.

As time went by, the jackal not only grew bigger and bigger, but also began to feel proud. "Don't I have four legs?" he asked himself. "Don't I have fangs? Why should I remain a pensioner living on another's bounty? From now on, I will kill elephants and other beasts for my own food. It is only because of the formula, 'Shine forth in your might, Lord,' that the lion, king of the beasts, can kill his prey. If I have the lion call out to me, 'Shine forth in your might, Jackal,' I'll be able to slay an elephant by myself."

The next day, he approached the lion and explained that, after having lived so long on what the lion killed, he now had the desire to eat an elephant of his own killing. "Please allow me to sleep in your golden den," he requested, "while you climb the mountain to look for an elephant. As soon as you see one, hurry back and call, 'Shine forth in your might, Jackal.' Please do not begrudge me this request."

"Jackal," replied the lion, "only lions can kill elephants. There has never been a jackal able to manage the killing of an elephant. Give up this fancy, and continue to feed on what I kill."

In spite of the lion's protests and sound advice, the jackal refused to give up his ambitious scheme. At last, from weariness, the lion gave in. He invited the jackal to rest in his den and climbed up the mountain. It was not long before he spotted an elephant in rut. Returning to the mouth of the cave, he called, "Shine forth in your might, Jackal." The jackal nimbly bounded from the golden den, looked around, and gave a howl. Then he sprang with all his strength at the elephant's head, but, missing his aim, he landed at the elephant's feet. The infuriated tusker raised his right foot and trampled the jackal's head, crushing his skull. Then, pounding the jackal's carcass into a pulp and defecating on it, the elephant trumpeted and hastened back into the forest.

"Now shine forth in your might, Jackal!" proclaimed the lion. "Ah, your mangled corpse proves how you've shone forth in all your might today!"

The lion returned to his old way of life and, living to a ripe old age, passed away to fare according to his deserts.

Having concluded his story, the Buddha identified the birth: "At that time, Devadatta was the jackal, and I was the lion."

58

Dousing the Birth-Fire
Nanguttha Jātaka

It was while staying at Jetavana that the Buddha told this story about the ājīvikas, or naked ascetics, who practiced austerities behind the mango grove. A number of bhikkhus saw them punishing their bodies in various ways—painfully squatting on their heels, swinging in the air like bats, reclining on thorns, and scorching themselves with five fires.[3] The bhikkhus asked the Buddha whether there was any value in such practices.

"None whatsoever," the Buddha answered. "Wise men used to go into the forest, expecting to benefit from austerities like these. One of them found himself no better off for all his sacrifices, so he doused his fire and gave it up. By practicing meditation, he won rebirth in the Brahma heavens." Then he told this story of the past.

Long, long ago, when Brahmadatta was reigning in Bārānasi, the Bodhisatta was born into a brahmin family in the northern part of the kingdom. On the day of his birth, his parents, in keeping with tradition, lit a fire.

---

3 One fire in each of the four cardinal directions and the burning sun overhead.

On his sixteenth birthday, his parents said, "Son, on the day of your birth, we lit a birth-fire for you. Now it is time for you to choose. If you wish to lead the family life, you should learn the three Vedas. If, however, you wish to attain heaven, take your fire with you into the forest, and care for it there. In that way, you can win Mahā-Brahmā's favor and reach his realm."

He told his parents that a family life didn't appeal to him, and he went into the forest and lived in a hermitage, tending his fire. After a while, some villagers gave him an ox. As he was leading the beast back to his hermitage, he resolved to offer it as a sacrifice to the deva of fire. He discovered, however, that he had no salt. Thinking that the Lord of Fire would not like his offering of meat without salt, he decided to return to the village to get some. Before going, he carefully tethered the animal.

While he was away, a band of hunters passed his hermitage. Seeing the ox, they killed it and roasted the best cuts for themselves for dinner. What meat they couldn't eat they carried away, leaving only the tail, the hide, and the hooves.

When the young ascetic returned with the salt, he found only these miserable remains.

"If this Lord of Fire cannot manage to look after his own sacrifice," he cried, "how can he possibly look after me? It is a complete waste of time to serve him!

"Wretched Jātaveda," he mocked, addressing the Lord of Fire by name, "through your own incompetence, your meat is gone. Now you will have to be satisfied with this offal. Enjoy your tail, skin, and hooves, and consider yourself lucky!" In disgust, he threw the miserable scraps onto the fire.

After this bogus ceremony, the young ascetic put out the fire and left the hermitage. He went into the Himavat and devoted himself to meditation. Through his efforts, he ensured his rebirth in the Brahma heavens.

Having concluded his story, the Buddha identified the birth: "At that time, I was the ascetic who quenched the fire."

59

Emptying the Sea
Kāka Jātaka

It was while staying at Jetavana that the Buddha told this story about a group of elderly bhikkhus.

In Sāvatthī, there were some rich landowners who were good friends and performed many good deeds together. One day, after they heard the Buddha teach, they decided to become bhikkhus. They reasoned that, since they were already old and they had no more use for the home life, it would be better for them to try to put an end to suffering.

They divided their property among their children and asked the Buddha to accept them into the Order.

After they ordained, however, they didn't devote themselves seriously to meditation, and they failed to master the Truth.

Having been friends during their household life, as bhikkhus, they lived together in a cluster of huts on the outskirts of the monastery. On their almsrounds, they usually went to the houses of their relatives and ate there. All these old bhikkhus depended particularly on the former wife of one of them. She regularly supplied them with delicious curries and provided them with the other requisites.

When a sudden illness took her life, the bhikkhus were devastated. Overcome with grief, they wept and wailed and carried on noisily over the death of their benefactress, who had cooked rich curries and tasty sauces for them.

Hearing their loud cries, other bhikkhus hurried to their huts to find out what was wrong. The elderly bhikkhus explained tearfully that their kind benefactress was dead and that they were crying because they would never see her like again.

Later, the bhikkhus were talking about the impropriety of the old men's sorrow. When the Buddha heard what they were discussing, he said, "Bhikkhus, long ago, too, this same woman's death made them weep and wail." Then he told them this story of the past.

Long, long ago, when Brahmadatta was reigning in Bārānasi, the Bodhisatta was born as a deva living in the sea.

One day, just after some people had made an offering of milk rice, fish, meat, and strong drink to the nāgas, a crow and his mate came to the seashore in search of food. The two crows were delighted to gorge themselves on the food. They drank so much alcohol, which they were unaccustomed to, that they both got very drunk and decided to play in the sea. As they were awkwardly trying to swim on the surf, a wave suddenly swept the female crow out to sea. A fish took advantage of her helplessness and swallowed her whole.

"Oh, my poor dear wife is dead," wailed the crow, bursting into tears.

Soon the whole flock of crows, drawn by his loud grieving, arrived to find out what was the matter. When he explained that his wife had been carried out to sea, they all began to lament loudly. Then it occurred to them that they were surely stronger than the sea. They could rescue their friend's spouse by simply emptying the sea. Resolving to do just that, they set to work. They scooped up water with their bills and dumped it mouthful by mouthful on the dry land. In no time, the salty water made their throats very sore. As they continued to toil, their mouths became dry and inflamed, and their eyes grew bloodshot from the sun. All of them were on the point of dropping from exhaustion. Turning to one another, they agreed that they were laboring in vain to empty the sea. No sooner had they gotten rid of the water in one place than more water flowed in, filling that space exactly as it had been before. It was obvious that they would never succeed in bailing all the water out of the sea. All they had for their trouble was sore mouths and weary wings.

They stopped their work and began to praise the crow's mate who had been swept away. They extolled the beauty of her beak, her eyes, her complexion, her figure, and her sweet voice. They agreed that all her virtues must have provoked the sea to steal her from them.

As they babbled on with such nonsense, the deva frightened them, and, completely forgetting about emptying the sea, they scattered in all directions.

Having concluded his story, the Buddha identified the birth: "At that time, the elderly bhikkhu's former wife was the hen-crow, her husband was the male crow, the other aged bhikkhus were the rest of the flock, and I was the sea deva."

60

Trapped!
Sigāla Jātaka

It was while staying at Jetavana that the Buddha told this story about controlling the defilements.[1]

Once, some five hundred friends, sons of wealthy merchants of Sāvatthī, heard the Buddha teach and decided to become bhikkhus at Jetavana. One night, at midnight, thoughts of lust overwhelmed all five hundred of them. Unable to control their desires, they all decided to return to lay life. At that same hour, as the Buddha was surveying the world, he perceived their distress and immediately understood the cause. Indeed, like a mother watches over her only child or a one-eyed man protects his single eye, the Buddha watched over his disciples, helping them, whenever necessary, to subdue the lust that beset them. With compassion and wisdom, he resolved to assist these bhikkhus to curb their passions and to lead them to arahatship.

The Buddha realized, however, that, if he summoned only those five hundred bhikkhus, they would know that he was aware of their lustful thoughts and would be too agitated to listen carefully to his words. Therefore, leav-

---

1   The occasion for this story is the same as that for Tale 113, 154, and 157.

ing his Perfumed Chamber, he called Venerable Ānanda and asked him to assemble all the bhikkhus at Jetavana. Venerable Ānanda went from cell to cell summoning the bhikkhus.

With stately dignity, the Buddha seated himself in the Hall of Truth. As the bhikkhus entered, they paid reverent obeisance and took their seats around him.

"Bhikkhus, a bhikkhu should not harbor the three evil thoughts, of lust, hatred, and cruelty," the Buddha began. "Never imagine that a desire is a trivial matter. A wicked desire is like an enemy, and an enemy is never trivial. Given an opportunity, an enemy wreaks destruction. A desire, even though small at first, needs only to be allowed to grow, and it will bring about utter devastation. It can be as dangerous as a little viper. Desire is like poison in food or the thunderbolt of Sakka. It is always to be avoided and always to be feared. When desire arises, do not give it a moment's opportunity to rest in your heart. Expel it by thought and reflection. Shed it like a raindrop which rolls off the lotus leaf. Long ago, a wise being realized the danger of greed and crushed it before it could destroy him." Then he told this story of the past.

Long, long ago, when Brahmadatta was reigning in Bārānasi, the Bodhisatta was born as a jackal and lived in the forest by the Gangā. One day, an old elephant died by the riverbank. Discovering the carcass, the jackal congratulated himself on finding such a great store of meat. First, he bit the trunk, but that was like biting a plow handle. "There's no eating here!" he cried. Trying a tusk, he found that he was just biting bone. Then he tried an ear, but that was like chewing the rim of a winnowing basket. He tried the stomach, but the skin there was as tough as a grain-basket. The feet were like a mortar, so he tried the tail, but that was like the pestle. The poor jackal was becoming extremely frustrated at not finding any toothsome spot on the entire beast when he happened to bite into the rear, which was like soft cake. "At last," he sighed happily, "I've found the right place." He continued eating the delicious meat right into the belly, where he made a plenteous meal off the kidneys, the heart, and the rest, quenching his thirst with blood.

When night came, he lay down inside. As he lay there, he thought, "This carcass is both food and shelter to me. Why should I leave it?" The jackal decided to stay there, eating as much as he wanted every day.

As time passed, however, the flesh and blood dried up. The summer sun and wind dried the elephant's hide, which hardened and shrank, closing the entrance by which the jackal had gotten in. Finding himself trapped in utter darkness, cut off from the world, and with no food left inside the carcass, the jackal panicked. In desperation, he rushed back and forth beating against the skeletal walls of his prison, trying to escape. While he was struggling helplessly inside the desiccated elephant, certain that he would die there, the weather outside was changing. A tempest was brewing and soon broke, sending torrents of rain from the heavens. The downpour moistened the carcass so that the skin became softer. Through the opening by which the jackal had entered, a ray of light appeared like a star in the night sky.

"I'm saved!" cried the jackal. Overjoyed at this chance of freedom, he backed up into the elephant's skull and made a mad dash at the hole. The force of his sprint was such that his head emerged, but he was still stuck. Struggling hard, through sheer desperation, he managed to get out, but only by scraping off all the hair of his body on the rough edge of the hole. As soon as he was free, he ran to get far away from his prison. Then he stopped and sat down, surveying his bare, scraped body.

"Ah!" he thought, "I've learned a great lesson. This misfortune comes of my greed and my greed alone. From now on, I will never be greedy again. I certainly will never again be tempted to crawl into the carcass of an elephant! I feared I would die in that black tomb! I'll never do that again." The jackal trotted off, and, true to his word, he never again gave in to greed.

Having concluded his story, the Buddha added, "Bhikkhus, never let desires take root in the heart, but pluck them out as soon as they spring up." Then he taught the Dhamma. Those five hundred bhikkhus attained arahatship, and the rest won varying lesser degrees of liberation. Finally, the Buddha identified the birth: "At that time, I was the jackal."

61
A Word of Advice
Ekapanna Jātaka

It was while staying at Kūtāgārasālā, the gabled-hall monastery in the great forest near Vesāli, that the Buddha told this story about a Licchavi prince.

In those days, Vesāli was a very prosperous city, surrounded by three walls, a gavuta apart. There were also three gates with watchtowers protecting the city. The city was governed by a council consisting of all seven thousand seven hundred seven Licchavi princes. The eldest son in one of the families was an extremely fierce and cruel youth. He was so volatile that none of his companions dared correct him in any way. Unable to reform him or to curb his temper and realizing that no one else could tame their son's fiery nature, his parents, at last, resolved to take the unruly young prince to the All-Wise Buddha. After paying their respects to the Buddha, they asked him to give the young man a lesson which would improve his character.

"Prince," the Buddha began, "human beings should not be passionate or cruel. A fierce man who is harsh to the mother who bore him, to his father, to his brothers and sisters, to his wife, to his relatives, and to his friends, inspires terror like a viper darting forward to bite, a robber springing from the darkness, or a yakkha attacking his prey. A fierce man will always ap-

273

pear ugly to others, no matter how much he tries to beautify himself. Even if his face is as handsome as a full moon, it will appear disagreeable, like a lovely lotus scorched by flames or a golden disc covered with grime. Those who injure others will always be hated.

"Rage may also drive a man to slay himself with a sword, with poison, by hanging, or by throwing himself off a cliff.

"Such a fierce man will be reborn in hell or another place of punishment and torment. When, at last, he is reborn as a human, disease and deformity will afflict him from birth. For these reasons, men should show kindliness to others and do good. Hell will not be their destination and punishment will cause them no fear."

The Buddha's words had a powerful effect on the prince. His fierceness vanished, and he became as gentle as a defanged snake or a bull with broken horns. After that, he treated his friends and family with kindness, and never again did he revile or strike at anyone.

Later, the bhikkhus talked about this in the Hall of Truth. They marveled at how the wicked Licchavi prince had been subdued with a single exhortation by the Buddha.

"Consider the elephant-tamer," they said. "He guides the elephant, making it to go right or left, backward or forward, according to his will. Thus, the Buddha guides the man he seeks to train wherever he wishes. For his incomparable ability, he is hailed as chief of the trainers of men, supreme in bowing men to the yoke of the Dhamma."

When the Buddha heard what they were discussing, he said, "Bhikkhus, this is not the first time that a single exhortation of mine has conquered that prince; the same thing happened before." Then he told this story of the past.

Long, long ago, when Brahmadatta was reigning in Bārānasi, the Bodhisatta was born as a brahmin in the northern part of the kingdom. When he grew up, he studied at Takkasilā and lived for a while with his parents, but, after they died, he became an ascetic in the Himavat, where he achieved extraordinary powers. After living in seclusion for quite some time, he left at the beginning of a rainy season to get salt and vinegar and to find a place to stay. He arrived in Bārānasi and slept in the royal garden. The next morning, he dressed himself carefully in his ascetic's garb and approached the king's gate for alms.

The king saw the ascetic from his window and was greatly impressed at how serenely he moved, with his gaze fixed in front of him.

"If goodness dwells anywhere," thought the king, "it must be in that man's heart." He ordered a courtier to bring the ascetic to him. The courtier approached the ascetic with due respect and tried to take his almsbowl.

"What is it, sir?" asked the ascetic.

"The king requests you," the man replied.

"I stay in the Himavat, and the king does not know me."

When the man reported this, the king was even more impressed with the ascetic's behavior and imagined him as a confidential advisor. Once again, he ordered the courtier to summon the ascetic. This time, he agreed to meet the king.

When the ascetic entered the royal chamber, the king greeted him with great courtesy, invited him to sit on a golden throne beneath a royal umbrella, and had him served delicious food which had been prepared for his own meal.

After the ascetic had finished eating, the king asked where he had come from and where he intended to go. Upon learning that the ascetic was in search of a place to stay during the rainy season, he immediately offered his pleasure garden, and the ascetic graciously accepted. The king took his own meal and accompanied the ascetic to the garden. He ordered his servants to build a hermitage with two rooms, one for the day and another for the night, and to provide the eight requisites of an ascetic. Asking the gardener to make sure that the ascetic had everything he required, the king returned to the palace. Thus, the ascetic stayed in the garden, and the king visited him several times each day.

The king had a son who was notorious for his bad temper. Neither the king nor any of his relatives could control the boy. Councilors and brahmins, as well as many ordinary citizens, had tried to show him the error of his ways, but their words were in vain. He paid no attention to anyone's counsel. The king was certain that this virtuous ascetic would be able to help in taming his son. One day, the king took his son with him when he visited the ascetic, but he returned alone.

The ascetic took the prince for a walk around the garden. When they came to a neem tree seedling with only two leaves, he plucked one of the leaves and handed it to the prince. "Taste the leaf of this little tree, Prince," he said, "and see what it is like."

The young man took the leaf from the ascetic, but scarcely had he put the leaf in his mouth, when he spat it out with a curse, gagging and spitting to get rid of the foul taste.

"What is the matter, Prince?" asked the ascetic.

"Sir, today, this tree only suggests a deadly poison, but I'm sure that, if it is left to mature, it will prove the death of many people," the prince replied vehemently. He bent over, pulled up the seedling, and crushed it. "If there is already poison in the baby tree, what will the full grown tree become?"

"Prince," the ascetic said, speaking slowly, "dreading what the poisonous seedling might grow into, you pulled it out of the ground and crushed it. Even as you behaved toward that tree, so the people of this kingdom, dreading what so fierce a prince may be if he becomes king, will do to you. Rather than place you on the throne, they will uproot you, as you did this neem seedling, and drive you into exile. Take a warning from the tree. You must begin to show compassion and to practice loving-kindness."

From that moment, the prince's behavior began to change. In his dealings with family and friends, he began to show humility. He practiced kindness toward everyone. In all his actions he became merciful and showed concern for the feelings of others. After his father's death, he continued to follow the advice of the wise ascetic, ruling righteously, practicing generosity, and performing many good deeds. At the end of a life well spent, he passed away to fare according to his deserts.

Having concluded his story, the Buddha added, "Thus, you see, Bhikkhus, that this is not the first time that I have tamed this wicked prince. I did the same in days gone by." Then the Buddha identified the birth: "At that time, the Licchavi prince was the wicked prince, Ānanda was the king, and I was the ascetic who exhorted the prince to goodness."

62

Raising the Dead
Sañjīva Jātaka

It was while staying at Veluvana that the Buddha told this story about
King Ajātasattu.

While still a prince, Ajātasattu had put his faith in Devadatta, the bitter
foe of the Buddha. Prince Ajātasattu honored Devadatta and spent vast sums
of money to build a monastery for him at Gayāsīsa. Following Devadatta's
advice, the prince even killed his father, the virtuous King Bimbisāra, who
had already attained the first path.

When King Ajātasattu heard that the earth had swallowed up Devadatta
for his great sins, he feared a similar fate for himself. He imagined the earth
yawning wide and the flames of hell reaching up for him. He pictured himself
chained on a bed of burning metal with iron lances thrust into his body. Suffering from insomnia, he wandered around the palace. Constantly shivering
in terror, jittery, and without a moment's peace, he neglected the kingdom's
welfare. In the midst of his suffering, King Ajātasattu felt a keen desire to
see the Buddha, to be reconciled with him, and to ask him for guidance, but,
because of the enormity of his crime, he was afraid to approach the Teacher.

During the Kattikā festival, Rājagaha was illuminated and decorated like heaven itself. Sitting on his golden throne, King Ajātasattu noticed his physician, Jīvaka, sitting nearby with his other advisors. Knowing that Jīvaka was a disciple of the Buddha, the king wanted to ask him to take him to see the Buddha, but, not wanting to admit that he was afraid to go alone, he hesitated to say anything outright. After thinking for a few moments, King Ajātasattu devised a plan. "How fair, sirs, is this clear cloudless night!" he exclaimed to those in attendance. "After months of rain, how delightful and charming is the clear night sky with the full moon rising. On such a perfect night, what sage should we seek out, to give our hearts peace?"

One minister recommended Purāna Kassapa, and another suggested Makkhali Gosāla. Others proposed Ajita Kesakambala, Pakudha Kaccāyana, Sañjaya Belatthiputta, and Nigantha Natuputta. In silence, King Ajātasattu listened to all their suggestions and waited for Jīvaka to speak. The great doctor suspected the king's intention, but, wanting to be sure, he kept silent.

At last the king said, "Well, my good Jīvaka, don't you have anything to say?"

Jīvaka immediately stood up, pressed his palms together in the direction of the Buddha, and said, "Sire, the Buddha is staying in my mango grove with one thousand three hundred fifty bhikkhus. Such, indeed, is the Exalted One: worthy, perfectly enlightened, endowed with knowledge and conduct, well-gone, knower of the worlds, supreme trainer of persons to be tamed, teacher of devas and men, enlightened and exalted. Let Your Majesty go to listen to him teach and to ask any questions you may have."

Having gotten Jīvaka to make the suggestion, the king immediately ordered elephants readied and rode in state with a full entourage to the mango grove.

As the king entered the grove, he was gripped with fear, and his hair stood on end. "Jīvaka," he cried, "you aren't deceiving me, are you? You aren't betraying me, are you? You aren't turning me over to my enemies, are you? You said that there were more than one thousand bhikkhus here, but I hear no sound of sneezing or coughing. There is no talking at all. How can that be?"

"Don't be afraid, Your Majesty." Jīvaka calmly replied. "I am neither deceiving you nor betraying you to your enemies. Go forward, Sire! You can see lamps burning in the pavilion."

In the pavilion, King Ajātasattu found the Buddha surrounded by bhikkhus, sitting in absolute calm, as quiet and still as the ocean without a breath of wind. There were more bhikkhus than King Ajātasattu had ever seen gathered together, and he was extremely pleased with their demeanor. The king bowed low to the Buddha, spoke words of praise, and sat down.

When the time was right, he posed his question: "What is the fruit of the religious life?"

In reply, the Buddha delivered the Sāmaññaphala Sutta[1] which greatly pleased the king. At the end of the discourse, King Ajātasattu made his peace with the Buddha, paid solemn obeisance, rose from his seat, and returned to the palace.

Soon after the king had gone, the Buddha addressed the bhikkhus and said, "Bhikkhus, this king is uprooted. Had King Ajātasattu, in his thirst for power, not slain that righteous ruler, his own father, he would have attained the first path before he got up from his seat today. Because he followed the wicked Devadatta, however, he has cheated himself of that attainment."

The next day, many bhikkhus were talking about King Ajātasattu's patricide, which had lost him liberation. They remarked that Devadatta had indeed been the king's ruin. When the Buddha heard what they were discussing, he said, "This is not the first time, Bhikkhus, that King Ajātasattu has suffered because he favored the wicked. Long ago, similar conduct cost him his life." Then he told this story of the past.

Long, long ago, when Brahmadatta was reigning in Bāranasi, the Bodhisatta was born into a very wealthy family. When he was old enough, he went to study at Takkasilā, where he received a complete education. Returning to Bāranasi as a teacher, he enjoyed great fame and had five hundred young students. Among these was one youth named Sañjīva (Having Life), to whom the teacher taught the charm for raising the dead to life. One day, when he went with his fellow students to the jungle to gather wood, they came upon the body of a dead tiger.

"Now watch me bring this tiger back to life again," Sañjīva boasted.

"You can't," his companions said.

"Of course I can. Nothing to it. Just watch me!"

"Well, do it if you can," the other boys said, quickly climbing a tree.

Sañjīva recited his charm and struck the dead tiger with a stick. Up jumped the tiger, and, as quick as lightning, it sprang for Sañjīva's throat, killing him on the spot. After the fatal bite, the tiger fell back dead, right next to Sañjīva's corpse.

The other young students raced back to their master and reported what they had witnessed.

"My dear boys," the teacher said, "by showing favor to the wicked and paying honor where it was not due, Sañjīva brought this calamity on himself.

---

1   Dīgha Nikāya 2.

Befriend a villain, help him when he's in trouble, and like that tiger which Sañjīva returned to life, he will devour you for your pains."

After a life of generous alms-giving, and performing other good deeds, the teacher passed away to fare according to his deserts.

Having concluded his story, the Buddha identified the birth: "At that time, Ajātasattu was the young Sañjīva, who brought the dead tiger to life, and I was the famous teacher."

63
The Kings' Virtues
Rājovāda Jātaka

It was while staying at Jetavana that the Buddha told this story about teaching a king a lesson.

One afternoon, the king of Kosala arrived in his splendid chariot at the monastery. After the king had paid his respects, the Buddha asked why he had come at that time of day.

"Venerable Sir," the king replied, "I am later than usual because I was sitting on a difficult criminal case. After passing sentence, I ate and came directly here, with my hands hardly dry, to wait upon you."

"Sire, you are correct in judging such a case with justice and impartiality; that is the way to heaven. In that you have the advice of a teacher such as I, it is not surprising that you judge your cases fairly. It is remarkable, however, that a king of the past, who had to rely on the advice of mere scholars who were not so wise, was, nevertheless, able to pass judgment fairly and justly, avoiding the four evil courses and observing the ten duties of a king."

At the king's request, the Buddha told this story of the past.

Long, long ago, when Brahmadatta was reigning in Bāranasi, the Bodhisatta was born as his son and was named Prince Brahmadatta after his father.

At sixteen, he was sent to Takkasilā, where he quickly mastered all branches of learning. When, on his father's death, he became king, he ruled with uprightness and administered justice without partiality. Because he ruled justly, his ministers were also just. Because everything was done fairly, no false suits were ever brought to court. All the bustle of litigation stopped. Ministers often sat on their benches for many days without seeing a single plaintiff. The courts were virtually deserted.

One day, the king reflected, "My government is just, and the courts are quiet. I wonder, however, whether I personally have any fault. If I do, I will give it up and live a better life."

He began asking everyone in the palace, but no one told him of any flaw in his character or behavior. He heard only praise of himself. "Perhaps," he thought, "they are all so afraid of me that they dare not say anything but good. Let me ask those in the city, outside the palace." There, too, he heard only praise of his virtues. He extended his quest into the suburbs, inquiring of the citizens at large, but, even there, no one spoke of any fault in the king.

Still not satisfied, he decided to try in the countryside. Before he went into the rural areas, he entrusted the government to his ministers. Mounting his chariot, accompanied only by the driver, the king left the city in disguise. He traveled all over the country, even as far as the very borders of the kingdom, but no matter how he phrased his question, not a single person found any fault in the king. Everywhere he went, he heard himself lauded, even though no one suspected who he really was. Satisfied at last, he turned back to return to the capital.

It just so happened that Mallika, the king of Kosala, had been doing the very same thing. King Mallika, who also ruled fairly, had been searching in exactly the same way for a fault in himself. He, too, had traveled to the edge of his kingdom, but had heard nothing but praise, and had decided to return to his capital. Riding in his royal chariot, he arrived at the very same spot as King Brahmadatta at the very same time.

The place where these two kings met was a narrow passage between two steep cliffs. The road was wide enough for only one chariot.

"Make way!" King Mallika's charioteer shouted, "Get your chariot out of the way! This is the vehicle of the great King Mallika, king of Kosala! You must make way and let our king pass!"

"My goodness!" King Brahmadatta's driver mused. "Here's another king! What in the world is to be done?" Then, announcing that his chariot contained the king of Kāsi, he asked King Mallika's age, thinking that the younger should give way. He discovered, however, that the two kings were exactly the same age. When he asked the extent of the other kingdom, he discovered that each of them ruled a country three hundred yojanas long. Furthermore, their wealth, power, and glory, were exactly the same. Then he thought that way might be given to the better man, so he asked the other driver to describe his master's virtues.

"King Mallika." the charioteer replied, "gives rough to the rough, and mildness to the mild. He masters the good with goodness and makes the bad suffer."

"Is that all you have to say about your king's virtues?" asked King Brahmadatta's charioteer.

"Yes," the other shouted.

"If these are his virtues, what must his vices be!"

"You call those vices, do you? All right. Let us hear what your king's virtues are."

"Listen, my good man! The king of Kāsi conquers wrath by mildness, and sways the bad with goodness. He overcomes the miser with generosity and consistently repays lies with the truth."

When they heard that, both King Mallika and his driver got down from their chariot. The driver unhitched the horses and moved the chariot out of the way so that King Brahmadatta could pass.

Before leaving, King Brahmadatta advised King Mallika on the ten duties of a king and urged him to rule wisely and with compassion.

King Brahmadatta returned to Bārānasi and continued giving alms and performing many good deeds all his life, until he went, at last, to swell the hosts of heaven.

King Mallika took Brahmadatta's lessons to heart. Returning to his own city, he ruled wisely, practiced generosity, and performed many good deeds. When he died, he, too, was reborn in heaven.

Having concluded his story, the Buddha identified the birth: "At that time, Moggallāna was the driver of King Mallika, Ānanda was the king, Sāriputta was the driver of the king of Kāsi, and I was the young King Brahmadatta."

64
Delusions of Grandeur
Sūkara Jātaka

It was while staying at Jetavana that the Buddha told this story about an elderly bhikkhu.

One night, after the Buddha had preached a discourse to a large gathering of bhikkhus, bhikkhunīs, laymen, and laywomen, he retired to his Perfumed Chamber. Both Venerable Sāriputta and Venerable Moggallāna also retired, but, after a brief rest, the two of them returned to the hall.

As a continuation of the teaching, Venerable Moggallāna asked Venerable Sāriputta questions regarding the Buddha's sermon. The Captain of the Teaching answered each question as clearly as though he were making the moon rise in the sky. The disciples were delighted with the clarity of this exposition of the sermon the Buddha had delivered in brief.

One elderly bhikkhu, however, was disgruntled and thought, "What if I were to ask Sāriputta a very difficult question? If I could puzzle him and stump him in front of all these disciples, everyone would think, 'What a clever fellow!' That would give me fame and reputation."

He stood up and stepped closer to Venerable Sāriputta. Standing on one side, he said loudly, "Friend Sāriputta, I, too, have a question for you. Will you let me speak?"

When Venerable Sāriputta nodded to him, the bhikkhu started babbling, "Give me a decision in discrimination or in nondiscrimination, in refutation or in acceptance, in distinction or in counter-distinction."

Venerable Sāriputta stared at him and thought, "This old man is stuck in the sphere of desire. He is empty and knows nothing. He should be ashamed!" Without saying another word, the Captain of the Teaching laid down his fan, got up from his seat, and returned to his room. Venerable Moggallāna did the same.

Instantly, a man sprang up and shouted, "This wicked old fellow has deprived us of the sweet words of the teaching! Seize him!" When the irate laypeople rushed toward him, the old bhikkhu ran off. Just outside the monastery, he tripped and fell through a hole in the corner of a cesspool. He scrambled to his feet, but he was completely covered with filth.

Feeling sorry, the laypeople went to see the Buddha. "Why have you come at this unseasonable hour?" the Buddha asked. They told him what had happened, and the Buddha replied, "This is not the first time that this old man has been puffed up and, not knowing his own limitations, has pitted himself against the strong, only to be covered with filth. Long ago, too, he challenged the strong and ended up exactly the same." Then, at their request, he told them this story of the past.

Long, long ago, when Brahmadatta was reigning in Bārānasi, the Bodhisatta was born as a lion in the Himavat. He lived in a mountain cave near a lake. Beside the lake, in simple huts made of leaves and branches, resided a company of ascetics, and, nearby, a herd of wild boars.

One day, after killing a buffalo and eating his fill, the lion went down to the lake to drink. As he was finishing, he noticed a hefty boar feeding near the water." Someday," the lion thought, "that boar will make a nice meal for me." Fearing that the boar, if he saw him, might be alarmed and not return to that spot, the lion quietly slipped away back into the jungle.

Out of the corner of his eye, the boar saw this. "That lion tried to sneak away," he thought. "He must have been frightened when he saw me. He dares not come near me but, instead, slinks off in fear! Today will witness a fight between that lion and me!" Raising his head very high, he shouted, "Lion! Both of us have four feet! We are the same, you and I! Turn, Lion, turn! Are you afraid? Why do you run away from me?"

The lion turned to face the boar and roared, "Friend boar, there will be no fight between you and me today, but, one week from today, let us fight it out right here in this very spot." Then he turned once more and stalked away.

The boar was delighted at the thought that he was going to fight a lion. He hurried to tell his friends and relatives about it, but they were horrified. "You will be the death of us all," they cried, "and you will get yourself killed, as well. You have no idea what you have done! If you did, you wouldn't be so eager to challenge a lion to battle! When that lion comes, he'll destroy you and the rest of us, too. Why are you so violent? Who do you think you are?"

This frightened the boar, and he began to doubt himself. "What should I do?" he asked them.

The other boars discussed the matter and came up with a suggestion. "Every day, for the next week," they advised him, "roll around in the ascetics' dunghill. Each day, let all of the muck dry on your body. Then, on the last day, moisten yourself with a little dew. On the morning of the fight, go to the meeting place before the lion arrives. Find out which way the wind is blowing, and position yourself upwind. Your only hope is that the lion, being fastidious in cleanliness, will spare your life when he gets a whiff of you."

The impetuous boar did exactly as they suggested.

Just as they had predicted, when the lion smelled him, he chuckled and said, "Friend boar, that's a neat trick! I fully intended to have you for my dinner today, but, since you are covered with dung, I cannot get near you, let alone bite you. I wouldn't touch you with my foot. Filthy creature that you are, I will spare your life. Today, I yield to you the victory."

The lion turned away and went off to hunt for his day's food.

The boar boasted to all his friends and relatives about his victory. He claimed that he had truly defeated the lion. Though pleased that the foolish boar had not been killed, the rest of the herd were still afraid. They knew that the lion could come back at any time for them, so they left and settled in another place far away.

Having concluded his story, the Buddha identified the birth: "At that time, the elderly bhikkhu was the boar, and I was the lion."

65

The Elephant Who Saved the Kingdom
Alīnacitta Jātaka

It was while staying at Jetavana that the Buddha told this story about a bhikkhu who had given up striving.[1]

The young man, who came from a good family in Sāvatthī, had become a bhikkhu after hearing the Buddha teach. He had accomplished all the tasks set by his teachers and preceptors, and had memorized the Pātimokkha, the Code of Discipline. After five years of study, he requested meditation instruction and chose a remote village near the border of Kosala, where he could retire to the forest for intensive practice. There he built a hut of leaves. When the villagers saw him, they were so pleased with his demeanor that they offered to supply all his needs.

During the three months of the rainy season, he zealously endeavored to perfect his concentration, but, at the end of that time, he felt that his efforts had been in vain. Concluding that he had no penchant for meditation, he resigned himself to failure. He decided to give up and to return to Jetavana

---

1 The occasion for this story is the same as that for Tale 178.

where he could, at least, see the beautiful face of the Buddha and hear his sweet words.

His teachers and friends were surprised to see him back at the monastery. When he informed them that he had given up meditating, they scolded him and took him directly to the Buddha.

Seeing them coming, the Buddha asked the bhikkhus why they were bringing him, obviously against his will.

His friends answered, "This bhikkhu has ceased striving."

"Is this true?" the Buddha asked the young bhikkhu.

"Yes, Venerable Sir, it is true," answered the bhikkhu.

"Why, Bhikkhu," the Buddha asked him, "have you quit trying? In my Sāsana, no success is possible for a slothful man. Only strenuous effort can lead one to Nibbāna. Long ago, you won the entire kingdom of Kāsi and presented it to a tiny baby boy. You did it by sheer determination. Now that you have embraced this great discipline leading to liberation, how could you possibly lose heart?" Then he told this story of the past.

Long, long ago, when Brahmadatta was reigning in Bārānasi, there was a village of carpenters who earned their livelihood by building houses. Every day they took a boat upriver and went into the jungle. There they cut trees and shaped beams and timbers for houses. Then they numbered all the pieces to be put together into a frame. Taking all the lumber back to the river, they loaded it on the boat and returned to town. They were very skillful at their work and earned substantial wages.

One day, near their jungle workplace, an elephant stepped on a splinter of acacia wood. The splinter pierced the elephant's foot, which began to swell and fester, causing him terrible agony. When the elephant heard the carpenters cutting wood, he thought, "Perhaps those carpenters can heal my foot." Limping with pain, he approached them and lay down. At first, the carpenters were very surprised at this, but, noticing his swollen foot, they looked closely and discovered the infected wound. With a sharp tool they made an incision around the splinter, fastened a string to it, and pulled it out. Then they cleaned the wound thoroughly with warm water, disinfected it, and wrapped it in clean bandages. In a short time, the elephant's foot healed completely.

Grateful to the carpenters for having saved his life, the elephant decided to repay them by helping them with their work. From that time on, he pulled up trees and rolled logs for them. Whenever the carpenters needed tools, he picked them up with his trunk and took them to where they were working. At lunchtime, the carpenters brought food to the elephant, so that he wouldn't have to forage.

After some time, the elephant realized that he was getting old and would not be able to continue serving the carpenters much longer. One day, he brought his son, a magnificent, well-bred white elephant. He said to the carpenters, "This young elephant is my son. Since you saved my life, I give him to you. From now on, he will work for you." After he had explained all his duties to his son, the old elephant returned alone to the jungle.

The young elephant worked faithfully and obediently, the same as his father had done. The carpenters fed him as they had fed his father, and he thrived.

At the end of each work day, the elephant bathed in the river before returning to the jungle. The carpenters' children enjoyed pulling him by the trunk and playing all sorts of games with him both in the water and on the riverbank.

Of course, noble creatures, be they elephants, horses, or men, never urinate or defecate in water. This elephant, being noble and pure white, was always careful never to do anything of the kind while he was in the river. He always waited until he came out.

One day, when it rained very heavily, flood waters caught a half-dry cake of the white elephant's dung and carried it down river. This piece of dung floated to Bārānasi, where it lodged in a bush, right at the spot where the king's elephant keepers brought the king's five hundred elephants to bathe. When these beasts caught the scent of the dung of the noble young elephant, they refused to enter the water. Instead, they extended their tails, fanned their ears, and ran from the river.

When the keepers explained what had happened to the elephant trainers, the trainers realized that there was something in the water. Orders were given to search the river, and the lump of dung was found in the bush. The trainers powdered the dung and mixed it with a little water. Then they sprinkled it over the backs of the other elephants. This caused the animals to smell very sweet, and they immediately went into the water to bathe. The trainers were sure the dung had come from a very noble elephant. They reported all this to the king and advised him to capture the elephant for himself.

The king ordered a raft prepared and set off upstream. When he reached the place where the carpenters had settled, he found the young elephant playing in the water. As soon as the elephant heard the sound of the king's drums, he came out of the water and drew near to the carpenters. They all went together to pay their respects to the king.

"Sire," the carpenters said, "if you wish us to do any work for you, you don't need to come yourself. You can send for whatever you need, and we will bring it to you."

"No, my friends," the king answered. "I've come not for wood, but for this elephant."

"He is yours, Sire!" they replied immediately, but the elephant refused to budge.

Addressing the elephant directly, the king asked, "What do you want me to do?"

"Order the carpenters paid for what they have spent on me, Sire," the elephant answered.

"Willingly, Friend." The king ordered one hundred thousand coins to be piled by the elephant's trunk, by his tail, and beside each foot, but this was not enough for the elephant; he still refused to go. Each of the carpenters was given clothes for himself and his wife. Then the king provided money for all the children.

Satisfied that his friends would be able to manage without his help, the elephant bade farewell to the carpenters, their wives, and the children, and departed with the king.

The king took the elephant to his capital, which was beautifully decorated to mark the occasion. He led the elephant around the city in a solemn procession and gave him a richly furnished stable.

The elephant served as the king's comrade, and no one else was ever permitted to ride him. With the help of this elephant, the king won supremacy over all of Jambudīpa.

After some time, the queen-consort became pregnant. When it was almost time for her to give birth, the king died.

Everyone realized that, if the elephant were to learn of the death of the king, his heart would break, so he was cared for as usual, and not a word was said.

As soon the king of Kosala heard rumors of the king's death, however, he thought, "Surely Bārānasi is at my mercy!" and he decided to attack the kingdom.

Marching at the head of a great army, he laid siege to the capital. The people of Bārānasi closed the city gates and sent a message to the king of Kosala: "The queen of Bārānasi is near the time of her delivery, and the astrologers have predicted that she will bear a son in seven days. If, indeed, she bears a son, we will fight to protect the kingdom. Please grant us seven days." The king of Kosala agreed to their terms.

Just as predicted, on the seventh day, the baby boy was born. Since he was born to win the hearts of his people, the queen named him Alīnacitta, which means "Inspirer."

On that day, the army emerged to begin fighting the king of Kosala. Without a leader, however, the soldiers were driven back and began to waver.

Shortly after the battle began, messengers went to see the queen. "Our army is losing ground," they reported, "and we are afraid of defeat. The state elephant, our late king's loyal friend, has not been told that the king is dead, that a prince has just been born, and that we are besieged by the king of Kosala. Shall we tell him?"

"Yes, the time has come," answered the queen. She quickly dressed her baby boy and wrapped him in a fine cloth. Then she went with all the court to the elephant's stable. She laid the infant at the elephant's feet, saying, "Master, your comrade, the king, is dead, but we were afraid to tell it to you for fear your heart would break. This is your king's son. Now the king of Kosala is besieging our city and making war upon us. Our army is losing ground. Either kill your son yourself or win back his kingdom for him!"

The elephant stroked the child with his trunk and gently lifted him up to his own head. Then, with lamentation for his dead master, he took the baby and laid him in his mother's arms.

The elephant told the officers to dress him in his armor and to prepare him for battle. They unlocked the city gate and escorted him out. The great beast emerged trumpeting. His awe-inspiring demeanor so surprised and frightened the invaders that they panicked and fled in retreat.

During the rout, the elephant managed to seize the king of Koala by his topknot. He carried his prisoner to the young prince and dropped him at the baby's feet. Soldiers sprang to kill the invader, but the elephant stopped them. "Be careful in the future," the noble elephant advised the captive king. "Never presume to take advantage of us because our prince is young." Then he allowed the king to go.

Prince Alīnacitta was consecrated king at the age of seven. Like his father, he ruled all of Jambudīpa, and no foe dared to rise up against him again. His reign was just, and, when he came to the end of his life, he was reborn in heaven.

Having concluded his story, the Buddha observed that any bhikkhu, strong in will and seeking a refuge in the Triple Gem, would prevail as did that determined elephant. Then the Buddha taught the Dhamma, and the weak-hearted bhikkhu attained arahatship. Then the Buddha identified the birth: "At that time, Queen Mahā-Māyā was the queen, this bhikkhu was the elephant who won the kingdom and handed it over to the child, Sāriputta was the father elephant, and I was the young prince."

66

One Good Turn Deserves Another
Guna Jātaka

It was while staying at Jetavana that the Buddha told this story about Venerable Ānanda receiving a gift of one thousand robes.

Venerable Ānanda had been preaching regularly to the women of the palace of the king of Kosala for some time. One day, one thousand robes, each worth one thousand coins, were brought to the king. The king gave five hundred of them to his queens. The queens put the robes aside and presented them to Venerable Ānanda after he taught them.

The next morning, when the women joined the king at breakfast, they were all wearing their old robes. The king remarked, "Yesterday, I gave you robes worth one thousand coins each. Why aren't you wearing them?"

"My Lord," they answered, "we have given them to Venerable Ānanda."

"Does Venerable Ānanda have them all?" he asked.

"Yes, he does," they replied.

"The Buddha allows only three robes," he said. "It seems that Venerable Ānanda is doing a little trade in cloth!"

The king became angry with Venerable Ānanda and, after breakfast, visited him in his kuti. After greeting him, the king sat down and said, "Venerable Sir, please tell me. Do my wives listen to your preaching and learn anything?"

"Yes, Sire, they listen to what they hear, and they learn what they need to learn."

"Oh, indeed. Do they only listen, or do they make you presents of upper garments or under-garments?"

"Sire, yesterday they gave me five hundred robes worth one thousand coins each."

"And did you accept them?"

"Yes, Sire, I did."

"Why? Didn't the Buddha make a rule about three robes?"

"Yes, Sire, the rule is that a bhikkhu is allowed to keep three robes. That refers to what he himself uses. No one is forbidden to accept what is offered. I accepted what was offered, and I will give them to bhikkhus whose robes are worn out."

"But when a bhikkhu gets a new robe from you, what does he do with his old robe?"

"He turns it into a cloak, Sire."

"And what about the old cloak?"

"That he turns into a shirt."

"And the old shirt?"

"That serves for a blanket."

"The old blanket?"

"Becomes a mat."

"The old mat?"

"A towel."

"What about the old towel?"

"Sire, it is not permitted to waste the gifts of the faithful. We chop old towels into bits and mix the bits with clay, which we use for mortar in building our kutis."

This conversation so pleased the king that he sent for the remaining five hundred robes and offered them to Venerable Ānanda, as well. After receiving anumodana, he paid his respects and returned to the palace.

Venerable Ānanda distributed the first five hundred robes he had received to the bhikkhus at Jetavana to replace their old, worn-out robes. There was one young bhikkhu, however, who was very helpful to him. This young bhikkhu swept out Venerable Ānanda's cell, brought him toothsticks and water for rinsing his mouth, cleaned the toilets and kept them filled with water, dusted and tidied the sitting and sleeping rooms, and did whatever else was necessary. To him, in recognition of his great service, Venerable Ānanda gave all of the five hundred robes which he had received directly from the king. That young bhikkhu, in turn, distributed the robes among his fellow students, who cut them up, dyed them yellow, and wore them when they next waited on the Buddha.

After greeting the Teacher, the young bhikkhus sat down to one side and asked a question: "Venerable Sir, is it possible for a bhikkhu who has attained the first path to show favoritism in giving gifts?"

"No, Bhikkhus, it is not possible for such a senior bhikkhu to show favoritism in giving gifts."

"Venerable Sir, Ānanda gave five hundred robes, each worth one thousand coins, to one young bhikkhu, and that bhikkhu divided them among us."

"Bhikkhus, in giving these robes, Ānanda did not show favoritism. That young bhikkhu is very useful, so Ānanda made the present to his attendant in recognition of his great service, for the sake of virtue. Ānanda was rightly thinking that one good turn deserves another, and he was doing what gratitude demands. Long ago, the wise also acted according to the principle that one good turn deserves another." Then, at their request, the Buddha told this story of the past.

Long, long ago, when Brahmadatta was reigning in Bārānasi, the Bodhisatta was a magnificent lion, and he lived in a cave on the side of a hill. At the foot of the hill was a great marshy swamp. Pools of clear water were broken up by patches of soft green grass which grew out of thick mud. Deer, rabbits, and other small animals often grazed on that rich grass.

One drizzly day, the lion stood at the mouth of his cave and looked down at the marsh. Right below where he was standing, a plump deer was grazing. After watching the deer's movements and carefully gauging the distance, the lion charged from the hillside directly toward the deer. Hearing the rush of air, the deer raised her head and bounded away, with a cry of fear. Having missed his prey, the lion couldn't stop the force of his rush, plunged into the treacherous mud just beyond where the deer had been standing, and sank so deep that he could not move. Unable to extract himself, there he was with his legs fixed like four great posts. The sun set and the sun rose and still the lion remained there, for a week, without a bite to eat.

On the seventh day, a solitary jackal approached the edge of the swamp. As soon as he saw the lion, he started to slink away. The lion called out to him, "Jackal! Don't go away. I'm caught fast in this mud and can't get out by myself. Please save me!"

The jackal approached cautiously. Seeing that the lion was, indeed, trapped, the jackal said, "I could pull you out, but I'm afraid of what you might do to me when you're free."

"Don't be anxious, Jackal," the lion replied weakly. "I won't hurt you. Actually, if you get me out of here, I'll do you a great favor. Please help me!

The jackal accepted the lion's assurance and started working the mud away from around the lion's legs. As he dug, water began seeping in and softened the hard, dried mud. Finally, the jackal was able to get under the lion's belly. "Now, Sire," he said, "you must make one great effort!" As the jackal pushed from below, the lion exerted every bit of strength he had left. He felt himself gradually rising from the mud, and, finally, he was able to scramble onto solid ground. After resting a moment to catch his breath, the lion plunged into the water and rinsed off the mud. Then he stalked and killed a buffalo. With his great fangs, he tore off a hunk of flesh from its flank. Offering the meat to the jackal, the lion said, "Eat, Comrade!" When the jackal had finished, the lion ate his fill.

As they were preparing to leave, the jackal took in his mouth a piece of meat that he had put aside. "What is that for, Comrade?" the lion asked.

"Your Majesty, this is for my mate, who awaits me at home," the jackal replied.

"Good idea!" said the lion, and he also took a chunk of flesh for his lioness. "First, let's go to your den. I want to fulfill my promise to take care of you." At the jackals' den, the lion took the meat from the jackal and offered it himself to the jackal's mate. When she had finished eating, the lion invited both of them to his cave.

After introducing them to the lioness and giving her a portion of meat, the lion established the pair of jackals in a cave near his own.

Every day, the lion and the jackal went hunting together. They caught all sorts of animals, always sharing what they killed and never forgetting to take some back to their mates. The two families lived happily and harmoniously in their adjoining caves. Soon, there were two cubs in each cave, and the children played together.

The lioness, however, began worrying. "My Lord seems to be very fond of the jackal, his mate, and their children," she thought. "I wonder why. It's just not natural for our two families to be living together like this. I fear that something is going on between them. Perhaps that is why My Lord is so fond of them. In any case, I should get rid of her. I'll have to find a way to drive them away!"

While the lion and the jackal were off hunting, the lioness started to intimidate the jackal's mate. Every day, she asked leading questions, such as, why the jackal stayed there, whether she was afraid, and why she didn't run away. These questions terrified the jackal's mate. Taking a cue from their mother, the lion cubs began frightening the jackal cubs as well. The lion cubs pounced so fiercely and roared so loudly that the poor jackal cubs were afraid to leave their cave.

One evening, the jackal said to her mate, "We have been living here for a long time, and it seems that we must have outstayed our welcome. The lioness has been asking some very pointed questions, and I'm frightened. Perhaps it is time for us to go back where we used to live." When her husband asked her to be more specific, she repeated exactly what the lioness had said and told him about the lion cubs.

The next day, the jackal talked with the lion. "We've been staying here for a long time. I'm afraid we've outstayed our welcome. I thought we were friends, but, if you want us to go, we will go!" When questioned, he reported exactly what his wife had told him.

The lion immediately called his family, and, in front of the jackals, asked, "Wife, do you remember that, once, I was gone for a full week?"

"Yes, My Lord," the lioness replied.

"Afterwards," the lion continued, "I brought this jackal and his mate back with me and moved them into their cave."

"That's right, My Lord," the lioness agreed.

"Do you know why I was gone all that week?" the lion asked.

"No, sir. I have no idea," the lioness replied. "I assumed you were hunting."

"I had tried to catch a deer, but I misjudged and got myself stuck fast in the mud. There I stayed, unable to move, for a whole week without food. I would have died, but for this jackal. I was helpless, and he rescued me. He proved himself a true friend, and I owe him my life. You must never again belittle or disparage my comrade or his wife or his children."

The lioness was very sorry for the suspicions she had had. She humbly apologized to her mate and to the mate of the jackal, and the two families once more lived together as one. The young jackals and the young lions played together while they were small, and, even after they grew up, they remained close. After the parents died, the children maintained the bond of friendship and lived together happily. Indeed, the relationship remained unbroken through seven generations.

Having concluded his story, the Buddha taught the Dhamma. Some bhikkhus attained the first path, some attained the second, some attained the third, and some became arahats. Then the Buddha identified the birth: "At that time, Ānanda was the jackal, and I was the lion."

67
On Dandaka Hill
Mora Jātaka

It was while staying at Jetavana that the Buddha told this story about a backsliding bhikkhu.

When the bhikkhu was taken to see the Buddha, the Buddha asked him, "Is it true that you have lapsed?"

"Yes, Venerable Sir."

"What led you to do so?"

"I saw a woman dressed in gorgeous attire, and I was shaken."

"Is it any wonder that a woman could addle the wits of a man like you! Even a wise being, who had maintained his celibacy for seven hundred years, on hearing a female's voice, backslid in a moment. If one who had made great attainments and achieved high honor could have come to disgrace, how much more the unholy!" Then the Buddha told this story of the past.

Long, long ago, when Brahmadatta was reigning in Bārānasi, there was a peacock's egg with a shell as yellow as a kanikara bud. When the shell broke, the Bodhisatta was born as a rare and magnificent golden peacock, with beautiful red lines under his wings.

In searching for a safe place to live, the golden peacock crossed three ranges of hills and settled on the plateau of a golden hill in Dandaka.

Every morning, he sat on the hill, watching the sun rise, and recited charms which he had composed. The first charm honored the sun:

"There he rises, the king all seeing, who makes all things bright with his golden light. You I worship, glorious being, who makes all things bright with your golden light. Through the coming day, keep me safe, I pray."

The second charm honored all the Buddhas who had passed away:

"Honor do I raise to all arahats, the righteous, fully enlightened. All honor to the wise, to wisdom, to freedom, and to all that freedom has made free. Through the coming day, keep me safe, I pray."

Only after uttering these charms to keep himself safe, did the Peacock go to feed.

In the evening, the peacock returned to sit on the hilltop. As the sun went down, he meditated and again recited charms:

"There he sets, the king all seeing, who makes all things bright with his golden light. You I worship, glorious being, who makes all things bright with your golden light. Through the night, as through the day, keep me safe, I pray.

"Honor do I raise to all arahats, the righteous, fully enlightened. All honor to the wise, to wisdom, to freedom, and to all that freedom has made free. Through the night, as through the day, keep me safe, I pray."

One day, Queen Khemā, the wife of King Brahmadatta had a dream in which she saw a golden peacock giving a religious discourse. She described her dream to the king and expressed her longing to hear the sermon of that golden peacock. The king asked his courtiers if there was such a thing as a golden peacock, but they did not know. They suggested that the brahmins would know. The brahmins told the king that golden peacocks did exist, but that they were extremely rare. When the king asked where such rare creatures could be found, they replied, "The hunters will certainly know." The king summoned all the hunters and asked them.

Only one hunter could answer. "Sire," he said, "on one of my forays in Dandaka, I once saw a golden peacock which lives there on a golden hill."

"Hunter," the king replied, "I command you to bring us that peacock. Do not kill it; you must bring it here alive."

The hunter went across the ranges of hills to Dandaka. He repeatedly set snares in the peacock's feeding ground, but, even when the golden peacock stepped in a snare, the snare would not close. The hunter tried for seven years to catch the golden peacock, but he never could. Eventually, he died on the Dandaka hill. Queen Khemā also died without having her wish fulfilled.

In his grief over the death of his queen, the king blamed the peacock for his loss and wanted revenge. He ordered that a golden plate be inscribed with this message: "In the Himavat, on the golden hill of Dandaka, there lives a golden peacock. One who eats the flesh of this bird will be immortal and will stay young forever." He placed this golden plate in a casket.

When the next king read the inscription, he became excited at the possibility of eternal youth and immortality. He sent one of his hunters to Dandaka with instructions not to return until he had captured the golden peacock. Like the first, this hunter not only failed to capture the peacock, but also died in the quest. The same thing occurred during the reign of six successive kings.

The seventh king also sent a hunter to catch the golden peacock, but this hunter was cleverer than the others. He, too, was puzzled that the snare did not close when the golden peacock stepped into it. As he carefully observed the peacock, however, he understood that the bird was reciting a charm every morning before setting out in search of food and every evening before retiring. Convinced that this charm was protecting the golden peacock, the hunter caught a peahen in the marshes and trained her to utter a cry when he snapped his fingers.

Early one morning, the hunter went to the place where the golden peacock recited his charms. Before the peacock arrived, the hunter set up the snare, fixing its uprights carefully in the ground. He released the peahen in the area and hid himself. As soon as the golden peacock appeared, the hunter snapped his fingers, and the peahen uttered her cry.

Having lived all his life alone in the Dandaka hill, the golden peacock had never heard such a cry from a female. The beautiful note awakened desire in his breast. Leaving his charm unsaid, he strutted toward the peahen and unwittingly stepped in the snare. Overjoyed that his trick had worked, the hunter snatched up the peacock and carried him to Bārānasi.

The king was delighted to see the golden peacock, and he was amazed at how beautiful the bird was. He ordered that a special seat be prepared for the peacock.

The peacock placed himself in the seat and asked the king, "Why did you have me caught, Sire?"

"It is written," the king replied, "that anyone who eats your flesh will have eternal youth and will become immortal! I intend to eat you and to gain that immortality."

"Let us grant, for the sake of argument, that one who eats my flesh will have eternal youth and will become immortal, but doesn't that mean that I myself must die?"

"Of course it does," said the king quickly.

"You see. There's a contradiction! If I die, how can my flesh give immortality to those who eat it?"

"Well," the king replied hesitantly, "since your color is golden, the one who eats your flesh will last as long as gold. That's proof enough!"

"Sire," replied the peacock, "there is a simple explanation for my golden color. Long ago, I held imperial sway over the entire world, reigning from this very city. While I was king, I kept the five precepts, and I commanded that everyone in my realm keep them as well. Because of that, I was reborn in Tāvatimsa. From there, because of some previous misdeed, I became a peacock in my next birth, but, because I had kept the precepts, I was born with this golden color."

"That is incredible! What proof do you have that you were an imperial ruler who kept the precepts! How can I believe that, because of that, you were born with a golden color?"

"I have proof, Sire."

"What is it?"

"When I was monarch here, I always traveled in a jeweled car which now lies buried beneath the waters of the royal lake. If you dig in the lake, you will find that car, and that will be my proof."

Accepting the golden peacock's challenge, the king ordered the lake to be drained. As soon as his men began digging, they found the jeweled chariot. When the king saw the chariot with his own eyes, he believed everything the peacock had said.

"Sire," the peacock continued as he instructed the king, "except for Nibbāna, which is everlasting, all things, being compounded by nature, are unsubstantial, transient, and subject to death." At the end of his lesson, he established the king in keeping the precepts, which filled the king's heart with peace. In gratitude, the king bestowed his kingdom upon the golden peacock and paid him the highest respect. The peacock, however, returned the kingdom and, after a few days' sojourn in Bārānasi, flew back to the golden hill of Dandaka. His parting words of advice were, "Your Majesty, be heedful!"

The king followed the peacock's advice, and, after a lifetime spent giving alms and performing good deeds, he passed away to fare according to his deserts.

Having concluded his story, the Buddha taught the Dhamma, and the backsliding bhikkhu attained arahatship. Then the Buddha identified the birth: "At that time, Ānanda was the king, and I was the golden peacock."

68

The Haughty Half-Brother
Vinīlaka Jātaka

It was while staying at Veluvana that the Buddha told this story about Devadatta's imitating him at Gayāsīsa.[1]

Long, long ago, when King Videha was reigning in Mithilā, the Bodhisatta was born to his queen-consort. When the prince grew up, he was sent to Takkasilā for his education. On his father's decease, he inherited the kingdom and also took the name King Videha.

At that time, the leader of a flock of golden geese from the forest mated with a crow in Mithilā and sired a son, who resembled neither of his parents. His feathers were blue and black, giving him the color of a bruised corpse. Thus, he was called Vinīlaka.

The golden goose king, who normally lived in the Himavat, had two other sons, golden like himself, but he often visited Vinīlaka, who lived with his mother near the capital city. One day, in the Himavat, the two sons approached the king and said, "Father, it seems that you are going to the city quite often. We wonder why you venture into the regions where men live."

---

1   The occasion for this story is told in detail in Tale 57.

"My dear boys," he said, "I have a wife there, a crow, and she has given me a son, a half-brother to you, whose name is Vinīlaka. I go to visit him."

"Father," said his sons, "we are afraid for you. It is dangerous to go where men live. A city like that is quite risky for you. You should let us go and bring our half-brother here for a visit. Where exactly do they live?" his sons asked.

The golden goose described the spot just outside Mithilā. "There is a very tall palm tree, and, at the top of it, my mate and Vinīlaka have a nest. But, my boys, he is not able to fly the great distances you can."

"Don't worry, Father. We'll manage to bring him back here."

With their father's blessing, the two young golden geese set out to fetch their brother. They easily found the palm tree and greeted Vinīlaka in the nest. They explained their mission and urged the young bird to perch on a stick they had brought. As soon as Vinīlaka was secure, each of the brothers grasped an end of the stick with his beak. Firmly holding the stick to keep it steady, the two geese took flight to carry their brother to the forest.

They happened to fly over Mithilā just as the king, in a magnificent chariot drawn by a team of four milk-white thoroughbreds, was making a triumphal circuit of the city.

When Vinīlaka saw the king, he blurted out, "What is the difference between King Videha and me? He is riding in state around his capital in a chariot drawn by four white horses, and I am carried in a vehicle drawn by a pair of golden geese."

This made the two geese so angry that they considered releasing the stick and letting Vinīlaka fall to his death. They remembered their promise to their father, however, and, not wanting to disappoint him, they held on to the stick and flew on to the forest.

After they had safely deposited their young brother in front of their father, they recounted what had happened.

"Who do you think you are?" shouted the father angrily. "Do you think you are superior to my other sons? How dare you consider yourself their master and compare them to horses drawing a chariot! It is clear that you don't belong here. Go back to your mother!" Turning to his other two sons, he said, "My boys, carry your brother to the dunghill just outside the city of Mithilā. Leave him there for his mother to find him!"

Having concluded his story, the Buddha identified the birth: "At that time, Devadatta was Vinīlaka, Sāriputta and Moggallāna were the two young geese, Ānanda was the father, and I was King Videha."

69

The Pet Elephant
Indasamānagotta Jātaka

It was while staying at Jetavana that the Buddha told this story about a headstrong bhikkhu who resisted correction.

The Buddha told the stubborn bhikkhu, "Long ago, you were trampled to death by a mad elephant because you ignored the advice of the wise." Then he told this story of the past.

Long, long ago, when Brahmadatta was reigning in Bārānasi, the Bodhisatta was born into a brahmin family. After he grew up, he left home to take up a religious life. In time, he became the leader of five hundred ascetics in the Himavat.

When the leader heard that one of his students, named Indasamānagotta, was keeping a pet elephant, he called the young ascetic to him and asked whether it was true.

"Yes, sir, it is true," Indasamānagotta replied. "I've had him since he was just a baby. I found him after his mother was killed."

"Elephants are dangerous beasts," the leader warned. "When they grow up, they may kill even those who have fostered them. You had better get rid of that elephant."

"But, Teacher, I can't live without him!" Indasamānagotta protested.

"You'll regret keeping him," the leader persisted.

The young ascetic was so headstrong and contrary that he paid no heed to his teacher's advice. He insisted on keeping the elephant.

"Well, mark my words," the teacher concluded, "elephants are dangerous."

Despite all warnings, Indasamānagotta continued rearing the beast, which grew to an immense size.

One morning, all of the ascetics went into the forest to gather roots and fruit and stayed away from their hermitage for several days.

While they were gone, the weather began to change. The wind came from the south and brought a storm, which greatly upset the elephant, who became more and more agitated at having been left alone. He went on a rampage, smashing his master's hut, water jar, and stone bench. Then he hid himself in the forest, watching for Indasamānagotta to return.

When the ascetics did come back, Indasamānagotta was the first to arrive. As soon as he saw the elephant, he rushed forward to offer him the food he had brought.

The huge elephant charged out of the thicket, seized the unsuspecting ascetic with his trunk, and dashed him to the ground. After crushing his master's body, the elephant trumpeted wildly and tore off into the forest.

Following closely behind Indasamānagotta, the other ascetics saw everything that happened and informed their master.

"Let this be a warning to you," the teacher said. "We should never try to befriend those who are wicked and dangerous. When you find a kindred spirit, who, like you, is inclined to learning and virtue, choose that one to be your true friend. Good friends bring the greatest blessings. Listen carefully to the advice of your friends, and do not let obstinacy lead you to ruin, as it did Indasamānagotta with the elephant."

After performing a funeral service for his unfortunate student, the teacher spent the rest of his life in meditation and was, at last, reborn in the Brahma heavens.

Having concluded his story, the Buddha identified the birth: "At that time, this stubborn bhikkhu was Indasamānagotta, and I was the teacher of the ascetics."

70

No Spot on This Earth
Upasālha Jātaka

It was while staying at Veluvana that the Buddha told this story about charnel grounds and cremations.

In Rājagaha, next to Veluvana, there lived an extremely well-to-do elderly brahmin named Upasālha, who, being a follower of another sect, never showed the slightest interest in the Buddha's teaching.

Upasālha had one son, who was a very intelligent young man. One day, he said to his son, "When I die, I don't want my body to be cremated in a charnel ground where outcastes can be burned. You must find a completely uncontaminated place for my cremation."

"Father," the son replied, "I know of no charnel ground that would be fit for your cremation. You will have to advise me and tell me where I should have your body burned."

The brahmin agreed, and, the next day, he took his son outside the city to the top of Gijjhakūta Peak. "This is the place, son," he said, indicating the very spot where they were standing. "No outcaste has ever been cremated here. I want you to burn my body here." Satisfied, he and his son started descending the hill.

That morning, as the Buddha was surveying the world to see who might benefit from his Teaching, he perceived that Upasālaka and his son were receptive. He went to Gijjhakūta and waited at the foot of the hill. When they reached the bottom, he greeted them and asked, "Where have you been, Brahmins?" The young man explained their errand.

"Very well," the Buddha replied, "please show me the place your father pointed out." The two brahmins escorted the Buddha back to the top of Gijjhakūta.

"Is this the place your father indicated?" the Buddha asked.

"Yes, it is, Venerable Sir," replied the son. "He said that this space among these three hills is the best place for his cremation."

"This is not the first time, my lad, that your father has been particular about his cremation," the Buddha told him. "Nor is this the first time that he has chosen this place for that purpose. Many times before, he has been cremated on this very spot." At the son's request, the Buddha told this story of the past.

Long, long ago, the Bodhisatta was born in a brahmin family in Magadha. After he had finished his education, he left home and became an ascetic in the Himavat. Through concentration meditation, he perfected the five extraordinary powers and the eight jhānas. One year, at the beginning of the rainy season, he left his hermitage and walked to Rājagaha, where he set up a temporary residence on Gijjhakūta.

At that time, in Rājagaha, there lived a brahmin named Upasālaka who had one son. Upasālaka and his son had exactly the same conversation as explained above, and they went to Gijjhakūta in the same way. When they reached the bottom, the ascetic was waiting for them.

Their exchange was the same as the exchange with the Buddha, and the three climbed the hill together. At the top, the son showed the ascetic the exact same spot, and the ascetic replied, "This piece of land is neither pure nor undefiled. There is no end to the people of every caste who have been cremated on this very spot. In fact, your father has himself been cremated here in fourteen thousand births. On the whole earth, there is not a single place to be found where a corpse has not been burned, which has not at one time been a charnel ground, and which has not been covered with skulls."

The ascetic knew this because he was able to recall his previous lives.

After instructing Upasālaka and his son and encouraging them to practice truth, justice, harmlessness, moderation, and self-control, the ascetic resumed his meditation on the Four Brahma Vihāras. When he died, he was reborn in the Brahma heavens.

Having concluded his story, the Buddha taught the Dhamma, and Upasālha and his son attained the first path. Then the Buddha identified the birth: "At that time, Upasālha and his son were Upasālaka and his son, and I was the ascetic."

71

One's Own Territory
Sakunagghi Jātaka

It was while staying at Jetavana that the Buddha told this story about the Four Foundations of Mindfulness.

"Bhikkhus," he said, "a bhikkhu must keep to his own pasture ground, his own territory, which is, namely, the Four Foundations of Mindfulness. Objects, sounds, and the rest are fraught with passion and incite lust.

"Long ago, when an animal failed to keep to its own territory and strayed into the preserves of others, it fell prey to its enemies, but, relying on its own intelligence and resources, it managed to escape from a deadly enemy." Then he told this story of the past.[2]

Long, long ago, when Brahmadatta was reigning in Bārānasi, the Bodhisatta was born as a quail. Everyday, he feasted on the insects and worms which had been exposed by the plowing in farmers' fields.

---

2 This story is also related in the Sakunovāda Sutta (Samyutta Nikāya, Mahāvagga, Satipatthāna Samyutta, 6).

313

One day, he wondered what kind of food he might find elsewhere. Noticing a forest nearby, he flew there and began searching for food at the edge of the forest. While he was feeding contentedly in the short grass, a falcon, circling silently overhead, spotted the quail and swooped down and caught the tiny bird in his sharp talons.

Terrified and unable to move a muscle, the quail bewailed his fate. "How stupid of me!" he cried. "I never should have strayed into another's territory. If only I had kept to my own place, where my fathers fed before me, this falcon would have been no match for me!"

"Little quail," retorted the falcon, "what is your own place, where your fathers fed before you, and why is it so special?"

"My place is a plowed field where the soil is turned up in clods," replied the quail, sobbing.

"Do you think you would be safe from me there?" asked the falcon sarcastically.

"Oh, yes!" cried the quail. "I am sure of it!"

Spotting a freshly plowed field, the falcon swooped down again and released the quail. "Off with you, little quail!" he shouted as he flew back up high. "I accept your challenge, but you won't escape me here either!"

The quail perched on an immense clod and bravely shouted, "Come along now, falcon! Catch me if you can!"

Circling back at a great height, the falcon spotted the quail and heard his challenge. The falcon poised his wings, strained every nerve, and swooped down toward the quail at tremendous speed.

The quail watched the falcon carefully and thought, "Here he comes with a vengeance!" As soon as he saw the falcon lock his wings for the attack, the quail jumped behind a large clod of earth. The surprised falcon tried to grab the quail, but, instead, he slammed into the hard clod of earth and shattered his breast, falling dead at the quail's feet.

The quail emerged from behind the clod and proclaimed, "Truly, by keeping to my own territory, I found a clever way to defeat my enemy."

Having concluded his story, the Buddha added, "Thus, you see, Bhikkhus, that even animals fall into their enemies' hands by straying from their proper place and that they conquer their enemies when they keep to it. Therefore, take care not to leave your own place and not to intrude into another's. When one leaves his own territory, Māra finds an entry point and gains a foothold. What is that foreign territory, which is the wrong place for a bhikkhu? It is the five sense pleasures—of the eye, of the ear, of the tongue, of the nose, and of touch. These are foreign territory for a bhikkhu." Then the Buddha taught the Dhamma, and many bhikkhus attained the paths.

Finally, the Buddha identified the birth: "At that time, Devadatta was the falcon, and I was the quail."

72

The Tinduka Tree
Tinduka Jātaka

It was while staying at Jetavana that the Buddha told this story about the Perfection of Wisdom.

When a devotee exclaimed that the Buddha was very wise, the Buddha replied, "This is not the first time that I have been wise. Long ago, I was also wise and resourceful." Then he told this story of the past.

Long, long ago, when Brahmadatta was reigning in Bārānasi, the Bodhisatta was born as a monkey and became the leader of a troop of eighty thousand monkeys in the Himavat. Not far from the forest where this troop lived was a village, which was sometimes inhabited and sometimes empty. In the middle of the village was a large tinduka tree, with unusually sweet fruit. Whenever there were no people in the village, the monkeys delighted in going there and eating the delicious fruit.

Once, when the season for tinduka fruit arrived, the monkeys knew that the tree in the village would be fully laden with ripe fruit. They sent a scout to see whether or not people were living in the village. When the scout returned, he excitedly reported to the other monkeys, "The tree is indeed heavy with magnificent fruit, but not only is the village full of people, there is also a new bamboo fence around the entire village, and the gates are closely guarded."

As soon as they heard that the tree was full of ripe fruit, the monkeys began longing for it. They decided that they would take the risk to satisfy their hunger. They approached the leader and told him of their intention.

"Is the village empty?" he asked them.

"No, Sire, it is full of people."

"Then you must not go," he replied. "Men are dangerous and cannot be trusted."

"But, Sire," the monkeys insisted, "we will go at midnight, when the villagers are all fast asleep. We'll proceed quietly and eat quickly!"

The leader repeatedly tried to show the monkeys the folly of their plan, but they would not be dissuaded. Finally, he reluctantly agreed, and, that night, he led the troop down the mountain. When they reached a great rock near the village, they stopped and waited until midnight. At last, they were sure that all the people had gone to bed. Very quietly, they crept toward the village, scaled the fence, climbed the tree, and began eating the fruit.

Unfortunately, one man came out of his house to answer nature's call. Seeing monkeys moving in the tree, he raised an alarm and roused the entire village. People immediately poured out of their houses, and, armed with bows and arrows, spears, knives, sticks, rocks, and even clods of earth, they surrounded the tree. "Make sure they don't escape!" someone shouted. "As soon as dawn comes, we'll have them!"

The monkeys were terrified. "Look at all those fierce men and women!" they cried to each other. "They all have dangerous weapons! We are doomed! Who can save us from disaster?"

"The only one who can save us is our chief!" one monkey exclaimed.

In desperation, the monkeys turned to their leader and asked for his advice.

"Don't be afraid!" he answered reassuringly. Then, realizing that the troop needed some crumb of comfort to keep them from despair, he added, "Human beings have a lot of things on their minds, and they usually find a lot of things to do. It is only a little past midnight, and they say that, now that they have us trapped, they will wait till morning. Be patient. Something will come up, and we will find a way to escape. In the meantime, there's a lot of fruit left. Keep eating, and don't worry!"

After a few minutes, he ordered his assistants to take roll call. The assistants quickly made a complete circuit of the tree and returned to announce that one monkey, the leader's nephew, Senaka, was not present.

"If Senaka is not here," the leader answered, "there is nothing to worry about. We can trust him to find a way to help us."

As a matter of fact, when the monkeys left the forest just before midnight, Senaka, who had not heard about the raid on the tinduka tree, was sound asleep. When he awoke, he was startled to find everything so quiet. He looked around, but could not find anybody. Then he noticed the signs and followed the trail down the mountain toward the village. When he got close, he could see all the villagers gathered around the tree with torches and weapons.

"This is certainly trouble for our troop," he said to himself. Very quietly, he crept closer to the village to see exactly what was going on. At last, he could see that all his friends were trapped in the tree, and he realized that he had to do something to help them. At the edge of the village, he passed a hut and saw that an old woman was fast asleep inside in front of a blazing fire. Pretending to be a child going to the fields, Senaka crept through the door and seized a burning stick from the fire. Holding the firebrand aloft, he positioned himself windward and set fire to several houses in that quarter. Very quickly, the fire spread throughout the entire village. The old woman awoke and immediately raised an alarm. As soon as the villagers surrounding the tree realized what was happening to their homes, they forgot about the monkeys and raced back to put out the fire. As quickly as they could, the monkeys scampered away. A bit shaken, but relieved to be back in the safety of the forest, each monkey gratefully presented Senaka with a fruit he had brought from the village.

Having concluded his story, the Buddha identified the birth: "At that time, Mahānāma the Sākyan was Senaka, my followers were the monkey troop, and I was their leader."

73

A Stick in the Mud
Kacchapa Jātaka

It was while staying at Jetavana that the Buddha told this story about escaping from a fever.[1]

At one time in Sāvatthī, a household was struck by a serious fever.[1] Although the parents had fallen ill, their son was still healthy. Knowing that they were going to die, the couple buried their treasure in a safe place. Then they said to their son, "Since the disease is hovering in the doorway, you must break a hole in the wall and flee. Go far away from Sāvatthī. Wait there until the fever has disappeared. Then, when it is safe, come back, claim this house as your inheritance, dig up the treasure, restore the family fortune, and live happily. Now, quickly, flee!" The young man did exactly as his parents had instructed. After he returned, he set up his household in that same house and again became wealthy.

One day, he prepared oil, ghee, robes, and other offerings, and went to Jetavana. After respectfully greeting the Buddha, he took his seat.

---

1   The word indicates "snake-wind disease," perhaps malarial fever, which in the Terai, the foothills of the Himalayas, was believed to be caused by a snake's breath.

"We heard that your family died from the fever," the Buddha said to him. "How did you manage to escape?"

The young man explained what he had done.

"Long ago, my good man, in a time of danger, there was an animal who was so fond of his home that he refused to leave and consequently perished. At the same time, there were others, who were wise enough to leave, and they saved their lives." Then, at the layman's request, the Buddha told this story of the past.

Long, long ago, when Brahmadatta was reigning in Bārānasi, the Bodhisatta was born in a potters' village near the capital. When he grew up, he, too, became a potter, married, and had a family.

Near the village there was a huge lake, which, in the rainy season, was no more than an inlet of the Gangā. In the dry season, however, the two became separate.

Animals inhabiting the lake instinctively understood this change of seasons.

One year, as soon as the water started receding in the lake, the fish and turtles in the lake sensed the coming drought. While the lake and river were still one, they all swam out of the lake into the river for their survival. All, that is, except for one turtle. As this stubborn creature saw his friends leaving, he shouted, "This is where I was born, and I grew up here! This was my parents' home, and I cannot leave it!" The water of the lake continued receding, and the turtle kept moving toward the center. When, at last, the water disappeared, the turtle escaped from the heat by burying himself in the mud.

One day, the potter arrived at that spot and was delighted to find exactly the right kind of clay for his craft. With his long-handled spade, he began digging the clay from what was once the middle of the lake. As he was digging, his spade hit something hard, and he heard a loud "Crack!" He dug a little further and discovered that he had split open the turtle's shell. With his spade, he gently lifted the mortally injured turtle out of the hole and laid him on the ground. The poor turtle looked like a large lump of clay. In his agony, the turtle cried, "Here I am, dying, all because I was too fond of my home to leave it! I took the damp clay to be my refuge, but it has proved to be no refuge at all! I should have given up my attachment to this place and gone where there was water and life! I was a fool, and I suffer for my folly!" With that, he breathed his last.

The potter picked up the turtle's body and carried it to the village, where he showed it to his friends. "Look at this turtle," he said. "When the other creatures went into the great river, he stayed behind. When the lake dried up, he buried himself in the mud. I was digging for clay, and I broke his shell with my spade. As he was dying, he lamented what he had done He came to his end because he was all too fond of his home. Take care not to be like this turtle," he taught the villagers. "Don't say to yourselves, 'I have sight, I have hearing, I have smell, I have taste, I have touch, I have a son, I have a daughter, I have servants, I have precious gold.' Do not cling to these things with craving and desire. We are all reborn, again and again, within the three states of existence—sensual, corporeal, or formless." This lesson spread throughout Jambudīpa, and, for seven thousand years, it was repeated and discussed. All the villagers who heard it that day followed the potter's exhortation, giving alms and doing good, until, at last, they went to swell the hosts of heaven.

Having concluded his story, the Buddha taught the Dhamma, and the young man attained the first path. Then the Buddha identified the birth: "At that time, Ānanda was the turtle, and I was the potter."

74
Ill-Gotten Gains
Satadhamma Jātaka

It was while staying at Jetavana that the Buddha told this story about the twenty-one wrong means of livelihood.

At one time, many bhikkhus were engaging in improper practices, such as running errands, acting as doctors, and telling fortunes.

When the Buddha learned about this, he summoned the community of bhikkhus together and said, "Bhikkhus, there are twenty-one ways in which you must not attempt to gain support and respect. These practices are not only unsuitable for you but also dangerous. Food gained through improper practice can bring neither joy nor contentment. It is no better than picked-over carrion. Such food is like deadly poison or red hot iron. Those who engage in any of these twenty-one wrong means of livelihood may be reborn as beasts of burden, as yakkhas, or as petas. They may even be reborn in hell." Then he told this story of the past.

Long, long ago, when Brahmadatta was reigning in Bārānasi, the Bodhisatta was born into a candāla family. One day, when he was a young man, his parents packed a basket of rice and curries for him and sent him on an errand.

At the same time, another young man named Satadhamma, the son of a wealthy family in Bārānasi, set out in the same direction, but he carried no provisions for his journey.

When the two met on the road, the brahmin asked the other about his caste, and he replied, "I am a candāla. What about you?"

"I am a Northern Brahmin," he answered haughtily. Then he added, "Oh, well, we might as well journey together."

When it was time for breakfast, the candāla found some fresh water, washed his hands, and opened his basket. "Will you have some?" he asked his companion sociably.

"Tut, tut," Satadhamma replied, "I want nothing from a low fellow like you."

"So be it." The candāla quietly placed a portion of rice and curry on a leaf. Then, careful not to waste anything, he fastened up his basket and proceeded to eat. When he had finished, he took a drink of water and washed his face, hands, and feet. Then, picking up his basket, he said to his companion, "Let's be on our way."

After tramping along the whole day, they stopped and had a bath in a pleasant spot. When they had dried off, the candāla sat down in a comfortable place, opened his basket, and began to eat, without offering anything to his companion.

The brahmin, having eaten nothing at all that day, was ravenously hungry. He stood, watching his companion, and thought, "If he offers me something, I'll take it." The candāla, however, did not even look up.

"That churl!" Satadhamma thought. "He's eating every bit himself! He must know I'm starving. Why doesn't he offer me some? Well, I'm so famished, I'll beg from him. I will be able to scrape off the outside, which has been defiled, and eat the rest, which has not been touched." Aloud, he asked, "May I have some?"

The candāla turned to him and replied, "This is all that is left."

"I'll take it!" The brahmin boy took the leftover food in his hand, scraped off the edges, and ate. As soon as he had finished, he felt pangs of regret. "I have disgraced my birth, my family, and my clan! I have eaten the leftovers of a low-born outcaste! What a wicked deed I have done, all for the sake of a bite of food, grudgingly given. How could I, a high-born brahmin, have done such a thing?" he cried as he vomited food and blood.

Overpowered by remorse and shame, which stabbed his heart like a dagger, Satadhamma plunged into the jungle, where he died, alone and forlorn.

Having concluded his story, the Buddha added, "Just as that young brahmin suffered great distress and lost all joy in life because he had taken food in an improper way, so, too, Bhikkhus, having entered this discipline, you will find neither happiness nor joy in this bhikkhu's life if you gain support by improper means; that is, by any of those practices which have been proscribed." Then the Buddha taught the Dhamma and identified the birth: "At that time, I was the young caṇḍāla."

75

The Skilled Archer
Asadisa Jātaka

It was while staying at Jetavana that the Buddha told this story about the Great Renunciation.

One day, the bhikkhus were talking about the Great Renunciation. When the Buddha heard what they were discussing, he said, "Bhikkhus, not only in this life have I made a Great Renunciation. Long ago, also, I gave up the white umbrella of royalty." At their request, he told this story of the past.

Long, long ago, when Brahmadatta was reigning in Bārāṇasi, the Bodhisatta was born to the queen-consort. He was named Asadisa, which means Peerless. About the time Prince Asadisa was able to walk, his mother had a second son, who was named Brahmadatta after his father.

At the age of sixteen, Prince Asadisa was sent to Takkasilā. Studying under a world-famed teacher, the prince mastered all the important subjects, but his skill in archery surpassed that of the other students. When he completed his education, he returned to Bārāṇasi.

On his deathbed, King Brahmadatta ordered that Prince Asadisa become king and that Prince Brahmadatta become the crown prince. Prince Asadisa declared, however, that he did not wish to be king. Allowing his brother to become king, Asadisa continued to live in the palace as a prince. The king's servants and ministers could not understand such behavior, and they warned their master, "Your Majesty, Prince Asadisa secretly envies you and wants to be king. We are sure he is planning to take the throne."

King Brahmadatta allowed himself to be deceived by these rumors and ordered that his brother be arrested.

When Prince Asadisa learned of this, he fled across the border to the neighboring kingdom. Making his way to the capital city, he asked to be announced to the king.

"Who are you?" asked the king.

"I am a skilled archer, and I wish to serve you," Asadisa replied.

"What salary do you ask?"

"One hundred thousand coins a year."

"That is quite a lot," replied the king.

"My skill is worth that much," Asadisa assured him.

"Very well, you may enter my service."

Asadisa faithfully attended his new master, but the other archers were jealous of his high salary.

One day, while the king was reclining on a magnificent couch beneath a mango tree in his pleasure garden, he noticed a cluster of mangoes at the very top of the tree. He could see that the mangoes were ripe, but he knew that no one could climb that high to pick them. He summoned his archers and asked, "Can any of you shoot an arrow and cut the stem of that cluster of ripe mangoes?"

One of the old archers immediately replied, "Your Majesty, any of us could easily do that, but the newcomer is being paid so much more than we are, why don't you have him show you his skill and bring down the fruit?"

"Asadisa!" the king shouted.

"Your Majesty," Asadisa replied, as he stepped forward and bowed.

"Can you shoot down that cluster of mangoes at the top of the tree?"

"Certainly, Your Majesty, but I must choose my own position, and I will need a screen."

"Where do you need to stand?"

"I must position myself in the place where your couch stands."

"Very well," replied the king, and he ordered that his couch be moved and that a screen be brought.

When everything was ready, Asadisa stepped behind the screen, took off his white shirt, and replaced it with a red one. Then he fastened a girdle and tied a red dhoti around his waist. From a bag he had hidden beneath his undergarments, he removed the pieces of a sword, his quiver, and the pieces of his great ram's horn bow. He swiftly assembled the sword and fastened it on his left side. Then he donned golden body armor and slung the quiver over his shoulder. After assembling his mighty bow, he fitted it with a string as red as coral. Finally, he put an elegant turban on his head and emerged from behind the screen, twirling the arrow in his hands. He looked, for all the world, like a magnificent nāga prince.

Stepping up to his chosen spot, he set his arrow in his bow. Then he turned to the king and asked, "Your Majesty, do you want me to bring this fruit down with an upward shot, or by letting the arrow fall upon it?"

"My goodness," the king replied, "I have often seen a marksman bring down his mark with an upward shot, but never with the downward. Please do so."

"In that case, Sire, my arrow, before returning to earth, will fly as high as the heaven of the Four Great Kings. You must be patient."

"I will watch and wait patiently," replied the king.

"Your Majesty," Asadisa continued, "on the way up, this arrow will pierce the stalk exactly in the middle. As it comes down, it will strike precisely the same spot, bringing the cluster of fruit with it."

Carefully drawing the red bowstring of the ram's horn bow, Asadisa aimed at the stalk and shot the arrow. Exactly as he had predicted, the arrow pierced the center of the mango stalk and continued flying upward out of sight. When he was certain that his arrow had reached the heaven of the Four Great Kings, he let fly another arrow with even greater speed than the first. Suddenly, the air was rent by a sound as loud as a thunderbolt.

"What is that noise?" asked the archers and the courtiers, nervously.

"My second arrow struck the feathers of the first arrow and turned it back," Asadisa replied. "What you hear is the sound of my first arrow falling."

"We must hide!" they shouted, looking for a safe place to jump.

"Don't worry," Asadisa reassured them. "I will see that it does not hurt anyone."

Everyone watched as the arrow descended. Just as Asadisa had predicted, it neatly severed the stalk of the mango cluster. With one hand, Asadisa caught the falling fruit and, with the other, the arrow, so that neither touched the ground.

"Incredible! Amazing! Remarkable!" cried the spectators, creating an uproar as they cheered, clapped their hands, and snapped their fingers. "We've never seen such shooting!"

"Wait a minute, Asadisa," shouted one of the other archers. "Where is the second arrow?"

"That arrow continued flying upward and was caught by a deva in Tā-vatimsa," Asadisa replied.

Again, everyone cheered and snapped their fingers.

Recognizing that Asadisa was far more skillful than they could ever hope to be, the other archers felt ashamed that they had begrudged him his salary. For his part, the king showered the archer with gifts and great honor.

At this time, the kings of seven kingdoms bordering Kāsi, realizing that Prince Asadisa was no longer in Bārānasi, combined their forces and invaded the kingdom. With their superior army, they quickly advanced all the way to Bārānasi and sent a message to King Brahmadatta that he must surrender or be killed. The young king, who had no experience with fighting, was terrified.

"Where is my brother?" he asked his advisors.

"He is in the service of a neighboring king," they replied.

"He is the only one who can save me," the king lamented. "If he does not come, I am a dead man!" Summoning a trusted messenger, he ordered, "Go! Find Prince Asadisa! Fall at his feet in my name! Tell him that I was completely wrong to mistrust him! Promise him anything! Bring him back with you! Go! Quickly!" No sooner had he finished speaking than the messenger sped away to do as commanded.

As soon as Asadisa heard the news, he took leave of his master and returned to Bārānasi. He assured his brother that there were no hard feelings and told him not to worry. He promised to rout the seven foreign kings and to drive them away. From his quiver, he extracted one of his best arrows and scratched a message on its shaft: "I, Prince Asadisa, have returned. With one arrow, exactly like this one, I will kill you all. Let those who wish to live escape now." He shot this arrow over the wall of the city so that it fell in the enemy camp in the middle of the golden dish from which the seven kings were eating. Without even finishing their meal, the seven kings mobilized their armies, mounted their chariots, and fled to their own capitals.

Thus, did Prince Asadisa, without shedding a single drop of blood, put to flight seven mighty kings.

Once more assuring his younger brother that there was no cause for fear or worry, Asadisa declared his intention to renounce the world. Then, laying down his bow and taking up the garb of an ascetic, he left Bārānasi for the last time. The rest of his life he spent in meditation, cultivating the Four Brahma Vihāras. When he passed away, he was reborn in the Brahma heavens.

Having concluded his story, the Buddha identified the birth: "At that time, Ānanda was the younger brother, and I was Prince Asadisa."

76

At Home on the Battlefield
Sangāmāvacara Jātaka

It was while staying at Jetavana that the Buddha told this story about Venerable Nanda.

One day, during his first return to his hometown of Kapilavatthu after his Enlightenment, the Buddha handed his almsbowl to his younger brother, Prince Nanda, who followed the Buddha to the monastery. Rather than returning home, Prince Nanda accepted the Buddha's invitation and ordained as a bhikkhu. When the Buddha left Kapilavatthu, Venerable Nanda accompanied him and the other bhikkhus to Sāvatthī and took up residence in Jetavana.

Even in Sāvatthī, however, Venerable Nanda kept remembering his betrothed, the beautiful Princess Janapadakalyānī. As he had left home, she had been standing with her hair half combed and looking out of the window. "Look!" she had cried with her melodious voice, "Prince Nanda is going off with the Master! Come back soon, my lord!"

As he recalled the scene, dwelling on each detail, Venerable Nanda grew increasingly despondent. Discontented and depressed, he became so thin and jaundiced that his veins stood out in knots.

When the Buddha learned of his younger brother's depression, he thought, "What if I could establish Nanda in arahatship!" He went to Venerable Nanda's cell and sat on the seat offered him.

"Well, Nanda," he asked, "are you contented with our teaching?"

"Venerable Sir," replied Venerable Nanda, "I am in love with Janapadaka-lyānī, and I am not contented."

"Have you been on pilgrimage in the Himavat, Nanda?"

"No, Venerable Sir, not yet."

"Then we will go."

"But, Venerable Sir, I have no miraculous power. How can I go?"

"I will take you." The Buddha took him by the hand, and together they traveled to the Himavat.

On the way, they passed over a burned field. There, on a charred tree stump, with her nose and tail half gone, her hair scorched off, and her hide burned like a cinder, sat a female monkey, not much more than skin and bone, covered with blood and scabs.

"Do you see that monkey, Nanda?" the Buddha asked.

"Yes, Venerable Sir."

"Take a good look at her," he said.

Then he pointed out the uplands of Manosila, the seven great lakes, the five great rivers, and the entire Himavat with its magnificent peaks and splendid scenery.

"Nanda," the Buddha asked, "have you ever seen Tāvatimsa, the Heaven of the Thirty-three?"

"No, Venerable Sir, never," Venerable Nanda replied.

"Come along, Nanda. Let me show you." The Buddha took him to Tāva-timsa. Accompanied by a host of devas, Sakka offered respectful greetings and sat down on one side. Sakka's handmaidens, delicate nymphs with slender feet, also greeted them and sat down. The Buddha pointed out the five hundred nymphs and encouraged Venerable Nanda to look carefully at them. The young bhikkhu was intoxicated by their beauty and burning with desire.

"Nanda," the Buddha asked, "do you see these doe-eyed nymphs?"

"Yes, Venerable Sir."

"Well, which is more beautiful, these heavenly nymphs or your fiancée, Janapadakalyānī?"

"Oh, Venerable Sir! Comparing these celestial nymphs to Janapadaka-lyānī is like comparing her to that miserable she monkey disfigured by the forest fire!"

"Well, Nanda, what are you thinking now?"

"Venerable Sir, I am wondering how it would be possible to win these nymphs?"

"By living as an ascetic, Nanda," the Buddha replied, "one might win these nymphs."

"If the Blessed One promises that an ascetic life will win these nymphs, I will lead an ascetic life!"

"Nanda, I give you my word."

"Then, Venerable Sir, I will become an ascetic."

The Buddha took him back to Jetavana, and Venerable Nanda began to live a strictly ascetic life.

The Buddha recounted to the eighty great bhikkhus how Venerable Nanda had made him promise that by living as an ascetic one would win the celestial nymphs. The Buddha told this to all the other bhikkhus at Jetavana as well.

Shortly afterwards, Venerable Sāriputta asked Venerable Nanda, "Is it true, as I hear, Friend, that you have the Buddha's pledged word that, by spending your life as an ascetic, you will win the devas in Tāvatimsa?"

Without waiting for a reply, he continued, "We could say, then, that your holy life is all bound up with womankind and lust? In fact, if you live chastely, simply for the sake of women, what is the difference between you and a laborer who works for hire?"

Venerable Sāriputta's question quenched all the fire in Venerable Nanda and made him ashamed of himself. When he heard the same remarks from the other great disciples and from all the other bhikkhus, he became even more ashamed, if that were possible.

"I have been wrong," he thought remorsefully. With that shame burning deep in his heart, he set himself to the task of developing insight. Soon, he attained arahatship.

He went immediately to the Buddha and said, "Venerable Sir, I release the Blessed One from his promise."

The Buddha replied, "If you have attained arahatship, Nanda, I am already released from my promise."

When the bhikkhus heard of this, they began to talk about it in the Hall of Truth. "How docile Venerable Nanda is, to be sure! Imagine! One word of advice awakened his sense of shame, and he began to live as a real ascetic. Now he is an arahat!"

When the Buddha heard what they were discussing, he said, "Bhikkhus, long ago, Nanda was just as docile as he is now." Then he told this story of the past.

Long, long ago, when Brahmadatta was reigning in Bārānasi, the Bodhisatta was born as an elephant-trainer's son and learned everything involved in the training of elephants. When he grew up, he entered the service of the king of a neighboring country and trained the royal elephant to perfection.

That king, who was an enemy of King Brahmadatta, decided to conquer Kāsi and led a mighty army to Bārānasi. He set up camp there and sent a message to King Brahmadatta: "Fight, or yield!"

Choosing to fight, King Brahmadatta ordered soldiers to defend the walls, towers, and battlements and to guard the city gates. He marshaled a great army to defy the enemy.

The invading king ordered that his royal elephant be prepared for battle. Then the king put on his own armor, took a sharp goad, and drove the great animal toward the city gate. "Now!" he shouted. "Let us storm this city, kill Brahmadatta, and take the kingdom as our own!"

As soon as the well-trained elephant saw the chaos of the battle, however, with boiling oil raining down from the top of the walls and huge stones and other missiles flying from the catapults, the huge beast was so frightened that he refused to advance.

Seeing the elephant balk, the trainer ran up and cried in his ear, "Son, a hero like you belongs on the battlefield! Remember all that I have taught you! It would be disgraceful for you now to give up. You are a champion! You have nothing to fear! No one can harm you! Go forward! Break through the gate! Carry the king into the city in triumph! You can easily do it!"

The elephant listened to his trainer. Just those few words were enough to dispel his fear. He charged forward, wound his powerful trunk around the pillars, and tore them up like toadstools. He beat against the gate until the doors broke down. Then he led the army through the city, all the way to the palace, and won it for his king.

Having concluded his story, the Buddha identified the birth: "At that time, Nanda was the elephant, Ānanda was the king, and I was the trainer."

77

The Drunken Asses
Vālodaka Jātaka

It was while staying at Jetavana that the Buddha told this story about eating leftovers.

In Sāvatthī there were five hundred laypeople who, having given their houses and property to their children, had taken the eight precepts in order to practice meditation and to study the Dhamma under the Buddha. All of them had attained either the first or the second path. When people invited the Buddha and his bhikkhus to a meal, these white-robed lay devotees were often invited as well. These lay followers, who were quiet and valued solitude, had five hundred attendants who looked after them, providing all their needs, such as toothsticks, water, and flowers. These young boys, however, were not in the least restrained in their habits. After eating the leftovers of a meal and resting a bit, they often raced to the Aciravatī River, where, shouting like fools, they wrestled on the bank.

One day, when the Buddha heard their shouting, he asked, "What is that racket, Ānanda?"

"It is the devotees' attendants, Venerable Sir."

"Ānanda," the Buddha replied, "this is not the only time those attendants have made a great noise after being fed on leftovers. They did the same once before. At that time, these lay devotees were as quiet as they are now." At Venerable Ānanda's request, the Buddha told this story of the past.

Long, long ago, when Brahmadatta was reigning in Bārānasi, the Bodhisatta became the king's advisor. Once, when there was a revolt on the frontier, the king led his army there, successfully quelled it, and returned to the capital.

Before retiring to his chamber, he ordered the grooms, "The horses are tired! Give them some freshly fermented grape juice to drink." The steeds drank the delicious juice, entered the stables, and stood quietly in their stalls.

The grooms asked the king what they should do with the dregs, which included the grape skins and the seeds.

"Mix it with water, strain it through a towel, and give the juice to the donkeys that carried the supplies."

The donkeys greedily drank the watery juice and immediately began galloping around the courtyard, kicking up their heels, and braying loudly.

When the king saw the donkeys, he called his advisor. "Look! Those asses have gone mad from that miserable drink! They're running around and hee-hawing like fools! My fine thoroughbreds drank the best juice, but they remain quiet in the stables. What does it mean?" the king asked.

"Whenever a low-class ruffian gets even a swallow of alcohol, he gets drunk and misbehaves. One who is gentle and well-bred will keep a steady head even if he drinks the most potent liquor!"

The king appreciated his advisor's perspicacity and ordered that the unruly donkeys be driven out of the courtyard.

Always abiding by the wisdom of his advisor, the king ruled righteously, gave alms, and performed many good deeds, eventually passing away to fare according to his deserts.

Having concluded his story, the Buddha identified the birth: "At that time, those attendants were the five hundred donkeys, these lay devotees were the thoroughbreds, Ānanda was the king, and I was the wise advisor."

78

A River of Curd
Dadhivāhana Jātaka

It was while staying at Jetavana that the Buddha told this story about keeping bad company.

"It is obvious that bad company has evil effects on human beings," the Buddha said, "but bad company can also ruin a splendid and valuable plant." To illustrate his point, the Buddha told this story.

Long, long ago, when Brahmadatta was reigning in Bārānasi, four brahmin brothers of Kāsi renounced the world and became ascetics. In the Himavat, they lived in four separate huts.

When the eldest brother died, he was reborn as Sakka. Even as the king of the devas, he remembered his brothers and visited them every week.

One day, as he was sitting with the eldest of the three remaining ascetics, he asked, "Sir, is there any way I can help you?"

"Yes, actually there is. Because I have jaundice," the ascetic replied, "I need a fire."

"Here you are," replied Sakka immediately. "Please take this special blade, which can serve as either a razor or an axe, depending how you fix it to the handle.

"But, Friend," the ascetic objected, "there is no one here to fetch firewood with that axe."

"Ah, but that is not a problem!" Sakka replied. "If you need a fire, all you have to do is strike the axe with your hand and say, 'Fetch wood and make a fire!' The axe will obey your commands."

Later, as Sakka was sitting with the second brother, he asked the same question, "Sir, is there any way I can help you?"

"Yes," the ascetic replied, "there is an elephant trail running past my hut, and the beasts often annoy me. I wish I could drive them away."

"Here is a drum," Sakka said. "If you beat it on this side, your enemies will run away. If you beat it on the other side, your enemies will become your firm friends and supporters, and they will serve you like a great army."

Next, Sakka asked the youngest brother, "Sir, is there any way I can help you?"

"Yes," the ascetic replied, "I have severe jaundice, and I would love to eat curd."

"Here is a bowl," Sakka said. "Whenever you turn this bowl over, a great river of curd will pour out of it. It might even win a kingdom for you."

Satisfied that he had greatly helped his three brothers, Sakka returned to Tāvatimsa.

Indeed, the three ascetics lived peacefully after that. The eldest used his axe whenever he needed a fire, the second was no longer bothered by elephants, and the youngest always had curd to eat.

At that time, there was a wild boar living in a deserted village. One day, this boar happened to find a magical gem. As soon as he put it in his mouth, he rose in the air and flew a great distance. In the middle of the ocean, he spotted an island and thought it would be a nice place to live. The gem carried him there, and he was able to survey the entire island. He was attracted to a pleasant site with a large mango tree, and, by the magic of the gem, he floated down at exactly that spot. For some time, he lived peacefully on the island.

Also at this time, in Kāsi, there was a young man who had been thrown out of the house by his parents for being lazy. This good-for-nothing had gotten a job on a ship as a deckhand, but, after a short time at sea, the ship had sunk in a storm, and that young man, clinging to a plank, had washed up on the shore of the island where the wild boar lived. As he was wandering around looking for water and for something to eat, he spied the boar sleeping soundly under the tree with the gem lying in front of him. The man very stealthily crept closer and seized the gem. Instantly, he found himself float-ing in the air! He alighted on a branch of the mango tree and thought, "The gem must have carried that boar to this remote island. Well, now I have the gem! Why don't I kill the boar, eat him, and go where I want?" He dropped a twig on the boar's head to see what would happen.

The boar woke up with a start and immediately realized that his gem was gone. Confused and trembling with fear, he ran back and forth, looking for his treasure.

From the top of the tree, the man laughed aloud at the sight.

The boar looked up and saw the gem in the man's hand. In his rage, the boar ran as fast as he could and struck the tree so hard with his head that he fell dead. The man climbed down and built a fire. After he had roasted the boar and eaten his fill, he picked up the gem once more. Instantly, he rose into the air and flew toward the Himavat.

From aloft, he saw the ascetics' huts and chose to descend in front of the eldest's. The ascetic received the man quite hospitably, and he stayed there for a couple of days. During that time, he saw the usefulness of the axe and decided to get it for himself. He showed his host the magic gem and offered to exchange it for the axe. The idea of flying through the air was so appealing to the ascetic that he agreed. As soon as they had made the trade, the man left.

Before he had gone very far, however, he struck the axe and commanded, "Smash the ascetic's skull and bring me back my magic gem!"

Instantly, the axe flew back to the hut, smashed the ascetic's skull, and returned with the jewel.

Delighted with his success, the man hid the axe and proceeded to the second brother's hut. While staying there for a couple of days, he learned the power of the ascetic's remarkable drum.

Again he made a bargain, exchanging his gem for the drum. As soon as he had left the hut, he again commanded the axe to smash the second ascetic's skull and to bring back the gem, and the axe obeyed.

During his stay with the youngest brother, he observed him using the extraordinary bowl and traded it for the gem. In the same way as before, he retrieved the gem and went on his way.

By the power of the gem, he rose into the air and flew with his treasures to Bārānasi. He sent a message to the king demanding that he surrender his kingdom or fight to defend it.

This message from an unknown wanderer so outraged the king that he himself led his army to seize the scoundrel. The vagabond beat his drum and summoned a huge army. As soon as he saw the king approaching, he rode calmly to the front of his forces and overturned his bowl. Out poured a great river of curd, which drowned the king's foot soldiers. Then he struck his axe and ordered it to bring him the king's head. The axe flew through the air, cut off the king's head, and returned, dropping the severed head at the young man's feet.

The king's army was in disarray. They realized that, without a leader and in the face of such weapons, they could offer no resistance, so they surrendered. Surrounded by a mighty host, the vagabond entered the city and had himself crowned king. Because he had been carried to the throne by a river of curd, he took the name Dadhivāhana. In spite of his treacherous past, King Dadhivāhana ruled righteously.

One day, while the king was amusing himself by casting a net in the river, he happened to catch a yellow mango, which had floated down from Lake Kannamunda in the Himavat. The king had never seen anything like it and wondered what it was. As soon as he tasted it, he was thrilled, for it was succulent, juicy, and fit for the devas. He immediately ordered that the seed be planted in his park and that it be sprinkled with milk-water. A sapling soon sprouted, and, after three years, the tree bore fruit which was of the color of fine gold and exceedingly sweet. The tree was shown great honor. Milk-water was poured on its roots, it was hung with perfumed garlands, and a lamp was kept burning nearby.

Whenever King Dadhivāhana sent a ripe mango as a present to another king, he carefully pricked the seed so that it would not germinate to produce another tree.

The other kings enjoyed the fruit immensely, and all of them planted the seeds, hoping to grow their own mangoes, but no one could get a seed to take root. One by one, the kings realized what King Dadhivāhana was doing.

One enterprising king asked his gardener whether it was possible to spoil the flavor of the fruit from this special tree and to make it bitter. The gardener assured his king that it was possible and that he knew how to do it. The king gave the gardener one thousand coins and sent him to Bārānasi to carry out the mission.

As soon as the gardener arrived in Bārānasi, he sent a message to the king that he was available for work. The king summoned him and, being satisfied with his experience and qualifications, gave him a position as assistant gardener.

The newcomer showed the chief gardener how to force flowers to bloom and fruit to ripen out of season, which greatly impressed the king. The park soon became so beautiful and productive that the king promoted the newcomer to chief gardener and dismissed the old gardener.

Having gained complete control of the park, the new gardener stealthily planted neem sprouts all around the special mango tree. These sprouts grew quickly. Their roots entangled themselves with the mango tree roots, and their branches entwined with those of the mango tree. In time, the fruit of the mango tree became as bitter as the leaves of the neem tree. Satisfied that he had accomplished his mission, the gardener returned to his former master.

One day, as King Dadhivāhana was strolling through the park, he plucked a ripe mango and eagerly took a bite of it. As soon as the bitter flavor touched his tongue, however, he spat out the pulp and cursed.

Unable to find the gardener, the king summoned his chief advisor and asked what had happened to his mangoes.

The advisor examined the tree and immediately understood the problem. "Your Majesty," he explained, "planted all around your special mango tree are small neem trees. The roots of these trees have become entangled with the mango tree roots, and the branches have likewise entwined. Bad company spoils the good, and your mangoes have been spoiled by the bitter neem."

The advisor ordered that all the neem trees be pulled up by the roots, that the noxious soil be replaced, and that the mango tree be frequently watered with fresh, sweet water. The mangoes soon grew succulent once more, and the king restored his former gardener to his post.

In time, the king passed away to fare according to his deserts.

Having concluded his story, the Buddha identified the birth: "At that time, I was the wise advisor."

79

A Good Friend
Sīlānisamsa Jātaka

It was while staying at Jetavana that the Buddha told this story about a pious lay follower.

One evening, when a faithful disciple came to the bank of the Aciravatī River on his way to Jetavana to hear the Buddha, there was no boat at the landing stage. The ferrymen had pulled their boats onto the far shore and had gone to hear the Buddha. The disciple's mind was so full of delightful thoughts of the Buddha, however, that, even though he walked into the river, his feet did not sink below the surface. He walked across the water as if he were on dry land, but, when he reached the middle of the river, he noticed the waves, his ecstasy subsided, and his feet began to sink. As soon as he again focused his mind on the qualities of the Buddha, his feet rose, and he was able to continue walking joyously over the water. When he arrived at Jetavana, he paid his respects to the Buddha and took a seat on one side.

"Good layman," the Buddha said, addressing the disciple, "I hope you had no mishap on your way."

"Venerable Sir," the disciple replied, "while coming here, I was so absorbed in thoughts of the Buddha that, when I came to the river, I was able to walk across it as though it were solid."

"My friend," the Buddha said, "you are not the only one who has been protected in this way. In olden days, pious laymen were shipwrecked in mid-ocean and saved themselves by remembering the virtues of the Buddha." At the man's request, the Buddha told this story of the past.

Long, long ago, at the time of Kassapa Buddha, a lay disciple, who had already entered on the path, booked passage on a ship along with one of his friends, a rich barber. The barber's wife asked this disciple to look after her husband.

A week after the ship left the port, it sank in mid-ocean. The two friends saved themselves by clinging to a plank, and they were, at last, cast up on a deserted island. Famished, the barber killed some birds, cooked them, and offered a share of his meal to his friend.

"No, thank you," the disciple answered, "I am fine." Then he thought, "In this isolated place, there is no help for us except the Triple Gem." As he sat meditating on the Triple Gem, a nāga king who had been born on that island, transformed himself into a beautiful ship filled with the seven precious things. The three masts were made of sapphire, the planks and anchor of gold, and the ropes of silver.

The helmsman, who was a sea deva, stood on the deck and cried, "Any passengers for Jambudīpa?"

"Yes," the disciple answered, "that's where we are bound."

"Then come on board," the sea deva said.

The disciple climbed aboard the beautiful ship and turned to call his friend the barber.

"You may come," the deva said, "but he may not."

"Why not?" the disciple asked.

"He is not a follower of the holy life." answered the deva. "I brought this ship for you, but not for him."

"In that case," the layman announced, "all the gifts I have given, all the virtues I have practiced, all the powers I have developed—I give the fruit of all of them to him!"

"Thank you, Master!" cried the barber.

"Very well," said the deva, "now I can take you both aboard."

The ship carried the two men over the sea and up the Gangā. After depositing them safely at their homes in Bārānasi, the deva used his magic power to create enormous wealth for both of them. Then, poising himself in mid-air, he instructed the men and their friends, "Keep company with the wise and good," he said. "If this barber had not been in company with this pious layman, he would have perished in the middle of the ocean." Finally, the deva returned to his own abode, taking the nāga king with him.

Having concluded his story, the Buddha taught the Dhamma, and the pious layman attained the second path. Then the Buddha identified the birth: "At that time, the disciple attained arahatship, Sāriputta was the nāga king, and I was the sea deva."

80

Even After Drinking My Blood
Culla-Paduma Jātaka[1]

It was while staying at Jetavana that the Buddha told this story about a backsliding bhikkhu.

When the bhikkhu was asked whether he had really lapsed in his practice, he admitted that he had.

"What caused you to lapse?" the Buddha asked him.

The bhikkhu replied that he had seen a woman dressed in fine clothes and that he had been overcome by passion at the sight.

"Bhikkhu, women can be treacherous and ungrateful. Once a wise man was so stupid that he gave his own blood to a woman suffering from thirst, yet he could not keep her heart." Then he told this story of the past.

Long, long ago, when Brahmadatta was reigning in Bārānasi, the Bodhisatta was born as his first son and was called Prince Paduma. Prince Paduma had six younger brothers.

As the princes matured into handsome, strong, and popular young men, they all married. For no good reason, their father, the king, became paranoid

---

1   Paduma means "lotus."

that they would try to usurp the throne. One day, when he looked out the window, he saw all seven of them together in the palace courtyard. The princes were merely on their way to wait upon him, but, when he saw the great following of courtiers around them, he became convinced that they were plotting to slay him and to take the throne for themselves. As soon as the princes arrived in his royal chamber, he ordered them to leave the kingdom. "After I have died," he told them, "you may return and claim the throne, but, until then, you must remain in exile."

The seven brothers were shocked by their father's harsh words and bewailed their fate. Nevertheless, they knew that they had to obey, so they returned home to inform their wives and to make preparations for their departure.

"Alas!" they cried. "We are doomed! What does it matter where we go!" Accompanied by their wives, the princes left the city. The road they followed took them into the forest, where they could find nothing to eat or drink. Overcome with hunger, the princes seized the wife of the youngest, slew her, and divided her flesh into thirteen parts. Prince Paduma and his wife shared only one portion between them, secretly setting aside the other portion. The next day, the princes killed the wife of the second youngest and divided her flesh into twelve parts. Prince Paduma and his wife again ate only one portion and set aside the other.

For six days, the princes continued this practice, killing and consuming six wives. Each time Prince Paduma and his wife ate only one portion and set aside the other.

On the seventh day, the other princes intended to kill Prince Paduma's wife, but before they could seize her, Prince Paduma brought out the six portions he and his wife had kept.

"Eat these," he told them. "We will manage." Satisfied, the six brothers ate the flesh and went to bed. As soon as they were asleep, Prince Paduma and his wife escaped together.

After they had gone a short way, the woman complained, "Husband, I can walk no further." Prince Paduma lifted her and carried her on his shoulders. At sunrise, they emerged from the forest. When the sun came up, it became hot, and the woman complained again, "Husband, I am thirsty!"

"Wife," Prince Paduma replied, "there is no water to be found here."

Again and again, she begged him for water. Finally, he stopped, took out his sword, and cut a gash in his right knee. "My dear," he said gently, "there is no water at all, but you can sit here and drink the blood from my knee." Grasping his leg, she put her lips to the wound and drank his blood.

The two of them continued on until they reached the mighty Gangā, where they drank, bathed, ate fruit, and rested in a pleasant spot. By a bend of the river, they built a simple hut and set up a residence.

One day, Prince Paduma heard someone moaning piteously, and the sound seemed to be coming from the river. "No poor creature should die if I can prevent it!" he exclaimed as he hurried to the bend in the river. He saw a boat drifting downstream, and in it was a man whose hands, feet, nose, and ears had been cut off. The prince immediately understood that the man must have been punished for some very serious crime, perhaps treason, and had been left in this miserable condition to die in the boat.

Prince Paduma rescued the wretched man, carried him to the hut, and treated his ugly wounds with herbal lotions and ointments. When Prince Paduma's wife saw the man, she spat in disgust and muttered, "Look at this nice lazy fellow my husband has fetched out of the Gangā to look after!"

While the man's wounds were healing, the prince let him stay in the hut with him and his wife. Every day, the prince went into the forest to gather fruit for the three of them to eat. Gradually, the woman became very fond of their guest and committed adultery with him. She fell in love with him and decided to get rid of Prince Paduma.

One day, she said to him, "Husband, when we first came out from the forest, you were carrying me on your shoulder, and I saw that hill over there. At that time, I made a vow that, if you and I survived, I would make an offering to the deva of that hill. My offering is long overdue, and now I want to thank the deva."

"Very good," said the prince. He prepared an offering for her, and together they climbed to the top of the hill.

"Husband," she addressed him when they had reached the summit, "you are my chief deva! Let me first offer wild flowers in your honor. Then I will walk reverently around you, keeping you on the right. After I salute you, I will make my offering to the deva of the hill." She placed him facing the precipice and stepped behind him as though she were going to pay her obeisance to him. Very quickly, she struck him hard on the back, pushed him over the cliff, and shouted triumphantly, "I am finally rid of him!" With a light step, she descended the mountain and joined her paramour.

Although the prince plunged over the cliff, he wasn't killed. He happened to fall into a sturdy fig tree which was growing from the mountainside. He was unharmed, but he could neither get down nor climb up. He was certainly stuck, but, fortunately, there were plenty of ripe figs, which were moist and delicious.

That fig tree happened to be a popular spot for a huge monitor lizard who also enjoyed eating its fruit. As soon as the monitor lizard noticed the prince sitting in the tree, he turned around and ran away in fright. The next day, he cautiously climbed back up the hill and ate some fruit on one side of the tree. Little by little, he inched closer to the prince, who called softly, "Don't be afraid! I would never hurt you."

Realizing that there was no danger, he climbed to the top of the tree, right beside the prince, and struck up a friendly conversation with him. He wondered how the prince managed to get into the tree, and Paduma explained all that had happened.

"Well, don't be afraid," said the monitor lizard. "I'll carry you down. Just cling to my back." As soon as the prince was securely in place, the monitor lizard carefully climbed out of the tree and down the mountain. He showed the prince the way out of the forest and returned to the fig tree.

The prince found lodging in a village and stayed there until he heard the news of his father's death. Then he returned to Bārānasi and claimed the throne, taking the name of King Paduma. He ruled wisely, observing the ten duties of a king. In order to distribute gifts to the needy, he constructed six almshalls in his capital. News of his generosity and his alms-giving spread throughout the kingdom.

In the meantime, confident that Paduma was dead, his wicked wife had picked up her paramour and was wandering with him on her shoulders. Without a means of livelihood, she begged for rice and scraps of food. When anyone asked what the man was to her, she replied, "His mother was my father's sister, so he was my cousin. My parents gave me to him, so now he is my husband. Of course, I will care for him, taking him on my shoulders and begging food for him."

"What a devoted wife!" people agreed, giving even more generously than before. After some time, several people told her about the new king. "Why do you struggle to get by here?" they asked her. "A great king now rules in Bārānasi. He has stirred up all Jambudīpa with his generosity. He will be touched to see your devotion and will surely reward you with rich gifts." They gave her a sturdy reed basket and suggested that she put her husband in it and make her way to Bārānasi. The wicked woman followed their advice and was able to live comfortably on what she got in the king's alms-halls.

It was King Paduma's custom to visit the alms-halls regularly, riding on the back of the royal elephant, richly caparisoned. After personally giving food to eight or ten people at one of the alms-halls, he would return to the palace.

One day, knowing that the king was coming, the woman placed her lover in the reed basket and went to stand where the king would pass. As soon as

King Paduma saw the woman, he recognized her, but she, convinced that he was dead, did not recognize him at all.

"Who is that woman?" the king asked an attendant.

"She is a devoted wife who comes here regularly to receive alms," the attendant answered. The king sent for her and asked her the question she had heard so often, "What is this man to you?"

"He is the son of my father's sister," she replied, giving her well-practiced answer. "My parents gave me to him, so he is my husband."

"Ah, what a devoted wife!" cried the crowd in praise.

"What?" shouted the king. "This scoundrel is your cousin? Your family gave you to him? Is he really your husband?"

Still not recognizing the king, she boldly answered, "Yes, Your Majesty!"

"Then this must be the son of the king of Kāsi," the king retorted, "since you are the wife of Prince Paduma!" Horrified, the woman fell on her knees before the king. "Didn't you once drink the blood from my knee?" the king continued. "Did you not fall in love with this rascal, whom I saved while we were together in the forest? Didn't you throw me down a precipice, leaving me for dead? Now here you are in my kingdom. I am quite alive, but I see that you have death clearly written on your forehead!"

"My friends," the king said, turning to his courtiers, "do you recall what I told you about the past? Did I not relate to you that my six younger brothers killed their wives one by one to keep from starvation and that I protected my own wife until we got safely to the bank of the Gangā? Do you remember that I saved a condemned criminal from death? I told you that my wife fell in love with that felon. Wanting to get rid of me, she pushed me over a cliff. I would have died there, but, by showing kindness, I was saved by a good and compassionate monitor lizard. This is that self-same woman. The miserable wretch in the basket is the same man I saved from the river. What kind of man rewards his benefactor by stealing his spouse? How dare this harlot masquerade as a faithful wife? This couple deserves to die!"

Soldiers rushed forward to seize them and to march them away to be executed, but the king held up his hand to stop them. "No," he said calmly, overcoming his wrath. "I will not have them killed. Strap that basket tightly to her head. Place that villain in the basket and let them wander, so that all can see and know their crimes." The soldiers did as the king commanded and drove the wicked pair out of the kingdom.

Having concluded his story, the Buddha taught the Dhamma, and the backsliding bhikkhu attained the first path. Then the Buddha identified the birth: "At that time, Ciñcā-Mānavikā was the wife, Devadatta was the criminal, Ānanda was the monitor lizard, and I was King Paduma."

81

The Jewel Thief
Manicora Jātaka

It was while staying at Veluvana that the Buddha told this story about Devadatta.

When the Buddha heard that Devadatta intended to kill him, he said, "Bhikkhus, this is not the first time that Devadatta has tried to kill me; he tried before and failed." Then he told this story of the past.

Long, long ago, when Brahmadatta was reigning in Bārānasi, in a village not far from the capital, the Bodhisatta was born as the son of a householder. When he became a young man, he married a well-bred young lady from Bārānasi. She was a fair and graceful maiden, named Sujātā. She became a virtuous wife, faithfully serving her husband and his parents. The young man loved his wife very much, and the two of them lived together in joy, harmony, and oneness of mind.

One day, Sujātā said to her husband, "I would like to see my mother and father again after such a long time."

"Very well, my dear," he replied, "please prepare food for us for the journey."

They loaded a cart with provisions and gifts. He sat in front to drive, and she sat behind. As soon as they reached the outskirts of Bārānasi, they stopped to rest, and he unyoked the oxen. After they had washed and eaten their meal, Sujātā changed her clothes and adorned herself. Quite refreshed, her husband yoked the oxen again and climbed up into the driver's seat. Sujātā sat down again in the back, and they resumed their journey.

As they entered the city, Sujātā stepped down from the cart and walked behind it. The king of Kāsi happened to be passing in procession on the back of his splendid royal elephant and saw her. He was so attracted by her beauty that he ordered one of his men to go and find out whether or not she had a husband.

"I am told she has a husband, Sire," the servant reported. "Do you see that man driving the cart? That is her husband."

The king could not control his passion. "I will get rid of that fellow," he thought, "and take the wife for myself." A vicious plan began forming in his mind, and he called his servant again. "Take this ornament," he said to the servant, handing him a beautiful jeweled crest, "and walk past that man's wagon. As you pass by, casually drop the jewel into the wagon without letting anyone see what you are doing. As soon as you have done it, report back to me." The servant did exactly as he was told.

"I have lost a jeweled crest!" cried the king. "Shut all the gates! Catch the thief!" The news spread rapidly, and the city was soon in an uproar.

The servant immediately set out with soldiers and accosted Sujātā's husband. "Hey, you!" he shouted. "Stop that cart! The king has lost a jewel, and we must search your wagon." Of course, he quickly found the jeweled crest which he himself had put there a few minutes before.

"Thief!" he cried, grabbing hold of the young man. The soldiers immediately seized him and beat him. They tied his arms behind his back and dragged him before the king.

"Here's the thief who stole your jewel!" they cried.

"Off with his head!" the king commanded excitedly.

The soldiers led the young man toward the southern gate, striking him with whips at every corner. Sujātā ran after him, stretching out her arms and wailing, "Dearest husband, it is I who got you into this wretched predicament!"

Just outside the city, the king's servants threw him down and prepared to cut off his head. When she saw her beloved husband about to be executed, Sujātā reflected on her own virtue and cried, "No devas are here! They must be far away. There can be no devas here, or they would stop these cruel men from slaying my innocent husband!"

While the virtuous Sujātā reproached the heavens in this way, Sakka noticed that his throne was growing hot. "Who is trying to make me fall from my position?" he wondered. He immediately became aware of what was happening. "Ah!" he thought, "The king of Kāsi is doing a very wicked thing. He is making the worthy Sujātā suffer. I must go there at once!"

Swiftly descending from his heaven, Sakka plucked the wicked king from the royal elephant and laid him down on the execution ground. In the same instant he snatched Sujātā's husband from the execution place, dressed him in the king's robes, and set him on the back of the king's elephant.

The executioner lifted his axe and cut off a head—but it was the king's head, and, as soon as the blow was struck, everyone realized that it was the king's.

Then Sakka appeared to the crowd, stood in front of the young man, and consecrated him as king, with Sujātā as his queen. All the courtiers, brahmins, householders, and other citizens rejoiced. "The unjust king is dead!" they cried. "Sakka himself has given us a righteous king!"

Sakka stood poised in the air and declared, "This upright king shall rule you virtuously. Because the former king was unrighteous, he was slain. If a king is immoral, the devas send rain out of season, and in season there is no rain. If the king is evil, three great fears torment men—fear of famine, fear of pestilence, and fear of the sword. This righteous king has been sent to you from heaven." Having thus admonished the people, Sakka returned to his divine abode.

The just king reigned wisely and, in due time, went to swell the hosts of heaven.

Having concluded his story, the Buddha identified the birth: "At that time, Devadatta was the wicked king, Anuruddha was Sakka, Rāhula's mother was Sujātā, and I was the king proclaimed by Sakka."

82

If She Is Dear
Pabbatūpatthara Jātaka

It was while staying at Jetavana that the Buddha told this story about King Pasenadi.

When King Pasenadi learned that one of his courtiers was misbehaving in the royal harem, he asked the Buddha for advice. In answer to his request, the Buddha told this story of the past.

Long, long ago, when Brahmadatta was reigning in Bārāṇasi, the Bodhisatta was his chief advisor.

One day, the king discovered that one of his wives was having an affair with one of his ministers. The king was, of course, very upset about this, but he hesitated to do anything because the minister in question was an important member of the court, and, furthermore, the king loved his wife dearly. "I don't want to lose either of the two," he thought as he pondered the delicate situation. "Let me ask my advisor. He is very wise and will give me good advice. I will do whatever he suggests." He sent for his advisor and asked him to be seated. "Wise sir," the king began, "I have an important question to ask you."

"Ask what you will, Sire, and I will answer," the advisor replied.

"Tell me what you think of this situation. At the foot of a lovely hill, there was a beautiful and very pleasing lake. A jackal dared to drink from the lake, even though he knew that a lion was constantly guarding its shores."

The advisor immediately understood what the king was asking and replied, "Out of the mighty river, all creatures drink at will. If she is dear, have patience. The river is still a river."

The king was very pleased with this answer and thanked his advisor. He talked to both his wife and the minister and, while admonishing them and giving them a stern warning, he forgave them for their misconduct. They apologized, broke off their liaison, and became faithful to the king once more.

For the rest of his life, the king gave alms and performed many good deeds, and, when he passed away, he was reborn in heaven.

After hearing the Buddha's story, the king of Koala forgave both his courtier and his wife. Having concluded his story, the Buddha identified the birth: "At that time, Ānanda was the king, and I was the wise advisor."

83

Fetters

Bandhanāgāra Jātaka

It was while staying at Jetavana that the Buddha told this story about fetters.

At one time, after a gang of murdering highwaymen had been captured, the king of Kosala ordered that they be shackled and imprisoned. The next morning, thirty bhikkhus, who had come from the countryside to see the Buddha, happened to pass the prison. That evening, they remarked to the Buddha on what they had seen. "Venerable Sir, today we saw a gang of criminals in great misery. All were wearing heavy chains and leg irons and could barely walk. Are there any fetters stronger than those?"

The Buddha answered, "Bhikkhus, those fetters are strong, but the craving for wives, children, wealth, and property are one hundredfold, even one thousandfold stronger. Even those fetters, however, were once broken by a wise man who became an ascetic in the Himavat." At their request, he told this story of the past.

Long, long ago, when Brahmadatta was reigning in Bārānasi, the Bodhisatta was born into a poor man's family. After his father died, he worked

361

for wages to support his mother, who, against his will, brought a wife home for him. Soon after he was married, his mother died.

Satisfied that he had fulfilled his duty toward his parents, he announced to his wife, "Now you must earn your own living. I am going to give up this worldly life."

"You cannot," she quickly answered. "Although I have not yet told you, I am expecting a child. Please wait until the baby is born. Then you may go." He agreed to wait.

As soon as the baby was born, he said to her, "Now, wife, you have safely delivered your baby. I will become an ascetic."

"Please wait," she begged, "until the child is weaned." Reluctantly, he agreed, but, before the first child had stopped nursing, she again conceived.

"If I continue to agree to her requests," the man thought, "I'll never get away. If I am to become an ascetic, I must simply go." One night, without saying anything to his wife, he got up and left.

Guards seized him, but, when he explained that he had a family, they let him go. He left the city and made his way to the Himavat, where he rigorously practiced meditation. Having experienced great happiness, he exalted, "At last, the bonds of wife and child, the bonds of wealth and property, and the bonds of passion, so hard to break, have been broken! Those fetters are mightier than ropes or chains and are harder to break than bonds of iron. Released from those heavy fetters, I am free!"

He continued his practice of concentration meditation, attained the jhānas, and, when he passed away, was reborn in the Brahma heavens.

Having concluded his story, the Buddha taught the Dhamma. Some attained the first path, some attained the second, some attained the third, and some became arahats. Finally, the Buddha identified the birth: "At that time, my parents were the mother and father, Rāhula's mother was the wife, Rāhula was the son, and I was the man who became an ascetic."

84
Gerophobia
Kelisīla Jātaka

It was while staying at Jetavana that the Buddha told this story about Venerable Lakuntaka.

Venerable Lakuntaka was well known by all the followers of the Buddha in Sāvatthī. Although he was a dwarf, he was an eloquent preacher and had a sweet voice. He possessed keen insight and lived with passions perfectly subdued.

One day, while Venerable Lakuntaka was waiting at the gate of Jetavana to pay his respects to the Buddha, thirty bhikkhus from the countryside arrived at the same spot. When they saw Venerable Lakuntaka, they mistook him for a little sāmanera and wanted to have some fun. They pulled the corner of his robe, caught his hands, tweaked his nose, shook him, and treated him like a child.

Later, after they had paid obeisance to the Buddha, they said to him, "Master, we understand that you have a disciple named Venerable Lakuntaka, who is a gifted preacher. Where is he?"

"Do you want to see him?" the Buddha asked.

"Yes, Venerable Sir."

"You saw him at the gate. Before you came here, you pulled his robe, tweaked his nose, and treated him with great rudeness."

Abashed to hear that, they asked the Buddha how such an outstanding disciple, who was so devoted to meditation and so greatly accomplished, could appear so insignificant?

"It is because of his own past deeds," the Buddha answered. At their request, he told this story of the past.

Long, long ago, when Brahmadatta was reigning in Bārānasi, the Bodhisatta was born as Sakka.

King Brahmadatta had one peculiarity; he could not bear to see anything old or decrepit. It didn't matter whether it was living or inanimate; if it was old, he could not endure it. He had old carts broken up and old houses pulled down. He was especially fond of playing nasty tricks on old people. Whenever he saw an old man, he made the poor fellow roll around on the ground like a ball. He ordered his soldiers to bring any elderly person they found to the palace for his amusement and the entertainment of his courtiers.

This behavior greatly upset the citizens. Those who could arrange it sent their parents far away beyond the reach of the king. Thus, as it became impossible for people to care for their aged parents, when they died, they were reborn in the four lower realms, and there were fewer devas in heaven.

Sakka quickly understood why no one was arriving in heaven and decided to teach King Brahmadatta a lesson by humbling him. Assuming the form of an old man dressed in rags, he put two jars of buttermilk in a rickety old wagon pulled by a pair of bony old oxen and set out for Bārānasi.

That day happened to be a holiday. The city was gaily decorated, and King Brahmadatta, seated on a richly caparisoned elephant, was riding in a grand procession. When the king saw Sakka and the wagon, he shouted, "Get that blasted cart out of the way, you old devil!"

"Who are you talking to, Sire?" his attendants asked. "We do not see any cart in the street."

Sakka, who had made himself and his cart invisible to all but the king, proceeded to taunt the king. He drove his cart in circles around the king's elephant and broke one of the jars of buttermilk on the king's head. When the king turned to catch what he thought was an old man, Sakka darted behind him and broke the second jar on the king's head. Looking ridiculous, with rancid buttermilk trickling down his face and into his ears, the king had to endure the laughter of the crowd, who could see him but couldn't see the cause of his discomfiture. King Brahmadatta was helpless against Sakka's torments.

When Sakka was sure that the king was completely miserable and thoroughly vexed, he made the cart disappear and, assuming his true form, poised himself in mid-air, thunderbolt in hand. "Brahmadatta!" he shouted. "You are a wicked and unrighteous man! Do you think that you yourself will never become old? Do you suppose that you are immune to aging? Of course, you're not! How dare you ridicule and mock those who are old! It is because of you that the people cannot care for their parents properly. Because of you, many people are being reborn in the four lower realms! If you do not cease your wicked ways, I will split your head with my thunderbolt! Let this be a warning to you!" Sakka fiercely shook his thunderbolt and returned to Tāvatimsa.

Sakka's warning had its desired effect. The king was completely reformed and never even thought of acting that way again.

Having concluded his story, the Buddha taught the Dhamma. Some of those bhikkhus attained the first path, some attained the second, some attained the third, and some became arahats. Then the Buddha identified the birth: "At that time, the virtuous Lakuntaka was the king who taunted the elderly and now has this deformity because of it, and I was Sakka."

85
Three Good Friends
Kurunga-Miga Jātaka

It was while staying at Veluvana that the Buddha told this story about Devadatta.

When the Buddha heard that Devadatta was plotting to kill him, he said, "It was the same long ago. Devadatta tried to kill me then, just as he is trying now." Then he told this story of the past.

Long, long ago, when Brahmadatta was reigning in Bārānasi, the Bodhisatta was born as an antelope and lived near a lake in a forest. A turtle lived in the lake, and in a tree nearby lived a woodpecker. The three animals were friends and lived together in harmony.

One day, a hunter, wandering through the forest looking for game, observed the antelope's hoof-prints going down to the water. Right at that spot, he set a snare with strong leather thongs and returned home. That night, as the antelope was going down to the lake to drink, he was caught in the snare. In fear and distress, he cried aloud.

Hearing their friend, the woodpecker flew down from the tree-top, and the turtle came out of the water. "Friend," the woodpecker said to the turtle, "with your strong beak, cut the thongs holding our friend captive. I will go and make sure that the hunter stays away while you are working. If we both do our best, our friend will not lose his life."

As the turtle began gnawing the leather thongs, the woodpecker flew quickly to the hunter's hut and waited. At dawn, the hunter, knife in hand, emerged from his hut. As soon as the woodpecker saw him come out of the front door, he uttered a cry, flapped his wings, and struck the man in the face.

"Ouch!" cried the startled hunter. "Some bird of ill omen has struck me!" Shaken, he went back inside and lay down again.

A little later, he got up and picked up his knife. Hoping to outwit the bird, he tried to sneak out the rear. The woodpecker, however, had suspected that the hunter would do just that and had positioned himself near the back door. As soon as he saw the hunter, he gave a loud cry, swooped down, and struck him in the face again.

"Curses!" the hunter exclaimed. "This creature will not leave me alone!" He went inside and lay down once again. When the sun was up, he resolutely picked up his knife and opened the door, cautiously watching for the bird.

The woodpecker, figuring that he had given his friends enough time, flew back to the lake and shouted a warning: "The hunter is coming!"

The turtle had indeed gnawed through all the thongs except the last, which was especially strong. His tough, leathery mouth was smeared with blood, and his jaws ached unbearably.

As soon as the antelope saw the hunter approaching with his sharp knife, he made a great effort, which burst the last thong, and he leapt to safety. The woodpecker flew up to the top of the tree, but the turtle was so exhausted that he could not move. Chortling at his fortune, the hunter threw the hapless turtle into a sack, which he tied to a tree.

The antelope had watched the hunter put the turtle in the sack, and, resolving to save his friend's life, he allowed himself to be seen. When the hunter spotted the antelope, he was overjoyed and darted toward him. The antelope pretended that he was weak and lame, but, keeping just out of reach, he led the hunter deep into the forest. When they reached a spot far away from the turtle, he gave the man the slip and ran as quickly as he could back to the lake by another route. He lifted the bag with his horns, tossed it on the ground, tore it open, and released the turtle. At the same instant, the woodpecker flew down to greet his two friends.

"My dear friends," the antelope said, "thank you for saving my life! You have been very good to me, but that cruel hunter will come back. It is still dangerous for all of us. I suggest that you, good woodpecker, fly with your family to another part of the forest. You, friend turtle, must dive into the water and stay out of sight. I will hide in the deep forest." Sadly, each of the three friends went his own way.

When the hunter found his way back to the lake, he picked up his torn sack and trudged back home, empty-handed and disgusted.

When the three friends were sure that it was safe, they reunited. They lived the rest of their lives in unbroken harmony, and they passed away to fare according to their deserts.

Having concluded his story, the Buddha identified the birth: "At that time, Devadatta was the hunter, Sāriputta was the woodpecker, Moggallāna was the turtle, and I was the antelope."

86
The Dung-Beetle Queen
Assaka Jātaka

It was while staying at Jetavana that the Buddha told this story about a bhikkhu who was distracted by the recollection of his former wife.

When the Buddha asked the bhikkhu how he felt toward the woman, the bhikkhu answered that he was still in love with her and longed deeply for her.

"This is not the first time, Bhikkhu," the Buddha said, "that you have been obsessed with desire for this woman. Long ago, your love for her brought you great misery." Then he told this story of the past.

Long, long, ago, Potali was the capital of Kāsi, and the king was named Assaka. His consort, Queen Ubbarī, was charming, graceful, extraordinarily beautiful, and very dear to him. One day, the queen suddenly died, and the king was plunged into grief and despair. He had her body embalmed with oils and ointments and laid in a coffin, which he kept beneath his bed. Weeping bitterly and crying aloud for his dead wife, the king languished in his bed and refused to take any food. Everyone in the palace, including his advisors, relatives, and friends, urged the king to stop grieving and to accept that all things must pass away, but nothing they said helped him.

At that time, at the edge of the Himavat, there was an ascetic, who had perfected the five extraordinary powers and the eight jhānas. With his divine eye, he was able to survey all of Jambudīpa, and, when he saw King Assaka in deep grief, he resolved to help him. He used his extraordinary power to travel in an instant to Potali and seated himself, like a golden image, on a ceremonial stone in the royal park.

A young brahmin from Potali happened to enter the park and saw the ascetic. After they had exchanged pleasant greetings, the ascetic asked, "Is the king a just ruler?"

"Yes, sir," the brahmin answered, "the king is righteous, but seven days ago, his queen died, and, since then, the king has been mourning over her body. How fortunate our king would be if a virtuous ascetic like you could cure him of his grief and depression!"

"Young man," the ascetic replied, "I do not know the king, but, if he were to come and ask me, I would tell him where the queen has been reborn, and I would make her speak to him herself."

"Marvelous, Holy Sir! Please stay right here, and I will bring the king to you!" cried the youth. The ascetic silently nodded assent, and the young man rushed to the king's palace.

As soon as the king heard about the ascetic, he summoned his chariot and ordered the driver to take him and the young brahmin to the royal park.

The king greeted the ascetic, sat down to one side, and excitedly asked, "Is it true that you know where my queen has been reborn?"

"Yes, I do, Sire," the ascetic replied.

"Please tell me," the king requested, breathlessly.

"Your Majesty, the queen was so intoxicated with her beauty that she neglected to perform good deeds or to behave virtuously. She has been reborn as a dung beetle in this very park."

"You're lying! I don't believe it!" declared the king indignantly.

"I will show her to you, and I will make her speak to you."

His desire to see his wife overcame his mistrust, and he reluctantly agreed, "Please do so, if you can."

"Let those two dung beetles that are busy rolling a ball of cow-dung come here before the king," the ascetic called out, and, because of his power, they obeyed and scurried toward the royal stone seat.

"There is your Queen Ubbarī, Sire," the ascetic said, pointing to one of the beetles. "The other one is her husband."

"That is impossible! Just outrageous!" cried the king. "How could my beautiful Ubbarī have become a dung beetle?"

"Please listen, Your Majesty," the ascetic replied. Then, raising his voice, he called, "Ubbarī! Ubbarī!"

By virtue of his power, the female dung beetle gained the power of speech in a human voice and asked, "What is it, Venerable Sir?"

"What was your name in your former life?" the ascetic asked her.

"My name was Ubbarī, sir. I was the consort of King Assaka."

"Tell me," the ascetic continued, "which do you love better, King Assaka or this dung beetle who is your husband now?"

"Venerable Sir, in my former birth, I lived with the king in the palace, and I loved him dearly. Together, in this very park, we enjoyed innumerable pleasures of sight, sound, scent, taste, and touch. Now, however, my memory has been confused by rebirth, and he is nothing to me. Now, I would gladly kill King Assaka and, with the blood that flowed from his throat, I would smear the feet of my beloved husband, this dung beetle!"

As soon as King Assaka heard this, he was shaken to the core. He immediately gave up grieving, and his gloom vanished. Profusely thanking the ascetic for his teaching, he paid his respects and returned to the palace. After ordering that the queen's body be removed and properly cremated, he bathed and resumed his royal duties. It was not long after this that the king took another queen, and, for the rest of his life, he ruled in righteousness.

The ascetic returned to his hermitage in the Himavat and continued his meditation practice.

Having concluded his story, the Buddha taught the Dhamma, and the distracted bhikkhu attained the first path. Then the Buddha identified the birth: "At that time, your former wife was Ubbarī, you were King Assaka, Sāriputta was the young brahmin, and I was the ascetic."

87
Give or Take an Ox
Somadatta Jātaka

It was while staying at Jetavana that the Buddha told this story about Venerable Lāludāyi.

Venerable Lāludāyi often joined discussions and debates with other bhikkhus, and sometimes even with the Buddha himself, but, more often than not, he was left speechless, took an untenable position, or came out with a foolish statement which utterly defeated him.

One day, in the Hall of Truth, a group of bhikkhus was talking about this peculiar behavior of Venerable Lāludāyi's. When the Buddha heard what they were discussing, he said, "Bhikkhus, this is not the first time that Lāludāyi has had difficulty speaking. It was the same before." Then he told this story of the past.

Long, long ago, when Brahmadatta was reigning in Bārānasi, the Bodhisatta was born into a brahmin family of farmers and was named Somadatta. He received his education in Takkasilā, but, when he returned home, he found that the family's fortunes had sharply declined. Resolving to restore their wealth, Somadatta bade his parents farewell and left for Bārānasi.

In the capital, he was not long in finding a position in the palace and, in time, became a trusted favorite of the king's.

One day, his father arrived in Bārānasi, very troubled. "Son," he said slowly, "as you know, I had only one pair of oxen. One of them has died, and I have no way of plowing. Please ask the king to give you an ox!"

"Father," Somadatta replied, "I have just now left the king, so it would not be appropriate for me to go back in and ask a favor. It would be better for you to ask him yourself."

"Dear Somadatta," the father said, "I am a very simple man. I have great difficulty trying to talk with other people. Usually, when I get into a discussion or try to explain something, I get it all wrong and make a fool of myself."

"Father, be that as it may, you have to do this. I cannot ask the king for you, but I will prepare you to do it for yourself." He took his father to a place in the charnel ground where there was a lot of tall grass. He cut several bunches of grass and tied them into sheaves, which he stood here and there.

"OK, Father! Let's imagine that this is the palace," Somadatta began. As he pointed to the various sheaves, he said, "This is the king. This is the crown prince. Over there is the commander-in-chief, and there are several ministers. First, you must bow and say 'Long live the king!'"

The father bowed to one of the sheaves and repeated, "Long live the king!"

"Then," Somadatta continued, "you should say, 'Sire, I am a poor farmer. I had two oxen to plow with, but one of them died. Please, Your Majesty, give me another ox.'"

The man repeated exactly what his son had said. He practiced bowing, greeting the king, and asking for the ox many times. Finally, he said to his son, "Dear Somadatta, I have learned my lines! Now I can say them in front of anyone at all. Take me to the king."

Somadatta arranged a suitable present for the king and led his father to the palace, and they entered the royal hall. The brahmin bowed, presented his gift, and cried, "Long live the king!"

"Somadatta," the king asked, "who is this man?"

"Your Majesty, he is my father."

"Why has he come here?" asked the king.

Before Somadatta could reply, his father shouted, "Sire, I had two oxen to plow with, but one of them died. Please, Your Majesty, take the other one!"

The king was startled at this outburst, but he realized that there must be some mistake. "Somadatta," he said, smiling, "your family must have plenty of oxen."

"If we do, Sire, they are your gift!" Somadatta replied with a bow.

The king was so pleased with this answer that he presented Somadatta's father with sixteen oxen, fine trappings, and an entire village. He sent the brahmin away with great honor.

Somadatta and his father returned home in a stately chariot drawn by beautiful white Sindh horses—also gifts from the king. On the way, Somadatta said, "Father, you rehearsed those sentences many times. I thought you had them memorized, but, when the time came, you got it wrong and offered your ox to the king! Truly, practice accomplishes nothing if the man has little wit!"

"My dear Somadatta," his father replied, "the man who makes a request takes his chance between the two extremes. He may get nothing, or he may get more. It's always the same!"

Having concluded his story, the Buddha identified the birth: "At that time, Lāludāyi was Somadatta's father, and I was Somadatta."

88

Condemned by Your Own Words
Kacchapa Jātaka

It was while staying at Jetavana that the Buddha told this story about Venerable Kokālika.

Once, at the beginning of the rainy season, Venerable Sāriputta and Venerable Moggallāna, wanting to avoid staying with many bhikkhus, took leave of the Buddha and went to the small monastery where Venerable Kokālika was living by himself. "Brother Kokālika," they said, "we would like to abide here for the retreat. It would be delightful for us to stay with you and for you to stay with us."

"Why would it be delightful for you to stay with me?" he asked.

"We would be very happy if you didn't tell anyone that we were here," they replied.

"And why would it be delightful for me to stay with you?"

"We will teach you the Dhamma for three months."

"Very well," Kokālika agreed. "Please stay here as long as you wish." He allotted them a pleasant residence, and they stayed there peacefully for three months. The three bhikkhus received generous alms every day on their rounds through the nearby village.

At the end of the rains retreat, they thanked their host, took leave of him, and announced that they would go to visit the Buddha.

After they had left, Venerable Kokālika went to the village and said to the people, "Lay disciples, you are no better than brute animals. For three whole months, the two chief disciples have been staying in this monastery, and you never came to pay your respects! Now they are gone."

"We had no idea! Why didn't you tell us, Venerable Sir?" the people asked.

Carrying ghee, oil, honey, and robes, they hurried after the chief disciples. As soon as they had caught up with the two bhikkhus, they cried, "Venerable Sirs, please forgive us! We did not realize that you were the chief disciples of the Lord Buddha. We learned it only today from Venerable Kokālika. Have compassion on us, and accept these small offerings."

Venerable Kokālika, knowing that the chief disciples were frugal and contented with little and hoping that they would suggest that the villagers give the gifts to him, followed behind. The chief disciples, however, realizing that the gifts were being offered at the instigation of a bhikkhu, neither accepted them nor suggested that they be given to Venerable Kokālika.

"Venerable Sirs, if you will not accept these gifts, please come here again later to bless us," the villagers requested.

The chief disciples promised to do so and proceeded to Sāvatthī, but Venerable Kokālika was furious.

After staying a short time with the Buddha, the chief disciples each selected five hundred bhikkhus to accompany him and returned to the village near Venerable Kokālika's monastery. The villagers met them, led them to the monastery, and showed them great honor, offering great quantities of robes, blankets, and medicine. The bhikkhus who accompanied the chief disciples divided everything among themselves. They gave nothing to Venerable Kokālika.

"Sāriputta and Moggallāna are full of sinful desire!" Venerable Kokālika grumbled. "Before, they wouldn't accept anything, but now look at what they accept! What's more, they have no regard for anyone else!"

The chief disciples, realizing that Venerable Kokālika was upset with them, decided to leave. The villagers begged them to stay even a few days longer, but they would not.

"Laypeople," one of the young bhikkhus remarked to the villagers, "where would the chief disciples stay? Your own bhikkhu does not want them to stay here."

When they heard this, the villagers rushed to the monastery. "Venerable Sir," they cried to Venerable Kokālika, "we have just heard that you do not wish the chief disciples to stay here. If you do not bring them back and allow them to stay here, you, too, must go and live elsewhere!"

Afraid of losing the support of the local people, Venerable Kokālika hurried after the chief disciples and asked them to return.

"Go back, Friend!" they replied. "We will not stay with you."

When Venerable Kokālika returned alone to the monastery, the villagers asked whether the chief disciples were coming back, and Venerable Kokālika had no choice but to admit that they were not.

This made the villagers think that good bhikkhus did not want to stay at the monastery because Venerable Kokālika was living wickedly. In that case, they thought, they should get rid of him. "Sir," they said, "please leave this monastery. We have nothing for you and do not want you to stay here anymore."

Disgraced, Venerable Kokālika left, taking only his robes and bowl, and hurried to Jetavana.

After paying his respects to the Buddha, he began complaining about the chief disciples. "Venerable Sir," he said, "Sāriputta and Moggallāna are full of sinful desire!"

"Do not talk like that," the Buddha admonished him. "You must be in harmony with Sāriputta and Moggallāna. They are both good bhikkhus."

"That's what you think!" Venerable Kokālika retorted. "You believe in your two chief disciples, Venerable Sir, but I have seen them with my own eyes! They are full of secret desires. They are deceitful and wicked."

Again the Buddha warned him against saying such things, but Venerable Kokālika would not listen. Indignantly, he repeated his charge three times. Then he stood up and left. As soon as he stepped outside the gate of Jetavana, his entire body broke out in boils. At first, the boils were as tiny as mustard seeds, but, quickly growing to the size of ripe bael fruits, they burst, oozing blood and pus. Groaning and writhing in pain, he fell down and lay on the ground in front of the gate. A great cry arose, "Kokālika has reviled the two chief disciples!"

In the Brahma heavens, a deva, who had been Venerable Kokālika's teacher and who had been reborn as an anāgāmī,[1] heard this cry and immediately descended to earth. Poised in the air, he gently called out, "Kokālika, you have done a great wrong. You must make peace with the chief disciples."

"Who are you?" Venerable Kokālika asked.

"I am Tudu Brahmā," the deva replied.

"Didn't the Buddha declare that you would never return?" Venerable Kokālika shouted scornfully. "Have you come back to be a yakkha on a dunghill?"

---

1 A non-returner, see "four stages of Enlightenment" in Glossary of Terms.

Realizing that he could not be of any assistance to Venerable Kokālika, Tudu Brahmā intoned, "May you be tormented according to your own words," and returned to his blissful abode.

When Venerable Kokālika died, Brahmā Sahampati[2] himself informed the Buddha that the reviling bhikkhu had been reborn in Lotus Hell, at the bottom of Avīci, and the Buddha told the bhikkhus.

One day, the bhikkhus were talking about how Venerable Kokālika had ended up in hell because of his own words. When the Buddha heard what they were discussing, he said, "This is not the first time, Bhikkhus, that Kokālika was destroyed and condemned to misery by his own words and with his own mouth. The same thing happened to him before." At their request, the Buddha told this story of the past.

Long, long ago, when Brahmadatta was reigning in Bārānasi, the Bodhisatta was the king's chief advisor. King Brahmadatta was so talkative that no one could ever get a word in edgewise.

At that time, there was a turtle living in a pond in the Himavat. Two young geese struck up an acquaintance with him, and the three became close friends.

One day, the geese said to him, "Friend turtle, we have a lovely home in another part of the Himavat. It's in a beautiful golden cave on a plateau of Mount Cittakuta. Would you like to visit?"

"How could I get there?" he asked. "You know how slow I am."

"We can take you there," they replied. Then they showed him a stick and said, "Grip this stick tightly in your mouth, and we can carry you. You must remember that you cannot open your mouth. You must not try to talk while we are flying. Can you do that?"

"Of course, I can do that," he said eagerly. "Let's go!"

Each of the geese took one end of the stick in its bill, and the turtle gripped the center. The geese took flight with the turtle dangling between them.

Their route passed over several villages and the great city of Bārānasi. When children saw them, they shouted, "Look! There are two geese carrying a turtle by a stick! How funny!" and they clapped their hands and laughed at the strange sight.

When the turtle heard this, he was furious. "How dare those ragamuffins laugh at me!" he thought. "What is it to them if my friends carry me this

---

2   A Mahā-Brahmā. Shortly after attaining Enlightenment, the Buddha appeared to hesitate as to whether or not to teach the Dhamma. Brahmā Sahampati urged him to teach for the welfare of devas and men. The Buddha wanted him to make the request because he knew that, when people learned that Brahmā Sahampati himself had begged the Buddha to teach, they would pay more attention to the Dhamma since the Mahā-Brahmā was so greatly honored.

way? I'll tell them a thing or two!" He opened his mouth to scold them, but, of course, as soon as he let go of the stick, he fell. He landed in the middle of the king's courtyard with a loud thud, and his shell split in two.

His fall created a tremendous uproar. People shouted, "A turtle has fallen from the sky!" The king and many courtiers rushed to the courtyard to see what had happened. Questions were buzzing all around, "Why did he fall?" "Can turtles fly?" "What was he doing up there?"

The king turned to his advisor and asked, "Wise sir, can you explain this mystery to us?"

The advisor looked up and saw the two geese flying away in the distance with the stick in their bills. Immediately, he understood what had happened. He briefly reconstructed the series of events to the king and concluded, "That turtle fell and died, Sire, because he opened his mouth. Even though he was supported by a stick in his mouth, he couldn't keep his mouth shut! Such is the fate for those with big mouths, who don't restrain their talkativeness. One should speak wisely and only at the proper time. Mark his fate well; the turtle talked too much."

"Are you actually referring to me?" asked the king.

"Whether it is you, Sire, or only a turtle," the advisor replied calmly, "one who talks too much comes to grief."

The king took this lesson to heart and, thenceforth, guarded his speech. Some even commented that he became a man of few words.

Having concluded his story, the Buddha identified the birth: "At that time, Kokālika was the turtle, Sāriputta and Moggallāna were the two wild geese, Ānanda was the king, and I was the wise advisor."

89

Can Mice Eat Plowshares?
Kūtavānija Jātaka

It was while staying at Jetavana that the Buddha told this story about a dishonest trader. In Sāvatthī, there were two traders who became partners. They loaded five hundred wagons full of wares, and journeyed to the west. After they had sold all their goods, they returned to Sāvatthī with a considerable profit.

When one of them suggested to his partner that they divide all they had brought back, including money and goods, the other trader, being a rogue, thought, "My partner has been roughing it with me for a long time. He must be fed up with bad food and uncomfortable beds. Now that we're back, he's goin†g to splurge. He'll overeat and kill himself. Then I can take everything for myself." He said to his partner, "The stars aren't favorable. Let's rest for a couple of days, and we'll see about it. Just enjoy yourself." Every day, the first trader suggested they make the division, but the second kept putting it off. Finally, after two weeks, the two divided everything in half and went their own ways.

The first trader immediately purchased incense and garlands and went to see the Buddha. At Jetavana, he paid his respects to the Master and sat on one side.

"When did you return?" the Buddha asked him.

"A fortnight ago, Venerable Sir" he answered.

"Why didn't you come to see me right away?" the Buddha asked.

"I could do nothing because my partner insisted on postponing the division of our profit," the trader explained.

"This is not the first time that that rogue has tried to cheat you," the Buddha replied. At the trader's request, he told this story of the past.

Long, long ago, when Brahmadatta was reigning in Bārānasi, the Bodhisatta was born as the son of a member of the king's court and, when he grew up, became chief justice.

At that time, a trader in Bārānasi became friends with another trader from the countryside and entered into business with him. The country trader left five hundred plowshares in his friend's storeroom in the city and returned to his village. The city trader secretly sold all the plowshares and scattered mouse dung all around the storeroom. When the country trader returned and asked for his plowshares, the city trader, feigning distress, replied, "My friend, I am very sorry, but mice have eaten them. Let me show you." He took his friend to the storeroom and showed him all the mouse droppings.

"Well, well, so be it," replied the country trader, showing no emotion whatsoever. "What can be done with things which the mice have eaten? It was not your fault."

That afternoon, the country trader went down to the river for a bath and took his friend's son with him. On the way, he stopped at the house of another friend and asked him to hide the boy for a short time. After bathing, he returned alone.

"Where is my son?" asked the city trader.

"Dear friend," the country trader replied, "I took him with me when I went for my bath. I left him on the river bank, but, while I was in the water, a huge hawk came and seized your son in his talons. I beat the water and shouted as loud as I could, but the bird just flew away with your son."

"Lies!" cried the city trader. "No hawk could carry off a healthy, grown boy!"

"I'm sorry, Friend, but it's true. It was not my fault. Yes, it's very unfortunate, but your son was carried off by a hawk. You'll just have to accept it."

"You've killed my son, and you will pay for it, you murderer!" shouted the city trader. "You can't get away with this! I will take you to court right now!"

"As you wish," the country trader replied calmly. "Let's go and see the king right away." The two of them went directly to the palace and were shown into the court.

The city trader immediately addressed the chief justice. "Your Honor," he began excitedly, "this man is a murderer! He took my son for a bath but came back alone. When I asked where my son was, he told me that a hawk had carried him off. That's obviously a lie! I am sure he has killed my son, and I demand justice!"

"What do you have to say?" the chief justice asked the country trader.

"Indeed, Lord," he replied, "I took the boy to the river for a bath. While I was in the water, a hawk carried him off."

"Where, my good man, are there hawks which can carry off boys?" the chief justice asked.

"If hawks cannot carry off boys," the country trader replied, "can mice eat iron plowshares?"

"What do you mean by that odd remark?" the chief justice asked.

"My Lord, the last time I was in Bārānasi, I left five hundred plowshares with this man. This morning, when I asked about those plowshares, he told me that mice had eaten them, and he showed me his storeroom full of mouse dung. If he expects me to believe that mice can eat iron plowshares, why can't he believe that a hawk can carry away a boy. I trust you to make a wise decision and to judge this case fairly."

The chief justice understood exactly what had happened and was impressed with the country trader's ruse. "Sir!" he said sternly, looking directly at the city trader. "If you pay this man for his plowshares, I am sure your son will come home."

Outwitted and undone, the city trader paid the money he owed and got his son back. Eventually, the two traders passed away to fare according to their deserts.

Having concluded his story, the Buddha identified the birth: "At that time, the rogue who tried to cheat you was the city trader, you were the clever country trader, and I was the chief justice."

90
The Four Great Virtues
Dhammaddhaja Jātaka

It was while staying at Veluvana that the Buddha told this story about
Devadatta's attempts to murder him.

One day, the bhikkhus were talking about Devadatta and his failed attempt
to take the Buddha's life. When the Buddha heard what they were discussing, he said, "This is not the first time that Devadatta has tried to murder
me, but has been unable to even frighten me. He did the same before." Then
he told this story of the past.

Long, long ago, when Yasapāni was reigning in Bārānasi, the Bodhisatta
was the king's spiritual advisor and was named Dhammaddhaja. King
Yasapāni was a good king, but his commander-in-chief was a corrupt and
wicked man named Kālaka. Whenever Kālaka judged a case, he ruled in
favor of the one who offered the biggest bribe, without considering the
merit of any claim.

One day, as Dhammaddhaja was passing the court, a man in obvious
despair came out. As soon the man saw Dhammaddhaja, he fell at his feet
and wept. When he regained enough composure to speak, he explained that

he had just lost his suit because the other party had given much more money to Kālaka. Dhammaddhaja felt sorry for the man and agreed to reopen his case at once. A great company followed them to the court. After examining the evidence and hearing the testimony of the litigants, Dhammaddhaja announced that the case was clear and reversed the unjust decision. The spectators applauded so loudly that the king heard the noise.

When he asked what had happened, courtiers told him, "Sire, there was a court case that had been wrongly decided. The wise Dhammaddhaja has just judged the case with complete fairness and reversed that decision. The spectators are applauding and shouting their approval."

The king was pleased and sent for Dhammaddhaja.

"They tell me," he began, "that you have judged a case"

"Yes, Sire, I found that Kālaka did not decide rightly the first time."

"That pleases me very much," replied the king. "From now on, I want you to serve as judge. That will bring happiness to me and prosperity to the kingdom."

Dhammaddhaja was reluctant to accept that responsibility, but the king insisted, and the advisor finally had to agree.

Kālaka was furious at having lost his judicial position from which he had received such lucrative bribes and gifts. At every opportunity, he slandered Dhammaddhaja. "Sire," he said one day, "the great Dhammaddhaja's head is turned by his new post."

The king refused to listen to him, so Kālaka tried to charge the advisor with more serious crimes.

"Your Majesty, Dhammaddhaja has had a taste of power, and now he covets your throne!" Kālaka exclaimed one day, accusing his rival of treason. Still, the king did not believe him.

A few days later, Kālaka rushed into the king's chamber and whispered a warning, "Sire, Dhammaddhaja is a treacherous man. If you do not believe me, look out of the window. You will see that he has got the whole city in his hands."

The king glanced out the window into the courtyard. Dhammaddhaja had just left the court and was surrounded by a great crowd. The king suddenly became afraid. "There is his retinue," he thought. "The whole city is behind him. Kālaka is right. Dhammaddhaja really could stage a coup!"

"Commander," he said aloud, "What are we to do?"

"Sire, he must be put to death."

"How can we put him to death without catching him in some great scandal or wickedness?"

"There is a way," Kālaka answered swiftly.

"What is that?" asked the king.

"Order him to do something impossible. Then you can execute him for failing to obey you."

"But Dhammaddhaja is very clever and skillful. What would be impossible for him to do?"

"My Lord, it takes two years or more of careful tending for a garden with good soil to bear fruit. Command that he provide you with a new pleasure garden tomorrow. He can't possibly do that."

A little later, when Dhammaddhaja arrived to pay his respects, King Yasapāni coolly said to him, "Wise sir, I have grown tired of my old pleasure garden. I want you to make me a new one. It must be ready tomorrow. If you fail, you must die."

Dhammaddhaja immediately realized that Kālaka, bearing a grudge against him, was behind this unreasonable demand. "Sire," he calmly replied, "I will do my best. If it can be done, I will do it."

Dhammaddhaja returned to his home, had a good meal, and lay down to ponder his hopeless task. In Tāvatimsa, Sakka's throne grew hot, and the king of the devas understood that it was because of Dhammaddhaja's predicament. Instantly, Sakka appeared in the advisor's chamber, poised in mid-air.

"Who are you?" Dhammaddhaja asked.

"I am Sakka. I understand that something is troubling you."

"Your Majesty, King Yasapāni has ordered me to create a pleasure garden by tomorrow. I have been lying here thinking, but it's an impossible task for me."

"Wise sir, don't worry. I will make a garden as beautiful as the celestial Nandana. Just tell me where it should be."

Dhammaddhaja pointed out an appropriate spot, and Sakka transformed it into a magnificent garden. Then he returned to his heaven.

The next morning, after inspecting the finished garden, Dhammaddhaja went to the king's chamber. "Sire," he announced, "your garden is ready for your enjoyment."

The king hurried to the spot and was amazed to find many beautiful trees, some laden with fruit and others in bloom with fragrant flowers. The garden, surrounded by a vermillion fence with elegant gates, was extremely pleasing and more glorious than anything the king could have imagined.

Later, when the king was alone with Kālaka, he said, "We set an impossible task, but Dhammaddhaja was able to it. What can we possibly do next?"

"Your Majesty," replied Kālaka, "now you understand how dangerous your advisor really is! If he can make a garden in one night, what's to stop him from seizing your kingdom?"

"Kālaka, I'm sure you are right, but what can we do?"

"Give him another impossible task."

"What might that be?"

"Order him to make a lake in one day."

The king agreed and summoned Dhammaddhaja. "Teacher," he said, "your park is wonderful. We are pleased. Please create a lake to complement the park. It must be finished by tomorrow. Your life depends on it."

"Sire, I will do my best. If it can be done, I will do it."

That night, Sakka created a splendid lake with one hundred landings and one thousand inlets and covered with lotuses of five colors.[3]

The next day, Dhammaddhaja announced that the lake was ready.

When the king again asked Kālaka what was to be done, the commander-in-chief suggested, "Command him to make a large house overlooking the lake."

"Dhammaddhaja," the king said, "your lake is splendid, but it lacks a pavilion. Please build me one of ivory, overlooking the lake. It must be as beautiful as the garden and the lake and must be ready tomorrow. You know what will happen if you fail."

"Sire," Dhammaddhaja replied, "I will do my best. If it can be done, I will do it."

That night, Sakka erected a magnificent pavilion of the finest ivory. As the king had commanded, it overlooked the lake and provided a perfect view of the entire garden.

The king was astonished. Again he conferred with Kālaka, and the commander suggested that the king demand a jewel to fit the house.

"Wise sir," the king said, "your pavilion is truly a work of art, but it must be illuminated by an exquisite jewel. Please find the perfect jewel to diffuse light evenly throughout it. If it is not in place by tomorrow, you must die!"

"Sire, I will do my best. If it can be done, I will do it."

That night Sakka placed a brilliant jewel in the center of the pavilion.

The king again asked Kālaka what to do.

"Your Majesty," answered Kālaka, "I think there is some deva who does whatever Dhammaddhaja wishes. You must order him to make something which even a deva cannot create. Even a deva is unable to make a man with the four great virtues. Command him to give you a park keeper with those four great virtues."

"Judge," the king said to Dhammaddhaja, "you have created a park, a lake, and a palace, and you have illuminated the palace with a splendid jewel. Now I need a man to take care of all of this. By tomorrow you must find me a park keeper endowed with the four great virtues. The price of failure is death. "

---

3 White, green, red, purple, and pink

"Sire, I will do my best. If it can be done, I will do it."

When Dhammaddhaja awoke the next morning, he pondered his predicament. "The great Sakka has made all that can be made by his heavenly power. Not even the king of the devas can create a man with the four great virtues. No one can help me now. It is better that I die in the forest than by the king's command." He secretly left the city, entered the forest, and sat down on a fallen log.

Sakka disguised himself as a forester and appeared before the judge.

"Young man, why are you sitting here alone in the forest. You look as though you have a prosperous and happy life, but here you are in the wild forest like a poor wretch whose life is a misery."

Dhammaddhaja replied dejectedly, "It must, indeed, appear that my life is happy, but here I am, preparing to leave home and to die alone in this forest like any poor wretch whose life is miserable."

"Let me be more direct. Why, young man, are you sitting here so forlorn?"

"Well, I will tell you. The king has ordered me to provide him with a park keeper who possesses the four great virtues. I am sure that such a man cannot be found so, rather than be executed by the king's men, I have decided to die a lonely death here."

"Young man, I am Sakka! I created your park, your lake, your ivory palace, and your jewel. Of course, even I cannot create a man endowed with the four great virtues, but that's no reason to despair. There is such a man! He lives right here in this kingdom. His name is Chattapani, and he makes ornaments for the king. Find this craftsman, and appoint him as the park keeper you need." Having revealed his secret, Sakka returned to Tāvatimsa.

Dhammaddhaja returned home, had breakfast, and went to the palace gate, where he found Chattapāni. Taking the craftsman by the hand, he asked, "Chattapāni, is it true, as I have heard, that you are endowed with the four great virtues?"

"Who told you that?" Chattapāni asked in turn.

"Sakka did."

"Why did he tell you such a thing?"

Dhammaddhaja recounted all that had happened.

"Yes," Chattapāni admitted, "I am indeed endowed with the four great virtues."

"Please! You must come with me," Dhammaddhaja said to the craftsman. Still holding him by the hand, Dhammaddhaja led him into the king's presence. "Your Majesty, this man, Chattapāni, is endowed with the four great virtues. May it please Your Majesty to appoint him as park keeper."

"Is it true, my good man," the king asked Chattapāni, "that you are endowed with the four great virtues?"

"Yes, Your Majesty, it is true."

"Please tell us what those four great virtues are," ordered the king.

"I have no envy, I never drink alcohol, I have no strong desire, and I never get angry."

"Did you say you have no envy at all?"

"That is correct, Sire. I have no envy."

"Please explain what you mean when you say that you have no envy."

"Certainly, Sire. Long ago, I was the king of Kāsi. My queen had affairs with sixty-four slaves. In my anger and jealousy, I imprisoned all sixty-four of those slaves. My queen's passion was insatiable, and she then tried to seduce my spiritual advisor. This virtuous man, however, was very loyal to me, and he refused her advances. Angry that she had been rebuffed, she came to me and claimed that he had taken advantage of her. Believing her, my jealousy again rose up. I arrested my innocent advisor and had him thrown into prison. When he was brought before me with arms bound, he told me what had really happened, and I immediately freed him. Furthermore, he encouraged me to release all the slaves whom I had imprisoned. Because of his wise teaching, I released them and completely forgave them.

"Then I began thinking, 'Here am I, a faithful husband, and yet I have been unable to satisfy this one woman's lust. In her anger at being spurned, she goaded me to jealousy, and I imprisoned an innocent man.' I understood that this was just the nature of things. There was no point in getting angry. One might as well become angry when a shirt becomes dirty after being worn all day. My anger arose from jealousy. Seeing this, I made a resolve that neither jealousy nor envy should ever arise in me again, for fear that I would fail to perfect my virtue. From that time on, I have been free from envy. This is what I mean when I say, 'I have no envy.'"

This impressed the king very much. Wishing to hear more, he addressed Chattapāni once again. "Dear sir, please tell us why you abstain from strong drink."

"Sire, long ago, when I reigned in this very city, I was addicted to alcohol. I was also very fond of eating meat, and I demanded that I be served meat at every meal. One day, a dog got into the kitchen and ate all the meat dishes which the royal cook had prepared for me the day before. It so happened that this was an Uposatha day, and animals were never slaughtered on those days. Thus, there was no more meat available. The cook was afraid to serve me a meatless meal, so he asked the queen's advice.

The queen thought about this for a moment and came up with a plan. 'Don't worry,' she said to the cook. 'The king is very fond of my son. I will dress up the boy and give him to the king to dandle on his knee. While he is playing with his son, he won't notice what he's having for dinner. Go ahead and serve whatever you have prepared. It will be fine!'

"At dinnertime, I was drinking as usual, and my wife handed me my favorite son. I was indeed very happy, and I continued drinking as I played with the boy. The cook served the food, and I began eating. I noticed, however, that there was no meat and demanded to know why. The cook apologized and explained that, since this was an Uposatha day, no meat was available.

"At this, I became furious. 'I am the king!' I shouted. 'How can there be no meat for me?' Being blind drunk as well as angry, I was completely unaware of what I was doing. Seeing my son in my hands, I wrung his neck, and threw his body to the cook. 'Here is some meat!' I shouted. 'Cook it for me, and bring it back. Be quick about it! I am starving!' The terrified cook obeyed, and I ate my own son's flesh.

"Afraid of my drunken fury, no one dared to weep or even to say a word. After I ate, I fell into a stupor. The next morning, having slept off my intoxication, I asked for my son. The queen fell weeping at my feet, and said, 'Oh, Sire, last night, you killed your son and ate his flesh!' Appalled at what I had done, I wailed with grief. I realized that I had committed that sinful deed simply because I was drunk. 'See,' I rebuked myself, 'what comes from drinking alcohol!' Having understood the perils of drinking, I made a vow that I would never again touch a drop of alcohol. From that time I never have."

"Excellent, my good man!" exclaimed the king. "Now tell us why you are without strong desire?"

"At another time," Chattapāni answered, "my name was King Kitavāsa. I had a son whom I adored. My fortune tellers and advisors predicted that my boy would perish from lack of water, so he was named Duttha (meaning "wicked"). When he was old enough, I made him crown prince. In order to defeat the prophecy, I kept my son close to me. To make sure there was always plenty of water available, I had tanks constructed at the city gates and many places inside the city. I had water jars placed everywhere within the palace compound.

"I knew that I was spoiling my son, but I loved him dearly with all my heart, and I tried to protect him as best I could. One day, the prince, dressed in his finery, went with his attendants to the pleasure garden. On his way there, he became very upset when he saw a huge crowd paying obeisance to a Pacceka Buddha beside the road. 'How dare those people pay such respect and attention to that shaven-headed beggar,' he cried, 'when I, the crown prince, am passing by!'

"He immediately ordered the procession to stop, got down from his royal elephant, and approached the Pacceka Buddha. 'Have you received your food today?' he asked rudely.

"'Yes, I have,' was the reply.

"The prince grabbed the Pacceka Buddha's bowl, threw it on the ground, and crushed the spilled rice and curries with his foot.

"The Pacceka Buddha looked into the prince's face and thought, 'In truth, this man is lost!'

"'I am Prince Duttha, son of King Kitavāsa!' declared the prince. 'What harm can you do to me by looking at me that way?'

"Without saying another word, the Pacceka Buddha rose into in the air and returned to his cave in the Himavat.

"At that instant, the prince's evil-doing began to bear fruit. He began crying, 'I'm burning! I'm burning! Somebody help me!' Suddenly, his body burst into flames, and he fell to the ground. Townspeople rushed to the tank, but all the water had vanished. All the tanks and ponds in that area were dry. With no water to quench his fire, the prince perished and was certainly reborn in hell.

"When I heard what had happened, I was at first overcome with grief. Then I thought, 'This grief has come because of my attachment to my son. If he had not been so dear to me and I hadn't had that great affection, I would feel no pain. I resolve that I will never again be strongly attached to anyone or anything!'"

"Excellent, my good man!" exclaimed the king once more. "Now tell us, why you are without anger."

"In another life, Sire," Chattapāni replied, "as the ascetic Araka, I developed thoughts of loving-kindness and practiced the Four Brahma Vihāras for seven years. Because of that I was reborn in the Brahma heavens and stayed there for seven eons. Thus, I am free from anger."

As soon as Chattapāni had finished explaining his four great virtues, the king made a sign to his soldiers, who jumped up and seized Kālaka. Instantly, the court resounded with cries of, "Wicked, bribe-taking villain!" "Because you lost your payoffs, you tried to trick our king into killing the wise Dhammaddhaja!" "Scoundrel!" "Wicked thief!"

The helpless commander was carried out of the palace and thrown down in the courtyard. Courtiers, brahmins, and laymen immediately began striking him with their fists, clubs, and stones, until someone finally killed him with a mighty blow. The angry mob dragged his broken body away and threw it on a dung heap.

The king appointed the virtuous Chattapāni as park keeper, and, following the advice of the wise Dhammaddhaja, he ruled in righteousness until he passed away to fare according to his deserts.

Having concluded his story, the Buddha identified the birth: "At that time, Devadatta was Kālaka, Sāriputta was the artisan Chattapāni, and I was Dhammaddhaja."

91

A Violent End
Culla-Nandiya Jātaka

It was while staying at Veluvana that the Buddha told this story about Devadatta.

One day, the bhikkhus were talking about how Devadatta had tried to kill the Buddha by rolling down a huge boulder and by releasing the fierce elephant Nālāgiri in the street. When the Buddha heard what they were discussing, he said, "This is not the first time Devadatta has been harsh, cruel, and merciless." Then the Buddha told this story of the past.

Long, long ago, when Brahmadatta was reigning in Bārānasi, the Bodhisatta was born as a monkey named Nandiya. He was the leader of a troop of eighty thousand monkeys in the Himavat. Nandiya had a younger brother named Culla-Nandiya, and the two of them cared for their blind mother.

Once, Nandiya and his brother left their mother in her shelter in the bushes and went with the troop to hunt for fruit. They were gone for several days, but, every day, they sent some of the fruit back to their mother.

When their foraging happened to take the troop back to the part of the forest near their lair, Nandiya stopped in to see his mother. He was shocked to find her starving. She appeared to be no more than skin and bones. "Mother!" he cried in distress. "Every day, we sent you sweet fruit. Why are you so thin?"

"I never received any fruit from you," his mother replied weakly.

Nandiya realized that he could not trust any messengers. He would have to look after his mother himself. He called Culla-Nandiya and said, "Brother! You must take over the leadership of the troop. I will care for our mother."

"No, Brother," he objected, "what do I care about being king? Let's both take care of our mother!"

Thus, the two of them left the troop and carried their mother out of the Himavat. When they reached the border of Kāsi, they found a huge banyan tree, and there they established a new residence, where they could look after her properly.

At that time, there was a brahmin named Pārāsariya in Takkasilā who, having completed his education under a famous teacher, had set himself up with a student of his own. After some time, Pārāsariya, who had the power of divining from physiognomy, perceived that his student was of a harsh, cruel, and violent nature. One day, he called his student and said, "My son, I can see that you are prone to cruelty and violence. People like you often have trouble in the world, and I fear you may come to a violent end. It is best that you not continue your study with me. Please go, and do what you can. Avoid cruelty and harshness. Do not be violent or commit deeds which you will later repent." With that advice, he sent the young student away.

The youth wended his way to Bārānasi, where he married and settled down. He tried several trades but was not able to earn a livelihood in the city. At last, he decided to use his skill with the bow by becoming a hunter. He moved to a border village so that, every day, he could easily go into the forest to kill animals and earn a living by selling their flesh.

One day, as he was returning home with nothing to show for a day's work, he noticed a huge banyan tree standing at the edge of a clearing, and stealthily drew near. "Perhaps," he thought, "there is something in that tree."

That tree happened to be the same one in which Nandiya and Culla-Nandiya were living with their mother. The two monkeys had just fed their mother and were sitting behind her in the tree, when they saw the hunter coming.

"Even if he sees our little mother," they said to each other, "he will not hurt her," and they quickly jumped to hide in the higher branches.

As soon as the hunter reached the tree, he saw the old female monkey and let out a cry of joy, "At least, I won't go home empty-handed!" He fitted an arrow into his bow and prepared to shoot her.

Nandiya immediately called to his younger brother, "Culla-Nandiya, I must save our mother. When I am gone, please take care of her. Good-bye!" He jumped down and placed himself directly between his mother and the hunter.

"Hunter!" he cried. "Don't shoot my mother! She is blind and old. Kill me instead! Please spare her life!" Resolutely, he sat there ready to accept the arrow in his chest.

Delighted at his good fortune, the hunter let his arrow fly and pierced Nandiya through the heart. As soon as the monkey had fallen, the hunter took out another arrow and coldly prepared to shoot the mother.

Culla-Nandiya could think of nothing but saving his mother's life. He, too, leaped down and placed himself in front of his mother. "Hunter," he cried, "don't shoot my mother! You have my brother's body; now be satisfied with mine! Without us to care for her, our mother may live only one more day, but grant her that gift of life. Please do not kill her. I give my life for hers!" He sat down and calmly faced the hunter.

Thinking he must be dreaming such good fortune, the pitiless hunter let his arrow fly and killed the second son as well. "That thin old monkey will be enough for my children," he thought and killed the mother with a third arrow. He tied all three monkeys onto his carrying pole and headed home, thoroughly pleased with himself.

At that moment, a bolt of lightning struck his house and set it afire. His wife and children were burned alive, and nothing was left of the house but the upright bamboo poles and the charred roof.

As the hunter was entering the village, a neighbor met him and told him what had happened. The hunter immediately dropped his carrying pole and bow, tore off his clothes, and ran madly toward his home. Deranged by grief, he flailed his arms and wailed loudly. When he reached the smoking ruins, he threw himself down in the ashes. Suddenly, the poles broke, and the roof collapsed on him.

At the same time, the earth opened under him, and flames rose from hell. As the hunter was being swallowed up, he remembered his master's advice. "So this is what my master meant! 'Avoid cruelty and harshness. Do not be violent or commit deeds which you will later repent,'" he moaned. "Too late do I understand that one will receive according to what he gives. Good for good and evil for evil!" With that haunting cry, he fell into the depths of hell.

Having concluded his story, the Buddha identified the birth: "At that time, Devadatta was the hunter, Sāriputta was the famous teacher Pārāsariya, Ānanda was Culla-Nandiya, Mahā-Pajāpatī Gotamī was the mother, and I was Nandiya."

92

The Liberated Wife
Asitābhū Jātaka

It was while staying at Jetavana that the Buddha told this story about a young woman.

In Sāvatthī, a supporter of the Buddha's two chief disciples had an extremely beautiful and charming daughter. When she grew up, she married into a family as good as her own, but her husband was not contented to stay at home with her. Completely ignoring his wife, he sought pleasure elsewhere. The young woman took no notice of this disrespect. She frequently invited the two chief disciples to her home, offered them meals, and provided them with the requisites. She always listened attentively to their preaching, and, in no long time, she attained the first path.

After that, she spent her free time in meditation, enjoying the bliss of the path and the fruit. One day, it occurred to her that, since her husband was not interested in her, she had no reason to stay at home. Informing her parents of her decision, she took herself to Jetavana, was ordained as a bhikkhunī, and soon became an arahat.

Shortly after this, some of the bhikkhus were talking about her in the Hall of Truth. "Friends," one of them said, "it is interesting how that young woman, even when quite young, was always striving to attain the highest goal. Fortunately for her, her husband was not interested in her, so she was able to devote herself to offering hospitality to the chief disciples and to listening to their teaching, thereby attaining the first path. It is really no wonder that, soon after she became a bhikkhunī, she attained arahatship. She never stopped striving for that goal."

When the Buddha heard what they were talking about, he said, "This is not the first time, Bhikkhus, that she has been diligent in her practice." At their request, he told this story of the past.

Long, long ago, when Brahmadatta was reigning in Bārānasi, he had a son of the same name, who surrounded himself with a great deal of pomp and ceremony. Observing this, the king became suspicious of what the young prince might do. One day, he summoned the prince and ordered him to leave the kingdom and not to return until he, the king, had died.

Prince Brahmadatta left Bārānasi with his wife Asitābhū to go into exile. Eventually, they reached the Himavat, where, finding plenty of fish and all manner of wild fruit to eat, they built a modest hut of leaves and lived comfortably.

They had not been there long, when the prince happened to see a kinnarī and became infatuated with her. Forgetting that he had a devoted wife, he pursued the kinnarī and resolved to marry her. When Asitābhū saw the prince cavorting in this way, she began to weep. "My husband," she cried to herself, "for whom I forsook the advantages and amenities of Bārānasi cares nothing for me!" Her tears, however, did not last long. Regaining her composure, she thought, "What is he to me? He is a fool! He has no need of me, and I have no need of him!"

With this realization, she went in search of an ascetic who lived nearby. It was well known that this ascetic, who had spent many years in the Himavat, was very skillful in concentration meditation. Arriving at his hermitage, Asitābhū paid him reverence and asked him to teach her how to meditate. Under his guidance, she quickly attained the jhānas. Pleased with her own achievement, she bade the ascetic farewell and returned to her own hut.

Meanwhile, Prince Brahmadatta had continued chasing after the kinnarī, but had lost track of her somewhere in the deep forest. Disappointed that the one he was so enamored of had eluded him, he turned back to the hut. When Asitābhū saw him coming, she rose into the air and seated herself on a ruby-red plank. "Because of you and your feckless nature, I have attained this ecstatic bliss! Thanks to you, I am rid of all passion; passion will never trouble me again." Without another word, she departed.

"She's gone!" the prince moaned. "Greed and lust confuse the senses and lead us to ruin. Through sheer folly, I have lost my devoted wife."

He continued living alone in the forest until he was able to return to Bārānasi to claim the crown.

Having concluded his story, the Buddha identified the birth: "At that time, that bhikkhunī was Princess Asitābhū, her former husband was Prince Brahmadatta, and I was the wise ascetic."

93
No Return
Mahā-Pingala Jātaka

It was while staying at Veluvana that the Buddha told this story about Devadatta.

For nine months, Devadatta had tried various strategies to kill the Buddha, but without success. Finally, just outside the gate of Jetavana, he was swallowed up by the earth and reborn in hell. When people heard this news, there was rejoicing that the enemy of the Buddha was, at last, dead.

One day, some bhikkhus were talking about this. When the Buddha heard what they were discussing, he said, "This is not the first time that multitudes have rejoiced at the death of Devadatta." Then he told this story of the past.

Long, long ago, a cruel and barbarous king named Mahā-Pingala was reigning in Bārānasi. Ignoring what was right, he ruled according to his own will and pleasure. Whenever he wanted money, he imposed oppressive taxes. He delighted in subjecting prisoners to sadistic torture. In every way, he crushed his subjects as if they were sugar-cane in a press, never showing the slightest sign of pity toward anyone. Mahā-Pingala was harsh to his wives, brutal to his children, and vicious toward his servants. He treated his ministers and advisors like slaves. People variously referred to the king as "the speck of dust in my eye," "the gravel in my soup," and "the thorn in my heel."

When, after a very long reign, King Mahā-Pingala died, there was a great sense of relief throughout the kingdom, and many people expressed jubilation. Crowds sang as they accompanied the king's body to the royal cremation ground. They laughed a great laugh as the body was burned with one thousand cartloads of wood. Everyone rejoiced as they quenched the ashes of the funeral pyre with one thousand jars of water.

Preparations were immediately begun to crown the king's eldest son as the new king. A drummer marched through the streets, declaring with a lively rhythm that, at last, the kingdom would have a righteous king. Citizens flew flags and colorful banners. The entire city was gaily decorated with flowers. For many days, the streets were filled with singing, dancing, and celebration.

On the day of the coronation, the crown prince sat on an exquisite couch on a great raised dais, shaded by the magnificent royal white umbrella. All around him were hundreds of courtiers and thousands of ordinary citizens.

In the midst of this splendor and rejoicing, the crown prince noticed that an old doorman standing near his couch was weeping and sobbing.

"My good man," the crown prince called out, signaling for the porter to step nearer, "everyone else here is celebrating and rejoicing that the old king is at last dead and gone. Yet you seem to be shedding tears from sadness. Is it possible that my father was kind to you so that you weep for him?"

"It is not sorrow that Mahā-Pingala is dead that makes me weep," replied the man. "My head is glad enough that he is gone. Every time the king entered or left the palace, he gave me eight blows on the head with his fist, not light taps, mind you, but blows like those of a blacksmith's hammer.

"I know that that was his habit, and I am afraid that, as soon as he arrives in hell, he will give Yama the gatekeeper eight blows on the head, as well. Then the inhabitants of hell will cry, 'He is too cruel for us!' and they will send him back to this world. When he comes back, he will beat me again every day in the same way. That is why I'm weeping."

"My good man," the crown prince comforted him, "my father's body has been burned with one thousand cartloads of wood, the ashes have been soaked with water from one thousand jars, and the ground has been dug up all around. He cannot return in the same bodily shape. Beings that have gone to another realm cannot return to this one, except by rebirth. Good porter, do not be afraid!"

Fully comforted by these wise words, the doorman joined the celebrations and added his voice to the songs in praise of Mahā-Pingala's successor.

The new king ruled many years in righteousness. After giving gifts and doing other good deeds, he passed away to fare according to his deserts.

Having concluded his story, the Buddha identified the birth: "At that time, Devadatta was Mahā-Pingala, and I was his son."

94

Subduing the World
Sabbadātha Jātaka

It was while staying at Veluvana that the Buddha told this story about Devadatta.

One day, some of the bhikkhus in the Hall of Truth were talking about how Devadatta, in spite of having won the favor of Prince Ajātasattu, had not been able to maintain his reputation or to retain the support he had enjoyed. When the Buddha heard what they were discussing, he said, "Bhikkhus, this is not the first time that Devadatta gained a great reputation and the support of many and then lost both." At their request, the Buddha told them this story of the past.

Long, long ago, when Brahmadatta was reigning in Bārānasi, the Bodhisatta was his chief advisor. The advisor had mastered all branches of knowledge and could even cast the powerful spell called Pathavījaya or "Subduing the World."

One day, the advisor, wanting to perfect his practice of this spell, went to a secluded spot in the forest and sat down on a flat stone. He carefully recited the spell again and again. When the advisor chose that spot, he had not realized that there was a jackal's den nearby. While the advisor was reciting his spell, the jackal was listening intently, and, since, in a previous existence, this beast had been a brahmin who had known that same charm, it was not at all difficult for him to relearn it even as a jackal. By the time the advisor had finished, the jackal knew it by heart.

As the advisor started to leave, the jackal emerged from his den and called out, "Ho, Brahmin! I have learned that spell even better than you know it yourself!" and off he ran.

The advisor set off in pursuit, shouting, "Stop thief!" but the jackal was too fast for him. The advisor returned to the palace, fretting, "That pesky jackal is going to cause a lot of trouble!"

Soon after that, the jackal found a female jackal and gave her a little nip with his teeth.

"What was that for?" she asked.

"Do you know me?" he asked her.

"No, I certainly do not," she replied coolly.

He recited the Pathavījaya spell, and she immediately became faithful to him. The jackal ran through the forest repeating the spell, and, soon, he had several hundred jackals under his control.

Many other animals, including elephants, lions, tigers, buffalos, deer, and wild boars, felt that something was happening and gathered to find out what it was. The jackal loudly repeated his powerful subjugating spell, and all those animals became his obedient followers. The jackal declared himself king and gave himself the royal name Sabbadātha, with the female jackal as consort.

Sabbadātha created a living throne for himself and his queen by perching a lion on the backs of two elephants. From the back of that lion, he gave orders to his army of animals, which extended for twelve yojanas.

Intoxicated by his power and the great honor he was receiving from all the beasts of the forest, the jackal decided to attack Bārānasi. He led his vast army to the gate of the city and sent a message demanding that the king surrender.

The terror-stricken citizens of Bārānasi barred the city gates and retreated to their homes.

As soon as the advisor heard about the impending attack, he rushed to the king. "Fear not, Your Majesty," he said. "Let me fight this jackal, Sabbadātha. I alone know how to deal with him!" This greatly comforted the king and reassured the panic-stricken citizens.

The advisor climbed to the top of the tower of the gate facing the jackal's army and called out, "Sabbadtha, how do you plan to conquer this city?"

"I will make my lion roar," the proud jackal shouted back. That roar will so terrify your citizens that I will be able to seize the kingdom with no trouble at all!"

"So that's it," mused the advisor. He descended from the tower and issued a proclamation that all the inhabitants of Bārāṇasi should plug their ears with flour paste. Everyone obeyed. They plugged not only their own ears but also the ears of their dogs, cats, horses, cattle, and even the royal elephants.

The advisor again mounted the tower and called out, "Sabbadtha!"

"What is it now, Brahmin?" snarled the jackal.

"Tell me again how you will conquer this city!"

"I will order all my lions to roar! That will frighten the people, and I will destroy them."

"Are you crazy?" the advisor shouted, taunting the jackal. "Those noble lions, with their long manes, their tawny coats, their great paws, and their sharp fangs, will never follow the orders of a mangy old jackal like you! Do you really think you can make them roar?"

"You ignorant brahmin!" the jackal shouted, his pride injured by this challenge to his authority. "Not only will all of these lions obey me, but even this one, upon whose back I sit, at my order, will roar loud enough to frighten all of you!"

"So you say! I dare you to try!"

The jackal tapped his foot on the back of lion as a command for him to roar.

That most magnificent lion immediately opened his mouth and roared three times. His mighty roar so terrified the two lead elephants that they tossed the jackal from his throne, and he fell at their feet. In their panic, they trampled him and crushed his head like an eggshell. When the sound of that one lion's roar reached the other elephants in Sabbadtha's host, they also panicked. In their wild stampede, the elephants not only injured each other but also killed every jackal, deer, boar, and hare in the entire army. Only the lions were able to escape unharmed into the forest.

The advisor ordered that a written proclamation be posted throughout the city allowing citizens to take the flour out of their ears. Then he had the city gates thrown open, and, by the beat of a drum, he ordered everyone to retrieve what they wanted from the massive heap of carcasses. People cooked as much meat as they could eat, and they dried the rest. According to tradition, this was the beginning of the custom of drying meat for later use.

Having concluded his story, the Buddha identified the birth: "At that time, Devadatta was the jackal, Ānanda was the king, and I was the royal advisor."

95
Maestro Guttila
Guttila Jātaka

It was while staying at Veluvana that the Buddha told this story about Devadatta.

Once, when some bhikkhus reminded Devadatta that the Buddha was his teacher and tried to dissuade him from showing enmity to the Master, Devadatta retorted, "Friends, what do you mean that Gotama was my teacher? That ascetic did not teach me anything! I have done everything by my own power!"

Later, discussing this in the Hall of Truth, the bhikkhus concluded that a miserable fate would certainly befall Devadatta.

When the Buddha heard what they were talking about, he said, "Bhikkhus, this is not the first time that Devadatta has repudiated his teacher and come to a miserable end. It was just the same before." Then he told this story of the past.

Long, long ago, when Brahmadatta was reigning in Bārānasi, the Bodhisatta was born as the son of two blind musicians, and he was named Guttila. While still young, he mastered all the branches of music. He was not only appointed Royal Musician to the court, but he was renowned as the finest musician in Jambudīpa. Wishing to care for his parents himself, Guttila never married, but continued living in their home.

At that time, some traders of Bārānasi traveled to Ujjeni on business. When a holiday was declared, they joined the local merchants for a feast. At the height of the festivities, one of traders shouted, "We need music! Bring a musician, and we will pay royally!"

The local merchants sent for a lute player named Mūsila, who was the chief musician in Ujjeni. Mūsila began playing, but the traders paid no attention to him. They were familiar with Guttila's playing, and Mūsila's music sounded like rats scratching on a screen.

Mūsila noticed their indifference and thought, "Perhaps that was a little sharp." He tuned his instrument to a lower key and began again. The traders seemed not even to notice. "The boors!" Mūsila cursed under his breath. "I suppose they know nothing at all about music." He loosened all the strings of his lute and played as though he were untrained and completely ignorant of music. The traders continued to ignore him.

Finally, Mūsila put down his lute and asked them, "Good merchants, don't you like my playing?"

"What?" they exclaimed. "Were you playing? We thought that you were taking your time tuning up."

"Are you too ignorant to appreciate my musical skill," he asked them, "or do you know a better musician?"

"We have heard the music of Guttila at Bārānasi, and he makes yours sound like tone-deaf village women groaning through a lullaby."

"In that case, take back your money! I don't want your fee, but," he said, pausing briefly, "when you return to Bārānasi, please take me with you."

The traders agreed and took Mūsila to Bārānasi. Then, pointing out Guttila's house, they left him and returned to their own homes.

Mūsila walked to the house the traders had indicated. Finding the door open, he stepped inside. He saw a lute hanging on the wall, took it down and played a few notes.

"Mice!" someone shouted from within. "Mice are gnawing the lute!" Guttila's blind parents hurried into the room, waving their canes and crying, "Shoo! Shoo!"

Mūsila immediately put the lute back and greeted the old couple.

"Where are you from, young man?" they asked.

"I am from Ujjeni."

"Why have you come here?" they continued.

"I wish to learn music at the feet of your son."

"Very well. Our son, the master Guttila, has gone out, but he will be back soon. Please wait."

Mūsila sat down and waited. When Guttila came in, Mūsila greeted him and asked the master to teach him to play beautiful music.

Observing the lines of his face, Guttila immediately perceived that Mūsila was not a good man. "Go, my son," he replied solemnly. "This art is not for you."

Mūsila clasped the feet of Guttila's parents and begged them to intervene with their son.

The couple urged their son not to send the nice young man away, but Guttila remained firm. Again and again, they implored him so strongly to teach Mūsila that, finally, he relented.

Having agreed to teach Mūsila, Guttila did not stint with his knowledge. He even escorted his student to the court and introduced him to the king.

One day, Guttila announced to Mūsila, "Your lessons are complete. I have taught you everything I know."

"At last, I have mastered the art of music," Mūsila gloated. "Now I know all there is to know, and I am as good as my teacher. Master Guttila is old, so I must stay here. After all, Bārānasi is the greatest city in all of Jambudīpa." Aloud, he said to his teacher, "Sir, I would serve the king."

"Very well, my son," Guttila replied, "I will inform him."

Guttila went to the king and announced, "Sire, my student Mūsila wishes to serve you. If it please Your Majesty, fix what his fee should be."

"His fee will be half of yours," replied the king.

When Guttila related this, Mūsila answered, "If I receive the same pay as you, I will play for the king. I will not serve for less."

"How can you say that?" Guttila asked in surprise.

"Have you not told me that you have taught me all you know?" retorted Mūsila.

"Yes, I have," Guttila answered truthfully.

"Then," Mūsila insisted, "if I know all that you know, why does the king offer me only half? I am as good as you!"

Guttila informed the king of Mūsila's demand.

"If, indeed, he is as perfect in his art as you are," replied the king, "of course, he will receive the same salary, but, first, he will have to prove it."

Mūsila accepted the challenge, and Guttila suggested to the king that a competition be held in one week. The king sent for Mūsila and tried to dissuade him from vying with his master. "There should never be rivalry between teacher and student," the king advised.

"Never mind that, Sire!" Mūsila answered haughtily. "Let there be a contest, and, seven days from now, you will know which of us, Guttila or me, is the true master of his art."

The king agreed, and it was publicly announced that in one week's time there would be an open competition between Guttila, the teacher, and Mūsila, the student. It would take place at the entrance to the palace, and all who appreciated music were invited to attend and to judge which was the more skillful musician.

Guttila was unhappy about the competition. "I know that I am a great musician," he reflected. "I have been honored by all the kings of Jambudīpa. Even if I play better than Mūsila, there is no great credit in that. On the other hand, Mūsila is young and fresh; I am old, and my strength is gone. I have taught him everything I know. Young men often succeed, and old men may fail. It would be better for me to die alone in the woods than to suffer the shame of defeat before the king and all his subjects." Slowly, he walked into the forest, intending to lose himself in its depths. As soon as he left the sunlight, however, he was struck by the fear of death and returned to his house. Once there, the fear of shame drove him back to the forest, but, again, he returned home. This continued for six days. His feet wore a path in the grass between his house and the forest.

This caused Sakka's throne to become hot. As soon as the king of the devas perceived the reason, he resolved, "I must help Master Guttila overcome this sorrow which is being caused by his student." Instantly, Sakka appeared in the forest and stood in front of the musician. "Master," he asked, "why have you taken to the woods?"

"Who are you?" Guttila asked him.

"I am Sakka. Please tell me what troubles you."

"Your Majesty," Guttila began, "I have a student named Mūsila to whom I have imparted all my knowledge and skill in performing on the seven-stringed lute. Now this student intends to show me up and to outdo me before the king. It is out of fear of shame that I have fled to the woods. Please, Sire, help me know what to do!"

"Don't be afraid, Master Guttila," Sakka comforted him. "A teacher deserves honor and respect from his student, not humiliation. Mūsila will not defeat you. I will protect you. You will prove to be the better man. While you are playing, you must break the strings of your lute, one by one. Continue to play, and your music will be just as beautiful as ever. Mūsila will also break his strings, but he will be completely confounded. He will no longer be able to play a single note. His lute will become silent, and he will be utterly defeated. Even from ends of broken strings, your music will enchant all of Bārānasi."

Before returning to Tāvatimsa, Sakka gave Guttila three dice and instructed him, "When the sound of your lute has filled the city, throw these dice, one by one, into the air. They will call forth devas who will enhance the glory of your music. I will also be there to witness your triumph. Master Guttila, proceed with this contest, and have no fear!"

With renewed confidence, Guttila returned home, bathed, anointed himself with sweet-smelling lotions, and ate a hearty breakfast. Then, taking down his lute, he walked to the palace.

In front of the palace, the king had erected a grand pavilion. In the center of the pavilion was a dais for the musicians. In front of the dais was a special throne for the king. Around the throne, the seats were reserved for the king's courtiers and ministers. The courtyard was filled with people. It seemed that all of Bārānasi had come to witness the competition. The great multitude waited patiently, seated tier upon tier around the pavilion.

Mūsila was already in his seat on the dais. Guttila mounted the dais and took his own seat. Sakka was also there, poised in the air, but only Guttila could see him.

First, each musician played the same piece, and their performances were identical. The audience was delighted and enthusiastically applauded them equally.

For the next piece, the musicians were to play alternately. Shortly after Guttila began, Sakka said to him, "Break one of your strings." Guttila broke his first string, but, as he continued playing, the broken ends of the string emitted a heavenly note, and there was no interruption in the music.

Not to be outdone, shortly after Mūsila began playing the second section, he broke one of his strings. He tried to continue playing, but that string was mute, and his music sounded sour.

When Guttila took up the third section, he broke a second string, but the ends of this string, as well, produced the proper note. If anything, his music sounded even more divine than before.

Mūsila followed suit and broke another string, but, for him, the broken string was silent. He tried to transpose the score to fit his remaining strings, but the result was disastrous.

Guttila successively broke all seven strings, but his lute continued producing beautiful music. Mūsila also broke all of his strings, but his lute became utterly silent.

Guttila continued playing on only the body of his lute, and his music filled all of Bārānasi.

Then, without the slightest interruption in his music, Guttila tossed one of the dice into the air. Instantly, three hundred female devas descended and began to dance to his heavenly music. When he tossed the second die, another three hundred descended. As Guttila concluded his performance, he tossed the third die into the air, and there were nine hundred devas dancing above the courtyard. The spectators were transported with delight. They waved their scarves, applauded, and shouted in appreciation of the spectacle.

Amidst the applause, the king stood up and shouted, "Mūsila, you made a great mistake in competing with your teacher! You do not know your own worth!" As one, the crowd suddenly rushed forward and mobbed the unfortunate student. They pulled him from the dais, beat him with sticks, and threw him onto a dustheap outside the palace grounds.

The king praised Guttila and showered him with gifts.

When Sakka returned to Tāvatimsa, he described Guttila's mastery of the lute to all the other devas. The younger female devas begged Sakka to fetch Guttila to heaven that they might also hear his superb artistry.

Sakka summoned Mātali and commanded him to drive the divine chariot to earth and to return with Guttila. When the teacher arrived in Tāvatimsa, Sakka greeted him and said, "The female devas here wish to hear you play."

"Your Majesty," Guttila replied, "we musicians make our living by our art. I will play only for a fee."

"Play on, Master, and I will pay you," Sakka agreed.

"My compensation will be only this," Guttila continued. "I would like these young devas to tell me what acts of virtue brought them here. If they will agree to do this, I will play."

"We will gladly tell you what you wish to know, but you must play first, Master."

For seven days, Guttila played his lute for them, and his music surpassed any they had ever heard before. Not even the heavenly musicians could compare with him. When he had finished, he put down his lute and asked the female devas to recount for him their virtuous lives.

"In the time of Kassapa Buddha," one said, "I gave an upper robe to a bhikkhu."

"I stood in the river and offered a drink of water to a bhikkhu who had eaten his meal on a boat," said another.

"I faithfully performed my duty to my husband's parents without ever losing my temper."

"I was a slave, and, with neither anger nor pride, I made generous donations whenever I could, though I possessed very little."

"I gave flowers to a bhikkhu on his almsrounds."

"I offered a scented wreath of sandalwood to a cetiya."

"I made an offering of delicious fruit."

"I offered rare incense."

"I listened to the discourses of bhikkhus and bhikkhunīs."

"I shared part of a meal before I myself ate."

Guttila was delighted. "How wonderful," he exclaimed, "to know that, even by a small meritorious deed, one may achieve great glory! What a wonderful pilgrimage this has been! How fortunate I have been to see and hear these delightful devas! I vow that, when I return to earth, I will be generous, kind, virtuous, and truthful!"

Then Sakka directed Mātali to return the music teacher to Bārānasi. Guttila told everyone all that he had seen and heard in Tāvatimsa, and he admonished them to give gifts generously and to be steadfast in performing good deeds.

Having concluded his story, the Buddha identified the birth: "At that time, Devadatta was Mūsila, Anuruddha was Sakka, Ānanda was King Brahma-datta, and I was Guttila, the music teacher."

96
The Wounded Ascetic
Sankappa Jātaka

It was while staying at Jetavana that the Buddha told this story about a backsliding bhikkhu.

One day, on his almsrounds, a young bhikkhu happened to see a beautiful woman in an elegant sari, and passion suddenly raged in his heart. Unable to forget her lovely face, he was no longer able to meditate, and he was constantly distracted. When his friends asked him what was wrong, he told them that he wanted to return to the world. The other bhikkhus took him to see the Buddha. Although the Master immediately understood, he asked what the problem was, and the young bhikkhu admitted that he had experienced passion from seeing a beautiful woman.

"Women have stirred up lustful thoughts even in pure beings who have achieved great powers of concentration," the Buddha told him. "It is natural for an ordinary man like you to feel this way. Will the wind that shakes Mount Sineru fail to stir up a heap of dry leaves?" At the bhikkhus' request, the Buddha told this story of the past.

Long, long ago, when Brahmadatta was reigning in Bārānasi, the Bodhisatta was born into a tremendously wealthy Brahmin family. After
completing his education in Takkasilā, he returned to Bārānasi and married.
When his parents died, he performed their funeral rites.

As he was making an inventory of his inheritance, the thought occurred
to him that the immense treasure had been accumulated and invested by
many generations, all of whom were no more. He was suddenly overcome
by a sense of futility, and he broke out in a sweat.

From that moment, he was a changed man. He continued living at home,
but he no longer took delight in business or in frivolous entertainment. He
gave alms generously and mastered his passions.

After some time, he left his weeping family and friends and went to the
Himavat, where he built a simple hut in a pleasant spot and lived on the wild
fruits which he gathered in the forest. Through concentration meditation, he
perfected the five extraordinary powers and the eight jhānas.

One year, at the beginning of the rainy season, he left to get salt and
vinegar and to find a place to stay. It was sunset by the time he reached
Bārānasi. He spent the night meditating at the foot of a tree in the royal park.

The next morning, after taking care of his bodily needs, he adjusted his
matted hair, his bark robes, and his antelope skin; picked up his almsbowl;
and started off in search of alms. His senses calmed, he carried himself nobly,
looking a plow's length in front of him as he walked. His poise drew the
notice of all who saw him as he begged from door to door.

When he stopped at the gate of the palace, the king spied him through
a window and was impressed with his bearing. "If there is such a thing as
perfect quietude, it must be in that man," the king said to himself and sent a
servant to fetch the ascetic. The servant hurried to the gate and announced
to the ascetic, "The king sends for you, sir."

"Friend," replied the ascetic, "the king does not know me!"

"Please wait," the servant replied and hurried back to the king.

"We have no resident priest here," the king told the servant. "Go, and
bring that ascetic here." At the same time, the king looked out the window
again and beckoned to the ascetic.

The ascetic gave his almsbowl to the servant and followed him inside the
palace. The king greeted the ascetic, sat him on the royal couch, and served
him from the dishes which had been prepared for his own breakfast.

After the ascetic had finished eating, the king asked, "Good sir, where
do you reside?"

"In the Himavat," replied the ascetic.

"Why have you come to Bārānasi?"

"During the rainy season, Sire, we need to find a proper dwelling place."

"In that case," the king replied, "please stay here in my royal park. You will lack for nothing. I will provide all that you need, and the merit I acquire will take me to heaven."

The ascetic accepted the invitation. As soon as the king had finished his own breakfast, he escorted the ascetic back to the park. The king instructed the park keeper to construct a hut of leaves with a covered walk and to provide all the necessary furnishings to ensure that the ascetic was comfortable.

For the next twelve years, the ascetic stayed in the royal park, and, every day, the king provided his meals.

Once, when rebellion broke out in a frontier district, it was necessary for the king himself to go there. The king summoned the queen and announced, "My dear, I must go to the border, but I am very afraid to leave the palace."

"Why is that?" she asked.

"Every day for twelve years, I have personally provided food for the ascetic who is staying in my garden."

"Have no worry on that account, My Lord. I will not neglect him."

While the king was gone, the ascetic took his meals in the palace. One day, the queen prepared his food and set a low stool for herself, as usual, but the ascetic did not come. After waiting for some time, the queen went to her own room, bathed, adorned herself, and lay down on her bed, with an exquisite robe thrown loosely over her body.

As soon as the ascetic, who had been meditating, noticed the time, he picked up his almsbowl, rose into the air, and entered the palace through a window. The queen heard the rustle of his bark robes and quickly rose, but, as she did so, her robe slipped down.

This unusual sight so startled the ascetic that he let it penetrate his senses, and he looked at her with desire. Suddenly, the passion that had been so long suppressed by the power of his meditation rose in him as a cobra rises from its basket. He felt like a plantain tree struck by an axe. The queen swiftly rearranged her clothes and invited him to sit down, but his passion continued to grow.

Unable to calm himself, he could not sit down to take his meal as usual. The queen urged him to stay, but he begged to be excused. The queen put all the food she had prepared into his bowl, and he started to leave, but, unable to concentrate, he no longer had the power to pass through the air. He had to go down by the great staircase and walk to the park. When he arrived at his hut, he was completely dejected and distraught. His senses had lost their purity, and he felt like a crow with a broken wing.

He still did not feel like eating, so he placed his bowl on the bench at the foot of his bed. He threw himself down and moaned, "What a woman! Such lovely hands and feet! How delicate her waist! How soft her thighs!" For seven days, he lay on his bed, without moving. The food in his bowl rotted and attracted a cloud of black flies.

It was at this time that the king, having restored order to the frontier area, returned to Bārānasi. The entire city was decorated to greet him. He paraded through the streets in a grand procession, beginning at the city gate and ending at the palace. Even before greeting the queen, however, he hurried to the royal park to pay his respects to the ascetic. When he saw the dirt and rubbish around the hut, he wondered whether the ascetic had left. Cautiously, he pushed open the door and stepped inside. When he smelled the rotten food and saw the ascetic lying motionless on the bed, he was sure that sage was ill. He ordered his attendants to throw the food away and to clean up the mess. He himself knelt bedside the bed and cried, "Venerable Sir, what is the matter?"

"Sire, I am wounded!"

"Oh, no!" the king murmured. "My enemies have done this! They could not hurt me, so they have attacked that which I hold most dear!" He gently turned the ascetic over, looking for a wound. "Where have they injured you?"

"No, Sire. No one has hurt me. I have wounded my own heart. No archer shot me with an arrow. There is no feathered shaft here, but this heart of mine has been pierced by desire. By my own will and determination, I had once cleansed it of passion, but now it burns with lust."

Then, feeling stronger, the ascetic said, "Your Majesty, please step outside for a few minutes." The king went out and closed the door. Alone once more, the ascetic summoned his determination and self-control and soon recovered his interrupted jhānic concentration. Emerging from the hut, he declared to the king that he could no longer stay there. He explained that, having suffered that lapse, he had to return to the Himavat. The king tried to dissuade him, but the ascetic replied, "Sire, see what humiliation has come upon me while staying in this place! I cannot remain here any longer!"

The ascetic spent the rest of his days in the Himavat, and, when he passed away, he was reborn in the Brahma heavens.

Having concluded his story, the Buddha taught the Dhamma, and the backsliding bhikkhu became an arahat. Then the Buddha identified the birth: "At that time, Ānanda was the king, and I was the ascetic."

Glossary of Terms

Abhidhamma: Abstract Teaching; the collection of texts in which the underlying doctrinal principles presented in the Suttas are reworked and reorganized into a systematic framework that can be applied to an investigation into the nature of mind and matter. The Abhidhamma Pitaka is the third division of the Tipitaka.

aggregate: See five aggregates.

Ājīvika: a sect of naked ascetics; followers of Makkhali Gosāla.

anumodana: a Dhamma teaching given by the Sangha following an offering, meant to encourage the donor, to rejoice in the donation, to dedicate the merit made, and to invite others to share in it.

arahat: a fully-enlightened one, who, having freed his mind of all defilements, has attained Nibbāna and is not subject to further rebirth.

Asadisadāna: the unmatched offering which occurs only once for each Buddha.

Āsālha: the eighth month of the Indian lunar calendar; the beginning of the rains retreat.

asseveration of truth (saccakiriya): a statement of truth, the force of which is used to obtain a desired result.

asura: a class of pugnacious, but cowardly and perpetually angry, beings, roughly equivalent to Titans. Sakka evicted the deva-asuras from Tāvatimsa while they were drunk. They continue to maintain a heavenly existence in a place outside, but equal to, Tāvatimsa. There are, quite distinct from this, beings called asura-kāya, sometimes referred to as peta-asuras and niraya-asuras. These beings lead a miserable life in the third woeful realm. Their suffering is very similar to that of the peta and niraya realms.

bael a Bengal quince; a woodapple.

bhikkhu: a fully ordained monk in the Buddha's order; a man who has left the household life to seek the end of suffering. He lives a life of discipline in accordance with the Vinaya.

bhikkhunī: a fully ordained nun in the Buddha's order; a woman who has left the household life to seek the end of suffering. She lives a life of discipline in accordance with the Vinaya.

Bodhi tree: the tree under which a Supreme Buddha attains Enlightenment. Within the Sāsana of that Buddha, saplings from that tree, wherever they are planted, are respected. For Gotama Buddha, the Bodhi tree was the pipal tree (Ficus religiosa).

Bodhisatta: one striving for Buddhahood; "a Buddha-to-be." The term is used to describe someone from the time he makes his aspiration and receives confirmation from a living Buddha until his full Enlightenment.

Brahmā: a deva in the non-sensual heavens of form or formlessness which are called the Brahma heavens.

Brahma heavens (Brahma-loka): the highest heavens, where beings enjoy blissful existence. Birth in these realms is achieved by practicing concentration meditation, particularly on the Four Brahma Vihāras to the point of attaining jhāna.

Brahma Vihāra: See Four Brahma Vihāras.

brahmin (brāhmana): a member of the highest caste in Indian society, respected as such and qualified to perform rituals and sacrifices. Rejecting the caste system, the Buddha used the term to refer to one who was worthy of respect, not because of birth, but because he had reached the goal and had become an arahat.

Buddha: one who attains full Enlightenment on his own. A Supreme Buddha is one who, having discovered for himself the liberating path of Dhamma, after its having been forgotten by the world for a tremendously long period of time, teaches others so that they, too, may attain Enlightenment. There have been and will continue to be innumerable Supreme Buddhas. The Bodhisatta made his aspiration to become a Buddha at the time of Buddha Dīpankara. From that time until he became the Buddha Gotama, there were twenty-four Supreme Buddhas, the last being Kassapa Buddha. The next Buddha will be Mettaya Buddha.

catumadhu: literally, four sweet things. This mixture of ghee, oil, honey, and jaggery is allowable as medicine for members of the Sangha in the afternoon.

candāla: an outcaste; an untouchable; someone born outside (below) the four castes.

caste: the system of social class in traditional India. The four main castes, said to have been created by Brahmā, are: brāhmana, brahmin, teacher, priest; khattiya, warrior, king, ruler; vessa, businessman, artisan, farmer; sudda, worker, servant to the others

cetiya: a stupa; a pagoda; a monument, originally a mound, enshrining the relic of an enlightened one or commemorating a great event. The term can also be used for a funerary mound, particularly in pre-Buddhist times.

craving (tanhā): the longing for sense pleasures, for existence, and for non-existence; the origin of suffering. Craving is the second of the Four Noble Truths.

crore: ten million.

defilement (kilesa): any of ten unwholesome, mind-defiling qualities. These are: 1. greed (lobha); 2. hatred; (dosa); 3. delusion (moha); 4. conceit (māna); 5. speculative views (ditthi); 6. skeptical doubt (vicikicchā); 7. mental torpor (thīna); 8. restlessness (uddhacca); and 9. shamelessness (ahirika); 10. lack of moral dread (anotappa). The first three are considered the root defilements from which all the others arise.

determination (adhitthāna): the resolute will-power which forces all obstructions out of one's path, such that, no matter what may come in the form of grief or disaster, one's eyes never turn from the goal. Determination is the eighth of the Ten Perfections.

deva: a heavenly being; a deity. This can be a resident of one of the heavens or a guardian or spirit of a tree, a hill, a doorway, or some other entity.

Dhamma: the Buddha's Teaching. Dhamma-vinaya is the Buddha's own term for the religion he founded.

dhutanga: the ascetic practices allowed by Buddha to be voluntarily undertaken. They are: 1. wearing only rag robes; 2. having only one set of robes; 3. eating only almsfood; 4. not skipping any house on almsrounds; 5. eating only one meal a day; 6. eating only from the bowl; 7. refusing any further food; 8. staying in the forest; 9. staying under a tree;

431

10. staying in the open (without a roof or a tree for shelter); 11. staying in a charnel ground; 12. accepting whatever accommodation is offered; and 13. never lying down.

Discipline: See Vinaya.

eight precepts: See precepts.

energy (viriya): the mental vigor or strength of character, which is the persevering effort to avoid or to overcome evil and unwholesome things and to develop and to maintain wholesome things. Energy is the fifth of the Ten Perfections.

Enlightenment (bodhi): the state of complete understanding, the supreme awakening from the stupor caused by the mental defilements, and the perfect comprehension of the Four Noble Truths; Nibbāna.

eon (kappa): a world-cycle; a world-age; the period between the formation and the destruction of the world.

equanimity (upekkhā): maintaining an even balance in times of happiness and adversity in the face of praise or blame; discerning rightly, viewing justly, and looking impartially, with neither attachment nor detachment, with neither favor nor disfavor; not to be mistaken for indifference or callousness. Equanimity is the tenth of the Ten Perfections and the fourth of the Four Brahma Vihāras.

first path: See four stages of Enlightenment.

five aggregates (pañca khandha): the five aspects or factors of clinging; the physical and mental components of the personality and of sensory experience, which make up individual existence: 1. form (rūpa), 2. feeling (vedanā), 3. perception (saññā;), 4. mental formations (sankhāra), and 5. consciousness (viññāna).

five extraordinary powers: the powers attainable by perfecting mental concentration. They are: 1. magical power (iddhi-vidha); 2. divine ear (dibba-sota); 3. penetration of the mind of others (ceto-pariya-ñāna);); 4. divine eye (dibba-cakkhu); and 5. remembrance of former existences (pubbenivāsānussati).

five precepts: See precepts.

five symbols of royalty: sword, umbrella, crown, slippers, and fan.

Four Brahma Vihāras: also called the Four Divine Abidings; the four sublime abodes that are attained through the development of meditation on: 1. loving-kindness (mettā), 2. compassion (karunā), 3. sympathetic joy (muditā), and 4. equanimity (upekkhā).

four elements (dhātu): the four physical properties which are the ultimate constituents of all matters. They are: 1. earth, solidity (pathavi); 2. water, cohesiveness (āpo); 3. heat, fire (tejo); and 4. air, wind (vayo). All four are present in every material object, though in varying degrees of strength. Sometimes, the Buddha spoke of five or six elements, in which case, space (ākāsa) or space and consciousness (viññāna) are included.

Four Foundations of Mindfulness (satipatthāna): the bases for maintaining moment-by-moment mindfulness and developing mindfulness through meditation. They are: 1. contemplation on the body; 2. contemplation on feelings; 3. contemplation on the mind; and 4. contemplation on mental objects.

Four Great Kings (cātummahārājikā): the four powerful devas who reign over the lowest plane of heaven and serve as guardians of the four quarters. They are: Vessavana of the north, Dhatarattha of the east, Virūlhaka of the south, and Virūpakkha of the west. Their retinues consist of, respectively, yakkhas, gandhabbas, kumbhandas, and nāgas. Life in this realm lasts ninety thousand years, and beings are reborn here because of various acts of faith, prompted by rather unrefined motives. Their realm is located mid-way up Mount Sineru.

Four Noble Truths (cattāri ariya saccāni): 1. All forms of existence are subject to suffering. 2. The origin of suffering is craving. 3. The extinction of suffering, Nibbāna, is possible by eliminating craving. 4. The Noble Eightfold Path is the way to bring about the extinction of suffering.

four stages of Enlightenment: the four levels of progress on the path to Nibbāna. They are: 1. stream-enterer (sotāpanna), one who has attained the first path and who will undergo no more than seven rebirths, none of which will be lower than a human being; 2. once-returner (sakādagāmi), one who has attained the second path and will be reborn only once more in the human world and will attain Nibbāna in that life; 3. non-returner (anāgāmi), one who has attained the third path and will attain Nibbāna without being reborn in any sensuous realm; 4. fully-enlightened one (arahat), one who has attained the fourth path, Nibbāna, and will not be reborn again.

fourth path: See four stages of Enlightenment.

gandhabba: the lowest form of deva, inhabiting the realm of the Four Great Kings. The Buddha described gandhabbas as dwelling in the fragrance (ganda) of plants and flowers.

Gang of Six (chabbaggiya): the six bhikkhus frequently mentioned as being guilty of various Vinaya offences. These bhikkhus—Assaji, Punabbasu, Panduka, Lohitaka, Mettiya, and Bhummaja—were notorious for causing trouble.

Gaṅgā: the modern Ganges River.

garula (Sanskrit, garuda): an enormous supernatural bird; the implacable foe of the nāgas.

gavuta: one-fourth of a yojana.

generosity (dāna): a virtue which confers upon the giver the double blessing of inhibiting the immoral thoughts of selfishness and of developing the pure thoughts of selflessness. Generosity is the first of the Ten Perfections and the first of the ten duties of a king. Dāna often refers to giving alms to ascetics and members of the Sangha or to the alms thus given.

good deeds (kusala kamma): the wholesome, skillful, and meritorious actions which are bound to result eventually in happiness and a favorable outcome, whereas bad deeds (akusala kamma) lead to unhappiness and unfavorable results.

Great Renunciation (abhinikkhamana): Prince Siddhattha's act of leaving home in search of Enlightenment.

hattha: a hand; a measurement, similar to a cubit; namely, the distance from the elbow to the end of the middle finger.

Himavat: the region of the Himalaya Mountains. It is said to be three hundred thousand yojanas across with eighty-four thousand peaks, the highest being five hundred yojanas tall. The region includes seven great lakes—Anotatta, Kannamunda, Rathakāra, Chaddanta, Kunāla,

Mandākinī, and Sīhappapātaka. Its forests have always been the refuge for ascetics. The region includes a mountain called Mahāpapāta where Pacceka Buddhas traditionally pass into final Nibbāna. The Himavat is inhabited by many supernatural creatures, and female nāgas go there to give birth.

impermanence (anicca): the doctrine that anything that has arisen will pass away. All conditioned things are in a constant state of flux and are of the nature to decay. Impermanence is the first of the Three Characteristics.

insight (vipassanā): the intuitive understanding of the reality of existence.

Jain: a sect of naked ascetics, followers of Nigantha Nātaputta.

jambu: a rose apple; a pink and green fruit. See Jambudīpa.

Jambudīpa: Land of the Rose Apple; the traditional name for the Indian subcontinent.

jhāna: mental absorption; a state of strong concentration in which the mind becomes fully immersed and absorbed in the chosen object of attention. There are eight jhānas (atthasamāpattiyo): four fine-material (rūpa jhāna) and four immaterial (arūpa jhāna).

kadamba: a tree with bright orange or yellow flowers, thought to reunite separated lovers.

kanavera: Indian oleander, a shrub with foul-smelling red flowers. A garland of these flowers (vajjhāmāla) was hung around the neck of a criminal on his way to execution.

kasina: an external device used to develop meditative concentration. There are ten kasinas in all: the elements—earth, water, fire, and air; the colors—blue, red, yellow, and white; and space and consciousness.

kathina: the ceremony marking the end of the rains retreat, when laypeople gather to express gratitude to the Sangha and to make a special offering of gifts, particularly new robes. Traditionally, the Sangha of a monastery receives an offering of cloth from laypeople and gives it to one of its members, who then dyes, cuts, and sews it into a robe before dawn of the following day.

Kattikā: in the Indian lunar calendar, the last month of the rainy season. It also refers to the constellation of Pleiades and to a traditional festival.

khattiya: See caste.

kinnara (female, kinnarī): a creature, half-bird and half-human, which lives in the Himavat.

kumbhanda: a low form of deva inhabiting the realm of the Four Great Kings. The name refers to a gourd or a pot (kumbha). They are so called, perhaps, because their bellies are like pots.

kuti: a bhikkhu's residence.

loving-kindness (mettā): a great regard, much deeper than goodwill, friendliness, or kindness, for all beings in all realms. It is the universal love through which one neither fears nor instills fear in any other being. Loving-kindness is the ninth of the Ten Perfections and the first of the Four Brahma Vihāras.

lower realms (apāya): woeful realms; states of deprivation; the four lowest planes of existence into which a being is reborn because of past unwholesome actions. They are: hell, the peta realm, the asura realm, and the animal realm. Of course, none of these states is permanent.

meditation (bhāvanā): mind training; mind development. There are two distinct types of meditation: tranquility (samatha) and insight (vipassanā). Tranquility meditation, which was practiced even before the Buddha's time, involves focusing the mind on an external object. Through this concentration, one can attain extraordinary powers and the jhānas. There are forty subjects suitable for tranquility meditation. Insight meditation requires concentration, but the goal is to develop purity of mind and insight into the Three Characteristics, which leads to Nibbāna. Meditation is the second section of the Noble Eightfold Path.

merit (puñña): the quality which purifies and cleanses the mind as the result of wholesome action. Accumulated merit can be shared with other beings, whenever that intention is expressed. There are ten meritorious actions:

1. generosity; 2. morality; 3. meditation; 4. reverence; 5. helping others; 6. sharing one's merit with others; 7. rejoicing in the merit of others; 8. teaching the Dhamma; 9. listening to the Dhamma; and 10. correcting one's views.

mindfulness (sati): self-collectedness; bare attention; the clear and single-minded awareness of what is actually happening in us and to us at the successive moments of perception.

morality (sīla): restraint through the precepts. For a layman, this means keeping the five or eight precepts. For an ascetic, there are additional rules, and, for a bhikkhu or a bhikkhunī, there are many more. Morality also includes all wholesome action of body, speech, and mind. Morality is the second of the Ten Perfections, the second of the ten duties of a king, and the first section of the Noble Eightfold Path.

nāga: a great supernatural serpent, capable of assuming the form of a human or a deva. The traditional enemy of the nāga is the garula. Sometimes a nāga swallows stones, hoping that, in that way, it will be too heavy to be carried away by a garula.

neem: a tree common in South Asia, considered beneficial for its medicinal properties. All parts of the tree are extremely bitter. Neem twigs are commonly used to make toothsticks for cleaning the teeth.

Nibbāna: Enlightenment; arahatship; the fourth path; liberation; the freeing of the mind from defilements (kilesas); the end of the round of rebirth (samsāra). The term refers to the extinguishing of a fire, so it also connotes stilling, cooling, and peace.

Nikāya: division, group. A group of texts within the Sutta Pitaka, the Collection of Discourses, of the Tipitaka.

Noble Eightfold Path (ariya magga): the Fourth Noble Truth. The factors are: 1. Right View; 2. Right Intention; 3. Right Speech; 4. Right Action; 5. Right Livelihood; 6. Right Effort; 7. Right Mindfulness; and 8. Right Concentration; This Path can be divided into three sections: Morality, 3–5; Meditation, 6–8; and Wisdom, 1–2.

non-self (anattā): the doctrine that neither within nor outside of the bodily and mental phenomena of existence can be found anything that, in the ultimate sense, can be regarded as a self-existing, real ego-entity, soul, or self. Non-self is the third of the Three Characteristics.

Pacceka Buddha: a fully enlightened Buddha who has attained perfect insight, but neither creates a Sangha nor establishes a Sāsana. Offerings to a Pacceka Buddha are of great efficacy. A Pacceka Buddha can also grant boons and make predictions.

panic: a type of millet which was made into a gruel. It was also used as a medicine.

Parinibbāna: a synonym for Nibbāna, though often used to refer to the passing away of a fully-enlightened one, particularly of a Supreme Buddha or a Pacceka Buddha.

path and fruit (magga-phala): the attainment (path) of one of the four stages of Enlightenment and the result (fruit) thereof.

patience (khanti): forbearance which includes enduring any suffering inflicted upon oneself by others. Patience is the sixth of the Ten Perfections and the ninth of the ten duties of a king.

Pātimokkha: the code of discipline for bhikkhus and bhikkhunīs, which is recited at every full and new moon.

Perfection (pāramī): See Ten Perfections.

peta: a hungry ghost; a miserable being born in the peta realm, one of the four lower realms. Petas are often depicted with huge bellies and tiny mouths which do not allow them to eat enough to ease their hunger. They are completely dependent for food and clothes on merit shared with them.

Plowing Festival: a festival in ancient India in which the king used a ceremonial plow to mark the beginning of the plowing season. Once, when Prince Siddhattha was a boy, he sat under a jambu tree during this festival and, for the first time, practiced meditation. The shadow of the tree continued to provide shade all day. Seeing this, King Suddhodana paid obeisance to his son.

precepts (sīla): virtue; morality; the training rules voluntarily undertaken to restrain one from doing unwholesome actions.

(a) five precepts (pañcasīla): 1. to abstain from killing, 2. to abstain from stealing, 3. to abstain from sexual misconduct; 4. to abstain from lying; and 5. to abstain from taking alcohol and drugs which cloud the mind. These are considered by Buddhists to be the minimum code of morality for a human being.

(b) eight precepts (atthasīla): the five precepts, except that the third becomes "to abstain from all sexual activity," plus 6. to abstain from eating after noon; 7. to abstain from indulging in music, singing, and dancing and from adorning the body; and 8. to abstain from using a large or high bed or chair. These are usually undertaken by laypeople on Uposatha days.

rains retreat (vassa): the period from July to October, corresponding roughly to the monsoon rainy season, when every bhikkhu and bhik-khunī is required to stay in a single place, without traveling, unless there is an urgent reason to do so.

rebirth (punabbhava): renewed existence in samsāra; the arising of a new group of the five aggregates after death. The consciousness aris-ing in the new person is neither identical to nor different from the old consciousness, but is part of a causal continuum with it. Rebirth, which is conditioned by intentional action (kamma), may take place on any plane. [See The Thirty-one Planes of Existence]

renunciation (nekkhamma): giving up certain luxuries and worldly pleasures. Ultimately, renunciation, which implies freedom from sensual lust, is withdrawal from worldly life and pleasures by adopting the ascetic life to practice meditation and to make spiritual attainments. Renuncia-tion is the third of the Ten Perfections.

requisites: (a) eight requisites (attha parikkharāni): the things which a member of the Sangha should have. They are: three robes, an almsbowl, a razor, a needle, a belt, and a water strainer.

(b) four requisites (cattāro paccaya): the things a member of the Sangha needs to sustain himself or herself. They are: robes, food, a dwelling place, and medicine.

Sakka's throne: the marble seat of the king of the devas, located in Sudhammā Hall. It grows hot and begins to shake for two different reasons. The first is the occurrence of a great injustice which requires Sakka's intervention. The second is that someone is performing an extremely meritorious act, which indicates, perhaps, that that person is striving to be reborn as Sakka in Tāvatimsa, in which case Sakka would be on the verge of losing his office.

sāmanera: a novice monk (sāmanerī, a novice nun), who keeps ten precepts, which are the eight precepts, with the seventh split into two, plus (10) to abstain from accepting gold and silver (money). A sāmanera or a sāmanerī is a candidate for higher ordination as a bhikkhu or a bhikkhunī.

samsāra: the round of existence through rebirth.

Sangha: the Buddha's order of bhikkhus and bhikkhunīs.

sāsana: dispensation; the legacy of a Supreme Buddha; the Buddhist religion. [See Dhamma]

second path: See four stages of Enlightenment.

seven precious things: gold, silver, pearls, gems, lapis lazuli, diamonds, and coral.

silk-cotton tree: a very large tree related to the kapok tree.

sudda: See caste.

suffering (dukkha): the doctrine that all phenomena and all experience are inherently unsatisfactory and lead to mental anguish. Suffering is the first of the Four Noble Truths and the second of the Three Characteristics.

Sutta: Discourse; a sermon attributed to the Buddha or to one of his closest disciples. The Sutta Pitaka, the Discourse Collection, is the second division of the Tipitaka. It is divided into five Nikāyas. The first four Nikāyas contain most of the actual discourses, or suttas. The Jātakas are included in the last Nikāya, Khuddaka Nikāya, or Minor Texts.

sympathetic joy (muditā): taking delight in the happiness or good fortune of others. Sympathetic joy is the third of the Four Brahma Vihāras.

tank: a man-made reservoir, usually rectangular, often with stone steps leading to the water for bathers.

Tathāgata: literally, "Thus Come One," an epithet which the Buddha used to describe himself.

Tāvatimsa: the Heaven of the Thirty-Three; the realm of Sakka, king of the devas.

ten courses of unwholesome action (dasa-akusala-kamma-patha): 1. killing any being; 2. stealing; 3. committing adultery; 4. lying; 5. slandering; 6. using harsh speech; 7. engaging in frivolous gossip; 8. being covetous; 9. having ill-will; and having wrong view. Abstaining from these constitutes the ten courses of wholesome action (dasa-kusala-kamma-patha).

ten duties of a king: the ten qualities a king must have to be considered a righteous ruler. They are: 1. generosity (dāna); 2. morality (sīla); 3. sacrifice (pariccāga), willingness to sacrifice everything—comfort, fame, even his life—for the people; 4. honesty (ajjava), integrity—neither fearing some nor favoring others and never taking recourse in any crooked or doubtful means to achieve one's ends; 5. kindness (maddava), gentleness which tempers firmness, so that a ruler is neither harsh nor cruel; 6. austerity of habits (tapa), self-control, shunning indulgence in sensual pleasures, and keeping the five senses under control; 7. freedom from ill-will (akkodha), bearing no grudge against anyone and acting with forbearance and love; 8. harmlessness (avihimsa), non-violence and a commitment to peace; 9. patience (khanti); and 10. non-opposition or uprightness (avirodha), ruling in harmony with the people, not opposing their will, and cultivating the spirit of amity among the people. (A different list is given in the text of Tale 210.)

Ten Perfections (dasa pāramī): the ten qualities of character which must be developed completely for one to attain Buddhahood, but of which the partial development is meritorious for any being. They are: 1. generosity (dāna); 2. morality (sīla); 3. renunciation (nekkhamma); 4. wisdom (paññā); 5. energy (viriya); 6. patience (khanti); 7. truthfulness (sacca); 8. determination (adhitthāna); 9. loving-kindness (mettā); and 10. equanimity (upekkhā). Each of these is given a separate entry in this glossary.

third path: See four stages of Enlightenment.

thirty-two parts of the body: one of the meditation subjects taught by the Buddha. They are: 1. hair of the head (kesa); 2. hair of the body (loma); 3. nails (nakha); 4. teeth (danta); 5. skin (taco); 6. flesh (mamsa); 7. sinew (nahāru); 8. bone (atthi); 9. marrow (atthimiñja); 10. kidneys (vakka); 11. heart (hadaya); 12. liver (yakana); 13. membrane (kilomaka); 14. spleen (pihaka); 15. lungs; (papphāsa); 16. intestines (anta); 17. mesentery (antaguna); 18. stomach (udariya); 19. feces (karīsa); 20. brain (matthalunga); 21. bile (pitta); 22. phlegm (semha); 23. pus (pubba); 24. blood (lohita); 25. sweat (seda); 26. lymph (meda); 27. tears (assu); 28 serum (vasa); 29. saliva (khela); 30. nasal mucous (singhānika); 31. synovial fluid (lasika); and 32. urine (mutta).

Three Characteristics (ti-lakkhana): the three basic facts of existence which are inherent in all conditioned phenomena. They are: 1. impermanence (anicca); 2. suffering (dukkha); and 3. non-self (anattā).

tinduka: an Indian persimmon.

Tipitaka: (literally, "Three Baskets"), the Buddhist canon; the collection of primary texts which form the doctrinal foundation of Buddhism. The three divisions are: 1. Vinaya Pitaka, Book of Discipline; 2. Sutta Pitaka, Book of Discourses; 3. Abhidhamma Pitaka, Book of Abstract Teaching. After the Buddha's Parinibbāna, the Teaching was arranged as the Tipitaka at the First Buddhist Council, a gathering of five hundred arahats. All the texts were memorized and, for about five hundred years, were transmitted and preserved orally. They were first written down in Sri Lanka about 100 B.C.E. when, due to hardship and famine, the number of bhikkhus declined to the point that it was feared that the Teaching would be lost.

toothstick: See neem.

Triple Gem (ti-ratana): the Teacher (Buddha), the Teaching (Dhamma), and the Order (Sangha).

truthfulness (sacca): keeping one's word and fulfilling a promise at any cost. It is said that a Bodhisatta may, at times, violate the other precepts but that he never tells a lie nor forsakes truthfulness. Truthfulness is the seventh of the Ten Perfections.

twenty-one wrong means of livelihood (ekavisati anesana): practices which bhikkhus are forbidden to perform. They are: 1. medical practice; 2. acting as a messenger; 3. doing things at the behest of laymen; 4. lancing boils; 5. giving oil for medical application; 6. giving emetics; 7. giving purgatives; 8. preparing oil for nose-treatment; 9. preparing oil for medicine; 10. presenting bamboos; 11. presenting leaves; 12. presenting flowers; 13. presenting fruits; 14. presenting soap-clay; 15. presenting toothsticks; 16. presenting water for washing the face; 17. presenting clay-powder; 18. using flattering speech; 19. speaking half-truths; 20. fondling children; and 21. running errands.

Uposatha: a day reserved for religious observance, corresponding to the phases of the moon (one, two, or four). In Buddhist practice, on Uposatha days, lay people gather to listen to the Dhamma and to observe eight precepts. On the new-moon and full-moon Uposatha days, bhikkhus assemble to recite the Patimokkha rules.

Veramba wind: a strong wind which blows at a great height.

vessa: See caste.

Verocanamani: the octagonal gem which Sakka gave to King Kusa (Tale 206). It is mentioned twice in Tale 216.

Vinaya: Discipline; texts concerning the rules of conduct governing the Sangha. The Vinaya Pitaka, the Collection of Discipline, is the first division of the Tipitaka. The Vinaya Pitaka also includes the story behind the origin of each rule. The rules are summarized in the Pātimokkha. There are 227 rules for bhikkhus and 311 for bhikkhunīs. Dhamma-vinaya is the Buddha's own term for the religion he founded.

water of donation (dakkhinodaka): water which the donor pours over the right hand of the recipient when a gift is made, indicating that the gift is freely given and dedicating the merit gained.

wisdom (paññā): right understanding of the real nature of the world; seeing things as they really are; ultimately, insight into the Three Characteristics. Wisdom is the fourth of the Ten Perfections and the third section of the Noble Eightfold Path.

yakkha (female, yakkhinī): a demon; an ogre; a superhuman being, often hostile to man. Some yakkhas resemble devas, but others resemble petas. They have strange characteristics; for example, they have red eyes, they cannot wink, and they cast no shadow. Sometimes, they are said to be repelled by palm leaves and iron. Their king is Vessavana, one of the Four Great Kings.

yojana: the distance a team of oxen can travel in one day; about twelve miles.

Glossary of Personal Names

This glossary includes those who were contemporaries of the Buddha. It does not include the innumerable characters who appear in the stories of the past. The two exceptions are Kassapa Buddha and Vipassi Buddha. (The numbers in parentheses at the end of each entry indicate the tales in this anthology in which the individual appears.)

Ajātasattu: the son of Bimbisāra, king of Magadha. Prince Ajātasattu became a generous supporter of Devadatta, who encouraged Ajātasattu to kill his father and to usurp the throne. Ajātasattu also aided Devadatta in his attempts to kill the Buddha. After Devadatta's death, King Ajātasattu repented and became a devoted follower of the Buddha, but his parricide prevented him from making any attainments. After a long rule, Ajātasattu was killed by his own son, Udāya, who had been born on the day that Bimbisāra died. According to the commentaries, Ajātasattu was reborn in hell, where he will suffer for 60,000 years, eventually becoming a Pacceka Buddha. (56, 62, 94, 130, 132, 179, 193, 212)

Ajita Kesakambala: one of the six teachers who were contemporaries of the Buddha. He taught materialism, stating that all is annihilated at death. (62)

Ālavaka: a yakkha in Ālavi, thirty yojanas from Sāvatthī. Vessavana, king of the yakkhas, had given him permission to eat anyone who stepped into the shade of the huge banyan tree near his mansion. The king of Ālavi, while hunting, did so, but avoided death by promising to send one victim daily. For twelve years, he sent prisoners, and later children. Finally, the only offering available was the king's own son. With compassion for the prince, the king, and the yakkha, the Buddha went there, but Ālavaka was away. When the gatekeeper went to inform Ālavaka, the Buddha entered the mansion and began teaching the yakkha's wives. Ālavaka returned and tried to kill the Buddha, first by frightening him and then by exhausting him. After going out from and reentering Ālavaka's house three times, the Buddha refused to leave again. Ālavaka then asked the Buddha a series of questions which had been handed down to him from Kassapa Buddha. The Buddha easily answered all of them. Ālavaka was delighted. He understood everything the Buddha said and attained the first path. The next morning, the king's men arrived and gave the prince to the yakkha. Ashamed of his former

445

practices, Ālavaka handed the child to the Buddha. The king gave the reformed yakkha a special house, and the people gave regular vegetarian offerings. His conversion is one of the Eight Great Victories of the Buddha referred to in the Jayamangala Gāthā. (181, 216)

Ambattha: a brahmin, proud of his lineage and his learning, and the follower of another teacher. When the Buddha taught the Ambattha Sutta (Dīgha Nikāya, 3), Ambattha's teacher and other students were converted, but not Ambattha himself. According to the commentary, the Buddha knew that Ambattha would not benefit and, therefore, wasted no time on him. (216)

Ānanda: an eminent bhikkhu; the last personal attendant of the Buddha [See Tale 177]; "Treasurer of the Teaching." He was a Sākyan prince and a first cousin of the Buddha. Soon after ordaining, Venerable Ānanda attained the first path, but it was only after the Buddha's Parinibbāna, just in time to attend the First Buddhist Council, that Venerable Ānanda attained arahatship. Most suttas begin "Thus have I heard" because, at that council, Venerable Ānanda recited each discourse as he had heard it from the Buddha.

Venerable Ānanda was foremost among the bhikkhus in 1. having heard many of the Buddha's discourses; 2. having a good memory; 3. having mastery over the sequential structure of the teachings; 4. being steadfast in study; and 5. being the Buddha's attendant.

Venerable Ānanda was accomplished in seven ways: 1. in the doctrine; 2. in knowledge; 3. in knowledge of causes; 4. in investigation; 5. in having an eidetic memory with penetrative comprehension; 6. in applied attention; and 7. in the potentiality of Buddhahood. (5, 6, 8, 10, 14, 15, 16, 17, 20, 30, 32, 33, 34, 36, 40, 42, 55, 60, 61, 63, 65, 66, 67, 68, 73, 75, 77, 80, 82, 88, 91, 94, 95, 96, 98, 99, 104, 105, 106, 109, 112, 113, 116, 119, 121, 126, 130, 136, 144, 145, 147, 148, 150, 152, 153, 154, 155, 156, 157, 158, 160, 162, 163, 165, 170, 171, 172, 173, 175, 176, 177, 179, 181, 182, 183, 185, 187, 188, 189, 190, 196, 197, 198, 199, 203, 206, 207, 208, 210, 211, 213, 214, 215, 216)

Anāthapindika: a wealthy merchant, the great patron of the Buddha who built Jetavana Monastery near Sāvatthī. He appears in the occasions for many of the stories and attained the first path, but he is not mentioned in the identifications. (1, 10, 21, 22, 36, 98, 105, 108, 134, 136, 161, 182,)

Angulimāla: a bhikkhu. He was a serial murderer who was converted by the Buddha and became an arahat. [See Tale 207] His conversion is one of the Eight Great Victories of the Buddha referred to in the Jayamangala Gāthā. (29, 147, 181, 207, 216)

Anuruddha: an eminent bhikkhu; a Sākyan prince and first cousin of the Buddha. He was foremost among bhikkhus endowed with the divine eye. [See Tale 8] (8, 81, 95, 102, 167, 170, 190, 191, 197, 207, 210, 211, 215, 217)

Asita: a brahmin ascetic. A few days after Prince Siddhattha was born, Asita went to the palace. Instead of paying respect, the baby turned and touched the ascetic's head with his feet, signifying that he was the nobler. Asita smiled and then wept. He smiled because he knew that Prince Siddhattha would become a Buddha. He wept because he was too old to live to become his disciple. (217)

Baka-Brahmā: a deva in the Brahma heavens. Correcting his wrong view is one of the Eight Great Victories of the Buddha referred to in the Jayamangala Gāthā. [See Tale 151] (136, 151, 181, 216)

Bandhula: a son of a chieftain of Malla, who became commander-in-chief of King Pasenadi of Kosala. His wife's name was Mallikā [See Tale 179] (179)

Bhaddaji: a bhikkhu. He was the son of a wealthy merchant of Bhaddiya, a city in Anga. The Buddha went there to teach him. After hearing the Buddha's discourse, Bhaddaji attained arahatship. When the Buddha explained to Bhaddaji's father that, on that day, Bhaddaji had either to ordain or to pass away, the merchant let his son ordain. (This is related in the occasion to Jātaka 264, which is not included in this collection) This is one of the few instances in which a layman became an arahat. [See Suddhodana] (214)

Bhaddakaccānā: See Yasodharā.

Bhaddā-Kāpilānī: an eminent bhikkhunī. She was the daughter of a brahmin in Sāgala, a city in Madda. She was married, but the marriage was never consummated. (This took place very much as in Tales 129 and 206.) Her husband was named Pippali-mānava. They left the home-life together. He ordained as Venerable Mahā-Kassapa, and she lived as an ascetic until the bhikkhunī order was established. Soon after ordaining as a bhikkhunī, she attained arahatship. She was foremost among bhikkhunīs who could recall former lives. (210)

Bhaddiya: an eminent bhikkhu. He was a Sākyan prince. He was foremost among the bhikkhus of aristocratic birth. [See Tale 8] (8)

Bimbisāra: the king of Magadha and a strong supporter of the Buddha. He attained the first path. He was killed by his son Ajātasattu. (62, 132, 188, 193, 212, 214)

Channa: a bhikkhu. He was born on the same day as Prince Siddhattha and became his charioteer. He accompanied the prince at the time of the Great Renunciation, but returned to Kapilavatthu. Refused permission to leave the household life, he did not ordain until the Buddha returned to Kapilavatthu. Because of his closeness to the Buddha, he became conceited and could neither overcome his pride nor fulfill his monk's duties. He was chastised and punished for his obstinacy several times, the last instance being just before the Buddha's Parinibbāna. When Venerable Ānanda informed him of the Buddha's declaration that he was to be shunned by the Sangha, he was completely tamed and attained arahatship, at which point the penalty automatically expired. (142, 198, 217)

Ciñcā-Mānavikā: a female ascetic in Sāvatthī. At the instigation of rival ascetics, she accused the Buddha of making her pregnant. Exposing her lie is one of the Eight Great Victories of the Buddha referred to in the Jayamangala Gāthā. [See Tale 182] (80, 182, 217)

Citta: a merchant in Macchikāsanda, a town in Kāsi. When Venerable Mahānāma visited Macchikāsanda, Citta built a monastery in his garden, Ambātakārāma, which he presented to the Sangha. While listening to Venerable Mahānāma teach the Dhamma there, Citta attained the third path. He was foremost among laymen in teaching the Dhamma. (190)

Culla-Nandikā: nothing further seems to be known. (216)

Dabba: an eminent bhikkhu. He was the son of a Mallan family in Anupiya. He was born while his dead mother was being cremated on the funeral pyre. He heard the Buddha teach when he was seven years old and asked to be ordained. Attaining arahatship at the age of seven, he had extraordinary powers. He assumed the post of meals' designator and was very good at it. He was foremost among bhikkhus in assigning lodgings. [See Tale 5] (5)

Devadatta: one of the Buddha's cousins. He became a bhikkhu along with the other Sākyan princes. [See Tale 8] He was a rival of the Buddha, and tried to kill him several times. He also created a schism in the Sangha. Finally, he was swallowed by the earth and fell into hell. The origin of the implacable enmity which Devadatta felt toward the Bodhisatta and the Buddha is related in Tale 3. (1, 3, 8, 9, 10, 13, 18, 28, 32, 44, 51, 54, 56, 57, 62, 68, 71, 81, 85, 90, 91, 93, 94, 95, 115, 118, 128, 130, 135, 140, 141, 153, 164, 173, 182, 183, 187, 193, 198, 199, 201, 204, 212, 213, 214, 216, 217)

Dhammadinnā: an eminent bhikkhunī. She was the wife of Visākha of Rājagaha. When Visākha heard the Buddha teach, he attained the third path. On returning home, he gave his consent for his wife to ordain. She became a bhikkhunī, stayed in a nunnery near Rājagaha, and soon attained arahatship. Later, she returned to Rājagaha to revere the Buddha and taught the Dhamma to her former husband. She was foremost among bhikkhunīs in teaching the Dhamma. (217)

Dhanuggaha-tissa: a bhikkhu. He was an officer in King Pasenadi's army. No more is known of him. [See Tale 193] (193)

Ditthamangalikā: no one with this name can be identified at the time of the Buddha. (195, 216)

Gotama: the clan name of Prince Siddhattha. After leaving home, the Bodhisatta was called Gotama the Ascetic during the six years before his Enlightenment. Even after his Enlightenment, he was called Gotama the Ascetic by followers of other teachers. The Buddha is called Gotama Buddha to distinguish him from other Buddhas.

Jīvaka: the physician to King Bimbisāra and to the Buddha. He became a prominent lay follower of the Buddha and built a monastery for the Buddha in his mango grove in Rājagaha. After the death of King Bimbisāra, Jīvaka continued serving King Ajātasattu. (4, 62, 199)

Kāludāyi: an eminent bhikkhu. He was the son of a Sākyan minister. He was born on the same day as Prince Siddhattha and grew up with him. After King Suddhodana learned of his son's Enlightenment, he sent ministers to invite him to Kapilavatthu. The first nine times, the messengers ordained, became arahats, and forgot the king's request. Finally, the king ordered Kāludāyi to make the invitation, but allowed him to join the Sangha beforehand. Kāludāyi became a bhikkhu and attained arahatship, but, at the proper time, he informed the Buddha of his father's request. Kāludāyi was foremost among bhikkhus at reconciling families. (190)

Kassapa Buddha: the twenty-fourth Buddha and the third Buddha of the present eon. (23, 79, 95, 169, 181, 207, 217)

Khemā: an eminent bhikkhunī; one of the two chief female disciples of the Buddha. As the chief consort of King Bimbisāra, she was so proud of her golden skin and her beauty that she would not visit the Buddha. Finally, the king persuaded her to go to Veluvana. The Buddha conjured up the image of a woman as beautiful as a deva, who stood facing him. As Khemā gazed at this woman, whose extraordinary beauty far exceeded her own, the woman passed from youth to extreme old age and died. This so dismayed Khemā that, when the Buddha preached to her on the vanity of lust, she attained arahatship. With the consent of Bimbisāra, she entered the Sangha. She was foremost among bhikkhunīs in insight. (138, 209, 217)

Khujjuttarā: a slave woman belonging to Queen Sāmāvatī, who was one of the wives of King Udena. When Khujjuttarā heard the Buddha teach, she attained the first path and, subsequently, taught the queen. She was foremost among laywomen for her extensive knowledge. It is her record of the Buddha's teaching that forms the Itivuttaka, part of the Khuddaka Nikāya. (138, 190, 206)

Kisāgotamī: an eminent bhikkhunī. She came from a poor family in Sāvatthī but married into a rich family. She was disdainfully treated until she bore a son. When the boy died, just as he became old enough to run about, Kisāgotamī was so distraught with grief that she carried his body here and there, seeking medicine to revive him. People laughed at her, but one wise man directed her to the Buddha. The Buddha asked her to bring him a handful of mustard seed from a house where no one had ever died. In the course of her search, she grasped the truth, laid the child's body in the charnel ground, and requested admission to the Sangha. She attained the first path, and, soon after, became an arahat. She was foremost among bhikkhunīs in wearing coarse robes. (217)

Kokālika: a bhikkhu. The commentaries differ on his identification. In some sources there are two bhikkhus with this name, so they are called Culla-Kokālika and Mahā-Kokālika. In other sources, all references are to the same person.

Culla-Kokālika was one of the chief supporters of Devadatta and a great friend of the bhikkhunī Thulla-Nandā, who also supported Devadatta. Once, Culla-Kokālika complained that he had never been allowed to recite the Dhamma. When the monks gave him the chance, he put on brightly colored robes and went to the assembly. He tried to speak, but perspiration poured from his body, and he babbled incoherently. His confusion proved that his learning was a sham. (57; though Kokālika is not mentioned, the same incident is related in 9, 44, 68, and 183)

Mahā-Kokālika quarreled with Venerable Moggallāna and Venerable Sāriputta and, as a result, fell into hell. [See Tale 88] (88, 101, 131, 186)

Kosala-Devī: the sister of King Pasenadi, a wife of King Bimbisāra, and the mother of King Ajātasattu. (132, 193)

Kumāra-Kassapa: an eminent bhikkhu. He became a sāmanera at the age of seven. He was foremost among bhikkhus in eloquence. [See Tale 10] (10)

Kundalī: a bhikkhunī with the name Bhaddā-Kundalakesā. She was the daughter of a wealthy merchant in Rājagaha. One day, she saw a young man being led to his execution and fell in love with him. Her father bribed a guard and had the man released to her. From that point on, her life parallels Tale 161. (His name was also Sattuka.) After pushing Sattuka over the cliff, Kundalī joined the order of Ajivikas (a group of naked ascetics). At her ordination, all her hair was pulled out with a comb. It grew back curly (kundali), hence her name. She left the Ājīvikas and wandered from city to city, seeking debates, in the manner described in Tale 111. In Sāvatthī, Venerable Sāriputta challenged her and converted her in the same way as in that tale. Venerable Sāriputta sent her to the Buddha, who taught her a discourse, and she attained arahatship. She was foremost among bhikkhunīs in swift intuition. (216)

Kutadanta: a learned brahmin of Magadha. The Buddha arrived in his village while Kūtadanta was making preparations for a great sacrifice, and, wishing this sacrifice to be successful, Kūtadanta consulted the Buddha. The Buddha taught the Kūtadanta Sutta (Dīgha Nikāya 5) to him, and he attained the first path. The conversion of Kūtadanta is considered one of the great spiritual victories of the Buddha. (216)

Lakuntaka: an eminent bhikkhu. He was born in a wealthy family in Sāvatthī. Though extremely short (lakuntaka = dwarf), he was very handsome and had a beautiful voice. Taking the body as the object of meditation, he achieved insight and attained arahatship. He was foremost among bhikkhus in having a sweet voice. (84)

Laludāyi: a bhikkhu, notorious for saying the wrong thing at the wrong time and place and for arguing with learned bhikkhus. He is cited as an example of a person who did no good either to himself or to others. (5, 47, 87)

Losaka Tissa: a bhikkhu who attained arahatship, but failed to receive enough to eat. [See Tale 23] (23)

Madhuvasettha: a brahmin of Sāketā in Kosala. His son, Mahānāga, became a bhikkhu and attained arahatship. (190)

Mahā-Brahmā: a great deva. This refers not only to a particular being, as indicated in Tale 195, but, perhaps, to any resident of the highest Brahma heavens. (195)

Mahā-Kappina: an eminent bhikkhu, He was the king of Kukkuta-vata, a large kingdom northwest of Takkasilā. Every morning, he sent men to question travelers about news of distant lands. One day, when traders from Sāvatthī were asked for news, they replied, "Sire, we cannot tell you with unwashed mouths." After rinsing their mouths and clasping their hands, they reported the appearance of the Buddha. Mahā-Kappina rewarded the traders, renounced the world, and went to find the Buddha. With an asseveration of truth, he and his companions crossed three rivers without getting the horses' hooves wet. The Buddha perceived them with his divine eye and met them on the bank of the Candabhāgā River, where he taught them the Dhamma, and they all became arahats. Venerable Mahā-Kappina was foremost among bhikkhus in teaching other bhikkhus. (181)

Mahā-Kassapa: an eminent bhikkhu. He was born a brahmin named Pippali in the village of Mahātittha in Magadha. He didn't want to marry, but was finally wed to a like-minded woman, Bhaddā-Kāpilānī.

(This took place very much as in Tales 129 and 206.) Never consummating their marriage, they slept separated by a chain of flowers and left the home-life together, When they came to a crossroads, they agreed that it was not proper to stay together and went in opposite directions. The earth trembled at their virtue. The Buddha felt the earthquake, understood its meaning, and traveled three gavutas to meet Pippali. Seated under a tree, Pippali listened to the Dhamma and was ordained as Mahā-Kassapa, On their way to Rājagaha, the Buddha wanted to sit, so Venerable Mahā-Kassapa folded his outer robe as a seat. The Buddha felt the robe and praised its softness. Venerable Mahā-Kassapa offered it to him. "And what would you wear?" asked the Buddha. Venerable Mahā-Kassapa requested the Buddha's rag robe, saying that he would prize it above the whole world. Venerable Mahā-Kassapa was foremost among bhikkhus in upholding minute observances of form. After the Buddha's Parinibbāna, Venerable Mahā-Kassapa called together five hundred arahats for the First Buddhist Council in Rājagaha. (102, 124, 126, 168, 175, 181, 190, 191, 207, 210, 212)

Mahā-Kosala: the king of Kosala and father of King Pasenadi. (132, 193)

Mahā-Māyā: the mother of Prince Siddhattha and the wife of King Suddhodana. As the mother of a Bodhisatta in his last life, she died seven days after the baby was born. She was reborn in Tusita heaven. After the Twin Miracle, she descended to Tāvatimsa to listen to the Buddha teach the Abhidhamma. [See Tale 188] (7, 20, 65, 83, 102, 163, 176, 188, 202, 206, 207, 209, 212, 217)

Mahā-Pajāpati-Gotamī: the first bhikkhunī. She was Mahā-Māyā's sister and was also married to King Suddhodana. After Mahā-Māyā's death, Mahā-Pajāpati-Gotamī nursed and cared for Prince Siddhattha. After having attained the first path, she requested ordination, but the Buddha refused twice. Finally, after Venerable Ānanda interceded, the Buddha agreed and ordained her as the first bhikkhunī, and she soon attained arahatship. She was foremost among bhikkhunīs in seniority and experience. (91, 141)

Mahānāma: a Sākyan king. He was the elder brother of Anuruddha and a great patron of the Buddha and the Sangha. He sent Vasabbha-Khattiyā, his daughter by a slave woman, to King Pasenadi. [See Tale

179] The Buddha declared that Mahānāma was foremost among laymen in giving choice alms to the bhikkhus. (7, 72, 179)

Makkhali Gosala: one of the six teachers who were contemporaries of the Buddha. He taught fatalism, stating that man is powerless in the face of predestination. (62)

Mallikā (1): the chief queen of King Pasenadi. She was the daughter of a garland maker in Kosala (mala = garland). At age sixteen, on the day she offered a portion of sour gruel to the Buddha, King Pasenadi made her his chief queen. She was always devoted to the Buddha, and, in her knowledge of the Dhamma, she was wiser than the king. She was one of the Buddha's outstanding female lay disciples. (33, 114, 119, 160, 197, 200)

Mallikā (2): the wife of Bandhula, who was King Pasenadi's commander-in-chief. [See Tale 179] (179)

Mantidatta: a bhikkhu. He was an officer in King Pasenadi's army. No more is known of him. [See Tale 193] (193)

Māra: a deva. Residing in the highest heaven of the sensuous worlds, he is the lord of the world of passion. He attacked the Bodhisatta with a great army hoping to prevent his Enlightenment under the Bodhi tree. Māra's elephant is named Girimekhala. The Buddha's victory over Māra is one of the Eight Great Victories of the Buddha referred to in the Jayamangala Gāthā. (22, 71, 204)

Mātali: Sakka's charioteer. (16, 95, 175, 181, 211)

Moggallāna: an eminent bhikkhu; one of the two chief disciples of the Buddha. He was born as Kolita in a village near Rājagaha on the same day as Sāriputta. The two were childhood friends and ordained together. Venerable Moggallāna was foremost among bhikkhus in extraordinary powers. [See Sāriputta] (9, 21, 32, 34, 57, 63, 64, 68, 85, 88, 101, 121, 128, 142, 149, 175, 185, 188, 189, 190, 191, 209, 212, 213, 214, 215)

Nālāgiri: an elephant from the royal stables of Rājagaha. In an attempt to kill the Buddha, Devadatta instructed the mahouts to give Nālāgiri extra alcohol and to release him on the street while the Buddha was going on his almsrounds. As Nālāgiri was charging, Venerable Ānanda stepped in front to protect the Buddha. Using his extraordinary power, the Buddha forced Venerable Ānanda aside and extended loving-kindness toward the elephant. Tamed by that loving-kindness, Nālāgiri knelt at the Buddha's feet, and the Buddha taught him the Dhamma. If Nālāgiri had not been an animal, he would have attained the first path. The townspeople were so impressed that they threw their ornaments and jewels on the elephant, completely covering him. From then on, he was called Dhanapāla (Treasurer). The Buddha's taming of Nālāgiri is one of the Eight Great Victories of the Buddha referred to in the Jayamangala Gāthā. (91, 130, 141, 198)

Nanda: an eminent bhikkhu. Being the son of King Suddhodana and Mahā-Pajapati-Gotamī, he was the Buddha's half-brother. When the Buddha returned to Kapilavatthu, he gave his bowl to Nanda to carry. Although Nanda was to marry that day, the Buddha asked him to ordain, and he could not refuse. Nanda ordained and became an arahat. He was foremost among bhikkhus in self-control. [See Tale 76] (76, 90, 102)

Nigantha Nātaputta: one of the six teachers who were contemporaries of the Buddha; now known as Mahāvīra, the founder of Jainism. He taught a doctrine of extreme restraint in order to avoid suffering, which is the result of wrong action. (62, 133)

Pakudha Kaccāyana: one of the six teachers who were contemporaries of the Buddha. He taught eternalism, stating that matter, pleasure, pain, and the soul are eternal and do not interact. (62)

Pārileyya: an elephant. Once, when two groups of bhikkhus refused to settle their quarrel, the Buddha went to stay alone in the forest near Kosambi. While he was there, Pārileyya and a monkey carefully looked after him. This incident is mentioned in Tale 143. It was on this occasion that the Buddha also told Tale 155. (190)

Pasenadi: the king of Kosala. Quite early in the Buddha's ministry, King Pasenadi became his follower. His devotion to the Buddha lasted until the king's death. (7, 10, 23, 28, 33, 40, 63, 82, 83, 98, 104, 114, 119, 132, 158, 160, 162, 179, 193, 197, 200, 205, 207)

Patācārā (1): a bhikkhunī. She had three sisters and a brother, Saccaka. Their parents were both wandering debaters, who had been encouraged by the Licchavi princes to marry and to settle in Vesāli. Patacara and her sisters became wandering debaters, too, but they were defeated by

Venerable Sāriputta. They became bhikkhunīs, and Venerable Patācārā attained arahatship. [See Tale 111] (111)

Patācārā (2): an eminent bhikkhunī. She was the daughter of a rich merchant of Sāvatthī and eloped with a servant. When her first baby was due, she wanted to return to her parents' house. She and her husband set out, but, after she delivered on the way there, they went back home. The second time she became pregnant, she again went into labor on the road. When a storm arose, her husband went to get branches to make a shelter and was killed by a snake. After Patācārā found his body, she continued to Sāvatthī with her two sons. She was weak after childbirth, but she had to cross the flooded Aciravatī River. Carrying her newborn baby across, she laid him down and started back for her elder son. In midstream, she saw a hawk swoop down and snatch the baby. She shouted to scare the bird away, but her shouts were misunderstood by the toddler, who thought she was calling him and ran toward her. Before she could reach him, he fell into the water and was swept away. Devastated by her triple loss, she reached Sāvatthī, only to learn that her parents and brother had also been killed when their house collapsed in the storm. Seeing their funeral pyre, she went mad and began raving with grief and wandering naked though the city. (Patācārā means "garment walker.") Eventually, she reached Jetavana, where, restored to presence of mind by the Buddha's Teaching, she attained the first path. She was ordained and attained arahatship. She was foremost among bhikkhunīs in knowledge of the Vinaya. (217)

Pilinda Vaccha: an eminent bhikkhu who was well-known for his extraordinary powers. He was a brahmin with some magical abilities, but when the Buddha appeared, he lost his powers. Hearing that the Buddha knew a greater magic, he became a bhikkhu in order to learn it. The Buddha gave him some meditation subjects, and he attained arahatship. King Bimbisāra built a monastery for him and provided a village with five hundred attendants to support it. It was in this village that the incident related in Tale 152 took place. He was foremost among bhikkhus in being dear and delightful to the devas. (152)

Pilotika: a Paribbājaka, a religious wanderer. He often served the Buddha and the Sangha. His conversation with Jānussoni, another Brahmin who was an eminent follower of the Buddha, was expanded upon by the Buddha to form the Culla-hatthipadopama Sutta: The Shorter Elephant

Footprint Simile (Majjhima Nikāya, 27). In the third century B.C.E., when Emperor Ashoka's son, Venerable Mahinda, arrived in Sri Lanka, it was this sutta which he first taught to King Devānampiyatissa. (216)

Pindola: an eminent bhikkhu. He was the son of the chaplain of King Udena of Kosambi and became a successful teacher in Rājagaha. Seeing the gifts bestowed on the Buddha's disciples, he became a bhikkhu, but continued to be greedy. By following the Buddha's advice, he conquered his greed and became an arahat. Then, with a lion's roar (a bold and thunderous declaration of his power), he announced his readiness to answer the questions of any doubting bhikkhus. He was foremost among the bhkkhus in making a lion's roar. (188, 195)

Potthapāda: a Paribbājaka, a religious wanderer, who was converted by the Buddha. (216)

Punna: an eminent bhikkhu. He was born in Kapilavatthu and was ordained by his uncle, Venerable Kondañña, one of the first five bhikkhus. He became an arahat and was close to Venerable Sāriputta. It was after hearing a discourse by Venerable Punna that Venerable Ānanda attained the first path. He was foremost among bhikkhus in teaching the Dhamma. (102, 190)

Purāna Kassapa: one of the six teachers who were contemporaries of the Buddha. He taught amoralism, which denies both reward for good deeds and punishment for bad.

Rāhu: an asura chieftain. He is jealous of the devas of the sun and the moon and stands in their path with his mouth wide open. Eclipses are said to occur when those orbs fall into his mouth. (152, 165, 207, 216)

Rāhula: an eminent bhikkhu. He was the son of Prince Siddhattha and was born on the day that the Bodhisatta left the household life. When the Buddha visited Kapilavatthu, Rāhula's mother sent the boy to the Buddha to ask for his inheritance, and the Buddha asked Venerable Sāriputta to ordain him. When his grandfather, King Suddhodana, heard of this, he objected, and the Buddha declared that no young man should be ordained without the consent of his parents. Venerable Rāhula became an arahat and was foremost among bhikkhus in being eager for training. (83, 109, 123, 129, 134, 138, 154, 156, 163, 172, 189, 209, 212, 215, 217)

Rāhula's mother: See Yasodharā.

Sabhiya: a bhikkhu. As a Paribbājaka, a religious wanderer, he was famous as a dialectician. From a list he had received from his mother, he devised twenty questions which he put before ascetics and brahmins, but none could answer them. He visited the Buddha in Veluvana, and, at the end of the discussion, he entered the Sangha and attained arahatship. (216)

Saccaka: a Nigantha of Vesāli. His clan name was Aggivessana. He was teacher of the Licchavis and the brother of Patācārā. After the Buddha defeated him in a debate, he became a follower. His conversion is one of the Eight Great Victories of the Buddha referred to in the Jayamangala Gāthā. (111, 216)

Sakka: the king of the devas. His realm is Tāvatimsa. Rather than belonging exclusively to a particular being, Sakka refers to the office of king which is held by different beings in succession. [See Sakka's throne in Glossary of Terms] (16, 22, 34, 60, 76, 78, 81, 84, 90, 95, 100, 102, 108, 110, 111, 114, 134, 138, 146, 156, 159, 167, 169, 170, 173, 175, 180, 181, 182, 188, 190, 193, 197, 201, 203, 204, 206, 207, 208, 209, 210, 211, 212, 213, 214, 215, 216, 217)

Sañjaya Belatthiputta: one of the six teachers who were contemporaries of the Buddha. He taught an evasive doctrine, denying both existence and non-existence. (62)

Sāriputta: an eminent bhikkhu; one of the two chief disciples of the Buddha; "Captain of the Teaching." He was born in a village near Rājagaha. His name was Upatissa, and he had a childhood friend named Kolita. One day, Upatissa met Venerable Assaji, one of the first five bhikkhus, heard him recite two lines of a verse, and attained the first path. He hurried to Kolita and, repeating the lines he had heard, established his friend in the first path. Together, they invited their former teacher, Sañjaya Belatthiputta, to visit the Buddha, but Sañjaya refused to go. Upatissa and Kolita (Moggallāna) ordained together. Venerable Moggallāna attained arahatship in seven days, but it took Venerable Sāriputta two weeks longer. He was foremost among the bhikkhus in wisdom. Venerable Sāriputta's wisdom was second only to the Buddha's. (6, 9, 21, 23, 32, 33, 57, 63, 64, 65, 68, 76, 79, 85, 86, 88, 90, 91, 98, 101, 102, 109, 110, 111, 113, 118, 119, 120, 121, 128, 136, 139, 142, 145, 146, 149, 150, 157,

160, 174, 175, 177, 178, 179, 182, 185, 188, 189, 190, 191, 194, 198, 201, 207, 208, 209, 212, 213, 214, 215, 216, 217)

Sātāgira: a yakkha. He was present at the birth of Prince Siddhattha and at the First Sermon of the Buddha. At the latter, he was distracted because he was searching for his friend Hemavata. Later that day, when he met Hemavata in Rājagaha, Hemavata suggested that they hurry to the Himavat because the region was covered with flowers. Sātāgira explained that the reason for the flowers was the appearance of the Buddha and enumerated the Buddha's qualities. Together, they went to Isipatana to hear the Buddha. Their conversation in Rājagaha was overheard by a laywoman named Kāli-Kuraragharikā, and, through it, she attained the first path. Sātāgira and Hemavata also happened to be in Ālavi when the Buddha converted Ālavaka. Unable to pass over the yakkha's mansion and perceiving the reason, they went inside and congratulated the Buddha on his victory. Kāli-Kuraragharikā was foremost among laywomen who achieved insight from hearsay. (190)

Siddhattha: the personal name of Gotama Buddha. He was born in Kapilavatthu, the capital of Sākya, as the son of King Suddhodana and Queen Mahā-Māyā. At twenty-nine, on the day that his son Rāhula was born, despite King Suddhodana's precautions, Prince Siddhattha saw the Four Sights—an old man, a sick man, a corpse, and an ascetic—which prompted him to leave home and to become an ascetic.

Suddhodana: the Sākyan king and the father of Prince Siddhattha. Mahā-Māyā was his chief queen, and, after she died, her sister Mahā-Pajāpatī-Gotamī took that position. King Suddhodana tried to prevent his son from leaving the world by shielding him from unpleasantness and surrounding him with luxury. Later, King Suddhodana invited the Buddha to Kapilavatthu. [See Kāludāyi] When the Buddha walked for alms in Kapilavatthu, King Suddhodana reproached him for begging, but the Buddha replied that going on almsrounds was the custom of all Buddhas. Hearing that, King Suddhodana attained the first path. Much later, on hearing the Buddha teach to him again, he attained arahatship just before he died. This is one of the few instances in which a layman became an arahat. In such a case, the person must, on that day, either ordain or pass away. [See Bhaddaji] (7, 20, 83, 143, 174, 202, 206, 207, 208, 209, 216, 217)

Sunakkhatta: a Licchavi prince of Vesāli. He became a bhikkhu but disrobed to follow other teachers. He publicly defamed the Buddha, complaining that the Buddha had neither performed any miracles nor shown him the beginning of things. The Buddha scolded him, enumerating his own extraordinary powers and saying that he had not promised to explain the beginning of things. The Buddha pointed out that he taught only suffering and the end of suffering. (214)

Thulla-Nandā: a troublesome bhikkhunī who was close to Devadatta. Although she was an eloquent speaker, she was also greedy and was accused of misappropriating gifts given to other bhikkhunīs. She enjoyed men's company and went out unattended. She was jealous of other bhikkhunīs and frequently quarreled with them. Her misdeeds led to the establishment of quite a few of the Vinaya rules. (52)

Upāli: an eminent bhikkhu. He was the barber of the Sākyan princes and ordained with them. [See Tale 8] He attained arahatship and was foremost among bhikkhus in Vinaya. (8, 188)

Uppalavannā: an eminent bhikkhunī; one of the two chief female disciples of the Buddha. She was extremely beautiful and had been sought by kings and commoners from all of Jambudīpa, but her father suggested that she ordain, and she readily agreed. One day, while she was sweeping the Ordination Hall in Jetavana, she concentrated on the flame of a lamp as a fire-kasina, attained jhāna, and became an arahat. She was foremost among bhikkhunīs in extraordinary powers. (102, 111, 138, 154, 171, 190, 198, 208, 209, 210, 212, 213, 216, 217)

Uruvela-Kassapa: a bhikkhu. He was an ascetic in Uruvela and had five hundred disciples. His brothers, also named Kassapa, were also ascetics and had three hundred and two hundred disciples, respectively. The Buddha spent an entire rainy season with them, performing many miracles and trying to convert them. Even after the Buddha had overcome two powerful nāgas, the Kassapas were unconvinced, and Uruvela-Kassapa still believed himself to be an arahat and the Buddha's superior. Finally, the Buddha was able to convert him, and the three brothers, with their one thousand followers, were ordained. A little later, the Buddha taught the Fire Sermon (Ādittapariyāya Sutta), and they all attained arahatship. Uruvela-Kassapa was foremost among bhikkhus in having a large following. (214)

Vessavana: one of the Four Great Kings. His kingdom is in the north, and he is king of the yakkhas. (6, 147, 168, 202, 215)

Vidūdabha: the son of King Pasenadi and Vāsabha-Khattiyā. [See Tale 179] (7, 179)

Vipassi Buddha: nineteenth of the twenty-four Buddhas. (217)

Visākhā: the chief laywoman disciple of the Buddha. When she was seven years old, she heard the Buddha teach in Anga and attained the first path. Later, her family moved to Sāketa in Kosala. She moved to Sāvatthī when she married into a family that followed the Niganthas. After she converted her father-in-law, Migāra, she became known as "Migāra's mother" (Migāramātā). In Sāvatthī, she built Migāramātupāsāda, a monastery in the Eastern Park (Pubbārāma), and gave it to the Buddha. She was foremost among laywomen who ministered to the Sangha. (10, 98, 182, 203, 217)

Vissakamma: a deva. He is Sakka's chief architect and builder. (188, 202, 208, 210, 217)

Yama: the king of hell. (93, 188, 206, 210, 214)

Yasodharā: the wife of Prince Siddhattha and the mother of his son, Rāhula. She was also called Rāhula's mother (Rāhulamātā), and Bimbādevī. After Prince Siddhattha left home, she showed her loyalty by abandoning luxury, wearing yellow robes, and taking only one meal a day. After the bhikkhunī order was established, she ordained as Venerable Bhaddakaccānā and attained arahatship. (83, 102, 109, 129, 134, 154, 156, 163, 172, 201, 206, 212, 215, 216, 217)

The Thirty-One Planes of Existence

The Immaterial World (*Arūpa-loka*)

Level	Realm	Inhabitants	Cause of rebirth there
28–31	*Arūpa*	Devas of the formless realms. Mind only; no body	Four immaterial jhānas

The Fine-Material World (*Rūpa-loka*)

	Level	Realm	Inhabitants	Cause of rebirth there
Brahma Heavens (*Brahma-loka*)	23-27	*Suddhāvāsa*	Devas of the Pure Abodes. Beings who have attained the path of non-returning are reborn and attain arahatship here. Brahmā Sahampati resides here.	Fourth jhāna
	22	*Asaññasattā*	Non-percipient Devas. Body only; no mind	
	21	*Vehapphala*	Devas of Great Reward	
	20	*Subhakinha*	Devas of Refulgent Glory	Third jhāna
	19	*Appamānasu-bha*	Devas of Limitless Glory	
	18	*Parittasubha*	Devas of Limited Glory	
	17	*Abhassara*	Devas of Brilliant Radiance	Second jhāna
	16	*Appamānābha*	Devas of Limitless Radiance	
	15	*Parittābha*	Devas of Limited Radiance	
	14	*Mahā-Brahmā*	Great Brahmā. Often refers to the first resident of this heaven, but all beings here and above can be called Mahā-Brahmā	First jhāna
	13	*Brahmā-purohita*	Brahmā's Ministers	
	12	*Brahmā-parisajja*	Members of Brahmā's Retinue	——

The Sensuous World (*Kāma-loka*)			
Level	Realm	Inhabitants	Cause of rebirth there
11	*Paranimmita-vasavattī*	Devas who wield control over the creations of others. Abode of Māra	Ten courses of wholesome action, generosity, morality, and wisdom
10	*Nimmānarati*	Devas who delight in creation	
9	*Tusita*	Contented Devas. Bodhisattas are reborn here prior to their final human birth	
8	*Yāmā*	Comfortable Devas. Devas who live in the air, at ease, free of all difficulties	
7	*Tāvatimsa*	The Thirty-three Devas. Abode of Sakka. Large numbers of attendant nymphs also live here	
6	*Catumahārājika*	The Four Great Kings, who guard the four qauarters. Yakkhas, gandhabbas, kumbhandas, nāgas, and deva-asuras also live here. This realm and all the above are divine heaven realms, *deva-loka*.	
5	*Manussa*	Humans	
4	*Asura*	Asura-kāya	Ten courses of unwholesome actions
3	*Peta*	Petas (Hungry ghosts)	Lack of virtue, holding to wrong views
2	*Tiracchāna*	Animals	Behaving like an animal
1	*Niraya*	(The hells, of which there are eight, *Roruva* is the fourth highest. *Avīci* is the lowest and worst. *Ussada* is the collective name for lesser hells that surround each of the great hells.)	Killing one's parents, killing an arahat, injuring the Buddha, creating a schism in the Sangha

Left margin: Happy Realms (*Sugati*) — spanning levels 5–11; Woeful Realms (*Apāya*) — spanning levels 1–4.

Map of Jambudīpa

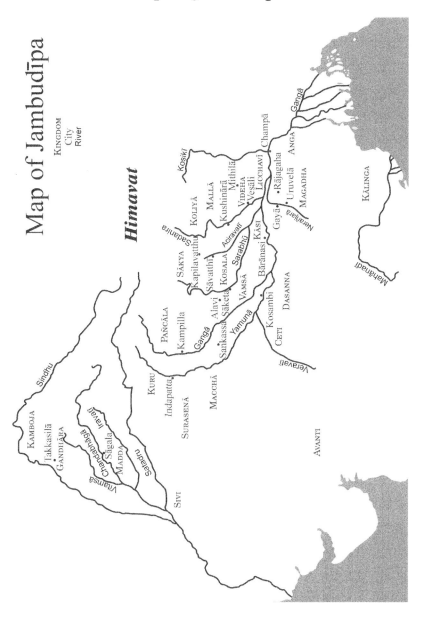

Map of Jambudīpa

KINGDOM
City
River

Himavat

Kosikī
MALLĀ
Kushinārā
Mithilā
VIDEHA
Vesāli
LICCHAVĪ Champā
Gangā
ANGA

Sadānīrā
KOLIYĀ
Aciravatī
KĀSI
Rājagaha
Uruvelā
MAGADHA
KĀLINGA

SĀKYA
Kapilavatthu
Sāvatthī
KOSALA
Sarabhū
Bārānasi
Gayā
Nerañjara

PAÑCĀLA
Kampilla
Alavi
Sāketa
VAMSĀ
Kosambī
DASANNA
Mahānadī

Ganga
Sankassa
Yamuna
CETI
Veravati

Sindhu
KURU
Indapatta
MACCHĀ

KAMBOJA
Takkasilā
GANDHĀRA
SURASENĀ

Candabhāgā
Sāgala
MADDA
AVANTI

Vitamsa
Satadru
Iravati

SIVI

465

Table of Correspondence
Jātaka Numbers from the Pāli

JTB = Jātaka Tales of the Buddha (This Anthology)
PTS = The Jātaka or Stories of the Buddha's Former Births, Pāli Text Society
Book = Nipāta, Division of the Pāli in which the Jātaka is included

JTB	PTS	Book	JTB	PTS	Book	JTB	PTS	Book
1	1	I	36	83	I	71	168	II
2	2	I	37	87	I	72	177	II
3	3	I	38	89	I	73	178	II
4	4	I	39	91	I	74	179	II
5	5	I	40	92	I	75	181	II
6	6	I	41	96	I	76	182	II
7	7	I	42	107	I	77	183	II
8	10	I	43	109	I	78	186	II
9	11	I	44	113	I	79	190	II
10	12	I	45	115	I	80	193	II
11	14	I	46	118	I	81	194	II
12	18	I	47	123	I	82	195	II
13	20	I	48	124	I	83	201	II
14	22	I	49	125	I	84	202	II
15	28	I	50	128	I	85	206	II
16	31	I	51	131	I	86	207	II
17	32	I	52	136	I	87	211	II
18	33	I	53	137	I	88	215	II
19	34	I	54	139	I	89	218	II
20	35	I	55	140	I	90	220	II
21	37	I	56	141	I	91	222	II
22	40	I	57	143	I	92	234	II
23	41	I	58	144	I	93	240	II
24	43	I	59	146	I	94	241	II
25	46	I	60	148	I	95	243	II
26	48	I	61	149	I	96	251	III
27	50	I	62	150	I	97	252	III
28	51	I	63	151	II	98	254	III
29	55	I	64	153	II	99	257	III
30	63	I	65	156	II	100	267	III
31	67	I	66	157	II	101	272	III
32	73	I	67	159	II	102	276	III
33	77	I	68	160	II	103	278	III
34	78	I	69	161	II	104	282	III
35	80	I	70	166	II	105	284	III

JTB	PTS	Book	JTB	PTS	Book	JTB	PTS	Book
106	286	III	144	379	VI	182	472	XII
107	288	III	145	385	VI	183	474	XIII
108	291	III	146	386	VI	184	475	XIII
109	292	III	147	398	VII	185	476	XIII
110	300	III	148	400	VII	186	481	XIII
111	301	IV	149	401	VII	187	482	XIII
112	302	IV	150	402	VII	188	483	XIII
113	305	IV	151	405	VII	189	486	XIV
114	306	IV	152	406	VII	190	488	XIV
115	308	IV	153	407	VII	191	490	XIV
116	309	IV	154	408	VII	192	491	XIV
117	312	IV	155	409	VII	193	492	XIV
118	313	IV	156	411	VII	194	493	XIV
119	314	IV	157	412	VII	195	497	XV
120	315	IV	158	413	VII	196	498	XV
121	316	IV	159	417	VIII	197	499	XV
122	318	IV	160	418	VIII	198	501	XV
123	319	IV	161	419	VIII	199	503	XV
124	321	IV	162	420	VIII	200	504	XV
125	322	IV	163	421	VIII	201	506	XV
126	323	IV	164	422	VIII	202	510	XV
127	324	IV	165	425	VIII	203	512	XVI
128	326	IV	166	427	IX	204	514	XVI
129	328	IV	167	429	IX	205	520	XVI
130	329	IV	168	432	IX	206	531	XX
131	331	IV	169	439	X	207	537	XXI
132	338	IV	170	440	X	208	538	XXII
133	339	IV	171	442	X	209	539	XXII
134	340	IV	172	443	X	210	540	XXII
135	342	IV	173	445	X	211	541	XXII
136	346	IV	174	447	X	212	542	XXII
137	352	V	175	450	X	213	543	XXII
138	354	V	176	455	XI	214	544	XXII
139	356	V	177	456	XI	215	545	XXII
140	357	V	178	462	XI	216	546	XXII
141	358	V	179	465	XI	217	547	XXII
142	359	V	180	467	XII			
143	371	V	181	469	XII			

Bibliography

Burlingame, E.W., translator, Buddhist Legends, London, The Pali Text Society, 1921, reprinted in 1990 and 1995; a complete translation of Dhammapada Commentary. About sixty of the stories are shared with the Jātakas.

Chandavimala, Ven. Rerukane, Analysis of Perfections, translated by A. G. S. Kariyawasam, Kandy, Sri Lanka, Buddhist Publication Society, 2003; a succinct treatment of the Ten Perfections and how they can be developed.

Cowell, E. B., editor, The Jātaka or Stories of the Buddha's Former Births, London, The Pali Text Society, 18951907, reprinted in 1990; a complete translation of the Jātaka Commentary, including all 547 stories.

Harischandra, D.V.J., Psychiatric Aspects of Jātaka Stories, Galle, Sri Lanka, Upuli Offset, 1998.

Karunaratne, David, translator, Ummagga Jataka (The Story of the Tunnel), Colombo, Sri Lanka, M.D. Gunasena & Co. Ltd., 1962.

Malalasekera, G. P., Dictionary of Pāli Proper Names, London, The Pali Text Society, 1938, reprinted 1960 and 1974.

Na-Rangsi, Dr. Sunthorn, The Four Planes of Existence in Theravada Buddhism, Kandy, Sri Lanka, Buddhist Publication Society, 2006.

Recommendations for Further Reading

Bhikkhu Bodhi, Editor, In the Buddha's Words, An Anthology of Discourses from the Pali Canon, Somerville, Massachusetts, U.S.A., Wisdom Publications, 2005; a collection of suttas selected to serve as an introduction to the Buddha's Teaching.

Dhammapāla, Ācariya, A Treatise on the Pāramīs, A Discourse from the Majjhima Nikāya, translated from the Pali by Bhikkhu Bodhi, Wheel No. 409/411, Kandy, Sri Lanka, Buddhist Publication Society (BPS), 1996; a lucid translation of a sixth-century discussion of the Ten Perfections, drawing from both Theravada and Mahāyana texts.

Dhammika, Ven. S., Middle Land, Middle Way: A Pilgrim's Guide to the Buddha's India, Kandy, Sri Lanka, BPS, 2008; A description of the sites important to the life of the Buddha.

Gunaratana, Ven. Henepola, Mindfulness in Plain English, Somerville, Massachusetts, U.S.A. Wisdom Publications, 1992; a practical and straightforward guide to vipassanā meditation and its benefits for everyone.

Kawasaki, Ken and Visākhā, Strive on with Diligence, The Buddha and His Teaching, Kandy, Sri Lanka, Buddhist Relief Mission, 2002; www.brelief.org; a multi-media presentation in DVD and VCD format, presenting the life of the Buddha and basic Dhamma through art and scenes from around the world.

Nyanaponika Thera and Hellmuth Hecker, Great Disciples of the Buddha, Their Lives, Their Works, Their Legacy, edited by Bhikkhu Bodhi, Kandy, Sri Lanka, BPS and Somerville, Massachusetts, U.S.A., Wisdom Publications, 2003; biographies of many of the Buddha's disciples who appear in the Jātakas.

Piyadassi Thera, The Buddha's Ancient Path, Kandy, Sri Lanka, BPS, 1974; a clear explanation of the Buddha's Teaching.

U Pandita, Sayadaw, In This Very Life, Liberation Teachings of the Buddha, Kandy, Sri Lanka, BPS, 2007; a guide to vipassanā meditation and an analysis of the workings of the mind.

ABOUT PARIYATTI

Pariyatti is dedicated to providing affordable access to authentic teachings of the Buddha about the Dhamma theory (*pariyatti*) and practice (*paṭipatti*) of Vipassana meditation. A 501(c)(3) non-profit charitable organization since 2002, Pariyatti is sustained by contributions from individuals who appreciate and want to share the incalculable value of the Dhamma teachings. We invite you to visit www.pariyatti.org to learn about our programs, services, and ways to support publishing and other undertakings.

Pariyatti Publishing Imprints

Vipassana Research Publications (focus on Vipassana as taught by S.N. Goenka in the tradition of Sayagyi U Ba Khin)

BPS Pariyatti Editions (selected titles from the Buddhist Publication Society, co-published by Pariyatti in the Americas)

Pariyatti Digital Editions (audio and video titles, including discourses)

Pariyatti Press (classic titles returned to print and inspirational writing by contemporary authors)

Pariyatti enriches the world by

- disseminating the words of the Buddha,
- providing sustenance for the seeker's journey,
- illuminating the meditator's path.